# Fate of the Silver Wolf

By: Sonya E. Destler

*I want to thank all those who have shown me support and encouragement, actually to do this and push through to reach my goal.*

*A special thank you to my kids, and Chris Datko, for putting up with me through all my ups and downs and hardships with writing this story, and for what is to come with future stories.*

*With all my love and gratitude,*

*Thank you!*

# Table of Contents

# Chapter One
## *Aylin*

Damn, that hurt. That is the first thing that runs through my mind as I lie on the ground for the umpteenth time today. I could feel the bruises already forming from where the blow landed, taking my legs out from under me, and from where I landed on my side. I already know what he is going to say. He knew that I was daydreaming again. Sometimes, I hated that he knew me so well, but at the same time, it was nice that someone did.

"You need to focus, Ay!" Lance called from the circle. The circle was a training area where we learned hand-to-hand combat along with training with daggers and short swords. Lance, my best friend, and his twin, Layla, my other bestie, have been training me in secret for about a year—ever since they started going with their dad to visit other packs to help train warriors. I have been able to get down the bow and daggers, but Lance is way too good when it comes to the short sword.

"I am focusing. I'm just tired." He knew I was lying, but I didn't care. My side was on fire where his wooden training sword had landed a previous blow. It was definitely already bruised, but thanks to our wolf's healing abilities, it would fade in a day or two. That ability is what I love most since it helps me hide the injuries I get from my bullies more often than I should. I would heal faster if only I had my wolf like others my age. I really wish I could fight back, but for now, I don't want to get Lance and Layla in trouble. My time will come.

"Bullshit, Ay. You're not focusing. Where is your head today?" He cocked his head at me and gave me one of his penetrating, all-knowing stares. "There is no way, even if I am better than you, as you say, that I would get this many hits in and knock you on your ass so many times."

Goddess, right now, I really want to knock him on his ass!

Lance was your typical warrior, with a tall and muscular build, reaching six-four—almost a head bigger than me at my five-foot-ten-inch height. He has blonde hair and brown eyes. I have always loved how, even though his and Layla's eyes are the same color, they still held a uniqueness of their own personalities. His were always deep and serious, and hers were doe-eyed and full of warmth and wonder. She had a unique view of the world and was far kinder than most others our age in our pack. She was tall like her brother but not quite—six foot even and just a few inches taller than me. She had a pretty, round face with a straight nose and full lips that even I was beyond envious of. She had a full, curvy figure—curvy but healthy, we would say. Like me, she loved her sweets, and we'd indulge often!

"You know where her head is, Lance. She can't stop thinking about Zander, hoping that with her birthday tomorrow, he will end up being her one. True. Love. Her mate." Layla giggled, and I turned about five shades of red, which only made her laugh harder.

She loved picking on me for my not-so-secret crush on Zander. He was the Future Alpha and my brother's best friend. I knew I didn't have a chance with him, but I couldn't help but feel there was a pull between us. However, if he has felt it, he never said anything to me or anyone I know. We do not really hang out, even when he is at my house with my brother, but come on, a girl can dream.

"I don't know what you see in him, Ay. So what if he is the Future Alpha of our pack? He is an utter ass and fucks around more than anyone because of his title," Lance said with his incredulous look. "He is way too entitled and really needs to be brought down a peg or two."

Layla just nodded her head in agreement, but I was a little upset about what he said. I thought he was taking great strides toward being a really good Alpha one day. From what my brother tells me, he is working really hard all the time with his Alpha training.

Zander was one of my brother Kevin's best friends. I basically grew up with him always around, just like Lance and Layla. He was never mean to me, but I did know it was mostly out of respect for my brother. When we were little, he even played with me, and I would have considered him to be a friend. His sister, Lizzie, however, was a complete and total bitch. She and her little band of cronies made my life miserable here. They were my tormentors, and even some of the other wolves would help hurt me to gain her favor. I think at some point when we were going to school and how everyone else treated me, that was what made Zander take a step back from our friendship. Like I said, he was never mean, and we got along. We just didn't hang out together unless it was because of Kevin.

Lizzie was the she-wolf all the guys wanted, the princess of the pack. She was tall and lithe, with long black hair and perfect angular features. She acted like a spoiled princess as she took advantage of the fact that her dad was the alpha. If someone upset her, she would run to Daddy and spin a story, acting innocent. Her fakeness always made me gag. Her friends were almost as bad—Amber Rae, and Kylie. The three of them loved to make my life miserable. Most people knew they bullied me verbally. No one really knew when they tried to gang up on me and beat me. I never fought back; I knew that it would be worse for me since they would spin a tale, and I would be the one in trouble. Again, my day would come. I knew it had to—well, at least I hoped it would.

Sometimes the beatings would be so bad that I had to wear long sleeves and pants to try to hide the bruising. Let me tell you, in the summer, when we are already burning hot, it is hard to explain why I am wearing such things. Broken bones healed slowly because I didn't have my wolf yet. On the rare occasion that one of the guys who followed her like a puppy really wanted to make it hurt, they would use a silver blade. I have a few scars along my back, torso, and legs that I constantly keep hidden from everyone. There is no way I want anyone to see those and think me weak. That is probably the worst thing that could come out of it all since I dreamed of joining the guard.

I am already not accepted by most of the pack for being adopted and not born of the pack; however, they went the extra mile in making my existence here shitty, daily reminding me just how much of an outsider I am. I roll my eyes at the thought. I really hate her, but Zander has the potential to be more, and I know I have caught him watching me. It had only been a handful of times over the years, but I couldn't help wondering if maybe he likes me too. Hey, a girl can dream. As I said, as much of a cliché as I know it is—having the hots for the future alpha of the pack—I just couldn't help it.

I got into my stance and let Lance know I was ready. We circled each other for a minute, and then he struck straight out. I spun away from his attack and brought up my sword, swinging it down at an angle. Of course, he blocked and then countered with a side swipe. I met his attack and struck back. This went on for a few minutes until I swung out, and he blocked. In a swift spin, he struck out low and got my leg, knocking me down to my knees.

"Better, but I think that is all for today." He was smiling at me, knowing I would keep going until I was bruised head to toe—even with my birthday tomorrow and having to wear a god-awful dress. My mother wouldn't appreciate that at all—looking like a bruised peach in a ceremonial dress for the coming-of-age birthday. "Besides, I am getting hungry, and your mom is making a roast for dinner that I just can't wait to sink my teeth into." I laughed at him.

My mom was a pretty good cook, and Lance loved her food. Then again, I didn't know of any food he didn't like. He was a bottomless pit. My mom had invited them over tonight since tomorrow is not only my birthday, but it's the Festival of the Moon Goddess as well, so no time for a birthday dinner. We will probably all eat there for the celebration tomorrow anyway, so my birthday dinner is tonight.

We placed the practice swords in a bag and put them in our hiding place in a hollow tree so we could practice again later. We used our feet to clear the practice circle so that if anyone came across it, they wouldn't know, and after another long look around to make sure everything looked good, we headed to my house. On the way, we passed the actual practice fields, and of course, there were people practicing as always—one of whom was Zander. I watched him as we walked by, how gracefully he moved across the field, attacking his opponent and dodging the blows. He didn't use practice swords; those were very real, and I have a feeling I would be cut in half if we had been using those to practice. I could use real daggers and throw them pretty accurately, too. But the damn sword—I just couldn't get the hang of it.

Not paying attention to where I was going as I watched the massive hottie on the field, I hadn't realized Layla had stopped until I walked into her. She looked at me and shook her head, laughing.

"You really don't pay attention when he is around, do you?" She loves laughing at my expense, but this made me laugh too.

"No, not really." I laughed with her.

Lance rolled his eyes at us and started walking away toward my house. I took one last look at Zander, sent a silent prayer to the moon goddess, wishing for him to be my mate, and followed behind Lance, arm in arm with his sister. My mind lingered on the male, currently shirtless and sweaty, whom I would have loved to just stay and watch.

At home, my mom was in full swing, getting dinner ready for us all. There weren't many people—my two best friends, my parents, and my siblings. I was looking forward to dessert more than anything, however. My sister was like Mom—great at cooking—and she excelled at desserts. She had been making my birthday cake for the last three years.

"What did you make me?" I asked her with a wide smile plastered on my face.

"You will have to wait and find out," she said back, placing her hand on her hip in the same way Mom did when she was talking to us seriously. "So why don't you get out of the kitchen for now?"

I stuck out my lip and pouted. "Come on, please tell me?" I all but begged.

Jolene shook her head at my silly antics. "Ok, ok, it's your favorite, but with my own little twist."

I couldn't wait. Strawberry shortcake was my favorite cake of all time, and I knew no matter what the twist was, I would love it.

Lance, Layla, and I went to my room and took turns getting cleaned up in my bathroom. We sat on my bed and talked about what we were going to do tomorrow at the festival. Layla and I planned to hit up the apple dumpling stand like we do every year, and Lance asked that this year I save him a dance, which I happily agreed to. I do love dancing. My parents got me into it young. They were amazing dancers and always took center stage with how beautifully they moved across the floor. I often walked in on them slow dancing in the kitchen, and I always hoped that whoever my mate was would do that with me.

I remember times when my father would stop dancing with my mom and twirl me around in her place. Those will probably always be some of my favorite memories—that and gardening with my mother. She truly loved her garden and was always changing it and adding to it.

"Hey, Mom says it's dinner time. You all should come downstairs," Kevin says from the doorway.

He looks in at us and shakes his head at what he sees. Lance is lying sideways along the foot of my bed, Layla sideways at the top, and I am lying lengthwise over both—my head on Layla's stomach and my legs draped across Lance.

"You three are so odd." He laughs and walks away.

I love Kevin. He and I are the closest in the family. Anyone would think he would be closer to Jolene, being his real sister, but he has never treated me differently. He has always been there and is very protective of me. He has gotten into several fights at school when he found out someone picked on me or put their hands on me—which is another reason I think Zander isn't a jerk toward me. Kevin is tough and could probably beat the tar out of Zander, even with him being the next Alpha.

"Ok, ok, coming! We will be down in a sec," I call as he walks away.

I got up and headed downstairs to see what my mom had prepared for my pre-birthday party.

In the dining room, my mom has decorations hanging all over the place—streamers, banners, and balloons in blues and purples, my favorite colors—and a big pot roast dinner in the middle of the table. She must have done the decorations while I was getting cleaned up because they were not here when we got back from practice.

"This looks great, Mom! You really outdid yourself. You really didn't have to! Thank you so much!" She always works so hard for all our birthdays to be special.

"It's not too much! Nineteen is a big year! You come of age, meet your wolf, and can find your mate!"

I blushed a little at the last comment as Layla elbowed my side and lifted her brows. We both laughed, and everyone took a seat at the table.

Everyone starts to dig in when there is a knock at the door. My brother jumps up to get it as we shovel the food into our mouths. I could hear him talking to someone at the door but couldn't make out who it was.

"So what did you get into today, Aylin?" my dad asked.

"We went for a hike in the woods on the far side of the pack." This wasn't a complete lie. We did have to hike into the woods, and it was on the far side of the pack. I just left out the part about training. "Figured we would scout the area for the run tomorrow when I first shift. I haven't decided if I want to go toward the cliff or the stream." The cliff was past the far end of the pack line and the edge of our border to the north, and the stream and meadow were behind our house a ways to the east—again, along the border of our lands.

"It may be safer to do the stream for your first run. If you have a hard time controlling your wolf, you will end up in water instead of the cliff's edge." He was obviously joking with me, but I still gave him a face. I had already planned on running to the river anyway. I was curious if I could see my wolf in the reflection of the water. I only really said that so they wouldn't ask more questions about what I was doing there again.

I had just taken another big bite of food when Kevin walked back into the room with none other than Zander. I felt my heart kick up and felt Layla nudge me under the table with her foot. I tried to close my mouth around the big forkful of food I had just shoved in it. I turned away, trying to hide my burning face. Damn it, did he have to come in at that moment? I finally swallowed and tried to act like nothing had happened. Zander was shaking hands with my mother and father. Then he turned to me.

"I hope it's okay that I am here. I know you are celebrating your birthday tonight. Kevin told me about it." He was smiling at me, and I glanced at Kevin, who just shrugged.

"No, I mean, yes, it's okay." That was all I could say before I turned beet red. I really couldn't believe he had spoken to me. He usually just nodded at me or would give me a small smile. Maybe he was just being polite because my parents were sitting here with us. Yes, that definitely had to be it.

"Thank you. Happy birthday, Aylin," he said a bit formally but still had that smile on his face. Kevin pulled up a chair next to him, and they started talking about the festival and everything they were going to do. I turned away and went back to my food and talked to my friends, even though all I could think about was the hot-as-fuck guy at the end of the table. I kept stealing glances at him, and twice, I locked eyes with him. I quickly looked away each time, and I could have sworn that he had a grin on his face. I hoped that I wasn't too red, as I could feel my face flush with warmth.

After dinner, everyone gathered around and sang "Happy Birthday." As promised, my sister made strawberry shortcake—chocolate-covered strawberry shortcake with homemade whipped topping. It was absolutely delicious, just like I knew it would be. I did get a little jealous when Zander gave her so much praise. The smiles they gave each other made me want to smash the cake in his face—and hers too. That would be a waste of a good cake, and besides, I knew I was being irrational. Zander wasn't mine.

My parents then had everyone go to the living room so they could give me my presents. My parents got me a new Nikon camera and some photo albums. I was over the moon! I loved photography. My friends Lance and Layla got me a charm bracelet with three charms to start: a crescent moon, a wolf, and a cupcake. I couldn't help but laugh at the cupcake. Layla picked that one, and Lance picked the moon. The wolf was a given because of what we were—this one had sapphire eyes.

Then there was Kevin. He walked over to me, handed me a box, and gave me a broad smile. I opened it and smiled back. It was a picture of him and me cuddled in my crib as a baby. He was only about a year old, still a babe himself, but he would cry anytime they tried to separate us. The picture next to it was us just a few months ago, covered in paint after he helped me repaint my dresser a vivid purple with light purple swirls and designs. He was better at the designs than I was. He had accidentally gotten paint on my arm, and I retaliated with a brush across his chin—then it was war. When my dad found us, he had been fitting lenses to his camera and took a picture of us before making us clean up our mess.

"Thank you, Kev. I love it." And I did. Kev was always by my side. I know Lance and Layla are my best friends, but no one could ever be as close to me as Kev was. When I looked up from admiring the photo, I locked eyes with Zander, who quickly looked away. I could have sworn he was smiling at me, but maybe it was my imagination again. Seems my imagination was running rampant today. I shook it off for the time being but still couldn't help the butterflies I felt.

Then Kev nudged Zander, who got up and walked over to me, holding out a small box. I was a little surprised, so I took the small box from him and opened it. Inside was a gold necklace with an elephant pendant that had an amethyst purple gem for the eye. It was beautiful, and my silly heart started racing. I couldn't believe that Zander got me a gift.

"Thank you so much. It's beautiful." I loved it. My favorite animal and color—I couldn't believe he even knew that about me. I felt over the moon.

"I didn't want to come empty-handed, and I remembered Kevin telling me about your stuffed elephant. When he showed me the gift he got you and explained that you guys were painting your dresser your favorite color, this just felt right," he said. My heart melted, and a bloom of blush filled my cheeks. It was beautiful and thoughtful. I was beyond surprised that he could do that for me and also a little mad at Kev for telling him about Archie. We would have to talk about that later—flush out what else he might have told Zander.

I looked at him, and all I wanted to do was stand and hug him for his thoughtful gift, but I didn't think it would be wise. I didn't want him to hug me just because he was surrounded by my family and Kevin. I gave him one of my brightest smiles, and for a moment, he looked completely frozen. I started to get worried at his reaction, but then Jolene got my attention. I was so grateful that she had—it was starting to get awkward. Out of the corner of my eye, I saw Zander sit down and then saw him and my brother lean in and whisper to each other. I wonder what he is saying. I truly hope he isn't saying anything bad.

A short time later, everyone was saying goodbye. I hugged Layla and Lance as they left. My mom and Jolene went into the kitchen to clean up, and Dad went back to the dining area to help clean up the table. I went back to the living room to gather up my gifts and take them upstairs to my room. When I got there, Kevin and Zander were laughing, and goddess, did I love how Zander's laugh sounded. I started grabbing the gifts, and then I felt a hand on my shoulder.

"Thanks again for allowing me to be part of your birthday dinner. I am glad you liked the necklace," Zander said.

I smiled at him, and I could feel myself blush for the umpteenth time this evening. Goddess, I must always look like such a rosy-cheeked idiot in front of him.

"Thank you for coming. I am really happy you were here. It made my birthday dinner so much better with you joining," I told him and then berated myself in my mind. Could I be any more obvious?

"I am going to head out. I have some last-minute things to handle before the festival tomorrow."

Zander turned and clasped Kevin's hand, giving him a quick bro hug. I turned and went to walk away, but he stopped me.

"Don't I get a hug?"

I almost lost my balance and dropped my gifts. The shock I felt must have been all over my face because I heard Kevin snort, trying—and failing—not to laugh at me.

"You, uh, you want a hug from me?" I asked.

"I thought you were giving everyone that came hugs. I kind of felt left out," he said.

At that moment, I knew he was just joking with me. There was no way he liked me. I felt my stomach fall. I put down the gifts, walked over to him, and gave him an awkward hug, but then he squeezed me, and I couldn't help but melt into his hold. I could swear I felt him shudder. Did he smell my hair? Why do I do this to myself? I must be imagining it. I know my imagination can run away with me sometimes, so that is not out of the realm of possibilities.

The hug lasted longer than I intended, and I hoped he didn't realize that I just didn't want to let him go. I finished saying good night, gathered my gifts, and went upstairs. I came back down and helped clean up the mess from the festivities. We all got ready and took off to bed afterward. Tomorrow is a big day for us all, and we need our sleep—especially me, after training and surprise guests.

Once again, I had a hard time falling asleep, which seems to be typical for me anymore. I rarely got a full night's sleep, and the fear I felt as I climbed into bed suffocated me more than normal. Something feels off. I hated going to sleep anymore, just laying there and praying for the nightmares to not come and give me peace for one single night. Please, not tonight. I just want to sleep. I don't know why these nightmares have become more frequent, but it's really starting to piss me off.

*My paws are wet and sore, and yet I keep moving through the forest. Faster, harder, I drive myself forward. I am not sure what is after me, yet I know I am scared. Dread washes over me like a thick cover of ice, freezing my limbs and insides. I feel something strong and dark—a presence—and I realize I am being hunted. I pray to the moon goddess for strength to keep running, to keep going.*

*It's so dark, and the moon is hidden behind thick clouds, causing the darkness to spread. My wolf's eyes should be able to see just fine, but this darkness is all-consuming and unnatural. The fear I feel continues to rise as I hear the steps of large, heavy feet following me, swiftly catching up— for something that sounds so heavy.*

*I can hear my heart in my ears as my blood pumps with every leap and every movement of my body. My muscles ache against my movements, but I keep going. I must push forward. I can't stop—not now. The fear swarming and consuming me is almost too much. Keep going, don't stop. I say this to myself again and again.*

*Soon, I come out into a large meadow with a beautiful lake at the far end. It's a large lake, and out in the center is an island shaped like a crescent moon. I feel the pull to the island, and I race forward, making my way to the lake. In the darkness, the lake looks like a sheet of black glass—so smooth and tranquil, barely a ripple. Next to no movement on it, with such a still night. The sight is beautiful and eerie at the same time. Knowing that this is where I need to go, I bolt for the water.*

*Stepping up to the edge of the lake, I peer into the water. At first, I see nothing, but then I see my reflection. It's just me—I am no longer a wolf, I am myself. My blue eyes, in my heart-shaped face framed by long silver hair, look back at me. Yet I am different somehow. I look older—my nose is smaller, my lips fuller, and I have a few more wrinkles around my eyes and forehead. As I look harder, I see someone standing behind me. Glowing red eyes are all I can make out; the rest of the features are hidden in the shadows, and I freeze.*

*The figure starts laughing—it's hollow and rough. A chill creeps over my skin and into my heart at the sound. Panic creeps over me, and I try to move, but my body does not respond. I am frozen in fear, but not just for myself. I try to speak, but my voice also seems to have left me. I watch as the stranger raises his hand, and I see the glint of a silver dagger in the moonlight. My terror spikes, and I feel the need to protect someone—but who?*

*I look down into my arms, and I am cradling a tiny babe. Her eyes are glowing blue, and her hair is silver like my own. As her eyes glow, her body pulses—a silver brand of wolves in a trinity circle surrounding a single wolf howling at the moon. I am mesmerized as the brand fades. I must protect her. I must keep her safe and away from this man.*

*In sheer panic, as the man draws near, I finally force my body to move and run away from the lake, knowing I will not be able to make it to the island. And I know that tonight is the only night I will be able to do so. I need to get her there. She will be safe—but how? All I can do now is run.*

*I take off and hear his laugh as I make my way around the lake. His voice flutters through my head and is all around me—You will never outrun me, princess. That voice makes my blood run cold.*

*I run as fast as I can and eventually come to the edge of a campsite. I can smell other wolves and pray to the moon goddess that they find her. Nearby, I* hide the baby in a small patch of wildflowers, hoping she will be safe and that the flowers will mask her scent enough that he will keep following me. I grab the extra blanket and quickly fill it with leaves, bundle it up, and get to my feet, taking off again. My heart aches, but I need to keep her safe. If I can get him far enough away, maybe she will stay safe and find her way home one day.

I try to throw off the scent by cutting my hand. Every now and then, I rub the blood on another tree, leading him further and further away. I can feel my strength waning—I just need to keep drawing him into following me and not look back. I can hear him gaining on me. I still need to push forward. Just a little further, just a little further—I can do it.

My fear rises, my heart pounds, and then I feel a large hand grab my hair and yank me off my feet. I land hard on the ground, and the air is knocked out of my lungs. I start struggling, kicking, and fighting hard to try to get away while I hold the fake bundle for dear life. I need to keep him busy and distracted for as long as possible so someone can find her.

Please, someone save her.

Please, find her...

I see his eyes in the dark and watch them flash red. He starts laughing again. He reaches for the baby. Struggling, fighting, and kicking, I try to get away from his reach. It's no use—he grabs the bundle and lets out a deep growl of anger when he sees the babe is nowhere to be found. His red eyes turn to me, and he raises the dagger. It glints in the moonlight that finally breaks through the clouds.

"I will find her, and she will be mine!"

He brings the dagger down.

I scream.

*And then...*

"No!" I shriek and bolt upright out of bed, covered in sweat. That was the third time this week I have had that same nightmare, and I have no idea why I am having it more and more often. I check my phone on the nightstand, and to no surprise, it is 1:37 AM. That seems to be the time that I wake every time I have this nightmare. Steadying my legs, I make my way over to my bedroom window and sit down on the seat in front. It is still dark and quiet, and for some reason, I cannot shake the feeling of being watched that always comes when I wake. I look out the window into the surrounding woods, as if I will see a pair of red eyes staring back. I take a deep breath and let it out slowly, trying to calm my racing heart.

After a few minutes, my heart and breathing slow, and I am able to relax a bit. What is wrong with me? Why am I so scared, and what is with that dream? It all just feels so real every time. It's more like a memory, but I know that it has never happened.

"You okay?" Kev is in the doorway, and I am still struggling to control my breathing.

"Yeah, I am okay. I'm sorry if I woke you. You should go back to bed." I was hoping no one would hear me when I woke up this time. I don't always yell out when the nightmare finds me, but when I do, it is usually Kevin that responds. It's like he knows I am in distress or upset.

"It's fine. I can sit with you for a while if you like." I do want company. I hate being alone after that dream. I always feel like those eyes will find me.

"Okay, maybe for a few minutes." I feel weak and silly for needing my big brother to chase away the monsters.

"You want to talk about it? Was it that dream again?" he asked.

"No... and yes, it was," I said with a shudder. "I don't know why I keep having the same one." I look at him, and he seems as perplexed as I am. He sits there with me for a little while, and soon my breathing is completely back to normal, and I feel less shaken. He can always make me feel safe.

I hate being so afraid to fall asleep. The nightmare is always the same, but it does not get easier to see. I am getting more and more scared, like somehow the man with the red eyes is going to actually get me one night, and I won't wake up. Like that dagger will hit its mark, and I will be gone forever.

"I really am sorry for waking you, Kevin."

"It's okay. I woke up just before I heard you, so you didn't actually wake me," he said as he handed me Archie, my stuffed elephant. I have had him since I was little. When I was small and would have a nightmare, I would hold him and rock him. I would pretend that he had the nightmare and that I was comforting him, just like my brother comforted me. I didn't have to do this a lot, as most of the time, my brother always seemed to know when I was awake and scared.

I lay there and let Kevin's presence soothe me, and eventually, I feel myself grow sleepy again. I focus on the peace I feel with Kevin close as I hold Archie and allow myself to drift off again for the night. At some point, I am aware of Kevin leaving, but I am no longer afraid. I let the nothingness surround me and drift off. Thankfully, the nightmare does not come back, and I sleep throughout the night.

# Chapter Two
## *Aylin*

The sun starts glaring through my window. Groaning, I pull my covers over my head. I don't want to get out of bed. I enjoy curling up in my soft comforter and snuggling in the warmth. If I were a cat, I would purrrrr. The last dream I had was a bit more pleasurable, and I want to get back to that.

"Rise and shine, loser." My brother laughs as he jumps and lands on my bed, effectively waking and pinning me under his weight. The huge oaf.

"Get off, Jerkface! You're crushing me!" He is laughing, and it causes me to laugh too while hitting him to get off. "Why are you so annoying?"

"Come on, Mom says it's time for breakfast, birthday girl."

I groan inwardly. I just want to go back to sleep and dream of soft lips and strong hands pulling me close.

I think about that for a minute. Today, I would know if I met my mate—I would finally be able to recognize him. I am honestly terrified of finding him. What if he doesn't like me? What if I don't like him? What if I get rejected? Although I have been shunned and rejected all my life, aside from my family and a few close friends, a rejection from a mate is far worse. It is a physical break, and some have a hard time coming back from it. They say in rare circumstances, you can find a second-chance mate if you are rejected or your mate dies. It is rare to find a fated mate; a second is nothing short of a miracle—one no one here has ever witnessed.

"Fine, I will be down in a few minutes. I need to get ready."

I kick my brother out and head to the bathroom. I have a funny feeling building, and for some reason, I really want to look nice today.

The water takes a minute to get hot to where I like it. Climbing in, I let the water cascade over me and ease my sore muscles. I have been training extra hard lately. My mother does not know it, but I plan on joining the guard. The exertion in the woods yesterday with Lance was definitely noticed.

After a few minutes of relaxing, I wash with my strawberry shampoo and vanilla body wash. I love the way the smell combines. It makes me think of the dessert from last night. I hope there is still some left.

After finishing, I turn the water off and grab a towel. Wrapping the soft material around me, I climb out of the tub and make my way back to my room to get dressed for the day. I throw on a powder blue camisole and black jeans. Simple, yes, but that is my style. I like to keep things simple.

Looking in the mirror, I wonder if I should try to do something with my face and hair. I look at my reflection, assessing myself. I don't feel any different. I don't know what I was expecting to feel, but I don't feel different—that is for sure. I still have the same pale skin, sapphire eyes that are big and round, set into my heart-shaped face, and thin lips. Oh, how I wish they were full. And my long silver hair.

This is why I am so different. This is how people here know I do not belong. I am the only one with silver hair.

I am not sure why I bother.

Shrugging, I run a brush through my hair, take another look in the mirror, and head out my door.

Downstairs, I can hear my mom and dad talking excitedly, but when they see my face, they stop and look over at me with big, mischievous smiles.

"What's going on, guys?"

They wait for me to sit down and start eating. Mom really went all out—pancakes with powdered sugar and strawberries, bacon, eggs, and hash browns. I take a big mouthful and wait for them to answer.

"We have a surprise for you!" my mother exclaims as she hands me a small box wrapped in green glitter paper. "Happy birthday, sweetie."

"I thought I got my gifts last night. What's this?"

I unwrap the gift, and it is a jewelry box. Upon opening it, I find a beautiful gold locket with a silhouette picture of a wolf howling at the moon.

"It's beautiful! Thank you guys so much!"

I absolutely love it.

I open the locket, and on one side is a picture of my family— my mom with me in her arms, my dad with my brother Kevin, and my sister Jolene. All of us are laughing, not even paying attention to the camera anymore. Those are my favorite kinds of pictures. Ones that are not staged—just real-life moments captured in time.

On the other side of the locket is an inscription: **"Forever our little girl, our daughter of the moon."** With a beaming smile, I jumped up to give them hugs. My chest swells with how much this little locket means the world to me. I blink away the tears that start to form in my eyes and hug them again.

**"The locket is wonderful. Thanks, guys! I truly love it."** They hug me back and both tell me how much they love me. No matter how old I get, I still love getting hugs from my parents. It makes me feel comfortable and protected.

At that time, my brother and sister walked in to sit down with us and eat, wishing me a happy birthday. Everyone is in such a good mood, laughing, joking, and talking animatedly about everything we are going to do today—even though I am dreading it. Any time I have to go to big events with the pack, I get this way. I don't like being stared at and talked about, and that always happens.

My sister, the youngest at sixteen, was going on about what she plans to do at the festival today. She is beautiful—tall with long, dark blonde hair that shines. She has slender, long legs and a small frame. She has high cheekbones, a small, straight nose, and big brown eyes. Her smile could light up a room—and often did—to go with her bubbly personality. She never had a problem making friends or entrancing boys.

My brother is the oldest, but not by much. He is only eight months older than me. He shares similar features with our sister, except his jawline is sharp, while my sister's is soft. They both take more after our father—except for the eyes. They have our mother's brown eyes. I wish I looked more like them.

Almost everyone in my pack knows I was adopted. This has caused a lot of people to treat me differently, as I am not originally from this pack. My parents told me they adopted me as a baby after finding me in the woods crying. They do not know where I came from or who my original pack was. This also made others even more uneasy. There were a lot of rogues, and the biggest fear was that I had rogue blood in me. My parents tried hard to make me feel like I belonged here, but it has not been easy for them. Most lost children do not get adopted. If you have no parents, you are usually sent to the orphanage and automatically become an omega who serves the pack. I still think this is an awful thing to do to a child. The only exceptions are usually those of high rank. They would never send an Alpha-born child to an orphanage.

My mother always tells me to ignore them, but honestly, sometimes it's hard. I do not like being different from everyone, and sometimes I wish I could find out who my original pack was. I have never said this to my mom for fear that I would break her heart. That is the last thing I would want to do to someone who has done so much for me.

"Are you excited, sis?" Kevin has not been able to shut up about his wolf for the last eight months and is eager to see mine. Everyone who lives here has gray and brown wolves except the Alphas. Their wolves are either a very dark brown, almost black, or black. It is a trait that only those with Alpha blood tend to have—which, in my opinion, is odd since white fur is what deems you as having royal blood in your family. So the dark fur in Alphas has always been an odd concept to me.

"Honestly, I am not looking forward to the first shift." I first sensed my wolf about a year ago, stirring inside of me. This is something that had my parents worried, since the wolf usually slumbers until around your nineteenth birthday. Yet mine has been talking to me and motivating me since just after my eighteenth birthday. The doctor seemed to think this was because I was more solitary, that the wolf had to be there for me. However, I think it was from the abuse I was dealing with from Lizzie and her friends—that my wolf showed up to give me strength to deal with them.

I cannot wait to see her. But again, I am so scared for this shift.

"I wonder what she will look like," Jolene says, mirroring my thoughts.

"How long does the pain last?" I have not asked before because I was scared to know.

"It's different for each person." My dad puts a reassuring hand on my shoulder. "For most, it's only a few minutes. However, the stronger the wolf, the longer the transition can take. An Alpha can take up to an hour or more for their first transition."

I groan, and my dad hugs me. "Sweety, we do not know what your lineage is. However, there are not many with alpha blood. I am sure you will be okay." My mom's words give me some comfort. She is right—the likelihood of my having alpha blood is low.

My siblings, on the other hand, are betas. My brother's transition took thirty-two minutes, and my sister's will probably be similar.

"We need to go over the itinerary again so we are all clear about what we are doing today," my mom chimed in. "The Festival of the Moon Goddess is going to start at about eight p.m. and will last well into the night. I know we all want to stay and enjoy this, but your sister's transition will be starting when the moon is at its zenith, so you all better find your way back home to watch her first shift."

Everyone agrees and promises to be back so they can be there for my first shift. Usually, this celebration is a big deal, and most of the community attends. It took a while, but I finally got my parents to agree to have a small gathering at home with a few friends and family. The Alpha gave his blessing for this—thank the goddess. Besides, it's not like the pack really wanted to be there. I often wonder if they agreed because no one wanted to come.

"Okay, everyone, it's time to get ready for your day. Aylin, you need to get changed into the ceremonial dress," my mom added.

"Why can't I wait until closer to my shift?" I really didn't want to go to the festival in the ceremonial dress. I know it's tradition to wear it on your birthday so everyone realizes you are coming of age, but I really didn't want to be any kind of center of attention.

"You know it's tradition, and we are not going to break all traditions for you. We have already agreed to have a small gathering here for you instead of in the yard by the pack house. I know you do not want to be around a lot of people, and you are scared of what may happen, but you will be okay."

My mom, again, is trying hard to set me at ease, but it doesn't work. I smile, though, and hug her because I do not want to let her know how I feel.

I groan inwardly and leave the kitchen to take refuge in my bedroom until it is time to go. I feel exhausted, and the day has not even started.

When I get back to my room, sitting on the bed is another gift box with two dresses inside. I take my time and try each one on. One is the traditional white dress, and this one has a beaded top and a tulle skirt that glittered. Pretty but not me. I will try it on to make Mom happy. The other dress is a spaghetti strap with white on top, and as you look down the body, it slowly fades to a Caribbean blue. It is soft cotton, and I enjoy the way it feels on my skin. It does not flare out far and just reaches the tops of my feet. I put on the matching ballet flats and thank my mom for not getting me heels. My mom went all out on this, and I know how much she wants it to be perfect. I am just happy she understands my style and gave me the choice.

"You look beautiful, sweetheart."

My mom is standing behind me as I look at myself in the mirror, and I can see her trying to fight back tears.

"Hey, Mom, can you help me with my hair? I am not good at that stuff."

She makes her way over to me, guides me to her room, and sits me down at her vanity. She brushes and curls my hair, sending big, bouncing silver spirals down my back. She pulls the front of my hair to the side and pins it back with a few sapphire-studded bobby pins.

She then gets out her makeup bag and applies a small amount of shimmer on my eyelids, draws a thin line of eyeliner across my lids, and then some mascara to fan my long eyelashes. Then she dabs a small amount of pink-tinted lip gloss on my lips and sits back.

I look in the mirror, and I am stunned at the girl looking back at me. This is not the girl who has been running off to the woods, learning to fight. This is a beautiful girl who almost looks like she is glowing. There is not a lot of makeup, but the little bit added makes my eyes pop, and I cannot help the smile that spreads across my face.

I was told not to wear my new necklace because, during the shift, it could break, and I didn't want that to happen. I would be heartbroken if anything happened to it, and I know my parents would be too. I had put both their necklace and the one Zander had gotten me on Archie for safekeeping.

After meeting the rest of the family downstairs, I inwardly groan again. I want to get this over with. I absolutely hate wearing dresses. And then I sense my wolf, Mona.

"You will be fine; we are strong and proud!" She is trying to help me stay calm, but I am still scared.

"My dad says the stronger the wolf, the longer the transformation can take."

"That is true, Aylin, but it gets easier. We will become one with each other and work together."

"Mona? Something keeps bothering me."

"Yes, Aylin?"

"You say we are strong. I know that means this transition can take a while. How strong are we? I cannot be alpha-strong. Someone would have sensed alpha blood in me, right?"

"Aylin, I promise no matter what, we will get through this. We are special." All I can think is, *What does she mean by that?*

I am brought back to attention by a loud knocking on the door. Smiling, I run over and yank it open. Standing there, Lance and Layla are bickering about something again. Goddess, I love these two. I appreciate them more than they will ever know.

I embrace them both in a big hug as they sing *Happy Birthday* to me—very loud and rather off-key, which I know Layla did on purpose since she actually has a very lovely voice.

As I step back, Lance lets out a loud whistle, and I have to fight a small blush. I never really thought of him in a romantic way, but I don't really get whistled at by others like most girls do. I definitely failed in hiding the blush—I can see it in his eyes when he grins at me and gives me a little wink, which only makes it worse.

"You clean up good. I had no idea you could look this hot!" He is smirking and enjoying my torment. Thankfully, his sister smacks his arm for me.

"Lance, you behave. Aylin, you look amazing!"

"I seriously can't wait for you to come running with us and start training with the pack."

Lance is really excited about my wolf coming. He, like my brother, cannot wait to see her. I think everyone is curious as to what she will look like since I was born an outsider. Most packs tend to lean toward one or two colors, just like regular wolf packs. We were not sure where I came from back then, so everyone is really curious.

I let them in, and we step into the living room with my family.

"All right, everyone, let's get a couple of group pics, and then we can head out."

My dad loves his pictures, and even though he may not be biologically related, it is something I got from him. We love taking walks and getting pictures together. I have a few of mine and his, all framed on the wall of my room.

After a few pictures, we all get our things and head out the door. I mentally give myself a shake. I look around at the decorations in the backyard. My family really went all out. Most of the decorations have been up since yesterday; however, Layla wanted to add a few more she thought I would like, and of course, she is completely right.

After I take another look, I hold my head up, straighten my shoulders, and head toward the pack house with my family and friends.

# Chapter Three
## *Aylin*

We finish some last-minute touches and help some others set up their booths. Now, it is off to the main lawn in front of the pack house. There are a few tables and things that still need to be finished. I just wish my mom would have let me put my dress on later. It has been hard helping others and not getting it messy.

As we finish the last of the centerpieces for the tables, I notice it getting darker. It's not like when a cloud covers the sun—it is like night is falling. But it can't be. I follow everyone's gazes and look up. To my utter amazement, right before us is a solar eclipse. I avert my eyes. I know that you can't look at it without causing damage to your vision.

The moon just had to make an early appearance, didn't it? You just can't wait for the party to start. I make myself laugh with that last thought.

The sun is almost completely covered when my wolf says something that gets my attention really fast and fills me with panic.

"It's time."

That is all she says in my mind.

**What?? No, not yet—not till night when the moon comes** out.

**"The moon is out, and it's out for us. It's time."**

What does she mean it's out for me—for us? I'm not ready.

Oh no, no, no—this can't be happening!

A burning pain starts in my abdomen and spreads through my body like I am being set on fire. I look around and see everyone still caught up in the eclipse, so I take off. I run, and I keep running. I can hear my brother yelling for me, but I ignore him. The pain is hot, and it throbs.

I fall to my knees, screaming. I try to get back up, to get to our house, but I can't.

Not here. Not now. Please.

I can hear people behind me, but aside from my brother, I am not sure who is there.

It hits me again and again—wave after wave of searing agony. I am on my knees, screaming, before I can make it home.

No. Not here. Please. I don't want people here. I don't want them to see me.

I am out of view from the pack house but not far enough away. People who were out and about for the festival begin to gather around me. I can hear whispering among them, but I cannot make out what they are saying. I am too focused on the pain.

Next comes a sharp pain, ripping through all of my muscles and deep into my bones—like I am being torn apart. I feel as though my skin is being peeled away. I guess, in a way, it is.

And everything hurts.

From my toes to my face—even my teeth hurt.

This is hell. Why would we want this?

I feel as though an eternity has passed, and I plead for the moon goddess to make it end.

I can hear my mom and dad telling me it will be okay, telling me to hang in there. I can hear my sister asking why it is taking so long.

How long has it been?

I can't tell if only a few minutes have passed or hours.

I can see others, but my focus is off. All I can seem to comprehend is the pain.

So. Much. Pain.

It's never-ending. Please, moon goddess, please help me.

Make it stop.

I beg you.

I feel my bones break and reshape. Each snap and break creates a pain so blinding I want to pass out. I know I am going to finish shifting for the first time as the last couple of bones reshape in my back and legs.

I hear growls and look around—until I realize they are coming from me.

And just as fast as the pain started, as soon as the last bone pops into place—it vanishes.

I am not sure how long it took, but it is over now. There is no lingering pain, and I huff a sigh of relief.

You would have never known I went through anything.

I try to stand, but my legs feel like jelly. I sway a little and catch myself. It's weird being on four legs instead of two. However, I hold myself upright.

I got this.

I will not look weaker than I already do in front of all these people.

And, of course, looking around, there are quite a few people who ended up watching. Most of them are gaping at me. I hear gasps and murmurs, and I could have sworn I heard the word *royalty.*

I shake my head, and I can feel my ears flopping around. That is such a weird feeling—with them hitting the side of my head. Then I feel my tail swish back and forth.

This is going to take some getting used to.

**"Oh my goddess! Your wolf is beautiful!"** Layla exclaims, jumping up and down.

I cock my head at her, and she smiles from ear to ear.

What do I look like?

I look down at my paws.

I am shocked when I see fur the color of snow with strands of what looks like silver shimmering throughout it.

I have never heard of a white and silver wolf.

Could I be from a pack far north or south, closer to the Arctic or Antarctica?

I wonder what the rest of me looks like.

I need to find out.

I look toward the forest and back at my family.

"It's time," Kevin says, understanding what I want.

He is definitely excited.

He, our father, and our mother all shift with me and lead me into the forest for my first run.

I follow Kevin's wolf excitedly. I can't wait to get started. Mona is chomping at the bit to be let out.

Everything is more intense, and it's hard to deal with at first. It's all louder and brighter, even in the dark, and I can smell, see, and hear so much that my senses are in overload. I vaguely realize, as I follow Kevin, that we are not alone. Two gray wolves are behind me, and I realize it is Lance and Layla joining us for my first run. I am beyond happy they are here with me.

After a few moments of getting used to running on all fours, I speed up, passing my parents and brother, taking the lead. I move faster and faster, yipping at the feel of the wind in my fur and the soil under my paws. I can't believe how good this feels. Mona presses against my mind, and I allow her to take over so she can enjoy her first run and finally being out.

After a few minutes, I make out a little clearing next to a spring, and we slow to sit next to the water. It is then that I realize we lost the others. I didn't even notice that they were not behind me anymore. I was so focused on Mona and her enjoyment. I wonder how long I have been on my own. I move to take a drink from the spring and stop. There, I can see a bit of my reflection.

*'Mona, you are breathtaking!'* I exclaim.

*'We are breathtaking,'* she replies. *'I told you we are strong and beautiful—not just in wolf form but as humans as well. You will see that.'*

Mona is always bringing me up and reminding me that we are more than what I can see. She makes me feel better when the world is against me. Mona gives me back control, and I turn my head from side to side, admiring the wolf.

I take a drink and relax by lying by the stream to wait. It only takes a few more moments for the others to catch up, their wolf senses allowing them to follow my trail. When they reach me, they are all panting, and even in their wolf forms, I can see they are a bit shocked.

Kevin's wolf is the first to come to me, and he nudges me with his head. *'We tried to call you through the mind link. Why didn't you slow down?'*

*'I'm sorry, I didn't hear you. I guess I was so focused on everything else around me that I didn't notice you guys were no longer with me.'*

He shakes his head at me, huffing.

*'I can't believe how fast you are,* my father exclaims through the link. *I don't even think our alpha is that fast.'*

That comment makes me swell with pride. I didn't even try, and I really think that if I wanted to, I could go even faster.

Lance and Layla come over and sit beside me, and for a moment, it is nice to just be here as our wolves by the stream. Everyone is talking about how fast I was and how they couldn't believe how my fur turned out. My mom is the only one who seems a little worried, and I'm not sure why.

*'I think it is time for us to head back. There is still a festival going on, after all, and we still need to celebrate your birthday, Aylin.'* My mom, as always, is the voice of reason.

We all get up and head back through the forest toward the pack house. On the way, Kevin jumps off trees and over logs, having me follow behind. I can see why he hasn't been able to shut up about his wolf. This is all so much fun, and I am excited to learn everything I can about being a wolf. Kevin has so many things he wants to do, and I am eager to have him teach me.

I am so happy to see that the crowd that had formed while I was shifting has dispersed. Everyone, aside from me, shifts back to human form, but I cannot seem to change. A whimper escapes me, and my dad is by my side in an instant.

*"It's okay, Aylin. Here's what I want you to do. Think of your human body—how it feels, what you look like—hands, arms, legs, and feet. Focus on that and picture changing back into your human self. It is all in your will—you have to will it to happen."*

I listen to what he says and focus. I think of my body, my long legs, curvy physique, and my heart-shaped face. Then I feel the cracking and breaking, and I howl, followed by a whimper. This lasts for a while, and then I am human again. Once again, as soon as I finish shifting, the pain is completely gone—like nothing happened.

*"That really sucks,"* is all I manage to get out.

My dad starts laughing and then helps me up, at which point I realize I am buck naked. I try to cover myself, which earns another laugh from my friends.

*"Let's get you inside and dressed. Thankfully, we have a backup dress for you."*

I know the dress she is talking about, and I do not want to put that thing on. Unfortunately, I ripped the one I liked when I shifted, which sucks since I was not expecting to shift until later—and I had really liked that dress.

Everyone heads inside and changes so we can all go back to the festival.

Twenty minutes later, Jolene knocks on my door. "You ready? Everyone is about to head out, and Mom wanted me to check on you. Lance and Layla had to go meet up with their parents, and the festival is about to start. They have a special guest for this year's festival, you know."

"Yeah, I am ready. Do you know who the guest is?" I took one last look in the mirror. The dress was not as bad as I thought it would be. The top was a little tight, but the tulle skirt was not as puffy as I thought it was going to be, which I was grateful for. I found the white flats that went with it—again, thankful for my mom not getting me heels—and two minutes later, we were out the door.

"It's Alpha Gideon." The Lycan lord who oversaw our pack and other packs in this region of the country? Why is he coming?

"That's interesting. I wonder why he is here and not celebrating with his own pack," I mused out loud.

"If the rumors she spreads about herself are to be believed, Lizzie says that he is supposed to be choosing her to be his Luna," Jolene shares. Poor guy. That would be awful—being mated to someone like her. However, if it is true, then she would leave this pack, and I wouldn't have to worry about seeing her. That could definitely be a good thing. I smile at my sister and nod, letting her know I was ready.

# Chapter Four
## *Trevor*

The Moon Festival, honoring the moon goddess, used to be one of my favorite celebrations. I always used to look forward to going with my parents every year. Now, it just seems like so much work. It's not the same since my father's passing.

That was five years ago. The rogue attack that took him from us was brutal. We were victorious in the end, but so many lives were lost, including my father's. I heard the stories from his beta over and over—how he went to the aid of one of the other warriors and lost his life in the process.

"Always remember, your father is a hero." His beta, Simon, would always remind me of that. He would remind me of how fair and wise he was as Alpha. He wanted me to be a great Alpha like my father was. Well, I am trying. For the past five years, I have been trying. Now, I am being pushed to find my Luna. That is the only reason I am here at this pack for the festival.

The car slows as we pull up to the North Woodland Pack gates and stop. We wait for them to allow us to enter. The guard who comes over gives a curt nod as he ushers us through.

Being this year's guest at the North Woodland Pack's Moon Festival was supposed to be an honor. I knew that Alpha Stephen was hoping that, since his daughter just turned nineteen, we might be a mated pair, thus uniting our packs. I have yet to meet my mate, and I am older than most when they do. I am now two hundred and twenty-two, and the elders want me to find a Luna for our pack. So, they agreed to this invitation on my behalf. All I know is that I do not want to be stuck with a spoiled princess for a mate. I pray it's not her. The moon goddess would indeed be cruel if it is her.

I have traveled throughout all the Lycan communities, trying to see if my mate was within them. Either she was not of age or simply not there. I am not happy with the thought that my mate may end up being a wolf. I know that by mating with me, they will become Lycan, but I just see it as a weakness.

With me are my trusted friend and beta, Nicolas, and his mate, Nikki. I always found it weird that their names were so similar, but it is what it is. They have been together since they were children, and the day they found out they were mates was an awkward one. They had been friends for so long that I don't think they had any romantic feelings for one another. It didn't take long for that to change, though, once the mate bond took hold.

My thoughts stray to my pack as we pull up the long drive to the packhouse here. The Blood Moon Pack is one of the strongest packs around after the Lycan Kings, and I can't help but wonder how the festival is going at home. I left my Gamma, Liam, and my mother, Carrie, in charge of everything. She has been enjoying planning the event—she always did. She kept saying this year is going to be special, and I can't help but think it was more intended for me and not for the festival itself. She always seems to know when something is going to happen and then is very cryptic about it.

Making our way to the end of the drive, we head up to the packhouse and meet with Alpha Stephen Black. He is a well-built, broad-shouldered man. His hair is slightly graying, and he seems to be happy by nature. His gray-blue eyes crinkle as he smiles at me and invites me inside and into his study.

I can see why he and my dad were friends. They always hoped that his daughter, Lizzie, and I would be mated. It would mean a safeguard for this pack to be allied with ours. I guess now we will see. I never cared for the spoiled girl, but if she is my fated mate, it is for a reason, and I will accept her.

I am surprised when I enter his study and find that she is not there. I thought he would want to know right away if we were compatible. I still pray that we are not. The last time I saw her was only two years ago, and she was too absorbed in herself to even remotely make a decent Luna. Lunas are compassionate and motherly and will defend the pack alongside their mate. This girl cares more about how to spend money and which style to follow than how to help someone else.

However, his son is sitting in the back corner. Zander is next in line to take over as Alpha here, and he looks every bit the part. He walks over and shakes my hand firmly.

"Good to see you, Alpha Gideon," he greets.

"Good to see you too, Zander. We will have to make some time to catch up." He nods and heads back to the corner as his father walks in. Zander was never as bad as his sister, but you can tell he still feels entitled, and I have seen him look down on others, especially Omegas, in the past. I wonder what kind of Alpha he will be. Hopefully, a decent one.

I sit across from Alpha Black at his desk.

"I am so happy you agreed to be our honored guest this year. We are very happy to have you here, son." He was always like this with me since I was a kid. Part of me wants to correct him that I am an Alpha — and not just any Alpha, but a Lycan Alpha. Now, I have the title like him, but he reminds me of my dad, so I just let it go.

"It's good to be back. I look forward to the festivities this year." I try to sound formal and nonchalant as I wish I was back home with my friends and family.

"My boy, you do not need to be so formal with me. We are like family! I have known you for years and watched you grow into a fine Alpha I know your dad would be proud of. I surely am!"

That sentiment made me smile, and I relaxed a bit. Maybe this won't be so bad.

We talk about the proceedings, when I will be announced, and what they have planned for the night. I just nod throughout the conversation and wait for him to wrap up so I can leave his office.

"Sounds good. I need to meet up with my Beta and the rest of my men. I will see you out front." With a polite smile and a nod, I walk out of his study.

"Don't go too far. I will be starting here in a few minutes and would like you by my side so I can introduce you as the honored guest tonight."

"No problem. I will just be out front waiting."

Heading outside, I meet up with Nicolas and Nikki. They are watching the pack members set up and get ready for the festivities tonight.

"Looks like they put a lot of work into making this a grand celebration." Nikki's tone was sarcastic. She knew — along with Nick — that the reason I was here was to see if I would find a mate, and they knew the Alpha here was pushing his daughter. They were as disgusted as I was at that thought. None of us really wanted to be here.

"I suppose they are going overboard so if you and Alpha Black's daughter end up being mates, they have more to celebrate. Maybe even a mating ceremony."

Nick's words made me want to punch him. I sent yet another prayer to the Moon Goddess not to stick me with a selfish brat.

"That's not where that goes! Why can't you do anything right?"

Speaking of the devil—Lizzie, dressed in a tight pink dress showing a very generous amount of cleavage, was standing just a few rows of tables away, yelling at an Omega finishing decorating one of the booths. Nothing about her calls to me, and I sigh in relief. She then looks up and sees me standing there and, with a quick wave, heads straight for me.

"Hello, Trevor. It's been a while," she says in a falsely sweet, sing-song voice that makes my teeth grind.

"That is Alpha Gideon to you. Please show some respect to your superior," Nikki growls and fumes. I can feel her anger at the Alpha's daughter being so informal, as if she had the right to call me by name.

To my enjoyment, she pales and turns red—by the looks of it, in both embarrassment and anger.

"Of course, I apologize, Alpha Gideon. I meant no disrespect. I guess I thought, with us being so close and growing up knowing each other, it slipped my mind."

I smirked at her and nodded.

"Be sure to remember next time." My no-nonsense tone broke no argument, and I can see her pale further.

That lasted all of two seconds before she gave a visible shake of her head and plastered a smile back on her face.

"Are you looking forward to the festivities tonight, Alpha? My father said he would like me to escort you around so you can see everything we have going on tonight."

I can't stand how fake she seems. Her voice is too high, and I can see the calculating look in her eyes, like she is trying to figure out the best way to get what she wants—me. Good luck, little girl. We both know now you are not my mate, and there is no way I would just choose you.

Just as I was getting ready to answer her, I smell the most amazing scent—a mixture of vanilla, strawberry, and moonflower. I lift my head away from her and look around, searching the crowd of people to see if I can tell where it is coming from. There are too many people, and it was a fleeting scent. I notice her trying to follow my gaze and stop looking.

"Alpha, are you seeing this?" Nick is standing beside me and looking above the people toward the sky. I follow where he is looking, and I can feel my jaw drop as we all watch the beginning of a solar eclipse. I look back at him, and he just shrugs. "I wasn't aware there was going to be a solar eclipse this year."

"To my knowledge, there wasn't supposed to be," I reply, just as curious as he is.

After a few moments, we hear a commotion over a group of people, and all I can see is a girl in a white and blue dress rushing off, a stream of silver hair flowing behind her. Silver hair? That's different. No one else here has silver hair. I watch as several others run after her, shouting.

"Ugh, leave it to her to make such a beautiful moment about her." Lizzie scoffs sarcastically and rolls her eyes at the girl who ran off.

"What do you mean?" I ask absently, wanting to learn a little more about the girl with silver hair. Part of me wants to go after her and make sure she is okay. Odd…

"That's just an outsider, not worthy of your time, Alpha. Why don't we go and see what Daddy is up to? I am sure he is going to want to start soon."

I don't like the way she talked about that girl. As we turn to head inside, we stop as we all hear a scream of pain. I look over at Nick and Nikki. Nikki nods and heads off to make sure everything is okay. Then Nick and I turn and head into the pack house after Lizzie.

Oddly, my wolf seems a bit uneasy, and I have an urge to go see where the silver-haired girl ran off to. Was it her that I smelled? Was it her that screamed? Was she okay? I will have to make this quick so I can get back out there and see if I can find her.

Following Lizzie, we locate her father, and we all head to the stage where the sun is now completely covered. I can sense Alpha Black's unease next to me and hear his sharp inhale. I don't think he believed us when we mentioned the eclipse on the way back out here.

Everyone waits for the eclipse to pass, and then Alpha Stephen steps up to the podium in front of the pack house and begins his speech. As I stand there next to him, I hardly listen as I search the people surrounding us, looking for the one with the silver hair. When I don't find her, I feel a bit more uneasy. I mind-link with Nikki to see if she found the source of the scream.

"Alpha, it was a girl. According to one of the people here, today was her nineteenth birthday. The moon being out caused her to shift early."

"Why didn't you reach out sooner and let us know what was going on?" I know she can tell I am irritated, and I don't care.

"I guess I was a little shocked by what I saw," she admits.

"You have seen wolves shift for the first time before." I am really irritated now.

"Yes, Alpha, I was getting ready to tell you what it was when I saw her. I have never seen a wolf like it before, and I was just frozen. I am sorry, Alpha."

"What do you mean?" Curiosity has me now, and I want to know why she froze up and didn't reach out. It must have been big for Nikki to freeze like that.

"The wolf was white and silver; it was like starlight in the dark. I don't know how else to describe it. I thought I was looking at a myth, but I could not be. She looked like the wolves from the stories my mother used to tell me of Crescent Moon." I could hear the awe in her voice, and it made me want to run to her and see what she was talking about. There was no way. With my hearing, I could hear people in the pack muttering about an all-white wolf and heard the term *royal* a couple of times.

"Where is she now?" I need to get out of here and find her. If she had silver fur, it was probably the silver-haired girl, and that is why she ran off when she was shifting for the first time.

"She ran into the woods with some other wolves." This news did not sit well with me, and a low growl built inside that I had trouble pushing down. Why am I so affected by a girl I have never seen? I took a deep breath and chalked it up to worry.

A few minutes later, Alpha Black finished his speech, and everyone started to cheer and clap. His wife, daughter, and son stepped up beside him and waved to the crowd.

Alpha Black turned to me then. "Why don't you show Alpha Trevor around, Lizzie?"

"That is a great idea, Daddy," she replied in that same sing-song voice.

"I was actually hoping to catch up with Zander, if that's okay."

Zander looked between me and his father and then shook his head.

"Sorry, Alpha, I am running over to my friend Kevin's place really quickly. It will be a few minutes. I will meet up with you later." He nodded toward me and then his father and ran off, leaving me with the bubbly blonde that is his sister.

"Follow me, Alpha," she says as she worms her arm into the crook of mine and walks me off the stage and into the crowd and festivities. I debated on removing her arm from mine, but with her father watching and me being ever the diplomat, I just had to deal with it. Goddess, did I loathe her touch.

# Chapter Five
## *Aylin*

As we head out of the house, I listen to my sister gush over how hot she heard the guest speaker is. All I can think about is the fact that he is rumored to be from the Blood Moon pack. That is not just any wolf pack. They are Lycans, and from what I know, he is directly related to the Lycan King.

Jolene stops talking when she notices someone running toward us. "Is that Zander?" I look up and feel butterflies when I see his sandy brown hair and toned, muscular physique headed toward us.

"Yeah, looks like it. He must be looking for Kevin."

Zander stops before us and, as usual, doesn't pay much attention to me as he asks where Kevin is. Goddess, he smells good—like cinnamon and pine. He reminds me of Christmas morning. Has he always smelled so good? Then he tenses, lifts his nose into the air, sniffs, and looks at me. Our eyes lock, and my stomach flips.

*It's him. Oh goddess, it's him.*

"MATE!" My wolf screams in my head, and I cannot help the smile that spreads across my face. At least, that is until I see his reaction. He does not look happy. In fact, there is definitely confusion on his face and what I think might be anger—and maybe even sorrow. That makes my heart sink. At that moment, I know what is going to come, and I want to run from it. I take an involuntary step back and shake my head.

"Jolene, can I talk to Aylin for a minute?" Zander looks at my sister and smiles warmly at her. The ache in my heart grows. She looks between us and nods.

"I'll see you at the festival, Ay!" she says, smiling before running off to join the music and noise and find her friends.

Zander looks back at me and offers a small smile. "Look, Aylin, you are a nice girl, but I am going to be the Alpha of this pack soon. I cannot have a Luna who came to us as an outsider. Maybe if we knew where you were from, it would be different, but no one will want me as their Alpha with you as my Luna."

His words hurt so much. The goddess paired us, and if she thought I was worthy of being a Luna, then that should have been the end of it. Mates are special and rare, and mine wants nothing to do with me.

"I understand," is the only thing I can get out as I do everything in my power to stand strong and not show how much he is affecting me, even though my chest is so tight I can't breathe. I watch as he closes his eyes and takes a deep breath.

"Okay, I am really sorry about this. I, Zander Black, future Alpha of the North Woodland Pack, reject you, Aylin Archwood, as my mate and Luna."

The howl from my wolf is the saddest noise I have ever heard, and the pain that rips through me is unbearable. It isn't just like a knife cutting out my heart, but more like my very soul is being torn in two.

I take a deep breath. "I, Aylin Archwood, accept your rejection to be your mate and Luna."

Everything inside me shatters. My eyes start to fill with tears, and I struggle not to let them fall. Zander looks at me one last time, and for a moment, it seems like he is just as sad and affected as I am. But then, just as quickly, it's gone, and he straightens himself up.

Besides, if he cared, he wouldn't have rejected me in the first place.

He looks away and then speaks one last time.

"I am so sorry to hurt you. It's the last thing I want to do. Please believe me." He turned and left. I couldn't believe him. If he didn't want to hurt me, he wouldn't have done it. Why even bother apologizing when this very action is so painful?

Mona and I watched him walk away, and the entire time, she howled in my head. Numbly, when he was out of sight, I turned to head back to my house. I walked through the garden that I helped my mom plant. I stopped for a moment at the moonflowers. They would not open till nightfall and were my favorites. I walked past the fence and sat in my backyard, close to the edge of the woods, for a while, listening to my wolf mourn the loss of her mate. My heart and soul were in pieces, and a strange numbness seeped into me. My eyes were red and swollen from the tears, and my throat was hoarse from screaming. I was surprised no one heard my meltdown.

An hour later, I still hadn't moved from the ground I sat on at the edge of the forest. Everything in me wanted to shift and run into the woods, like that was where I would find some semblance of peace. The only thing is, I knew if I went into them right now, if I shifted and allowed my wolf to take over, I wouldn't stop. I would run and keep running.

I don't belong here. I never have. This is not my pack. I may have been raised here, but I have always been an outsider. These thoughts keep spinning around in my head, along with thoughts of where I could go and what I could do if I left. Then I think of my family—the only parents I have ever known. They loved me and raised me as if I were their own daughter. I think about Kevin, Layla, Lance, and Jolene. I do have people here who care about me. Could I just leave them?

This is how Kevin finds me. I don't even hear him come up behind me, which shows how distracted I am. He can never sneak up on me, and yet this time, when he touches my shoulder, I start in surprise.

"What are you doing? You're missing one hell of a festival. Mom and Dad were looking for you, and—" That's when he sees my face. "Ay, what's wrong?" He went from carefree to serious in a nanosecond. Could I really bring myself to just leave him? All of them?

"It's nothing, Kev. I'm okay. I just need a few more minutes, and I will join you." I tried to make myself sound steady and sure so he would not see how broken I was. I should have known, though, that I couldn't fool him.

"Bullshit. What's going on? You know you can talk to me. Haven't I always been there for you?" He has. From the very beginning, he has been there for me. But how do I tell him one of his best friends just rejected me?

"Kev, please, I can't! It hurts too much!" Tears start to well in my stupid eyes. I hate feeling weak, like some damsel needing saving. I was no damsel in distress, and I didn't want anyone to look at me that way.

"Hey, hey, it's okay." He wraps his arms around me and pulls me closer. "It's okay. Tell me what's going on. I'm here for you, Ay." At his word, I release a sob, and he sits there in the dirt and rocks me. A few moments later, I am able to calm myself again with some great strength and look up at him.

"I found my mate," I said.

He seemed confused at first, and then he smiled.

"Ay, that is great news. I don't understand…" Then understanding hit him. I saw it in his face. The smile slowly faded into realization, and then his face turned sad for me. Finally, anger radiated from him.

"Who?" was all he said.

I could feel him shaking with anger—the same anger I was feeling. However, mine was mixed with the sorrow my wolf was supplying me. I shook my head at him and lowered my face. He put his fingers under my chin and tilted my head back up to meet his eyes.

"Who, Ay? Please tell me who did this to you." Tears brimmed my eyes yet again, but I refused to let them fall. I let the anger start to take over more instead.

"Zander," was all I managed at first. His reaction was of shock and then back to anger and rage.

"Jolene and I were walking to meet you all after I finished getting ready in this horrid dress." That made him huff a small laugh.

"He was coming to see if you were at the house or not, and he couldn't find you. Then, when he looked at me, it was like a shock went through me. My wolf knew instantly and was so happy that we found our mate so fast. He asked Jolene if he could talk to me, and she left. That is when he rejected me." I was starting to breathe heavily, trying hard not to cry and get it out. "He said that he could never have me as a Luna and the pack would never accept it." I took a deep, shaky breath, trying to find calm again.

Kevin was staring into the woods. I could feel him shaking, and I knew it wasn't because he was cold. "I'm going to kill him. I am going to rip out his heart and feed it to him." His eyes flashed red for a moment, and I honestly believed he would do just that.

"Kevin, I love that you want to protect me and fight this for me, but you can't." He looked at me in disbelief, and then he slowly calmed down.

"I can try," he said finally. "I will always be there for you, sis. I love you." He held his forehead to mine for a moment, and we calmed.

"You know, if we don't head toward the pack house soon, Mom and Dad are going to come looking for us," he said, trying to bring out some kind of smile from me. "Honestly, I can't wait to see what Mom's reaction is going to be when she sees you got your dress dirty."

That made me smile. She will be mad that I hadn't even made it five minutes without getting my dress dirty.

"It's not that bad," I said, looking around me. And it wasn't. I had sat in the grass, and it was mostly fine. He helped me to my feet, wiped the lingering tears from my cheeks, and we walked in silence toward the pack house. I continued to take deep breaths and tried everything in my power to keep myself steady.

As we got closer, we could hear the music and the laughter as everything was in full swing. My brother led me over to the side of the dance floor, and we watched our parents moving gracefully around it. I couldn't help but smile at how carefree they looked as they swayed and spun around the others. In this moment, I forced a smile for them and the joy they were having. Inside, I was in knots, and I couldn't help but think: This is the worst birthday ever.

After a few more moments on the dance floor, my mother noticed us standing to the side. To my relief, Kevin didn't leave me alone. He knew I was a mess, and I knew he would not leave until I was with others he knew were safe and had my back. I also knew that when he was scanning the crowd, he was looking for Zander, and I didn't want him to do anything that would get him in trouble.

"Please leave it alone, Kev." He looked down at me and sighed. "I know you, and I know whatever you're thinking is going to get you in trouble. He is the Alpha's son, and you can't do anything to him." He shook his head at me.

"Oh, I most definitely can do something, but I promise I will control myself enough not to kill him. Even though we both know he deserves nothing less. A mate is so rare, and the Moon Goddess herself chooses them. There is always a reason for her pairing, and you would have been an amazing Luna for us. You have to see that."

I smiled up at him. Always my champion. Kevin saw only the best in me. I never understood how he could have so much faith in me. He once told me somehow he just knew I was special—he could feel it—and my type of special needs to be treasured.

"What has taken you so long?" My mom stops before us, panting a little from all the dancing. Both she and our dad have the biggest smiles on their faces. What cheeseballs.

"I had a klutz moment and hurt my ankle," I said quickly before Kevin could say anything. He looked at me and narrowed his eyes, letting me know that this wasn't over.

"Honey, are you okay?" Going into full mom mode, she takes my arm and leads me to the table to sit.

"Yeah, Mom, I'm fine. I just needed to take a few minutes and let the pain subside so I could walk over. Thank God for quick healing, and as long as I just twinged it and didn't really damage it, then it was believable. I could also explain my red eyes and why I was crying if asked—tears of frustration for being such a klutz, I would say.

"Honestly, Mom, I feel much better."

She gave me a questioning look and then sighed, threw up her hands, and let it go. Thank the Goddess. I didn't feel better, though—I really didn't want to be here. My heart and soul were in a million pieces.

"If you truly feel better, then I suppose you would grace your old man with a dance?" my dad asked, holding out his hand to me. "It's only fair I get a dance from the birthday girl."

I smiled up at him and put my hand in his. His hand was warm and calloused from training and work. There were a few small scars on his hand from fights when he was younger. From what I understand, he was quite the scrapper.

"Okay, Dad, I would love to, but you know I have two left feet. I won't be anywhere near as graceful as Mom."

He smiled at that and leaned in close to me.

"She isn't as graceful as you think. I just make her look good," he whispered loudly.

My mom batted his arm and acted offended by what he said, making us all laugh.

"Besides, I know you are a beautiful dancer. After all, I taught you," he smiled cockily.

"Shall we?"

He wraps one arm around my waist and holds my hand in his other. The band started the next song, and my dad led us out onto the floor, swirling me around like I was a little girl again. The feeling of dancing and moving around the dance floor was phenomenal, and for a little while, I was able to get my mind off my heartache. I focused on my dad, on the dancing, and on the joy of the people surrounding us.

Somewhere in the circling and spinning, another tantalizing smell hit me. It was like the forest in the morning — coffee and dark chocolate. It made my mouth water, but just as quickly as I smelled it, it was gone. The scent faded in and out several times over the course of the dance. It was mesmerizing and distracting, and then it was surrounding me.

I turned around and looked up into a pair of sea-green eyes that took my breath away.

No, this can't be. It is impossible… MATE.

# Chapter Six
## *Aylin*

"Mate?" my wolf said in my head.

No, there is no way we were just rejected by our mate. This Adonis of a man couldn't possibly be my mate.

"MATE," Mona cried louder in my head. "We have another mate! He could heal our soul." She was way too excited for this.

"Or he could kill us," I reminded her. If you are lucky enough to find a second-chance mate and they also reject you, your soul cannot take the fragmentation, and you die. Fear spiked through me as he looked at me like he was trying to read my thoughts. My instincts were telling me to run after what just happened. I couldn't take another rejection so close together, and I knew I would not survive.

"He hasn't rejected us," she said simply, yet was what I thought in response. I couldn't stop staring at him. Tall, dark, and handsome did not do him justice. He was gorgeous, with bronze olive skin, slicked-back lush hair the color of midnight, and a jaw that could cut glass. His high cheekbones and slightly crooked nose only added character, and his eyes were a dark green like the lush forests I love and long to be in. I was entranced by his features and presence — all dominating and consuming.

"I am so sorry we did not see you there," he said to me and my father. My dad looked at him for a moment and then seemed to realize who was standing before us.

"Ah, Alpha Gideon, I am sorry I was not there earlier for the meeting. Today is my daughter's birthday, and we were spending some family time together before the festival. I hope you will forgive me. It's not every day your daughter turns nineteen." My father beamed down at me with joy and love in his deep blue eyes that crinkled at the corners.

"It is very lucky that I am here today on this special day of yours, Miss?" He was looking for my name, and I wanted to give it to him. I was still in shock. What was he playing at? Did he not know I was his mate?

"Aren't you going to introduce yourself, Ay?" my dad asked, nudging me.

"Sorry, yes, my name is Aylin. My friends call me Ay," I said in response.

"Aylin," he said like he was testing it and smiled. "It's a beautiful name." He gave me a small smile. "Would you honor me with a dance on your special day?" he asked.

That was when I noticed he was not alone. Lizzie was standing slightly behind him with a hand on her hip, scowling at me.

"That is a wonderful idea," my dad chimed in. "I would like to go snag your sister and get a dance with her before she gets too involved with her friends. She did, after all, promise to amuse me with a dance." He bowed toward the

Alpha, kissed my forehead, wished me another happy birthday, and walked off to find Jolene.

I turned back to the Alpha and glanced behind him at the female glaring daggers at me. "It really would be an honor, Alpha Gideon, but I think your date wouldn't be too happy with it," I said, taking a step back. Lizzie narrowed her eyes at me. Yeah, she definitely wouldn't like it, and I would probably be in for it when she and her friends caught me alone again.

"I am not here with a date," he said, taking a step toward me. His comment made Lizzie blanch and turn red.

"I am sorry, I just thought that you and—" He held up his hand and cut me off as I motioned toward Lizzie.

"Ms. Black was showing me around and fancied a dance. As a gentleman, I obliged. Now, I would like to dance with you," he said matter-of-factly.

Lizzie looked completely dejected, and I was enjoying her dismay. Even if it did cost me, I wanted to be in my mate's arms.

"Ok, it would be rude to refuse an Alpha," I said, trying to justify wanting to dance with him. Even though I shouldn't have to—he is my mate and has not rejected me. Lizzie went back to glaring daggers at me, and I knew she would make me pay for it later.

"Please, Alpha, you do not want to waste time with this outsider. We really should move on," she started, but again, he held up his hand to silence her—something she really did not take well.

"I think I can decide for myself what it is I want to do next, and I would like to dance with Aylin." He smirked at me, and for some reason, I felt like he was enjoying her misery, too. She gave a curt nod, stepped to the side of the dance floor, and watched our every move.

He wrapped his arm around my waist and took my hand in his other one. Sparks ran through me at the touch of our skin, and I took in a sharp breath. The only thing that made me aware he felt anything was the slight widening of his eyes and the tick-up at the corner of his lips. Then, just like my father did, he led me out onto the dance floor, spinning and turning me in time with the music. Everything fell away, and it was just us. I was lost in his eyes, drowning in them, and I didn't want to come up for air.

The song drew to an end, and reluctantly, we separated from each other.

"That was way better than dancing with my dad," I laughed. "But don't tell him I said that."

I couldn't help the smile on my face. It felt so good being in his arms—warm, safe, and wanted were the words that came to mind.

"Your secret is safe with me." He held up his hand in a Boy Scout salute, and I couldn't fight the giggles that burst from me. He smiled down at me then—a full smile that showed a dimple on his left side—and my breath caught. So mesmerizing.

"Well, thank you for the dance, Alpha Gideon," I said, smiling up at him.

"Please, call me Trevor."

I grinned more. I liked that he didn't want me to be so formal. You don't get a request from an Alpha often to call them anything other than their title. But then again, being his mate, I guess that is a normal request.

"Well, now that that is over, we should probably go." Lizzie appeared by our side within seconds. The smile left my face, and reality started to sink in. Of course. Why would he want to spend time with me, even if I was his mate when he could have the Alpha's daughter?

"I have plenty more to show you with the festival." She beamed up at him.

"Actually, Lizzie, I think I would like my mate here to show me around."

Both our heads snapped up to him in disbelief. He just called me his mate. Mona was running, leaping, and yipping in joy in my head, and the smile that had faded was back— along with two pink marks on my cheeks.

"I'm sorry, did you just say that she is your mate?" Lizzie asked in disbelief. "That can't be. She is nothing—an outsider. An Alpha should be with someone of a strong bloodline."

This got his attention, and he did not look happy at all.

"Do not talk down to my mate again. You are talking about my future, Luna." His tone brokered no room for argument.

She looked between us, her face turning red. I knew she wanted to say something, but instead, she stormed off toward the stage. I watched her walk off—up to her father and… him… her brother, Zander, who only a few short hours ago rejected me.

My breathing stopped, and my heart ached. Trevor looked to where I was looking and saw the Alpha family.

"Are you okay?" he asked.

I nodded and gave him a smile.

I looked back at them. You could see she was upset and was starting to throw a fit, which her dad tried to contain so he wouldn't be embarrassed. You could see the moment she got to the point in her tirade because both her father and brother looked up at Alpha Trevor and then… to me.

Zander's eyes widened when he saw I was the one his sister was talking about, and I stiffened as our eyes connected. I still had an urge to run to him. I had to force myself to look away.

"Are you sure you are okay, Aylin?" Trevor asked concern etched on his handsome features.

I tore my gaze from Zander and back to the eyes that offered so much more and gave him a small smile.

"Yes, I am alright. What would you like to see first?" I asked.

He smiled at me and lowered his mouth to my ear.

"Nothing you can show me here, little wolf," he said in a teasing tone that made me flush with the knowledge of what he was insinuating.

A delightful shiver ran down my spine, and when I glanced up, his eyes were heated, and he looked like he would devour me. My pulse picked up at the sight.

Calm down. Breathe. Calm down.

I chewed on my bottom lip while I thought about what he would like to see, and again, he leaned into my ear.

"You shouldn't bite your lip like that." He wrapped his arm around me. "It makes me want to bite it," he said as if he was talking about the weather.

Oh, Goddess.

His words made me feel hot, and I knew it was all wildly inappropriate. But I cannot deny that I liked it.

"I think, for the time being, we should focus on the festival," I said in a small, breathy voice.

He smirked at me.

"You're right. After all, there is always time for me to find out everything I want to learn about you later."

We were walking away from the dance floor now, and I could feel three sets of eyes boring into our backs, but I couldn't be bothered enough to care about any of them. Not anymore.

# *Zander POV:*

As I stand there, listening to my father go on about his plans, my mind wanders to Aylin. Did I do the right thing? No one would take me seriously as Alpha. No one would accept her as Luna. I would be looked at as weak. I kept telling myself this and telling my wolf. He was not having it. He didn't care that she was an outsider. He wanted her, and he was fighting me when it came to her. He wanted her, and he was not accepting the rejection.

My father commented on something and then snapped his fingers in my face to get my attention.

"Did you hear a word I just said?" he asked me.

I hadn't heard anything he said. My wolf is so loud in my head I can't concentrate.

"Sorry, Father, it's been a long day," I said, hoping he would let it go.

Just then, my sister stormed up, and I could tell she was going to throw one of her famous "Daddy, fix it" tantrums.

"Daddy, the worst thing possible just happened to me! You need to deal with it now." She was waving her hands around, and my dad reached out, trying to calm her.

"Okay, princess, tell me what's wrong," he said, placating her.

"Trevor found his mate on the dance floor and cast me aside! Isn't there anything you can do, Daddy? He was supposed to be with me — mate or no, we were supposed to get married and unite the packs. You said so yourself!" She was getting louder and really moving her arms now.

"Calm down, princess. Don't make a scene. You are better than that. Now, tell me, who is his mate?" my father asked.

"That outsider bitch!" She jutted her chin up toward the dance floor, where Alpha Gideon was standing way too close to MY mate.

My whole body tensed, and then her eyes locked with mine. My wolf howled in disbelief, and it was like another knife pierced my chest. Rejecting her was harder than I could have ever thought, but seeing her with someone else — I didn't even think about that possibility.

"NO!" I say out loud as I watch him pull her gaze from mine and lean in close to her, the smile on her face telling me he was saying things to her that only I should be. Watching the flush spread across her face made me see red.

"He isn't her mate! I am!" I growl.

My father and sister stare at me for a moment.

"That is really disgusting," Lizzie said with a scowl. "How can such a piece of trash have two mates? And how did she get two Alphas at that?"

Lizzie unintentionally had a great question. She was just being snide, but I wonder the same thing.

"Father, he can't have her! She belongs to me!" I told him, fuming and wanting to run after her and rip her out of the arm that was wrapped around her, ushering her away.

"Why didn't you tell me you found your mate?" My father was looking at me now questioningly.

Something seemed to dawn on him when I didn't answer and just looked away. He understood.

"What did you do, Zander?" he questioned.

Lizzie was looking at me now, too.

"I, um, I rejected her," I said, still keeping my head down like a pup, knowing I was in trouble.

Lizzie started laughing.

"YOU WHAT???" my father bellowed.

Several people stopped what they were doing and stared at us.

My father grabbed mine and Liz's arms and led us away to the other side of the packhouse, trying to get a little privacy.

"Please tell me you are not so dim-witted as to reject a mate the MOON GODDESS herself picked for you. What the hell were you thinking?" he fumed.

"I was thinking that she is an outsider, that no one would accept her as the Luna of our pack, and therefore, they would think I am a weak Alpha," I defended myself, trying to show him the logic of it.

"A mate picked by the Moon Goddess would strengthen the pack more than a mate of your choosing. **She** would be the backbone of everything and give you more strength — and I do mean actual strength and power — than you could think possible." He was really mad, looking at me like he wanted to knock me into tomorrow. "How could you throw that away?" he asked.

"I don't get it. You're strong, and you and Mom are not fated mates," I said, trying to grab onto anything to help me justify what I did.

"Yes, and imagine how much stronger I could have been if I had found my fated mate. I love your mother, but the bond of a fated mate would have strengthened our pack beyond measure."

I lowered my head again. How could I fuck up so bad?

"Dad, what are we going to do? I want to take it back. I don't want her with him. My wolf is fighting to get out to claim her as his own. I almost couldn't contain him when I saw them together." This can't happen. I made a mistake.

"I don't know. A Lycan's claim is absolute. They only have one mate and no chance of another. It is even rarer for them to find one, so I don't see how he will give her up," he said, and any hope I possibly had vanished.

"Well, you better figure out something. I want to be his Luna. You promised me I would be," Lizzie piped up.

"We have more problems than getting what you want, Lissette!" My dad's use of her full name and not a pet name got her attention, and she shut up quickly.

I looked back toward the area where I last saw her, searching while my dad stood next to me, thinking about anything we could possibly do to take Aylin back.

# Chapter Seven
## *Trevor*

I still can't believe that I found her. I was sure that I was going to have to choose a Luna, but here she is, and she is beautiful—so much more than words can describe. Her unique silver hair flows down her back, her heart-shaped face, and her expressive blue eyes—it's like looking at sapphires that can see into my soul. Her body is the perfect balance of fit and curvy. Goddess, I want to run my hands down her frame to her full, round ass, grab her, and pull her close to me. Later, I tell myself.

The feel of her in my arms is utter perfection. The sparks I feel wherever our skin touches make me crave more contact. I love the fact that she has erased the feel of that princess from me. I know I am trying to keep good relations with this pack for my father's sake, but I really cannot stand that girl. I have never met anyone as stuck-up and fake as her, and I have met a lot of people, being the Alpha of a pack of Lycans.

My uncle, the Alpha King, would send me on jobs to take care of squabbles between other Alphas. I take that role seriously, but it does mean I have to put a lot more on the shoulders of my Beta, Delta, and Gamma. I trust them to do my job in my stead and only them.

The thing that is bothering me is the way she reacted to Liz and how she looked at Alpha Stephen and Zander. What was going on between her and them, and why did I sense so much pain? I can see it radiating from her, and my Lycan, Bane, is demanding I take care of her. I wanted to know, but I knew better than to pry. Even being her mate, we have only just met, and the last thing I wanted was to do something that could push her away. I would ask her later.

After a little implied banter, we walked away from the dance floor for her to show me around the festival. The first thing she took me to was a stand that serves apple dumplings. I couldn't help but admire the way her face lit up when she saw the stand. I hope one day to see her light up like that—or more—when looking at me.

"This is my favorite food at any festival, and I get them every year. I usually get one with my best friend, Layla, but I don't see her anywhere." She looked around at the people nearby and then shrugged. "Do you mind if I get one?"

"Not at all. You don't need to ask me for permission, Aylin," I said with a small smile.

"It's just... you're an Alpha, and I am supposed to be showing you around, right? Not getting stuff for myself," she said in a slightly worried voice.

"It really is okay. Besides, waiting in line for something that makes you happy makes me happy. I want you to show me what you love doing here at the festival."

She looked at me for a moment, brows pinched.

"What about you?" she asked.

"I tell you what—if there is something that catches my eye, I will let you know. But I doubt I will want to see anything other than you and your smile."

It was cheesy, but I didn't care. It made her smile and even blush a little. I like her blush. I am going to have so much fun making her do that as often as possible.

"Okay, deal," she agreed. Then she looked around again. This time, she seemed to have seen someone. She smiled and, jumping up and down, waved someone over.

Two people ran up to her. The girl gave her a quick hug, but the guy picked her up and spun her around, making her laugh. This did not sit well with me. I didn't want any other male touching her. As soon as he set her down, I wrapped my arm around her waist and brought her to my side.

They all stopped smiling and looked at me. I didn't even realize I had growled. My Lycan half is already very protective of her. The guy gave me a quizzical look and then looked back at Aylin.

"Lance, Layla, this is Alpha Gideon of the Blood Moon Pack," she informed them. They both wore slightly shocked expressions and then bowed their heads in respect.

"He is my mate," she added.

Their heads shot up together, and they looked between the two of us with mouths hanging open. It was quite comical.

"I'm sorry, did you say mate?" Layla replied.

"Yes, we met on the dance floor just a few moments ago," she said, and that blush crept its way into her cheeks.

"Hold on, I'm confused," Lance said. "We just ran into Kevin! He was really worked up and told us that you were just..."

"Kevin was looking for his friends earlier, and I wasn't sure where they were and couldn't help him. He has a problem with one and wants to call him out on it, even though I told him not to—that it's just a waste of time." She cut him off, and it seemed to confuse him even more, but he stopped talking. Lance and Layla looked at each other and then back at her.

"Brat, are you getting apple dumplings without me?" Layla asked, and they started to banter as the line moved forward.

As they talked and giggled in front of me, I looked over toward Lance. He had made no move to get closer to her after learning I was her mate. Smart.

"I am not very good at striking up conversation. I usually just give orders or deal with matters between packs," I said to him honestly.

"It's cool." He shrugged. "Can I say something without you, I don't know, ripping me to pieces?" He looked a little scared of me, and I understood why. I have an extremely strong presence, and most wolves cannot even meet my gaze, but he didn't back down.

"Go on."

"Don't hurt her!" he said, and I grew a little respect for him. Some of the animosity I was feeling toward him lessened. "She has dealt with a lot, and I am happy she found you. But Lycan Alpha aside, I don't care if I am only a delta-born—I will die for her."

I knew then that he had a deep love for her, and part of me did want to rip him apart—not for the threat, but for the closeness they shared and the love in his eyes as he looked at her. But I respected him for wanting to protect her.

"I will never harm her! What exactly has she had to deal with?" I asked, wanting to know what he had meant.

"I am sure she will tell you what she wants you to know. It isn't my place," he scoffed. "Technically, this isn't my place either, but she is our world. There is something about her that we cannot walk away from—not me or my sister," he said, motioning with his head toward Layla.

"I can admire that," I replied. "I know it will be hard on you when she leaves with me, but she will be safe, and she will be allowed to have visitors and visit with her friends and family," I assured him. I didn't know why I was. Part of me still wanted to rip him apart. I didn't like how he looked at her—almost worshiping.

"That's good! She doesn't have a lot here, and maybe starting over somewhere new will be best for her. I always hoped she would get out of here and away from the judgment of our pack." He must have realized he slipped up and stopped talking.

"I see. Well, I am looking forward to introducing her to my pack as their Luna, and I am sure they will adore her." I knew I already did.

Aylin and Layla got their apple dumplings and led us over to a picnic table. Then I watched as they devoured the desserts and realized they were talking about Lizzie's reaction to my wanting to dance with her and when I told her that I wanted to spend tonight with my mate. They were laughing and enjoying themselves so much that Aylin didn't notice she had dropped some of her apple dumpling sauce on her dress.

"Here, let me get that," Layla said, grabbing a napkin.

"Crap, my mother is going to kill me. I seriously can't keep anything nice," Aylin replied.

"Yeah, but usually, that's dirt and grass stains, not food stains," Layla replied. They cleaned her dress and looked up at Lance and me, realizing we had both been watching them talk and eat with such animation. It was rather amusing.

"I'm really sorry," Aylin said, pink staining her cheeks. "I am ready to show you around if you would like." She gave me a small smile, and I reached out and, with my thumb, wiped away a bit of sauce next to her mouth.

"I am ready whenever you are, little wolf." I smiled down at her, watched the pink seep in again, and knew I would never get enough of how innocent and beautiful she looked when she blushed like that.

She got up and hugged her two best friends with earnest promises that they would talk later, and we were off on our own again.

"So, tell me something about yourself." I wondered how much she would open up to me.

"Well, as you know, they think of me as an outsider here." Well, she is diving right in. Ok. "They will tell you soon enough, so I may as well. I am adopted, and not only am I adopted, but I am not of this pack. My parents found me in the woods upstate when they were traveling back from meeting with the king." This surprised me. Most orphan wolves do not get adopted, and even fewer packs take in pups from other packs. "They were camping and heard crying and found me. My father had smelled blood and followed the trail, and he found who he assumed was my mother. He says I resemble her now that I am older and that he will never forget her face. She was dying when he found her, and he said the only thing she kept saying over and over was, 'Keep her safe.'

"Most people do not know the latter half of that; they know I was found in the woods and adopted. Some fear I was an abandoned child of a rogue. Most just avoid me. So that is something you should know since they are bound to tell you."

"I see. Well, I can see you are not a rogue and that you are very lucky to have such wonderful parents," I told her. "I am sorry that others have let fear dictate their actions." Fear was always hanging around when there was talk of rogues, and for them to believe her parents could have been—no wonder Lance had said she has dealt with a lot.

"Tell me something else." I wanted to change the subject. It was clear she was unhappy about it.

"Ok, umm, my favorite colors are blue and purple. I love sweet foods. Strawberry shortcakes are my favorite dessert, but I love all sweets. I love photography. In fact, my parents just got me a new camera for my birthday." She had a big smile plastered across her face now.

"What kind of pictures do you like to take?"

"Mostly nature, but I really love real-life pictures. You know, the ones where people do not realize the camera is out—they are just living in the moment." She looked up at me with those big blue eyes, and I stopped walking. I raised my hand and caressed her cheek. She leaned into my touch, and my Lycan approved.

"I would love to see some of your work," I told her, and she lit up again.

"So, tell me about you," she said.

"As you know, I am an Alpha. I had to take over my pack when my father passed away a few years back. We had a rogue attack, and he died aiding another." She gave me a sympathetic look, which I usually can't stand, but from her, it made me feel better in a way. "My favorite color is black, and I am not a big sweets guy. I prefer meat."

The conversation went back and forth like that for a while longer. We stopped at a few vendors, and I bought her a rose at one vendor selling flowers and a few more treats at others. Mostly, I just enjoyed being in her company. She had a very calming effect on me and my Lycan. It was like a balm over my frayed nerves — one I hadn't really realized I craved until now.

The night went by quickly — too quickly for my liking — and as I walked her to her house, I could not help but want to keep her with me. The urge to mark and claim what is mine was potent and it was all I could do to keep my Lycan calm. He seemed to sense something was wrong and wanted to make sure everyone knew she was ours.

"I think this is going to be my most memorable birthday," she said with a slight smile, looking ahead as we drew nearer to her house.

"The day you shift and meet your wolf usually is, and you were lucky enough to find your mate the same day. That is not common at all, so I can see why," I replied, squeezing her hand in mine. Goddess, her hand was so warm and dainty in mine.

"Yeah, that is very true. I honestly was not expecting to have a mate, and yet here you are," she replied with a shrug. "I am thankful to the goddess for you!" she said. She had stopped walking now that we were outside her house and looked up at me. Her features were earnest yet serious at the same time.

"I am thankful as well. I honestly thought I was going to have to choose a Luna before long. An Alpha cannot rule indefinitely without a Luna, and the elders were pushing for me to claim one," I told her. "Thankfully, you came into my life just in time, or I would have never had the chance to find you."

I cupped her cheek and brought my face to hers, claiming her lips with mine in an all-consuming kiss. The sparks that radiated through us caused us both to gasp at the intensity. I consumed her. It didn't take much prodding with my tongue to get her to open, and then the taste of her was delicious—cinnamon, apple, vanilla, and HER! I nipped her bottom lip and pulled away.

We were both panting for breath, like in the process of kissing, we forgot how to breathe. I put my forehead to hers and wished her a good night. With one last peck, I watched her walk into her house, and I started to make my way back to the pack house, where I was staying with my Beta.

I was halfway there when I bumped into someone headed in the direction I had just come from. I started to get a feeling in my gut—an uneasy feeling—and I decided to go back to make sure she was okay. I was probably overreacting since I had just found her, but I needed to make sure.

# Chapter Eight
## *Aylin*

The house was dark when I went inside. I shrugged my shoulders—everyone must still be at the festival. So, with that in mind and my blissful mood, I took off my shoes and headed to the kitchen for a glass of water.

As I took my first drink, I felt a shiver run down my spine, and the hair on the back of my neck stood up. I felt eyes watching me. Looking around, I made my way around the counter and into the living space. There, on the end of the couch in the dark, sitting quietly, was Zander.

My heart kicked up in pace, and I turned the light on so I could see him better. Not that I couldn't see him—my eyesight was amazing, thanks to my wolf—but this made me feel a little less scared. What was he doing here, and why was he sitting in the dark?

"I see you finally made your way home for the night," he said, almost sarcastically.

"Uh, yeah. What are you doing here, Zander? If you're looking for Kevin, obviously, he isn't here, and you should try the festival," I said, a little snarky. He narrowed his eyes at me then.

"Is that any way to talk to your mate and future Alpha?" he said, and my stomach dropped. He had what I could only imagine to be a fake smile, as it did not touch his eyes, and warning bells started to go off.

"You are not my mate. You rejected me, remember? I accepted your rejection so you could find someone you thought worthy. You said you didn't want me, that I was no good to be your Luna, remember?" I took a step back as he stood from the couch.

"It was a mistake, Aylin. I changed my mind. We can still be together and fix this. I shouldn't have rejected you, and I didn't want to. I thought I needed to, but I want you!" he said earnestly.

I was baffled. How could he possibly expect me to accept him? The pain he caused me was excruciating. I had dreamed it would be him, and then when I got my wish, my dream turned into a nightmare.

"No, I think you were right. The people here will not accept me, and you can still lead them as Alpha without me," I replied.

He was so quick to reject me. How can he sit here and say he wants me? Why would he play with my heart like this? His face fell as anger and hurt flashed through his eyes for a brief moment. But I noticed it. My hackles rose more.

"No, I won't. I need you. My father explained it: I am the first to find a fated mate in generations, and I need to claim you to have the power that comes with a fated mate. You and I must be together!"

I gaped at him. This wasn't a change of heart at all. He wanted me because the bond of a fated mate was stronger and gave the wolves more power and strength than that of a chosen mate. I rolled my eyes.

"Well, that is definitely going to get me to want to take you back," I said, my tone dripping with sarcasm. Not gonna happen. I crossed my arms and cocked my head. "Knowing you are so deeply in love with the power I can give you makes me sooo weak in the knees," I said, rolling my eyes.

"That is not what I meant, and do not speak to me that way!" he ordered, and I rolled my eyes again.

"You will be mine. You are my mate, and I will not allow you to be a whore and go around letting others touch what belongs to me!" he was yelling now.

And the rage I felt at his words was red-hot.

"I belong to no one! You do not get to reject me and make me feel like I am not worthy of you and then come back and demand I be with you because you want the power you didn't realize would come with claiming me! You do not get to tell me who I can be with or what I can do! You lost any right the moment the rejection came from your mouth, and furthermore, even if Trevor was not my mate, I wouldn't take you back."

He looked dumbstruck for a brief moment, then hurt. Then the anger came back. He took a step toward me and looked like he was getting ready to say something when the door opened.

Kevin walked in and looked at me with a quizzical expression, then looked toward Zander.

"YOU!" he growled and started toward him. I grabbed his arm and shook my head, keeping him close to me. I think he sensed I needed him, and he stepped half in front of me protectively.

"You need to leave before I teach you a lesson for hurting my sister," Kevin demanded.

"That is why I am here, Kev. I was trying to take it back. I made a mistake, and I want to be with her! I want her to be my Luna!" Zander said earnestly.

Kevin looked between me and him, and I tensed. He may want that, but I don't. Not anymore.

"You don't deserve her! She is too good, too pure for someone who cannot see it!" Kevin growled.

"I think that is something we can agree on," a new voice said from the door.

We all three looked over as Trevor entered the house. Kevin pushed me back more. He didn't know of Trevor yet, and it seemed he thought the threat just got bigger. At his reaction, Trevor and Zander growled, and Kevin growled back. He was preparing to fight not one but two Alphas to protect me. I needed to defuse this situation—and fast.

"Someone better tell me what is going on here and why you are keeping my mate behind you. Who are you?" Trevor was too calm as he said this, with a lethal look in his eyes.

Kevin straightened, looked over his shoulder at me, and lifted an eyebrow. "Is there something you need to tell me, sis?" he asked.

I could see some of the tension in Trevor relaxed, but he was still on guard with two other wolves in the room and one blocking him from me.

"I, um, didn't get a chance to tell you yet. Kevin, this is Alpha Trevor Gideon. My mate." I could feel my cheeks burn, and Kevin looked from me to Zander and then to Trevor—then smirked.

"Two mates in one day. Looks like you're too late, Zan," he said, shaking his head.

I stiffened, which did not go unnoticed by the two looking at me—or the one standing in front of me.

"What do you mean, two?" Trevor asked, at which point Kevin realized his mistake.

"She didn't tell you?" Zander asked, half-laughing. "We found out I am her mate as well—a few hours before you met her," he said matter-of-factly. "That's why I am here—to claim that which is mine."

That earned a growl from both my brother and Trevor, one that made every hair on my body stand at attention.

"You have no claim to her!" my brother growled. "You lost your claim when you told her she was no good and rejected her."

I bristled, and my heart ached at his words. I slowly looked up toward Trevor, who was staring at me with shock, sorrow, and betrayal in his eyes. I hadn't even done anything to earn that, and how was I supposed to tell him that just hours ago, someone rejected me?

My traitorous eyes started to fill with tears, and I turned and ran from the room.

I headed for the back door, ignoring the men calling my name. I can't stay here. If he rejects me now, I will not survive it. My heart was pounding, and the pain that was starting to fill me was unbearable. I burst through the door and ran. I ran through the garden and shifted into my wolf. I leaped over the fence and lost myself—in the run, in the wind, and in the pain.

I didn't hear them for a few minutes as I let all of the pain consume my being. My wolf was adding to the heartache. After all, two of us lost a mate and found a new one. The pain from the first loss was both ours and if we lost another, that pain would rip us apart. Just the thought that he was going to leave us was enough to cripple me by the time we reached the meadow I loved so much—the one with the stream I played in as a little girl.

I let Mona take over, and I listened as she howled her pain to the Goddess.

The pain I felt cracked my chest wide open, and something I had never felt before poured from that crack in my chest. I was vaguely aware that the three of them came barreling from the trees — then stopped and stared.

A blinding light from behind my eyes made it impossible for me to see. I could hear my brother's wolf whimper and feel him trying to reach me through the mind link. I could hear him calling for me with worry and fear in his voice. Then, the pain in my chest radiated through my whole being. I felt my body jerk, and then... then I was weightless — like I was floating. A feeling of light and warmth seeped from that crack in my chest and washed over me.

I went from feeling like I was struck by lightning, every fiber of my body being ripped apart, to feeling like I was wrapped in the warmest, softest blanket I could imagine. That's when I opened my eyes. I hadn't even realized I had closed them, but I must have when the pain took me. I looked up at the moon, full and high in the sky. It looked so bright, almost as if it were beckoning me. Then I heard a voice — silky and musical in a way.

"You are beautiful, my child," the silky-smooth voice said to me. "You are strong and have much courage in your heart! Believe in yourself and your wolf. Let her guide you. She will know what to do when the time comes."

The voice and presence were all around me, giving me a feeling of love and life one moment, and then the next, they were gone. And with them, it was like a small piece of me was empty.

The feeling of weightlessness left me, and I could feel the ground beneath me—the grass against my skin. Skin? I was no longer in my wolf form. I tried to stand shakily, but my head felt dizzy, and the world spun around me. Then the ground came up to meet me as the black nothingness found me.

## *Kevin POV:*

We made it to the clearing and watched as my sister's body started jerking. All I wanted to do was get to her. Something inside me told me she needed me, and I was powerless to get closer. Her body jerked again, and she whimpered. Then she started to glow—actually fucking glow—like a star lit up inside her. Then it got bright—not just from her light, but the moonlight seemed to shine brighter. The moon was directly over us right now, and between the two, the lights were starting to hurt my eyes, but I couldn't look away.

Then Aylin's body was raised off the ground. In a matter of seconds—that's all it took, seconds—she shone so bright we had to avert our eyes, and then she slowly lowered back down, now in her human form.

Her body moved, jerking, and then she slowly started to get to her feet. I watched her shaking, and then she fell. I bolted. I knew I needed to get to her and protect her. Something in me just had to. I saw a black blur pass me, and then Trevor's Lycan was standing over her, picking her limp form up from the ground and cradling her to its chest. He sniffed her, then looked at me and Zander and growled in warning.

I shifted to my human form to speak. "I am her brother. I would never harm her. I just want to make sure she is okay. We need to get her back to the house," I said to him, motioning back through the woods. He nodded, and I shifted back into my large brown wolf. I turned to lead the way back to the house and bared my teeth at Zander as I walked by. That fucker is not getting anywhere near her.

It took a lot longer for us to get back to the house as we weren't running and had to be careful not to jostle Aylin too much. We didn't know what had happened, and we needed to get my parents.

When we finally made it back to the house, Zander and I shifted back into our human bodies and went inside. There, we ran into my little sister, Jolene, who gawked at the sight of Zander naked. What was with my sisters and this guy?

"What were you two up to?" she started, then her eyes grew into saucers as she looked behind us at the giant black Lycan. It took a moment for her to realize what he was holding.

"Oh my goddess! Aylin? What happened?" she started to panic and ran toward our sister, only to get growled at by the Lycan. This irritated me, but I understood. He didn't know any of us, and his mate had just gone through... well... I had no damn clue, but she was unconscious, and that was enough for him to become extremely protective.

It also didn't escape me that Zander had tried to block her as well. Was he protective of her? Or was this a show? How could he reject her and then change his mind within a span of hours? What was he getting at? All I knew was if he was so willing to throw her aside once, he wouldn't treat her with the respect and love a mate should in the future, and I didn't want that for her.

We all backed up, Zander less so. It was like he was looking for an opening to get to her, which again, was not going to happen. At least he was smart enough to realize he was not going to get near her with the Lycan present.

Trevor took her toward the living room and looked around.

"Bring her up here to her room," I told him and started up the stairs for him to follow. Then I stopped and looked at my sister.

"Jojo." This was our pet name for my baby sister. "Go get Mom and Dad. Tell them something happened to Aylin, and we need them home immediately. I will explain everything when they get here. I am not sure if we need a healer or an elder, but they are not going to believe what we have to say, and I don't want to leave this house till we speak with them."

She nodded and ran out toward the front door.

I showed Trevor to her room, and he laid her on her bed. We both looked down at her, and he finally shifted back into his human form.

"I called my beta as well. He should be here soon," he said, not taking his eyes off Aylin. "His mate will probably be with him," he added as an afterthought.

I just nodded.

Thankfully, Zander had enough sense to stay out of her room as he waited in the hall. With one more look at her, I turned to Trevor and spoke calmly. "Come with me. I will get us all some clothes from my room. I am not sure how well they will fit you, but it's something for now."

He nodded, and we left her room.

## *Aylin POV*

The run was exhilarating, and now I am back at the stream, looking down at my wolf. I love that we are unique and beautiful, but I wanted to be normal, too. Why couldn't my human side be as beautiful as my wolf? I shift back to human and enter the stream to swim.

Suddenly, I feel strong, warm hands wrap around me from behind and slide around my waist and over my stomach, sending sparks over my skin. Trevor must have followed me.

"You should not run off, my little wolf." He is laughing, and I enjoy the sound. "That was very naughty of you."

"What are you going to do about it?" He laughs again and continues to move his hands over my belly and around my hips. His touch is driving me crazy, and my body reacts to it. My nipples harden even more than they already were in the cold water, and my sex is pulsing with need.

"Why don't I show you what I can do about it?" With another chuckle, he kisses the back of my neck and down my shoulder. He continues back up and moves to the other side. He brings a moan out that starts from inside my chest, all while caressing my midsection with his strong hands.

The coarseness of his hands feels good across my soft skin, and I inwardly beg him not to stop. His hand moves up my front and cups my large breast, kneading and testing the weight. Then he pulls my nipple between his thumb and index finger, rolling and pulling on it. I moan again and grind my backside against him, feeling his hard length straining against his britches.

He has barely begun, and my body is already shaking from his touch. His other hand moves down my stomach and heads toward my apex. He swirls one finger around my swollen clit, making me buck back against him.

He continues to circle my clit, pull on my nipple, and kiss my neck. My body starts to move of its own accord with what he is doing to me, and I start to rub my back end against his front again.

"Oh, my little wolf, I am not going to be able to take my time with you if you keep that up. I am trying to be good for you." I inhale deeply at his words. I want him to continue, but my body is on fire, and I want him to take away the heat I am feeling at my core—now.

"Please, Trevor," is all I can seem to get out as he pushes a finger inside of me, causing me to gasp and then moan. I can hear his sharp intake of breath as he finds me soaked just for him.

"I am very pleased to find you so ready for me, little wolf. I can't wait to be inside you." This man is going to torture me with his words and hands. I need more now.

He turns me around and looks down into my eyes. I can lose myself in the pools of his big green eyes. He lowers his head to mine and crushes his lips to mine in a hungry and intense kiss. He bites my bottom lip, and I gasp at the unexpected pain and pleasure of it. Taking advantage of my mouth opening, he slides his tongue in to caress and play with mine. Before we know it, we are battling for dominance, and with neither conceding, we break away to draw much-needed air into our starving lungs.

He lowers his hands to the back of my thighs and lifts me, causing me to wrap my legs around his waist. He walks us over to the bank, and when he gets farther into the meadow, he lowers me onto the soft pillow of grass.

He gently kisses my lips, then the tip of my nose, and a few on my jawline, down my neck, over my jugular, down to the base of my neck where his mark will one day go. He nips and sucks on the spot, causing me to moan, my back to arch, and me to push my breasts forward against him. My sex is dripping for him.

He continues down to my collarbone, and then I feel both his hands cupping my breasts and rubbing his fingers over my hard nipples. His eyes dart up to mine, and a mischievous smile plays across his sexy face, mesmerizing me. As I watch him, he lowers his mouth and licks one of my waiting, hardened nipples, then takes it into his mouth, sucking and biting, applying enough pressure that there is the smallest amount of pain, yet I can feel far more pleasure. I gasp as the slight pain radiates through my breast.

The hand on my other breast works its way down to my apex, and then he thrusts a finger into my wet, waiting sex. I begin moaning instantly. Then he works in another. He works them in and out and starts to rub circles around my clit with his thumb. I can't focus too much. His hands are working my pussy and my breast, and his mouth is taking me to heaven. The heat in my core is spreading, and I can feel myself building, my hips moving in time with his fingers, trying to get him deeper.

"Let go, baby, let go for me." At that moment, he withdraws his fingers and pinches my clit between his thumb and index finger, and I fall over the cliff as lights explode behind my eyes, bringing forward my first orgasm.

He crushes his lips against mine and devours my cries and screams. His fingers are right back inside me and already working me.

"You are so wet for me, little wolf. I want more. I need to taste you." He works his mouth back down my body, and when his tongue flicks over my clit, I buck my hips at the sensations he causes. He slides his tongue up and down my slit, and my hips start moving again. I hear him let out a low growl, and he tries to hold my hips down as he slides his tongue inside my sex.

"Yes, Trevor!" My legs are already starting to shake, and I can feel myself starting to build again. I don't want him to stop, but I know I am about to go over the cliff again.

"Please, I am so close." I am standing on the edge when he pulls away, and I feel myself come back down. I am aching and full of need.

His smile is dark and erotic, and he slides a finger back inside. I notice he is stroking himself now, bringing himself closer, getting ready to enter me. I lift my hips in welcome, and he places his mouth on mine, kissing me with more fire and passion than I thought possible.

"I am going to enjoy this."

**Buzz**

"I am going to make you scream, little wolf."

**Buzz buzz**

"I will show you who owns this pretty pussy." He moves forward and gets ready to enter me.

**Buzz buzz buzz**

He rubs himself up and down my slit, getting his cock wet, and positions himself at my sex.

**Buzz buzz buzz**

He starts to push himself inside, and I lift my hips to meet him.

**Buzz buzz buzz**

# Chapter Nine
## *Aylin*

My eyes flutter open, and I am dazed for a minute. I look around and realize I am back in my room, in my bed, and covered in sweat. My phone is going off on the nightstand next to me. How did I get here?

Then the memories leading up to the stream come flooding back, and I look down at myself. I no longer feel the pain that radiated all over, and I seem okay. But how am I in my room? I stand and make my way to my bathroom, wash my face, then go back into my bedroom and get dressed. I check my phone and see three missed calls—two from Layla and one from Lance—and several texts from both. I type them both a quick text, telling them I am okay and will call later.

I open the door and come face-to-face with Trevor. Speak of the devil. The one that just consumed me in my dreams is now standing outside my bedroom door. How long had he been standing there?

"Thank God you're awake," he exclaims, wrapping me in a hug. "I was just getting ready to come back in and sit with you. I just left your brother," he says. I hug him back and love the little tingles and shocks from his skin touching mine. He stiffens and lifts his nose, sniffing the air. He looks down at me and smiles.

"Little wolf, what were you dreaming about?" he asks, and I know I am as red as a tomato. He can smell my arousal. He shakes his head and wraps his arm around my shoulder.

"Come, let's go downstairs. Everyone is waiting for you."

I look up at him, curious. "What do you mean everyone is waiting for me?" What is going on?

"We will explain what happened. Let's just go downstairs, please," he says, not letting me go.

"Okay, let's go," I say, letting him lead me down the stairs to my waiting family.

When we get to the living room, I see my parents, Kev and Jojo. Zander is there, though I wish he wasn't. Two others I don't know are present, but I can tell by their presence that they are powerful—and Lycans.

"Does someone want to explain what's going on?" I ask the room, which is now staring back at me with looks of worry and awe.

"Do you remember what happened last night?" Kevin asks. He is sitting by Dad on the couch, and they were talking to each other when we came downstairs.

"Yeah, of course—all the way up to getting to the stream. I felt so much pain I must have blacked out. Before I did, I saw you, Trevor, and Zander there, but who was the woman?" I ask, and he looks at me in confusion.

"What woman?" he asks in response.

"The one that was talking to me. She said I was reborn and that I need to listen to my wolf. She will guide me. That was when the pain subsided, and I blacked out. I don't remember anything after that. I don't even remember how I got home," I say as they all watch me.

"I carried you home and put you to bed after you lost consciousness," Trevor speaks up then, squeezing my hand reassuringly.

"There is more that happened. I am not sure who you heard. We didn't hear anything, but what we saw was... well... it was impossible."

Kevin looks at me, waiting, and when I don't speak, he continues.

"When we broke through the clearing, you were whimpering, and we all seemed to have this overpowering urge to get to you, comfort you, and protect you. Then you started to glow—kind of like a star was shining within you."

I look at him like he has grown another head. Was he for real? People didn't glow.

"For a moment, we all swear we saw you float into the air! The moon got bright, and you got brighter—so much that we had to look away," he continues seriously. "When it dimmed and we looked back, you were back on the ground and trying to stand. That is when you lost consciousness, and we all ran to get to you."

He finishes, looking from me to our parents, shifting back and forth under my stare.

"You're messing with me, right?" I ask in disbelief. "Like, you are all pulling some kind of joke? People don't glow or float!"

I am having a hard time with this. They absolutely have to be fucking with me. I don't know why, but I don't like it.

"No, Aylin, he's not. It's not a joke, and whatever happened to you—I feel it," Zander speaks next. "I still feel the mate pull toward you, even after the rejection."

That makes everyone in the room tense, and several of them glower at him.

"Your claim, even if you didn't reject her, does not matter. A Lycan who has found his mate is absolute and cannot be challenged," says my dad.

I didn't know this.

"How is that?" Jolene asks, and she seems just as confused as I am. "Wouldn't she be allowed to choose?"

"Unlike us, a Lycan only has one fated mate. They do not have a chance to find a second, even with their much longer lifespans. This makes their mates extremely coveted. The law that makes it absolute came around with the previous king of Lycans over a thousand years ago and is one of the most absolute laws to this day," my dad explains.

He looks around and, after a pause, continues.

"To answer your question—no, Aylin would not have a choice. Once a Lycan locks eyes with their mate, they will start to change very slowly until they are marked and mated. Then, the transformation will take place more rapidly."

Kevin, Jolene, and Zander are just staring at him now.

"What do you mean change?" Zander asks.

"I mean she is becoming a Lycan. The process started the moment they locked eyes and his Lycan formed the mate bond with her wolf."

This revelation makes my heart stop for a minute.

"I only just met my wolf. What happens to her? Is she going to be okay?" I am beginning to panic.

"She will be fine," Trevor says calmly. "She will evolve — that's all. From wolf to Lycan. And her and your life will be expanded to accommodate my long life. Like Nick said, she is already changing."

He looks down at me with a smile, but his eyes hold an apology.

"It's not something we can help, and I know you had no choice, but I do not regret meeting you," he adds.

"So, she is going to be a Lycan and has no choice but to be with Alpha Gideon. Even if she wanted to, she cannot choose Zander? Why? What would happen to them if she did?"

Thank God Jolene is so curious. On one hand, I am very curious about it myself, but on the other, I don't care — because I am not going to choose Zander.

"It's simple. She would eventually kill him."

This comes from the tall, blonde, and beautiful Lycan female in the back corner.

"WHAT?" Jolene and Zander say together.

"We haven't met yet, Luna. My name is Nikki. Nick here is my mate and Alpha Gideon's Beta."

She smiles warmly at me, and the seriousness in her face is all but gone as she looks at me instead of the room.

"My mother, like you, was not born a Lycan. She had a mate in a wolf pack, and they were already bonded and even had a child—my older brother. She met my father by accident when they requested an audience with the Lycan king. He was one of the Lycan king's guardians."

She speaks with compassion and wariness, and I have a bad feeling about where she is going. I think we all already know.

"When mated wolves visit the kingdom, they are instructed to keep their heads downcast and not look any Lycan in the face. It sounds bad, but there is a reason for it. We can smell our mates like other wolves, and like other wolves, when mated, that smell goes away. For a wolf, you could meet your second chance mate if it is a wolf and never know, even if you make eye contact. It is not the same for a Lycan. If you are mated, we can still find you, but only by looking in your eyes."

"So, wait." My sister interrupted. "I'm sorry, I am just trying to keep up. A mated wolf will not recognize a possible second chance mate if it is a wolf but can if it is a Lycan?" she asked.

"Yes, that's right," confirmed Nikki. "My mother and her mate visited and kept their heads down until they got to the king's throne room. My mother said she just couldn't help herself and looked around, wanting to see the beauty of a space that most never get to see. She locked eyes on the guardian standing next to the king's throne, and they knew. She tried to downcast her eyes and ignore what just happened, but my father announced it to the king when they fully approached. She loved her mate but had no choice—she had to stay with my father. Her mate tried to fight and get to her, but the guards took him away." She looked sad at this but was not done yet.

"My mother tried to run from my father and made her way back to her pack. She had already started to turn. They were happy to be back in each other's arms and lay together that night. Like everyone else, the mate mark is a sensitive place, and they bit each other. A Lycan's bite is fatal to the one that is not their Lycan mate." Understanding dawned on everyone present. She had tried to mark and mate with the mate she already had, and her bite killed him in the process.

"My mother was forced to go back to the Lycan kingdom to be with her Lycan mate, but she grieved for the mate she lost for a long time. Eventually, the new bond with my father formed, and they still love each other very much. He was there for her through the mourning and did everything he could to comfort her. He knew it wasn't her choice and felt bad for her, but he would never give her up."

Everyone looked at me then, and Zander just shook his head.

"I don't think that would be a problem for us. I could mark her; she just can't mark me," he said with a shrug. I scowled at him.

"First, for the mate bond to be at its strongest, both need to be marked," Nick interjected, looking at him like he would a nasty insect he wanted to squash. "Second, even if that is what she decided and Trevor tried to honor it, eventually their bond would supersede yours, and their pull to be together would win out. Your mark on her will fade no matter how many times you place it on her skin, as she is no longer yours," he said, crossing his arms over his chest.

"This all makes no sense. So even if I didn't reject her and claimed her last night, I would have lost her the moment she saw Trevor?" he asked, and Nick nodded. "Okay, but I did reject her, and she accepted—why didn't the link between us fully sever? It felt like it did at first, but when I saw them together last night, I just wanted to claim her, and I can still feel it now." He was getting angry, but he was right. I could still feel his mate link to me, even though I know I am choosing Trevor.

"He's right, I can feel it too." Trevor tensed at that and looked at me with worry and hurt.

"Do you want him?" he asked worriedly.

"No, I know I have already chosen you, and so has my wolf. So why do I still feel this?" I asked.

"I'm not sure," my dad chimed in. "Maybe it's something to do with it all happening the same night or something with what happened to you in the woods. Kevin said all three of them were drawn to you with an overpowering need to be there for you." My dad was pondering out loud, and we were just trying to see if anything he said would make sense, but it was a lot of unknowns.

"Yeah, but I don't want to mate with her. I just have this need to be there for her, to comfort her, and guard her," Kevin added. "I haven't been able to leave here since whatever happened in the woods keeps pulling me back," he said, and my parents looked worried. I noticed Nick looking at him with an odd expression.

"I feel that too," Zander added. "I know I am not wanted here and tried to leave several times last night and this morning, but I didn't make it far and ended up right back here." Nick's eyebrows furrowed, and then he looked at me.

"Aylin, do you feel a pull to Kevin?" I stared at him for a moment.

"Like a mate pull?" He laughed at me.

"Not just any kind of pull to him. Focus on how you feel and how you react to his presence," he said. I looked at Kevin and tried to focus on him. There—I felt it, like a tether between us, a link, but it didn't feel the same as with Zander and definitely not the same as Trevor.

"Yeah, I do. What does that mean?" My mom looked between us in horror, and Nick chuckled.

"I think I know why he feels that way. It is very rare, and all we know is that it happens with someone of great power or importance. Usually, that means of a royal bloodline. And with your fur coat being what it is, you are definitely of royal descent." We all looked at him, shocked and waiting for more of an explanation.

"I think he is your guardian," Nick said.

"Like Nikki's dad is to the king?" Jolene asked. I didn't even put that together yet—bravo, Jojo.

"Yes, exactly like that. The king has several and has found them over his many years of ruling. It is not uncommon for there to be multiple, depending on the strength of the wolf or Lycan," he said.

"But I am not a royal," I interjected, and I was starting to feel lightheaded. I walked toward the loveseat and sat down. I don't know how much more I can handle.

"You said you were adopted," Trevor said thoughtfully. "Maybe it is because of your biological parents."

"That still isn't possible," I said. "There are no royal wolves anymore. They have fallen into legend, and that is why we are ruled by the Lycans now. They keep both the Lycans and wolves in check," I said earnestly.

My parents glanced at each other nervously, and this caught my attention. "What is it?" I asked them. They looked at me, and my mom smiled tentatively.

"When we found you that night, there were some things we left out of the story." I looked at them with disbelief. "You see, we didn't hear you crying. We both seemed to feel like something was wrong. We had this need to find out what it was. When we found you, your eyes were glowing the brightest blue, and you had this mark on your inner forearm. It was a trinity symbol with a wolf in the middle, howling at the moon," she said. "We knew right away that you were important and that we needed to keep you safe. It is why we fought so hard to adopt you," she added.

"We also think it is related to whatever happened last night," my father chimed in. "And when we finally brought you home and met Kevin for the first time, your eyes shone blue again. Hearing Beta Nick talk about him being a possible guardian makes sense now. Kevin has always been protective of you and has gotten in a lot of trouble fighting others to do so."

Kevin looked stuck in thought for a moment, his brows creased in concentration. "Last night, when I came home, I had a feeling to find you, and when I came in and saw Zander, I had wanted to tear him apart. I was ready to, and then you placed your hand on my arm. The rage in me calmed, and an immense feeling to stay by your side came over me.

It was like I knew you needed me there to comfort you, and I wanted to protect you. Especially when he came in next, and I didn't know who he was, but I knew he was a Lycan and a dangerous threat." He looked at me with wonder and awe in his eyes, then confusion. "What does this mean for me?" he asked, looking back at Nick.

"It means Aylin isn't the only one going with us or the only one changing." This caught everyone's attention.

My parents are worried now. "Aylin is very powerful, that much is given, or she wouldn't have a guardian. How powerful, we have no way of knowing because we do not know who her parents are. Her guardian will need to be by her side, especially as she is in transition, as this is when she will be at her weakest. After her transition, he will be marked by her, similar to a mate mark, but it's different. He will be marked because he will need to tie his life to hers so he can be her protector for as long as she draws breath. Only her death will release him from this."

Kevin growled at the last comment, and Nick raised his hands in a gesture to show he was no threat. "It is just a fact, not that it will happen anytime soon," he said, calming Kev. "There is probably more to all of this, but it is something our elders would know more about," he added.

"The elders!" my sister chimed in. "Why didn't you talk to the elders about Aylin?" she asked our parents.

"We were worried that if they knew about what we saw, they would take her. We wanted to keep her safe until she was old enough to make her own choice about her future and what she wanted to know and do. We had planned to talk to her within the week of her birthday and give her the choice."

My dad looked up at me. "We wanted to make sure you had your wolf and would be at your strongest before you made your choice. Maybe we should have told you sooner, but you had such a hard time here, and we didn't want to make it worse. I am so sorry this is how we had to tell you."

My heart constricted with the concern and love coming from my father. I knew they were only trying to do what was best for me, and it was a hard choice to make, but that didn't make it suck any less. A large part of me wanted to be angry, but right now, it was just too much to take in. I wasn't sure if I was angry, hurt, scared, or just in disbelief. I kind of felt like someone was going to scream, "Got you!" with all of this.

"Wait, I have a question," said Zander. I had almost forgotten he was here for a moment. "You said Kevin was going with you when you leave because he is her guardian," he said to Nick, who just nodded in response. "What does that mean for me? I had the same feelings and urges to protect her and keep her safe. Could that be what we feel instead of the mate bond? Could I be a guardian as well?"

Nick looked deep in thought at this, his brows furrowed as he considered it. Eventually, he sighed and looked back at Zander. "I am not sure. I have never heard of this kind of situation. It may be something we need to discuss with the elders, and you may need to come with us as well."

"Over my dead body," Trever exclaimed.

"Trev, we may not have a choice in this. There are too many factors here. If he is a guardian, he was chosen by the Moon Goddess and by her. That cannot be undone. The problem is, I do not know how it affects them with the fact that they were mates and he rejected her. I do not know how this works, and only the elders have those answers," Nick replied. Trevor looked murderous.

"He can still remain here until we have the answers," Trevor interjected.

"Trev, if he is her guardian, he will eventually be drawn to her. His need to protect his ward will overpower him, and that could put people in danger. What if he shows up and tries to get through the border? He is an Alpha who will have additional strength as a guardian. Even you know a guardian's strength increases if there is a fear that their ward is in danger, and if he does not know what is going on with her, then he will only be able to assume that she is."

Nick was speaking to Trevor as if he was trying to calm and reason with a dangerous predator, and in a way, he was. Nothing is more lethal than someone trying to protect their mate. I suppose second to that, based on what he said, would be a guardian.

"I can't just go, though," Zander interjected. I didn't want to look too hard at why that comment made me feel dejected.

"Again, you may not have a choice," Nick told him. "You could become a danger to others. You would start by lashing out, and you would become consumed by the need to see that she is safe."

"That is a lot of could's and maybes," Zander replied. "I am next in line to take over as Alpha here. I cannot just leave. What would happen to my pack?"

He looked at me then, and somehow, I knew he wanted to come. He wanted to be close to me, and the pull I felt told me that he still wanted me as his mate. I shuddered as my wolf whimpered in my head. She was confused; it was like she was being torn in two.

"You don't have a choice, at least not yet," Nick answered.

This got his, Trevor's, and my attention.

"Yet?" I asked before thinking.

Trevor glanced at me and then back at Nick expectantly. I think he assumed I was hopeful that Zander wouldn't have to stay with us, and I would let him think that, but the truth was, even though he ripped my heart out, my wolf did not like the idea of him not being with us.

"Again, I am not sure how this all works with the circumstances surrounding you, and I am not sure if you are a guardian or not. We need to see the elders for the answers. They should know something."

Nick looked like he was starting to get irritated. He didn't know all the answers, but it seemed we all hoped he would.

"Okay, well, I think that is the first thing we need to do then," I said to Nick, who looked at me with what looked like a "thank you" in his gaze. "Let's go see the elders and find out if they know what is going on and what all this means for everyone."

Nick nodded, and there were some other murmurs of agreement.

"Fine, but I don't want you alone with Zander until we find out how to have him come back to his pack."

This pissed me off. We weren't even mated yet, and he was trying to control me. I had no intention of being alone with him, but I would be damned if I let him tell me what I could and could not do.

Not wanting to argue in front of everyone, I gave him a disgusted look, stood, and walked away from him. "I need some air," I said, still glowering at him.

"I will come with you," he said, looking confused.

"No, I want to be alone," I told him.

This got a few looks from the others, and I noticed a slight smirk on Zander's face.

You know what? Fuck them all. I didn't ask for any of this.

I walked off and left them all to finish talking. I didn't care what else needed to be said. I could only hear a question asked and hear, "We need to talk to the elders," so many times. So why continue listening to this cycle?

I was mentally exhausted with all of this, and I didn't need or want any of it.

# Chapter Ten
## *Aylin*

I walked outside and into the garden I helped my mom with. It was beautiful this time of year, with everything in bloom. I sat in my favorite spot, cross-legged on the ground, and thought about everything that had happened in the last twenty-four hours. Yesterday, I had just wanted to meet my wolf and enjoy the festival with my friends. I was training to join the guard and prove myself to this pack, and maybe even see if I had a mate here. Now, none of that mattered.

Now, I was going to leave, and it seemed that there was more about my past that would have something to do with my future. With that thought, feelings of uncertainty and fear started to fill me. A shiver went down my spine, and the thought of someone watching me made me look around. I knew I must be reacting out of fear with everything I had just been told, but I couldn't shake it. I looked around, stood up, and walked back inside and up to my room. I still wanted to be alone.

There, I messaged Layla to tell her about everything that had been going on. She quickly called me.

"This is way too much to talk about through texts. I have so many questions," she said with a grumble.

"Right. How are you handling it all?" Lance asked. Of course, she had me on speaker, and her brother had joined the conversation. Not that I minded, but I did just need some girl time.

"Honestly, I don't know, but I have so many more questions than answers, and we need to figure them all out."

"Do you want us to come over?" Layla asked.

"No, not right now. I need some time to think. I just wanted to let you know what is going on. I am not sure what we are going to do from here, but I will keep you both updated," I sighed heavily.

After a few more minutes of talking and them telling me how the rest of their night went, we ended the call. I then went back to my thoughts. The more I thought, the more upset I became at the events that had happened just a few moments ago. Nothing in my entire life had been normal. Why start now?

A short while later, there was a soft knock on the door.

"Ay, can I come in?" Kevin asked hesitantly. I knew he just wanted to check on me, and he wasn't the cause of my anger. I still wanted to be alone, but I knew my brother would not be okay until he made sure I was.

"Yeah, Kev, come on in." He opened the door and walked through. I was sitting on my bed, holding Archie, my stuffed elephant. He was one of the few things I couldn't part with from my childhood. I was playing with the necklace my parents had given me, debating on putting it on. Zander's still hung on him as well, but I didn't bother with it. I debated taking it off but just couldn't bring myself to do it yet.

"That bad, huh?" he asked, nodding at Archie. I only really held him when I was really upset or angry at something. You would think that would be often, but it really wasn't. Lizzie and her cronies bothered me, but it's not often that I really got upset by them anymore.

I rolled my eyes and just went back to looking out the window across from my bed. He walked over and sat on the bed next to me. He watched me for a moment, assessing me.

"You know, Trevor looked like you punched him in the gut when you told him no and that you wanted to be alone. I don't think anyone has told him no in a while," he said with a small laugh.

I just shrugged.

"Come on, Ay. I know there's a smile in there. Do not make me drag it out," he said.

I narrowed my eyes at him. I knew what he would do, and I wasn't in the mood.

"Kev, I know you want to help, but I don't think you can this time. I just had bombshell after bombshell dropped on me, we have more questions than answers, and apparently, my mate does not trust me and is already ordering me around like he owns me." I gritted my teeth at the last statement, and Kevin nodded his head.

"I know. I just hate seeing you so upset. Mom told Trevor that he has his work cut out for him if he thinks he can tell you what to do like that."

That did, in fact, make me grin. I loved how well my family knew me. My parents had a hard time telling me what to do the last couple of years. My mom absolutely hated that I was always covered in dirt. I never could tell her why, but the few times I had bruises that I couldn't hide or cuts that needed a bit more attention, I knew that she knew I wasn't telling the whole truth about how I got them.

"Good. He should know that he isn't going to boss me around. I will not let him think he can tell me what I can or cannot do. He should be a decent person and talk to me. I can understand where he is coming from, but I refuse to be ordered around by my mate, no matter who he is."

Kevin looked at me with pride on his face.

"Good! I would hate to think my sister could be some weak girl that submitted to anyone."

He was laughing at me, and this time, I cracked more than a smile. I don't know how he did it, but he always made me feel better. He was the only one who could. My mom tried, and so did my dad, and sometimes they could cheer me up, but when I was really upset or angry, only Kevin could get me out of my head.

"Come on. I think they have come up with a plan on what we are going to do," he said to me. I nodded and followed him back downstairs. As I walked down the hall and down the stairs after him, I looked at the pictures along the walls. Memories of us swimming and camping. My dad trying to teach Jolene to fish and failing. She could never bait a hook and would cry if the fish got hurt. I smiled as I looked at them all. I would miss making these memories with my family.

We entered the living room together, and I saw Trevor look up at me expectantly, but I walked past him and sat next to Kevin on the couch. This inadvertently put me closer to Zander, which was not my goal. I just wanted to be with Kevin. He was keeping me grounded and calm. Trevor, however, scowled, and Zander just stood there with a smirk on his face and his arms crossed over his chest. They could both get lost.

"Kevin said you guys decided on what we were going to do about all this," I said, only looking at Nick. He looked from me to Trevor, then nodded.

"We are going to leave tonight so that the Alpha here does not have time to interfere with those plans since Zander will need to come with. We know he is not going to be happy with us taking the future Alpha and Beta with us, but we do not have a choice in this right now. We are going to contact the head Elder of our pack and make sure he is available first thing in the morning."

"Not tonight?" I asked.

"No. It will be very late when we get there, and we will all want to rest. The answers we are looking for may take time, and he will not be able to focus on little sleep. He is pretty old, after all."

I nodded, a little disappointed, but I understood. I would hate for someone to wake me up in the middle of the night to ask questions that could wait.

"You will also have to meet with Trevor's mother and be introduced to the pack. They will already be starting preparations for your Luna ceremony, which will be held at the end of the week," he continued.

I just stared at him. I knew we would have to do it soon, but I didn't think it would be less than a week. With today being Sunday, it seemed like such a short time away.

I looked over at Trevor, who was smiling at me. My stupid heart sped up, and I could feel what felt like a flock of birds in my stomach. So much for butterflies. My wolf seemed to like this idea and perked up. I wanted to squash it because I was still mad at him for being an alpha asshole, but damn, did I want his touch. What really irritated me was knowing his touch would actually help with my anger, which made me more irritated since he was the one to piss me off in the first place.

"It's good that we don't wait," Mona said to me.

"I don't know about that. I thought we would have a month or more to get ready for this," I replied.

"I don't think we can wait that long. Something is happening to me, and I think it would be wise to do what they said."

I thought about that for a moment.

"What do you think is happening? They said we would change from wolf to Lycan. Could that be what you are feeling?" I asked her.

"I am not sure. It could be. It's hard to describe, but I think it could be more."

That was the second time in two days she said something that made my stomach sink. I truly hoped it was nothing bad or painful.

I didn't really hear anything else they had said while Mona was talking to me. I nodded and tried to pay attention to the rest. Kevin and Zander would come with us to figure out what was going on with all of us. I would start Luna training and be mated, which my family was invited to attend. This made me feel a little better, knowing they would all be there.

After we were done, Zander left to pack and let his father know what was going on. Trevor would go with him when he spoke to his father to make sure he could broker no argument. This was why he was packing first, so that he didn't have someone trying to stop him. Kevin and I went upstairs to pack our things. We were all only taking necessities for now so we could leave in a few hours. We could come back for the rest. Even knowing that, I still made sure to pack Archie and a few pictures of my family that I had on my dresser.

I put the pendant my parents got me for my birthday on and looked around my room. This had been my safe space all my life. Now I was leaving, and it felt weird to think I wouldn't have it anymore.

I messaged Lance and Layla to let them know what was going on. There was no way I was going to leave without saying goodbye to them too. They had been my rocks here, aside from my family, and I would miss them both so much.

I met Kevin downstairs with my bags, and we spent the afternoon with our family. Jolene was talking excitedly about the Luna ceremony, what kind of dress she would wear, and what kind of dress I could wear. My mom would chime in with hair and makeup ideas. My dad and brother were talking about the possible outcomes for the pack if Kevin ended up having to stay with me at the Blood Moon Pack. It looked like the job of Beta could go to Lance as long as Zander came back. I was more interested in what they were talking about than dresses and makeup. I really was not into that kind of stuff.

"How do you think the Alpha is going to take it?" I asked, having had enough talk of makeup and letting my mom and sister plan.

"Definitely not well," Kevin said, shaking his head. "He is probably going to have a coronary about it, and that will be bad since his successor will be gone," he added.

"If push comes to shove, he still has options," our dad said. "His daughter is also Alpha-born, and she could technically take over if she found a mate," he said. "The other option is, instead of Lance being Beta, he has the ability to take over as Alpha. Then he would need to choose his Beta," he said.

"Wow, that is a lot to put on Lance," I said. I knew Lance had dreams of being a guard and one day leading them, just like his dad. He loved traveling to the other packs, helping his dad teach their soldiers, and learning other fighting styles. How would he truly feel about being an Alpha?

"I just hope whatever is going on, we can figure it out and take care of it so everyone can go back to living their lives," I said. I didn't want anyone to be obligated to be around me because the Moon Goddess made them.

Kevin looked at me with big eyes. "Ay, I am honored to be a guardian! I will do anything and everything to keep you safe," he said earnestly.

"But I don't want you to have to, Kev! I want you to have the life you dreamed about!" I insisted.

"Ay, I can't describe it, but this feels right to me. I would be happiest being your guardian. I will miss this place and miss our family, and yeah, I did want to be Beta, but I will still have you, and you will have me," he said with a smile. "I don't think you know how much of an honor it is to be selected as a guardian! There are so many guards, even royal guards, that would kill for this. To be chosen means the

Moon Goddess herself believes in you above all others, and to protect someone that is so very important is an honor — more so than being the Beta of this pack." He was beaming at me.

"He is right, honey," my mom said next to us. She put her hand on my shoulder and squeezed. "I know you want what is best for your brother and want him to follow his dreams. This surpasses any dream he could have, and he will always be with you. This is painful for us, losing the two of you at the same time, but we are also very happy that you will not be alone and will have each other," she said, her voice full of love and acceptance.

"Thank you, Mom. I don't know how I am going to do this without you and Dad, but with Kevin there with me, it will be a bit easier."

"You and Kevin have always been close and had a strong bond, and this will only strengthen it." My mom hugged me, and for a moment, everyone got a little emotional. A knock on the door made me jump. Kevin got up and went to the door. When he opened it, Nikki walked in. She looked between all of us and, with a small smile, let us know it was time to go. She helped me and Kevin with our bags and headed outside.

As we finished loading the last of it in the trunk, I was lifted off the ground and spun around. I knew it was Lance based on his scent. Layla laughed and told him to put me down. I started to laugh too. However, Nikki looked like she was about to tackle him.

"Ugh, I am so going to miss you guys!" was the first thing I said to them after he stopped spinning me. I hugged them both tightly.

"Thank God we live in an age of technology!" Layla said. "We will be able to text and call and video chat!" she said. But I knew she was having a hard time saying goodbye. She was like me; she did not like showing emotion in front of others. Behind closed doors or with people she trusted, she could be a blubbering baby, but with anyone else, she deflected.

"I know, and I plan to call and text all the time! If we go without talking for even a day, I might die!" I said to her dramatically. "I have to have my daily bestie fix." This made her smile, and we both seemed to calm a little. No more choking back tears.

"Don't forget about me! I better be part of that fix you need," Lance said with mock offense.

"You will be!" I promised. We didn't get much time as Nikki stepped forward, letting us know we needed to meet Alpha Trevor, Nick, and Zander at the pack house.

I looked at my best friends, my parents, and my sister. I started with my sister.

"Look after them for us, okay?" I asked her, hugging her tightly. "I am going to miss you so much, sis! I love you." She squeezed me back and replied the same.

"Mom, Dad, I am so happy that you gave me a chance, that you took me in and supported and loved me. I am thankful for everything you have done and sacrificed for me, even though you didn't have to! Thank you for being the best parents I could ever have had! I love you!" I hugged my mom, who had started to cry, and then my father.

"We love you too, kiddo, and we will see you later this week for your coronation!" I was looking forward to that fact. I had never been far from my parents, and this was going to be hard for me. I never realized how much I had come to rely on them being there.

"Layla, Lance, I am going to miss you guys so much! You have been by my side since we were little, and I don't know how I am going to do this without you! I love you guys." I hugged each in turn, lingering on Layla while Kevin said bye to our parents.

We got into the SUV and waved to our family as we drove off toward the pack house to get the others.

# Chapter Eleven
## *Trevor*

I really didn't want to leave Aylin behind, but knowing that Zander was with us here made me a little more relaxed. I am not sure about the fact that they still have some kind of bond after the rejection, and I really don't like the idea of her choosing him over me. I don't think she will; she was outright pissed that he was around last night, but my words upset her. The last thing I want is to cause her to run into the arms of someone else — especially someone who did not appreciate being given such a gift as her as a mate.

This has been quite an interesting trip, and here I thought I was going to be miserable while here. As we make our way up to the pack house, I stop and face Zander. I watch him look between me and Nick with a worried expression on his face.

"I am going to be honest with you. I don't know what is going on with your bond with Aylin, but I do know you do not deserve her. You gave her up, and the Moon Goddess brought us together. She will be my mate and Luna." I was glowering at him, and I didn't care if I was asserting my dominance. I wanted him to know she was mine.

"I will not interfere unless she decides she wants me after all," he said, straightening his shoulders. I had to admire his conviction, but it wasn't going to happen. Aylin was my mate, and I will not give her up without a fight.

"I made a mistake, and I can't take back what I did, but I can only assume the Moon Goddess meant for me to be part of her life since she seems to be giving me a second chance. And if Aylin does choose me, I will spend the rest of my life showing her that I do choose her. Not her power, not the power she will give me like she thinks — I am after her. I choose HER!" He did not back down as I glowered at him. He was more than serious with his words, and I didn't know if I should respect him or rip him limb from limb.

"I will not give her up. Not ever. She is it for me, and I would never let others influence my choice of mate. The fact that you did speaks volumes about your character as a mate and Alpha," I replied, the barb hitting its mark. "Now go pack what you need and meet me in your dad's office. We will need to inform him of what is going on, and he is not going to like it. So be ready for a fight." He looked like he was going to say something back, but wisely, he just nodded and walked off.

"Would you really keep her from him if she chose him?" Nick asked the moment Zander was out of sight.

"I don't know, to be honest. I don't think I could ever let her go, and I pray that does not happen. I don't envy him and this link between them because I honestly feel a deep connection with her and believe she will be happy with me. I just can't help this fear that he is right about the second chance given to him and what that could mean," I replied.

"I am not sure what kind of bond they have, though. That is the reason I think he should come to see the Elders. I don't know if it is the mate bond or if the bond shifted somehow to a guardian. He obviously cares about her and is a bit protective, so I can't tell what is driving him, and I don't think he can truly tell either," Nick said thoughtfully. He was looking up at the pack house, where we watched Zander enter, and then shook his head.

"I hope the Moon Goddess knows what she is doing," I said after a moment. I walked into the pack house with Nick and headed toward Alpha Stephen's office. I knocked on the door several times, but there was no answer.

"He's not in there right now," a voice came from behind me. I didn't need to look to know that too-sweet, too-high, fake voice came from the one person here I really didn't want to see.

"He is in a meeting with his head guard at the moment," she added. I turned and looked down at Lizzie.

"Can you let him know I need to see him as soon as possible? It is urgent, and we will be taking our leave this afternoon."

Her smile fell and changed to one of shock, which she quickly replaced with a pout.

"But we haven't even gotten to spend any time together," she all but cried. I cringed.

"Daddy said you would want to get to know me better, and I thought we could go for a stroll to the lake and take a swim together," she said flirtatiously. "I even bought a new bikini." She leaned in and whispered that last part with a coy smile on her face, all but throwing herself at me. My nose wrinkled, and I could feel myself physically recoil from her proximity.

Did men actually want her? Judging by her scent, they did.

"I am sure your dad had plans for my time here that I was unaware of. However, since I did, in fact, find my mate, I will no longer need to spend any amount of time with another female. I am sure you understand," I said rather formally while taking a step back. I didn't want her scent anywhere near me. I felt like I was already on rocky ground with Aylin, and I didn't need anything else coming between us.

She pouted again. "I don't know what any of you see in that mutt. She isn't pretty or Alpha-born like me. I would make a better mate for you and bring you Alpha children," she said, crossing her arms in front of her. "Seriously, Trevor, you should be with someone of our class. It is rather distasteful for you to go after an adopted omega."

With that comment, I almost lost it. The fact that Aylin is purely white in color marks her higher than any Alpha or Alpha-born alive today.

"You have absolutely no fucking right to say anything about my Luna, who, at this moment, is of higher rank than you!" I roared at her. "What's more, even if I didn't find my mate here this weekend, I would never take you as a mate!

You are a self-centered princess who thinks the world should hand her everything instead of working for it! A Luna is the mother of a pack and works alongside her Alpha to help the pack and take care of them. You only care about how much money you can spend, how you look, and how much power you have over someone. You are the worst sort of female out there! I honestly feel bad for whoever does become your mate since you would make a terrible Luna. The only saving grace for any pack you could possibly become a Luna of is that Aylin and I will be overseeing it and can stop in from time to time to make sure the pack under my care is doing well."

I could see the tears swimming in her eyes from embarrassment and anger, and I couldn't care less. She insulted my mate and future Luna, and that level of disrespect is something that usually earns a severe punishment.

"You can't talk to me that way!" she yelled back. "My father is the Alpha of this pack, and I deserve respect." She was trying to be tough, and all she was doing was pissing me off. Trying to assert her status and power, and that of her father's, was a mistake she would have to learn the hard way.

"You are getting all the respect you deserve from me. You have to earn respect; it is not just given to you, especially by another Alpha. As for your dad's position, let me fill you in and remind you who I am. I am Alpha Trevor Gideon of the Blood Moon Pack. I am a Lycan and royalty in our world! My uncle is the King of Lycans, and if you want to keep trying my patience, I can and will remove your father as Alpha, demoting him and, by extension, you! DO NOT try my patience, little girl!" I half-snarled, half-growled.

She visibly paled. "You can't do that!" Her voice was shaking now.

"I think you will find he can do just that," said a new voice. It was Alpha Stephen. He must have heard us yelling. "I was going to ask what is going on, but it seems my daughter has forgotten herself," he said, narrowing his eyes on her. "Why don't we all go into my office and talk about what just happened?" he said amicably.

Liz was fidgeting now. She waited for her father to open the door and then walked in with her dad, keeping her head low.

His office was a large space with a desk toward the front, close to the door. Across from the desk were two brown leather chairs. The back of the room had several large bookshelves covered in all kinds of books, but mostly history. To the far side were two windows and a chaise under each for additional seating. It was a large but cozy space that made you feel welcome, even though it was an Alpha's office.

"Now, what is this all about? What led to my right as Alpha being brought into this?"

I looked at his daughter for a moment, allowing her the chance to explain her actions. When she didn't, I spoke.

"It would seem that your daughter thinks she has the right to tell me who I should and should not be with or choose as my mate. Then, she had the audacity to insult her," I stated.

He looked at his daughter and then back at me. "That hardly seems a reason to bring my right as Alpha into this," he said.

I looked at Liz again, waiting to see if she would talk. She still didn't.

"That was not what led to that comment. She continued to tell me that I had to show her respect because of who you are. I then reminded her of who I am, and to prove my point, I let her know the kind of authority I have here, even in your pack," I finished.

Again, he looked between me and his daughter. I could see the anger he was trying to keep under wraps. He was better at it than I was, and the thing was, I was not sure if his anger was at me or her. I would assume the latter, but who knows with how he dotes on her?

"I am profoundly sorry for my daughter's insolence, Alpha Trevor. You have every right to be upset with her, and I can assure you she will be dealt with if you permit me to take care of her punishment." He was looking at me with a pleading expression.

He knew what she did could earn her at the very least twenty lashings just for what she said about my mate.

Lizzie's head shot up. "Daddy, you are taking his side? He yelled at me and disrespected me in our home—your home! He should be the one to—"

She was cut off by a hand across her face. She was not the only one in shock at this action. It shocked me that he would raise a hand to her.

"Have you not done enough? Did you not hear what he said to you? He is an Alpha-born Lycan. In our world, that is royalty! Add to the fact that he is part of the royal family! You could be chained and whipped or locked up for talking to him like this and for insulting his mate! He could remove me from my birthright and exile our family, and to top it off, you have the nerve to question me as well? In front of a visiting Alpha? Do you really have so little respect for me? I am ashamed and appalled by your behavior."

He yelled at her. She recoiled as if he had slapped her again. Tears were streaming down her face, and not one person in the room felt the least bit sorry for her. She lowered her head and stood there silently.

"I must apologize again, Alpha. I have obviously failed in my role as both Alpha and father to her."

Lizzie blanched at his words, and I watched as he tried hard to rein in his temper and his worry. I could see he was starting to sweat, and he splayed his shaking hands on his desk to try to keep them still.

"I will not hold your daughter's words against you or your family this time, out of respect for yours and my father's friendship," I told him, and I watched him visibly relax.

"However, there was a reason I needed to speak with you before this mishap took place, and we need to deal with it now, as I plan to leave this afternoon."

He looked up at me and nodded, then looked at his daughter.

"Go to your chambers and do not come out until I send for you," he told her.

She nodded and made for the door. She stopped and looked up at me.

"I am sorry, Alpha Trevor," was all she managed to say, and she actually looked like she was sincere. I nodded, and she left the office.

"Now, what is it you wanted to talk to me about?" he asked.

"We have come to find out a few interesting things about my new mate, and they may have an effect on your pack until we figure them out," I informed him.

He looked confused. "What do you mean? How could they affect us? She would be going home with you, wouldn't she?" he asked.

I nodded, and just as I was about to speak, there was a knock at the door.

"I am in a meeting. It will have to wait," Alpha Stephen yelled at the door.

"It's just me," said Zander, opening the door. "I actually need to be part of the meeting you're having, if it's with Alpha Trevor."

His dad's brows furrowed as he watched his son cross the room and sit on a chaise by the window.

"Okay, can you tell me what is going on now?" Alpha Stephen was looking more confused now that his son was involved.

"I am sure you are aware that your son rejected Aylin at the festival last night when he found out that she was his mate," I started. "Well, shortly after, it seems I found she was also mine."

He nodded that he was aware of these things.

"What does that have to do with my pack?" he asked again.

"It appears Aylin is rather special," I continued. "She has a very strong wolf inside her, and the Moon Goddess has gifted her guardians."

Stephen's eyebrows shot up at that.

"One of these guardians is her brother, Kevin," I informed him, and he nodded.

It took him a minute to put it together.

"Kevin will have to leave with you to protect her," he said, then looked at his son. "You will need to find a new Beta when you take over," he said to Zander. Zander looked at me, and I nodded at him.

"Father, I am also going with them," he said a little hesitantly. His father looked at him like he had a second head. "The thing is, there is still a bond between me and Aylin, and we are not sure if it is the mate bond giving me a second chance or if I am also a guardian," he said. Stephan looked like he was going to be sick.

"So let me understand this for a moment. You are leaving this afternoon, and when you leave, you will be taking my son and future Alpha of this pack and his future Beta with you?" He really looked like he was going to vomit now.

"We need to see the Elders," Nick spoke up for the first time since coming inside. "Our first stop when we get home is to see the Elders. We will need everyone involved there so they can ask any questions and get any details that may help them find answers for this current predicament," he explained.

"So there is a chance that Zander will not need to stay? He could find a way to break the mate bond and come home?" Stephan asked hopefully.

"That is what we are hoping for," I told him. "I know we need answers because all we have are questions. We would tell you more, but we would not be able to answer any questions you have right now either." I didn't like leaving him with no answers and a large problem for his pack. "It is important you have a backup plan in case there is no way to break their bond. I don't want to consider it either, but it could be a possibility. You may need to choose a successor." He looked down at his hands for a moment.

This man — this Alpha — had just gone from dealing with his errant daughter to finding out he could possibly be losing his heir. All in a matter of minutes. I felt for him. None of this could be easy, and he now had some difficult choices ahead of him.

"It doesn't look like I have any say in this," he said finally. "Is there nothing we can do? Couldn't he stay here and just call in when you see the Elders?" he asked.

Nick shook his head. "The Elders will need him there in case they need anything from him or need to test anything. If they ask him to do something so they can see what happens, they will need to be able to witness it themselves. We will see what they say, and hopefully, he will be able to come back and take over. We just think you should prepare for both the best- and worst-case scenarios," Nick told him.

He nodded again. Nick and I stood and offered him and his son some privacy and time to say their goodbyes, as well as for the rest of his family. We let them know we would be waiting out front and that we would be leaving in roughly two hours. That would give Stephan little time to try to persuade Zander from going — not that he would be able to. Zander looked like he hated the idea of coming back and leaving her behind. For me, that was the most ideal thing that could happen.

We walked outside into the sun, and I mind-linked with Nikki to let her know we were finishing up here and to meet us soon with Aylin and her brother. I knew it would be a long goodbye for them as well, so they might as well start now.

One thing was for sure: this was going to be a long drive home. Thankfully, we had two vehicles, because right now, I really wanted to just leave without Zander and deal with whatever consequences came later. I didn't want him anywhere near Aylin. The feeling I had growing inside—that I was not going to like the outcome of him coming with us— just kept growing.

# Chapter Twelve
## *Aylin*

We pulled up to the pack house and picked up Trevor and the others. Zander, thankfully, was in the other vehicle. I didn't know if I could handle being around him right now. I am still reeling from the fact that he rejected me and now wants me to be his mate, and, to top it off, he thinks I would be — even after not only that but admitting it was because his father told him he made a mistake. He believed he would be more powerful with a fated mate than a chosen one. How could I ever believe that he wants me?

Besides, Trevor, from the moment I met him, hasn't been able to take his eyes off me. Even though he did say something I didn't like, I am not going to hold that against him. He is an Alpha and male, so his overprotective instincts are going wild. I definitely want to give this a chance — see what he is like and get to know him. My wolf purrs in my head, and I know she agrees. She wants to know her mate and is happy that we have not been rejected a second time.

Trevor climbs into the SUV and smiles at me when he sits next to me — a big, cheesy smile showing his perfect set of straight, white teeth. I loved how his entire face lit up with it, especially his eyes.

"Why don't you sit over here?" he said, patting the empty seat next to him—the middle seat between us. I tried to hide my smile.

"I am already sitting next to you," I replied with a smirk.

"Not close enough," he said and then leaned over, un-buckled my seat belt, and pulled me onto his lap. "This is what I consider close enough," he said and nuzzled the space between my neck and ear, making me giggle.

"This isn't safe. What if we are in a car accident?" I pro-tested weakly. I really did like being in his lap. God, his body felt so good—big, warm, strong—and I couldn't help imagining him pinning me with this body. Nope… I need to stop right there. For God's sake, I just met him. I mean, I know that mating happens fast—hell, with some mates, the same day—but I possibly had two mates right now, and I didn't know what would happen if I let one mate with me. I tried to remind myself that we had to wait until we spoke to the elders.

He started to kiss my neck. One of his hands was on my leg, and his thumb was making soft passes on the inside of it. His other hand, on my back, kept stroking up and down, making me shiver and burn. This was going to be so damn hard.

He picked his hand up from my thigh, lifted it to my chin, and turned my face to look at him. His eyes were so beautiful—I could just get lost in them. The way they were looking at me, with such open lust and longing, made me lose all train of thought. I may have even stopped breathing.

After just the briefest of moments, he kissed me. It started soft and searching, and I lost myself in it—the feel of his mouth against mine and his hand now at the back of my head, holding me to him. I lifted my hands and wrapped them around him, leaning against him. He bit my bottom lip, and I gasped, which he used as an opportunity to explore my mouth with his tongue. I responded instantly, and soon, we were battling for dominance.

I am not sure when it happened that I went from sitting sideways on his lap to straddling him, but I found myself rubbing and grinding against him. I had completely forgotten where I was and was lost in the feel of his lips, hands, and body—and the impressive length beneath me. That was until we heard the clearing of throats from the front seat.

My entire body went rigid, and he chuckled. He knew I had forgotten about the others—Nick and Nikki—who were sitting up front. I slowly slid off of him and back onto the car seat, but when I made to move back over to where I was sitting before he got in, he grabbed me and pulled me next to him.

"I know you guys want to jump each other with the mate pull, but can you wait until we are not around? I really don't want to be a witness to it," Nick said jokingly.

Nikki nodded in agreement and was trying hard not to laugh. I, on the other hand, was as red as a tomato. I couldn't believe I had forgotten that we were not alone. I also wondered how far I would have let him go after just telling myself that we needed to wait. I knew the answer, though. In that moment, with how hot I was burning for him, I would have let him have me. I had no self-control, and I needed to get it together.

"Sorry, guys, we kind of forgot you were there for a moment," Trevor laughed, and they joined him. I was still too embarrassed to laugh at it.

"I will try to compose myself and keep it from escalating too far until we are alone," he joked with them and winked at me. With his wink, I relaxed a little.

"I am really sorry. It won't happen again," I told them, and Trevor looked at me with a *you wanna bet* look on his face that made me squirm in my seat. I pulled my gaze away from him, out the window, and watched the scenery roll by.

Around half way there, we rolled into a human town to refuel and get food. A little diner caught my eye, and I asked if we could eat there. Inside, it was all 50s-themed, with records and neon lights all over the walls. There were a few pictures of old cars, girls in poodle skirts, and guys in letterman sweaters and leather jackets.

One of the pictures caught my eye, and I had to laugh. It was a picture of a group of guys. Half of them wore leather jackets and had their hair slicked back, while the other half were in letterman sweaters and looked all preppy. The two in the front reminded me of Zander and Trevor—Zander, the preppy jock in school, and Trevor, the out-of-town bad boy. I laughed again.

"Want to tell me what's so funny?" Trevor asked as he looked at the picture.

"Not really. I think I will keep this one to myself for now," I told him with a mischievous smile.

His answering smile of wickedness almost made me swoon right there. He led me over to a table they had set up for our whole group. Thankfully, they weren't very busy. Trevor sat toward the end of the table, and I sat next to him. Next to me was Kevin, then Zander. Again, I was thankful for the space. Across from Trevor was Nick, then Nikki, and two warriors I hadn't met yet.

"Aylin, this is Thomas and Julian. They are some of my personal guards," Trevor says when he sees me glancing at them.

"Nice to meet you." I nodded at them and smiled.

"It's nice to meet you, Luna," said Julian with a broad smile.

"It's an honor," Thomas says with a slight bow of his head.

"Oh, you don't have to call me that. I am not your Luna yet," I told them, but they both just smiled at me. "Please call me Aylin." I felt weird being called Luna.

"They call you Luna out of respect, and they will probably keep doing so. Whether or not you are yet is not going to dissuade them, since you are my mate, and that makes you the true Luna of our pack with no one to contest your right," Trevor explained when they did not call me by my name or agree to.

"It just feels weird, is all," I said.

The waitress came up to our table, and I could see her eyes practically pop out of her head at the abundance of hot men sitting at the table. Werewolves and Lycans were pretty attractive— even the ones we think are plain are usually attractive to humans. However, these Lycans were definitely up there. They were hotter than most male models.

"Hi, my name is Jemma, and I will be your waitress today. What can I get you started with?"

I had to admire her professionalism. I don't think I would have been able to form a complete sentence. Everyone gave her their drink order, and she left to put it in and get them for us.

We took a few minutes to look at the menu, and light banter started between the Lycans.

When she came back, she passed out the drinks and took our orders. She lingered over by Julian and Thomas, and I couldn't blame her when she smiled flirtatiously at them. When she was done, she left to put in our orders, and conversation picked back up.

"How soon do you think we will be able to see the elders?" Zander asked.

"I am hoping we will be able to see them tomorrow, but I cannot make any promises. If not tomorrow, Tuesday would be the soonest with such short notice," Trevor told him.

"If you are the Alpha, can't you make them make time for us?" I asked. It didn't make sense to me that we would have to wait.

"The elders have been notified about the main issue and some concerns with what we saw. They may be looking up information, and if they are not ready or need to look up more to be able to get us answers, they may need the time to do it," Nick chimed in. "They already know quite a bit already, being elders, but they have libraries and histories that are kept safe, and they always double-check with the records to make sure they never give false information."

"Oh, that makes more sense. I guess no one can know everything, and we do have a very odd situation." I felt a little embarrassed that I didn't think about the need to do research.

"It's okay. Most people think along the same lines, that the elders just know and remember everything, but they are more protectors of knowledge passed through the ages," Nikki chimed in. She gave me a kind smile, and I felt a little better. At least I am not the only one who thought that way.

"When did you talk to them about this?" I asked.

"My dad went back last night. He had a conference with them first thing this morning while you were still asleep," Nick said.

"Your dad was here?" I asked curiously. "Why?"

"In case there were any problems with Trevor and Alpha Black." Nick laughed like he made a joke, but I didn't get it.

"Ha ha, very funny. He was here because my dad was friends with Alpha Black, and he wanted to visit with him as well. He got to a little at the festival last night, but when everything happened, he decided that he would go back early," Trevor said, giving Nick a sideways look.

"Yeah? So then why are you glaring at Nick like that?" I asked, teasing him.

"Because he is a pain in my ass. Maybe I should have let his dad stay on as Beta a while longer," Trevor said.

The waitress arrived then with our order and had to make a few trips to make sure everyone got what they wanted. The burger I ordered was huge, but, goddess, was it good. Everything was pretty good — from the Oreo shake to the burger to the fries and even the dill pickle that came with the meal. Everyone seemed to agree because talking took a back seat. Either that or everyone was just really hungry.

After we finished, Trevor paid, and they left a really generous tip for the waitress. We all piled back into the SUVs and were back on the road. Trevor took out his phone and started checking emails, and I messaged Layla and Lance in our group chat to let them know that, even though it had only been a few hours, I was still alive and missed them like crazy.

They both responded in turn— Layla going on about how it already wasn't the same without me and Lance reminding me to keep practicing. He doesn't want me to get lazy without him there to motivate me by kicking my ass.

After a while, I started to get tired. I leaned my head against Trevor's shoulder and just watched the scenery again. At some point, I guess I dozed off. I woke up with my head resting on his leg and his hand caressing my arm. I sat up, yawning, and stretched out my limbs the best I could in the back seat.

"Where are we?" I asked, looking around. It was dark now.

"Not too far from home," he said, looking at me, and again he made my heart and brain stop. How could someone so gorgeous be mine? "We have maybe another twenty minutes until we arrive," he added, smirking at me like he knew what I was thinking. He gave me a little wink. Yep, he knew right where my mind was.

"How long have I been asleep? I didn't realize I was tired. Sorry for falling asleep on you." I looked out the window to see our surroundings.

"I didn't mind you sleeping on me, and maybe about five hours— not all that long, considering the ride here," he said. He was smirking again, and I knew where his head was now. Of course, he didn't mind that my head was in his lap.

"Oh gee, I wonder why that was?" I replied, a bit sarcastically.

He laughed, then reached over, grabbed my waist, and pulled me over to his side.

"I like you being close to me, and if you want to sleep on any part of me, I will be more than happy to be your pillow," he added, then kissed my forehead before laying a trail of kisses down my nose and to my lips, where he kissed me deeply.

He tasted so good, and I loved how his soft, luscious lips felt against mine. I wanted to give in again to the sensation of him, but I remembered this time that we were not alone and somehow found the strength to break the kiss. We were both panting. I let the smile show. I wanted him bad — and so did my wolf.

A few minutes later, we turned onto an old dirt road, and after a few more minutes, we were surrounded by trees. I couldn't see much of the forest, with it being dark, even with my enhanced eyesight. I cuddled next to Trevor for the remainder of the trip through the forest.

Soon, a large gate came into view. It looked like gates of old, made out of wood and iron. Large walls made out of stone extended beyond my sight through the trees. As we approached, I could hear the sound of wolves howling, and then the gates opened for us to enter. My heart kicked up, and all I could think was, *Here we go.*

# Chapter Thirteen
## *Aylin*

Once inside, the pack's gate closed behind us, and we soon came up to what looked like a castle, but it was made out of different stones and wood, similar to the beautiful small stone cottages I have seen in movies. It was beautiful and huge. I felt kind of like I was in another world entirely — a magic one with fairies. I guess when you think about it, because we are werewolves and Lycans, we are part of another world of magic, so it makes a little sense. The pack house was definitely huge. It must have been an effort to build and must have taken a long time. I wonder how old it is.

The castle-like manor had several towers and was rather tall. I didn't know how many floors it had, but I bet I could live an entire lifetime roaming the halls and never find all its secrets. It had a large wooden porch that reminded me of log cabin porches. There were chairs everywhere, set in groups. Off to the side, there was a large wooden gazebo with tables and chairs set up, and beyond that was the forest. Same on the other side. I loved that I could come outside and sit even in the rain.

My mom had often talked about adding an overhang to our porch so that we could sit outside, drink tea or coffee, and enjoy the rain. It was something we both loved. I wish

that would have been something we got to do together before I left.

We got out of the SUVs and all stood in front of the large,
beautiful castle, admiring it and the land around it. Kevin
and Zander both had their mouths hanging open as well.
The look of awe was definitely not just from me. Julian and
Thomas drove the cars off to wherever they kept them.

"What do you think?" Trevor asked, and I just gaped at
him. He laughed and nudged me with his elbow. "Really,
what do you think?"

"I think I just walked into a fairy tale. Am I a Luna or a
princess?" I asked, feeling a little overwhelmed.

"Actually, wouldn't you be the queen?" Zander added
playfully.

I laughed at that but then gulped. Um, no, I am having
a hard enough time accepting Luna. I noticed Trevor gave
Zander a glare with his comment before looking back at me.
I cleared my throat and got his attention.

"You are my Luna, little wolf, and I am thrilled to bring
you home. Hopefully, you will find your fairy tale right here
with me."

Trevor took my hand in his and led us into what was
going to be my home for, hopefully, the rest of my life.

Once we were inside, my breath was stolen again. I
swear my eyes were going to pop out of my head. We
walked through a foyer that led to an open greeting area.

There were spacious lounge areas, beautiful large oil paintings on the walls, some old weapons crisscrossing here and there, and even a few columns with large potted plants. In the center, a grand staircase split at the top and went to the left and right. I could see several doors on the landing, and I assumed more stairs were on either side.

"So, the first floor here has the common room, dining room, ballroom, kitchens, and a game room. The second floor is the staff and omegas' lodgings. The third floor is for guests, and some of the warriors' lodgings are there as well—at least the ones that usually patrol here or serve as personal guards. The fourth floor is divided into sections: there is a section for the Beta and his family, one for the Delta and his family, and a wing for the Gamma. There is also a wing for the former Alpha and Luna and a wing for the King of Lycans or his dignitary if they visit. The last floor, the fifth floor, is ours; it's set up like an apartment of sorts," Trevor said while we took it all in.

"You said some of the warriors are on level three. Where are the rest?" Kevin asked, curiosity etched on his face.

"They also have lodgings on the second floor, and some have homes elsewhere. Not everyone lives in the castle—most actually live in the villages," Trevor informed him.

"Villages? As in more than one?" Zander asked.

"We have three now. The main one is right down the road and is also where the shops are. The other two are add-ons and more toward the back of the pack," he said.

"That is really impressive," Zander said in a tone of admiration.

"It would be if it were because we ourselves were growing. We needed to add on because we took in families from packs that were destroyed a few years back. There were attacks on several packs, and whoever hit them just left carnage. There wasn't much anyone could do, so I gave them a choice. They could try to rebuild, or they could come and stay with me in my lands and earn a place here. We had plenty of space that wasn't being utilized, but it has been a long process getting werewolves and Lycans to coexist."

I looked at Trevor and beamed at him. That was probably one of the most amazing things I had heard of. I was shunned in my old pack for being an outsider and different. Here, they embraced the people that needed a home.

"That is very merciful of you and your people," Zander said. He looked at me and then looked away, sadness and pain in his eyes.

"I am just pleased my father allowed me to do it. He was still Alpha then. It was not something he wanted, but in the end, it added to our numbers and saved a lot of families. Most of those that were left were women, children, and the elderly, so rebuilding on their own was not something they wanted to do."

I looked up at him in shock.

"How long ago did this happen?" I asked.

"It had to have been about eighteen years ago now," Trevor replied.

I heard Kevin's breath hitch along with mine. Could I have come from one of these packs?

"What is it?" Trevor looked at me, concerned, and then glanced at my brother, who was also watching me.

"Aylin was found about eighteen years ago, and no one knew what pack she came from. During the investigation in the surrounding packs, they couldn't find anyone who was missing a child. However, my parents did hear about packs that had been devastated in rogue attacks," Kevin answered. He reached out and grabbed my free hand.

I gave him a reassuring smile to let him know I was okay. I had a feeling he could sense my growing unease.

"Maybe we can ask some of the older pack members that are here from the—"

"Trevor, darling, you're home!" A loud, high-pitched voice squealed, and she ran into him, wrapping her arms around his neck. He dropped my hand, and my wolf went on edge, our hackles rising. Then she kissed his cheek, only because he moved his head out of the way, and I growled low in warning. The girl's head snapped to me.

"Who is this?" the female asked, still draped over Trevor, and I was starting to lose my patience.

"You should have heard, along with everyone else, that I have found my mate. This is Aylin, your future Luna," Trevor said, removing her arms from around his neck and stepping close to me. He rested his hand on my hip possessively, and I relaxed a little into him but stayed on guard around this female.

"Oh, I apologize, Trevor," the female said in a sing-song voice. "I thought they were just rumors spreading again," she said sweetly. This girl could give Lizzie a run for her money with the overly sweet facade. She looked at me, assessing, and in her eyes, found me lacking. She gave me a small smile and a nod. I will have to watch out for this one.

"You are to call him Alpha Gideon. You are not to be so informal with the Alpha when in public!" Nikki said sternly, stepping forward. The girl looked down and then nodded.

"I apologize again," she said.

"Now, Nikki, be nice," Trevor said to her, and I felt a bit of anger run through me at that. I knew this girl knew he had found his mate, and playing stupid was just a game for her.

"Aylin, this is Ruby," he said as a way of introduction.

I just nodded at her like she did me, assessing and finding her lacking. Her fake sweet smile faltered for only a minute, and I could see the dislike in her eyes. I let her see mine as well.

"Nice to meet you, Ruby," I said, not pretending to be sweet and innocent. I won't pretend to like her. She can see just how much I don't care. Trevor tensed a little beside me and looked at me with a raised eyebrow. The anger in me spiked again, and with that, I took a step away from him, closer to my brother and Zander. I crossed my arms over my chest, and my brother put a hand on my shoulder. Zander even took a step closer to me. That seemed to affect Trevor — him getting closer to Zander. If he was going to be all nice and sweet to a girl who was being beyond obvious, then I wanted no part of him.

"I think it is time for me to show our new packmates and my Luna to our rooms," Trevor said. "Excuse me." He stepped toward me, placed his hand around my waist, and tried to pull me close to him. I didn't budge. He looked down at me, and I could see the concern in his eyes. My heart squeezed, and I decided to let it go this one time. I let him lead me toward the stairs. The others followed, walking past Ruby without another word, except for Nikki, who glared at her as she walked by, which got a smile from me.

We headed up the stairs and reached the third floor, where Trevor turned to Kevin and Zander.

"You two have rooms made up here until we talk to the Elders and figure out if we need more permanent accommodations," he told them.

We looked at each other, a bit confused.

"I thought they would have rooms in our apartment. Kevin is my family, after all, and my protector is supposed to be close by?" I was not comfortable with this situation. I also didn't like Zander being down here—my jealousy getting to me—but I would not voice that opinion. I shouldn't be jealous when it comes to him. Hadn't I decided that I was going to choose Trevor? Then again, if he had this Ruby girl, then why the hell should I? I didn't have to worry about a jealous girl with Zander—just his annoying sister. And if I was her Luna, she would have to watch how she and her friends treated me or face punishment. I liked that idea.

"This is just temporary until we find out more about what is going on," Trevor said. "I think we should get answers, and these rooms are already made up for guests. It will take a few days to get their rooms ready in our suite if they end up staying."

I didn't miss the **if** in the sentence, and neither did Kevin or Zander, who both looked put off and ready to say something.

"I see. Well, I am sure we will be able to get the rooms ready in no time. After all, if it is anything like my old pack, we are talking about bedding and a few small pieces for each person, maybe some additional clothes depending on the jobs they end up taking on here. I will see you both in a little bit. Nick, will you please bring them to my room in an hour? I would like to talk with them before we go to eat. If that is okay?" I added the question at the end toward Trevor since he seemed to think that having them room down here would keep us apart or something. I didn't think so.

Trevor's jaw set in a tight line, and he just nodded. "I wasn't sure if you would like to rest after the journey and thought you would all like to just get accommodated in your own rooms before we head down for dinner," he said.

"Thank you, but I have rested enough on the drive in, and I haven't had a lot of time to talk to my brother or Zander, for that matter, about what is going on and how they are doing with all this. It is, after all, not something that any of us understands," I replied, keeping my cool and reigning in my anger.

I knew I was mostly still upset about Ruby and the lack of respect for someone who was about to become her Luna, but I also felt disrespected by Trevor since he didn't even seem to care that she blatantly lied and flirted with him, even after introducing me as his future Luna. He even defended her. My anger spiked again at that, and my brother looked at me and cocked his head.

"I will take you to our suite so you can get cleaned up then. See you both in an hour or so." He nodded to Kevin, then to Zander, and then dismissed Nick and Nikki for the time being.

"Okay, I will follow you." I motioned for him to lead the way and folded my hands together so he wouldn't try to take my hand in his. I still needed time to calm down since he clearly didn't see that what happened downstairs was not okay.

He led me upstairs two more floors, and I was greeted with a large living space with three large blue couches surrounding a square coffee table and a large fireplace against the far wall. There was a hallway to the left and one to the right, along with a door on either side of the fireplace, closer toward the entrance of the hallways. The walls were a cream color, bringing light to the room as I noticed there were no windows around the walls, but there were a few on the ceiling, letting some natural light into the space. It was beautiful.

"So this is the living room. The door to the left is a guest bathroom, and the door to the right is the dining room. The kitchen is attached through another door in the dining room. The hallway to the left leads to the Alpha and Luna's chambers, each having their own attached bathroom. They also both attach to an additional living space, and there are three other rooms that can be used however you see fit—eventually, possibly a nursery for the large one for our pups and rooms for the kids," he said, almost sounding hopeful.

He definitely has thought about what he wants with his Luna. I don't want to talk about kids right now, though, since I don't even know what is going on with Zander. It almost feels like a betrayal to be talking about something like that without him.

"I can't wait to see it all. What is down that hallway?" I ask, attempting to change the subject.

"Down that hall are a few more rooms, a small office for each of us, and at the very end is an attached gym with some exercise equipment and a small pool for laps. There is also a jacuzzi and sauna room," he explains and shrugs one shoulder like it's nothing.

"Wow, I don't even need to go outside to train," I laugh, and he smiles at me.

"Now let me show you to your room so you can get refreshed. I did have the head maid gather a few clothing items for you, and I will take you to town to get more. You will need a gown for the ceremony, and they will make a few options for you so you have choices for some future events as well."

He led me down the hall toward our rooms and opened the door to my room.

I think my jaw hit the ground. It was beautiful. The large four-poster bed had dark blue curtains and a dark purple bedspread with lilac and lavender paisley designs outlined in gold. On either side of the bed were bedside tables with small lamps. On the far wall, by the large windows, sat a blue chaise with some light and dark purple throw pillows. In the corner, there were bookshelves filled with books and a few figurines—one of a moon and one of a Lycan holding a heart. Some of the shelves were empty, ready to be filled. On the opposite wall were two doors; one, I assumed, led to the bathroom.

I walked over and opened the first door, leading to a large walk-in closet. Trevor was not kidding when he said they had brought some clothes already. Mostly dresses. I wrinkled my nose at that. I am not a dressy person. I am a hands-on person, and I guess I will have to get some more pants and activewear when he lets me go shopping. I am sure there are plenty of dresses in here for what I will need when I have to attend special occasions. My day-to-day wear, however, will not be dressy. I know a Luna should take pride in her appearance, but I am not going to spend my days behind a desk doing the bare minimum. I am going to be out there helping the people as much as I can to both prove I am one of them and show them I care.

I opened the second door, revealing a beautiful and spacious bathroom. It had black tile floors and white and black marble paneling on the walls with gold accents throughout. The cabinets were matte black with gold fastenings to open the drawers. The countertop was black and white marble with gold glitter inlay, matching the walls perfectly. There was a large clawfoot tub along one wall, and in the corner, a walk-in shower. Across from the sink was the toilet. It was all so nice, and I was having a hard time believing that this was all mine. The room, the closet, the bathroom — it was all so beautiful.

"What do you think?" Trevor asked. He sounded and looked nervous.

"I love it. I never in a million years thought I would have anything like this," I told him honestly, not hiding the awe in my voice. "I will say, though, I'll have to pick up clothes more to my taste. I am not a pastel-flower-dress kind of girl." I laughed at that, and he visibly relaxed.

"Anything you want. This is your home now, and I want you to be happy here with me," he said as he walked up behind me and wrapped his arms around my middle. I leaned back into his embrace, and the anger I had been holding onto faded. His scent and body were addictive, and soon, all I was thinking about was what he would feel like on top of me instead of just holding me. I had to give myself a shake and remember that we were supposed to just come shower and get ready for dinner.

"I am going to go get ready. See you in a minute," I told him, walking out of his embrace even though I just wanted to stay.

He grabbed my wrist, turned me around, and spun me back into his arms, facing him. He leaned down and claimed my lips in a searing kiss that left me breathless and full of want and need. Ass. He then smiled at me knowingly and walked through the door I had missed—the one that must lead to his adjoined room.

I rolled my eyes at him, gathered some clothes, and headed into the bathroom. I took my time getting ready. I may not like dresses, but this one didn't look half bad on me. It was a pretty dark purple, and I liked how it hugged my hips and then flared out just a bit. I put my hair up and added the little makeup I wore around my eyes. I was just looking over my appearance again when there was a knock at the door.

"Come on, Aylin, I am starving," Kevin grumbled from the other side. I shook my head at the bottomless pit.

"I'm coming, I'm coming. Hold your horses," I yelled back, then opened the door.

He stood there and gaped at me. That's when I noticed Zander and Trevor standing further into the room, both of them gaping as well.

"What's wrong?" I asked, looking down to see if something was wrong with the dress.

"Nothing is wrong, Ay. You are stunning," Zander said, not taking his eyes off me.

I blushed at the way he stared, his eyes full of desire. That look pulled at me, and my body responded. I looked him over and loved the way his jeans fell on his hips, paired with a black button-up dress shirt left untucked. It was almost like he had tried to look dressed up and casual at the same time—and it was hot.

"I agree, little wolf. You are breathtaking in that dress."

I smiled at them both and nodded to my brother. I took a minute to look at Trevor. As before, he wore dress pants and a white button-up dress shirt tucked in with a black tie. Ever the professional, I guess, but goddess, was he gorgeous.

I followed them out of the room and out of our little apartment toward the dining hall used for the pack.

# Chapter Fourteen
## *Aylin*

Dinner with the pack was loud and happy. Almost everyone seemed to want to meet me. I did get a few curious looks from some of the she-wolves—well, curious and a little hostile. They definitely didn't like that I was here. I'm betting they were either friends with Ruby or that they wanted Trevor to look their way.

Trevor, Nick, Jullian, and Thomas were going over everything they needed to do tomorrow and were planning out their day, so I was talking to Nikki, Kevin, and Zander when another male sat at our table with his food, up by Trevor. He jumped into their conversation about what was going on tomorrow. Nikki saw where my gaze went and leaned over to me.

"That is our Gamma, Liam," she explained.

Upon hearing his name, he looked up, smiled at me, and waved. I waved back and gave a small smile in return. He went back to talking to Trevor and Nick, and I went back to my conversation with the others.

"I am just looking forward to answers. I don't know how any of this is possible, and honestly, I am a little scared of what is coming. I just have a bad feeling about something, and I can't place my finger on what or why," I said to Kevin. He, like me, could not stop thinking about the past day. It's

163

hard to believe that is all it has been, and even then, not even a full day just yet.

"I know. I think we will all feel better once we have them. I just never thought I would leave the pack. I don't know what I am going to do here if we stay. Our pack will lose both the Alpha and Beta, and that isn't good. We could have challenges and discord; it is going to be a mess." He shook his head back and forth and then took another bite of food. He was already on his second plate, and it was piled just as high as his first—mostly meat, as usual.

"Let's not get ahead of ourselves," Zander chimed in. "We don't know what is going on, and we do not know if this is something that will be permanent or if there is a way out of any of this."

He said it, and I couldn't help the sharp pain in my heart and the disappointment in his words. He didn't want to stay? Did that mean he didn't want me? What am I saying? I can't have him and Trevor. I had already said no to Zander for rejecting me, so why does it hurt? And why do I want him to stay? I need to get a hold of myself. I need to stop my stupid infatuation with this male.

At that moment, Zander gave me a dazzling smile, and all thought left me. For a moment, all I could think about was the crush I had on this man for most of my life. The hurt he caused me was unbearable, but the idea of losing him a second time hurts too. When the time comes, will I be able to let him go? Trevor already said that he will never let me go. I am his one and only. What am I going to do? I am so selfish to have a mate and still long for Zander. Yet I feel like being with Trevor is a betrayal as well. Moon Goddess, please help me here.

"I would never make you stay with me, either of you. I know you have a pack to run and go back to, so if that is what you want, you know I am okay with it," I tell them, even though it's not completely true. I am rather selfish, as I want them both to stay. No one understands me like my brother, and the thought of losing Zander still hurts. I would let them go and deal with it for their happiness, however.

"What if we don't want to go? Or what if we do and want you to come with us?" Zander asked. He already knew I couldn't go with him. The hope in his eyes, however, stole my breath.

"She cannot go back to your pack. As future Luna here, she will have to stay," Trevor cut in, making me jump. "If we cannot find a suitable solution, you are welcome to stay or go. That is your choice," he added.

"If we stay, what would we do here? You already have an Alpha and a Beta. What would you need from us?" Kevin asked. He always had a hard time sitting still. I know not having something to do will drive him crazy.

"There are always positions to be filled in a pack, but for now, I do believe we need to get answers before we make any decisions," Trevor said, and I nodded in agreement. I wanted answers, and I wanted to know what we could do from here, but it was also hard thinking about all the possibilities that could come from getting answers—including losing Zander. Why does that thought hurt me so much? This stupid bond sucks.

The rest of dinner went by with talk of what we could expect from the elders and about the tour we were going to get tomorrow from Liam. I was especially interested in the training yard, while Trevor and Nick caught up on some pack business.

Once everyone was done eating, we all went up to our rooms. I stopped with Kevin and Zander and said good night, hugging Kevin and thanking him for being here with me. Even if he technically didn't have a choice, I still loved that he was here. Part of me wants to believe that he would have come if he could anyway. Our bond has always been strong.

Zander waited for me and stood there awkwardly by his door. He looked like he wanted to say or do something, but he hesitated. I wanted to hug him like I did with my brother, but we have never had that kind of relationship in the past. I mostly admired him from afar, and when we did hang out, it was at my house because he was there visiting my brother. So, we really didn't get close enough to have that kind of intimacy. But, Goddess, did I want to.

I gave him a small smile and wave and wished him a good night. He said good night as well, and with a sigh and a glare at Trevor, he went inside his room.

Trevor and I made the rest of the way to our apartment in a flirtatious silence. We kept sneaking looks at each other and kept catching each other doing it. I was blushing so badly I knew my face and neck were as bright as a tomato. Goddess, what this male did to me.

Trevor grabbed my hand, and the jolt of electricity caused me to suck in a sharp breath. I don't think I will ever get used to that. He held my hand the remaining short distance to our apartment and then to my bedroom door. He paused and stood there, not letting go of my hand. His brows were furrowed, and he looked like he wanted to say something.

"I am looking forward to the tour tomorrow," I told him to see if that would break him out of his thoughts.

"I just wish I could be the one to take you," he said, looking at me intensely.

"I think Liam will do a fine job," I replied with a smile. I liked that he wanted to be with me, even when he couldn't. Alpha responsibilities and all that obviously would keep him away at times.

"If I could, I would have him take your brother and his friend around, and I would take you so we could have some time just to learn about each other," he said, his voice low and gravelly. He gave me a mischievous smile, and I couldn't help the need that spread through me and to my core. Goddess, this man is making it impossible to wait.

"I have a feeling if that were the case, we would not be doing much touring." I was leaning back against my door now. He let go of my hand and moved his to the door beside my head and the other to my hip, keeping me in place.

"And what is it that you think we would be doing instead?" he asked, a smirk on his face, his eyes burning into mine.

"I am sure you have all manner of things you would have us doing," I replied. I couldn't look away. I watched as he slowly trailed his lower lip with his tongue. It caused me to bite my own to keep me from moaning out loud. His eyes flickered to the action, and his smile turned feral—wicked even.

"I think that is my cue to go to bed." I was laughing and blushing. I wanted more than anything for him to follow through with those wicked thoughts, whatever they may be. My body was responding to him, and the mate bond was calling me to complete the mating. I knew it was going to be just as hard for him. Fortunately, he seemed to take pity on me and nodded his head.

He bent and kissed me, his kiss searing my lips and devouring my rational mind. It took every ounce of willpower to pull away from his lips and his touch. Goddess, please give me the strength to wait. Just one more day. Just one more day. I repeated this to myself over and over. Just one more day, then we will have our answers, and I can move forward. We can move forward, and I will let him show me what those wicked thoughts were.

With one last longing look at my mate, I went into my room and closed the door behind me. I changed into a pair of sleep shorts and a tank top. Then I took care of my bathroom needs and went to bed. The bed was amazing. It was like lying on a large marshmallow with the softest blankets surrounding me. It didn't take long, with how comfortable I was, for me to fall asleep.

*The darkness seemed to go on forever. I felt the grass and dried leaves on the bottom of my feet as I walked forward. The trees were thick, and I had to take my time. Why couldn't I see? My wolf sight should allow me to see in the dark.*

*The way ahead starts to open, and as I walk through the tree line, I see a massive lake ahead of me. I recognize this lake. Usually, when I see it, I have a sense of foreboding and fear. Standing by the lake is a young woman. She has long silver hair, and I can't make out her features. Is that me? I keep walking toward her, and then I stop. Frozen, unable to move. I watch as a large brown wolf stalks up behind her. She turns toward him, and for a moment, I think the wolf is about to pounce; however, it transforms into a man. A very naked man.*

*The two stare at each other for a while. I realize they are talking. Then everything shifts. We are in a house, and the silver-haired woman is looking down at a mangled body. It was the man from the lake. I feel her tears run down her cheeks and realize now it is me standing over the body, crying. I can feel the ache in my heart and soul, like it had been torn in half, and I couldn't breathe — the pain was so suffocating.*

*"You will be mine. Come," said a deep and menacing voice. I was shaking. Then I could hear a baby cry. Fear spiked through me.*

*"You bred with this mongrel!" A deep voice boomed around me. I ran to the babe, picked her up, clutching her to me. The growl I heard made the hairs on the back of my neck stand up. My fight-or-flight instinct kicked in, and I ran from the house into the woods. I was fast. I knew I could outrun him, but for how long? He was a god and had more stamina than I could hope for. He wouldn't tire as fast as me and would eventually catch up.*

*Fear spiked through me as I tried to outrun the man with the red eyes. He was furious, and I couldn't let him hurt my little girl. I had to find a way to protect her and keep her safe. My little girl? I didn't have a little girl. Is this my future daughter? No, it can't be. This feels more like a memory, like it already happened.*

*Everything shifted again, and I was on my back, fighting the man with the red eyes, trying to keep him from grabbing the babe in my arms. That's right—the bundle. I hid the babe. He grabs it and roars when he finds the babe gone. I watch the emotions play through those red eyes—hurt, betrayal, anger—and I feel a tear roll down my face. Then I hear myself tell him that I'm sorry.*

*Then, nothing but darkness.*

I wake to my name being called and my shoulder being shaken. When I finally open my eyes, I see Kevin. He has a very worried look on his face.

"I couldn't wake you, Ay. What happened?"

I look around and notice Trevor and Zander are also there.

"It was that dream again, but different," I tell him.

"What do you mean it was different? How?" Kevin asks.

"The woman with silver hair — the one that looks like me but isn't — was standing by a lake, and a wolf came upon her. They talked, and then the dream changed. She — or I — was standing over his mutilated body, crying. The man with red eyes was there, and then I heard the baby cry. I could hear him talk this time — the man with the red eyes."

I hadn't realized I was crying while telling him about the dream until I felt him wipe away my tears.

"He said I was his. I grabbed the baby and ran into the woods. That is usually where my dream starts — running through the woods. All I know is it felt so real." I was shaking.

Kevin wrapped an arm around me, and Trevor and Zander both sat on the bed near me, placing their hands on my arms. Their combined touch seemed to calm me. It took only a few minutes for me to settle down with the three of them there.

Kevin looked around and got off the bed. He went over to my bags and started going through them. I hadn't unpacked yet. He grabbed Archie and brought him to me.

I smiled at him and took Archie from him. I held the stuffed elephant and took a few more deep breaths, steadying myself the rest of the way.

"Are you okay?" Kevin asked, his eyes searching.

"I am now," I tell him honestly. He seemed to believe me but had a skeptical look in his eyes.

"Is there anything else about the dream?" Trevor asked, looking at me curiously.

I nodded. "Usually, at the end, I see the dagger he kills me with, but this time, I only focused on his eyes. He looked so hurt and angry, like I betrayed him. This time, I told him I was sorry, and then it went dark," I told him.

Kevin was rubbing circles on my back, and I let my head fall onto his shoulder.

"Would you like me to stay till you fall asleep?" he asked.

Both Zander and Trevor growled low and gave him quizzical looks.

"Will you two calm down? He's my brother. He has been there through most of my nightmares, and his presence has always helped calm me. I have a hard time sleeping after the nightmares. His presence just helps," I explained.

"I am here now. I could stay with you till you fall asleep," Trevor said, getting territorial.

Zander growled again but was ignored by Trevor.

"Maybe we should all stay," Zander said, narrowing his eyes at Trevor.

This was going to get out of hand. Trevor looked like he was about to jump to the other side of the bed and rip Zander in half.

"That would be fine," I said quickly. All eyes turned to me.

"When you all touched me, it calmed me — faster than I have ever been able to calm down before. Sometimes, I even have panic attacks after a nightmare, and it was like you all stopped it from coming. Maybe you all staying will allow me to sleep."

Trevor didn't look happy, but he nodded. Zander looked undecided but also seemed happy that I didn't kick him out, and Kevin just shook his head but didn't say anything.

All three men climbed into my bed — Trevor on one side of me, Kevin on the other, and Zander lying next to Kevin. I knew Zander wanted to be next to me, but he also knew I still needed time. I didn't trust that he wouldn't hurt me, and I also didn't want to continue to be attached if he was leaving.

It took no time at all for their combined breathing to lull me into a deep sleep.

This time, when I slept, the nightmare didn't come back. However, the feeling of someone watching me remained. It was a thick and suffocating entity, and I couldn't shake it.

When I woke up, only Trevor and Zander were there. Kevin had left sometime during the night, and I really couldn't blame him. A queen bed was barely big enough for two people, let alone four.

Zander was sitting cross-legged on the bed on one side, and Trevor was still lying next to me.

"Good morning, little wolf," Trevor said, brushing a hand across my face and tucking my hair behind my ear.

Zander glared at him.

"How did you sleep, my queen?" Zander asked.

This time, Trevor glared at him. These two were barely able to keep from hurting each other.

I am so done. We need to speak with these elders before one of them gets hurt or killed from their jealous rage.

"Better with all of you here. I am sorry — I know it was awkward for both of you, but I am glad you were here. I just had this feeling like I was being watched, like those red eyes would find me."

I knew it sounded crazy, and I was being selfish for wanting them all to stay with me, but I felt safe when they were all there.

"Let's go to breakfast. After breakfast, Liam is going to take you on a tour of the grounds," Trevor said.

I nodded and got out of bed. The guys left to give me privacy, and I got dressed. I put on yoga pants and a sporty tank top that said, *Don't mess with me — I bite.* I pulled my hair back and went down to meet the guys for breakfast.

# Chapter Fifteen
## *Trevor*

Breakfast went by rather fast. I listened to Liam's plan for the tour and nodded my approval. Aylin, Kevin, and Zander would ask questions, and together they made a plan for the day. The thought of Zander spending time with her, even being watched by Liam, agitated me and Bane. He was ready to mark and claim her as his, even knowing it could upset and hurt her in the process. However, I cannot deny I wanted the same. I was just able to put her needs ahead of my own—at least for now.

After everyone was done eating and ready to start their day, I pulled Aylin into my arms and kissed her. I could hear the damn wolf growl low behind her, and I couldn't bring myself to care. He will be gone soon anyway. She is mine, and I am doing my best to hold it together and not just claim her as mine—mostly because I know she would be furious with me. But I could spend the rest of my life making it up to her. Maybe I would do just that and spend my days showering her with my desire for her now that she is here.

I bid her and the others goodbye and looked at Nick, Thomas, and Jullian. I jerked my head toward my office, and we both headed upstairs to get to the piles of work we needed to sort through. Walking away from her to the office was the hardest thing I had done in a while. Every ounce of my being—and my Lycan—demanded I stay with her, especially with the wolf so close.

Once in my office, I sat at my large desk and panned through the folders I needed to deal with first. I needed to focus and get my mind off my mate. One was a dispute between two wolf packs and the orchard that ran into both properties. Another was on the funds we had set aside to help with projects and deciding which projects got our attention first. The last was a request from the king for us to send over our head warrior, who handled our training. I didn't like that he would make this request when he did. There were other trainers, and I liked having my head warrior here.

Thomas and Jullian went to take their spots outside the door, but instead, I had them make rounds. When I am not away from the pack, I absolutely hate having guards. In my pack, it just seems to be a useless waste of manpower since my Beta or Delta are always with me. I have developed a friendship with them, but there are better things they can do with their time. I already had my Delta at the king's palace for other business. I didn't like so many of the higher pack members being away. I didn't even like taking them with me when I went somewhere.

"Where should we start?" Nick asked. He was also thumbing through some folders. They were smaller disputes with residents here or requests. We would get to those later. These three things needed to be handled first, as they were on a tight timeline. We wanted to avoid any fighting between packs, and the king hated being kept waiting. However, he would need to for the moment.

"Let's start with this dispute." I handed him the folder I was just looking at. Usually, I would handle the king's request first. However, it was not marked urgent, so I knew I would have some time to look at it.

"This one isn't going to be easy. Alpha Richardson of Winterhaven is too hardheaded and doesn't like to see reason," Nick said, still looking through the folder.

"He will need to work with us one way or another, or we will have to deal with him," I replied. I had no problem removing thorns. If the Alphas under my protection couldn't see reason, they could—and would—be replaced. I hated doing it and had only had to once since I took over as Alpha.

"From what I am reading and the property lines I am seeing here, I have a few ideas on how we can handle it," Nick said and looked at me to see if he should proceed. I nodded my head. This was why I had him here—to help me brainstorm and get this work done faster.

"Well, neither pack is going to give up territory space; we already know that. So we could make them build a wall or fence going through the property line so that no one goes over to the other side, and we divide the orchard." I nodded and thought about it.

"Alpha Richardson will probably have a problem with that, as in his statement, he said he started the orchard, and the new trees he sees as his property. He doesn't want Ashwood to have access to any of them," I said. Nick thought about it for a minute.

"We could give him an ultimatum. They build the fence, or we remove the orchard—all of it. If he did start it, he started it too close to the territory line as it is," Nick said. That wasn't a bad idea. I also agreed with his assessment about starting it too close to the border.

"What is your other idea?" I asked.

"This one also will not go over well between them, but it's worth a shot to at least possibly present the option. We take the territory and change it. We give the Winterhaven pack the area with the orchard, and to make it fair, they have to relinquish the same square footage along another area that borders the territory line," he said.

This was also a decent idea. I liked them both, and in each, both parties win and lose. It's as fair as we can be with something like this. We cannot just give one pack whatever they want and take from another. That will escalate. No, we have to be the voice of reason.

"I doubt they will go with either option, but in the end, if they do not decide, I will make the choice for them." I then typed up two contracts—one with each plan—and left a space open for the one with the territory change. I made three copies of each.

"Do you know what you will decide if they cannot agree?" Nick asked.

"I like your idea of removing the orchard. I think if they cannot agree, we will have to remove or destroy it. I would hate to see an orchard of fruit go to waste, however, so if we can remove it and bring some of those trees here, it would also help us in the process," I said. It could harm the pack that has been so used to having an orchard with their food supply, but if they cannot come to an agreement, then that will fall on the Alphas as a failure on their part.

"What if they fight because we removed the orchard and they blame each other?" I gave him a knowing look, as that was a possibility. If they wanted to have that fight, then I would take matters into my own hands and deal with the Alphas.

"I will present them with the options. I will let them know they have a limited time to come to an agreement, or I will choose for them. I will let them know what my choice will be if they cannot come to an agreement, and maybe that will motivate them to work together. I will also let them know that, after all is said and done, if they are still not happy with the choice made and want to fight further, one or both parties will be removed and outcast."

Nick's eyes widened at that. He knew that I hated removing an Alpha from power. It could lead to a battle in the pack for the next Alpha; sometimes, it turned into a bloodbath when an heir or appointed replacement was challenged. This was, however, how pack business was handled, and if there was a dispute, I had to let it play out — which was why I hated doing it at all.

"So, when do we go to the pack and present the options?" he asked.

"I am thinking early next week. My Luna's ceremony is this weekend, and I would like to take the weekend to celebrate and spend time with my mate. Monday should be fine to make the trip. We can give them some time to think about it and go from there."

Nick nodded in agreement.

"I will have messengers send word to the Alphas to prepare for your arrival," he said.

I placed the contract in the folder and put it aside. That one problem had taken up most of the morning. Really, drawing up the drafts for the agreements had taken most of the time, and the sad thing was that we could end up doing something completely different. I still had two more problems to deal with and then a mountain of small but no less important ones.

"Okay, now that we have that planned, let's look at the king's request to train more guards," Nick said, opening that folder. "So, it looks like he wants twenty new recruits trained. However, his request is that our trainer go to the castle."

That request bothered me. If I sent him to the castle and the king ordered it, he could be there for a while, leaving me without my head guard. He already had my Delta there. I would have to think of something.

"I don't think that's wise," I said. "I will talk to Liam about this and see about putting together the new recruits, but I will not send our trainer. I am sure there will be something else we can do with that. It is not marked urgent, so we will have some time to respond."

"We could always send his second," Nick suggested.

I knew that O'Brien's second was his firstborn son. He might not like the idea, but he was unmated, and even though it would be a loss, it wouldn't be as big of a loss for the pack as a whole.

"Why don't we present the king with the options? We could let him know that, due to the newest situation here, we need our head warrior. So, we can send his second, or the king could send his new recruits here to be trained with our guard," Nick said.

I liked that idea. However, I didn't know how my uncle would take it. He was not usually one to be questioned. However, he could be level-headed, and he knew how it was with new mates.

I wrote out the response to the king, explaining the upcoming situations and that it would be best to train them here. But if he insisted on the trainer coming to the castle, we would send the trainer's second—his son—to fill in at the king's request. Hopefully, he would just send the guards here, and we would have the added numbers just in case, while also sending some of our own to the Winterhaven and Ashwood packs to keep an eye on them.

"Have this sent to the king as soon as possible," I told him.

Nick grabbed the sealed letter and the two letters I had written to the Alphas to expect us this coming Monday, along with the current proposals and a request that, if they could think of something better, they should have it ready.

"Let's handle this last folder, and then I will take these to our messengers," he said, placing them in his jacket pocket for safekeeping.

I nodded and lifted the last folder. This one was about which project we were going to proceed with for the pack. I had two at the top of the list — one for a greenhouse so we could grow some vegetables even in the winter and the other for a second playground for the pack.

We had expanded so much that those staying toward the back of the pack's property had to come to the pack house to use the playground there. Sometimes, there were so many kids and parents that the playground became over-crowded. A few kids had even gotten hurt from being accidentally knocked off the equipment.

"I know you are leaning toward the playground. However, I have to say that the best option would be the green-house. I know that means waiting on the playground for a little while longer, but it would help the pack through the winter. We wouldn't have to go to town as often to buy food," he said.

I understood this, and I agreed. However, I was still leaning more toward the playground.

"We have been going to town to buy food for as long as we have been here. We both know that if we had to do it for one more year, we could manage. Kids are getting hurt, and I don't want the pack hospital dealing with kids with broken bones or worse daily. I have multiple reports in that pile of folders—complaints from parents of the kids who have been hurt," I told him. He sighed and nodded.

"Look, we may be able to do both if we have help from the pack," I told him.

"How so?" he asked.

"If we have volunteers instead of paid laborers, it would cut costs. I know some of the pack were looking to get a bit more income, but we could do both if we had the pack work together to build them with volunteers."

Nick looked out the window and thought for a few minutes.

"People look forward to the projects for that added income. It will be hard getting people behind it. I am sure some will, but you will have those that are angry," he said in return.

"I know it will cause waves, but I will present it as an option to them as well. We can choose one or both. It will benefit the pack to do both in the long run. We will be able to have some of them tending to the greenhouse, making a wage as well. If they don't like it, then we proceed with the playground, and next year we will do the greenhouse," I said simply.

Today has been a day of presenting options. Usually, I tell the pack how things are going to be done, and they just have to deal with it, but for this decision, I think they would like the chance to be heard. I know there will be quite a few people who will be upset that we are putting off the greenhouse, so maybe that will motivate volunteers.

"Well, now that we have that all settled, when are you going to address the pack to let them know?" he asked.

"I thought about tonight after dinner, but it's Aylin's first full day here, so how about tomorrow? We will send word of a mandatory pack meeting. That will give the pack plenty of time to accommodate the request into their plans," I told him. "Better to get it out of the way. I need to let them know my choice on the playground, that I will be leaving next week, and introduce them all to their future Luna."

We should have done it last night, but Aylin was already tired, and I didn't want to overwhelm her on her first night here.

"Okay, I will talk with the guard and have them make announcements right after I give these letters to the messengers. I will have them tell the pack that they are to all be present to meet their Luna and to hear about the upcoming project," Nick said, standing. He bowed his head to me and left my office.

I went to writing my speech. Thirty minutes later, I was done with my speech and pulled all the folders with complaints about the playground and hurt children. I was making my way through them when there was a knock at my office door.

"Come in," I said loudly, closing the folder in front of me.

The door opened, and in walked Ruby. She walked in like she owned the place, sat herself on the edge of my desk, and fluttered her eyes at me. I could see she was trying to get my attention. She was wearing a revealing dress and was pushing her breasts out to entice me. Too bad it wouldn't work. The only one I had eyes for now was my little wolf.

"Ruby, please remove yourself from my desk and take a seat," I told her coolly.

Her eyes widened a fraction, and her smile faltered for just a second before she composed herself.

"Why would you want me to do that, Trevor? You used to like when I came in here and interrupted your boring workday. If I remember correctly, it would involve you taking me right here on this desk," she said seductively, placing her hand on the area of the desk in front of me.

"That is in the past and will not happen again," I told her flatly. "Now, please get off my desk."

I stood and took the pile of folders over to my filing cabinet, where I stored them for later. I would deal with them later—most of it would be handled with the new playground, but I liked to make sure there was nothing else that needed my attention. I hate anything being overlooked. It cut the mountain of paperwork down quite a bit, knowing most of it would be about the playground.

When I turned around, Ruby was standing right behind me.

"Trevor, you know it should be you and me together," she said sweetly, placing her hand on my chest and moving it slowly up to my shoulder.

I grabbed her wrist, and her smile grew.

"We were made for each other. Even if the Moon Goddess didn't bless us with a mate bond, you and I have something special."

She reached out again and ran her hand down my chest. I grabbed her wrist and removed her hand from me. This time, I was a bit rougher. I saw her wince in pain, and a very small part of me felt bad.

"You do not have the right to touch me. I am your Alpha, and you will show me and your future Luna respect."

I was starting to get mad. It had been a long day, and I didn't need this she-wolf's attention-seeking right now. Not to mention, with her touching me, I knew Aylin would smell her, and I was already on thin ice with what happened back at her pack. I didn't need a reason for her to run into that wolf's arms.

"Trevor, you know it should be us. You can keep her and lock her up or something so you have the mate bond, and then we can be together. I should be the Luna here, not her!"

She was yelling now, and I was reaching my breaking point.

"You will never be my Luna. You were a way to pass the time while I searched for my mate—nothing more."

Her eyes flashed red, and then she smiled at me.

"You don't mean that, and I will prove it." Before I could see what she was going to do, she walked up to me, threw her arms around me, and kissed me—just as the door to my office swung open. I pushed her off me and looked to see Aylin staring at us, hurt and anger swimming in her beautiful blue eyes. The howl that ripped from her was utterly terrifying.

Ruby stepped behind me for a moment. I thought I saw fear in her eyes. She was a Lycan afraid of a wolf. It would have been comical if Aylin hadn't looked at me with accusation before running from my office.

"Aylin, wait!" I yelled after her. I went to run after her when Ruby grabbed my arm.

"Let her go, Trevor!" she said. "Stay with me and let her go."

I rounded on her. She shrank back from the look I gave her. I was promising pain and was beyond mad. This she-wolf thought she could come in here, demand to be Luna, and try to start something between me and my mate. The sad thing was, she had now succeeded in doing just that, and I was not going to have it.

"You will remain here, and you will not leave until I, Nick, or Liam come for you. YOU will NOT touch anything in my office, and you will remain quiet," I told her in my Alpha tone. She nodded and sat in one of the chairs.

I left the office and called for Thomas and Jullian to stand watch by the door. I told them no one was to go in or out of the office unless it was one of those sent to retrieve her. They nodded, and I left to go find my mate. I hoped she would listen to me and believe me when I explained what happened.

# Chapter Sixteen
## *Aylin*

Liam started to lead us out of the pack house after I said goodbye to Trevor. That kiss still had my brain in a haze. I wasn't paying much attention and didn't realize that Ruby and several other she-wolves were walking up to us. She stepped in front of Liam and gave him a big, playful smile.

"Hey, Liam, where are you off to?" she asked sweetly. I rolled my eyes.

"I am taking our Luna and her comrades on a tour of our pack so they get to see where they will be living," he said stiffly to her. He seemed really uncomfortable being around her.

"Oh, I am so sorry you got stuck with that job," she said, looking sympathetic. Her friends nodded in agreement.

"Couldn't Alpha Gideon get some omega or guard to do it?" one of the other girls asked. He shook his head and looked at them with disbelief.

"This is an honor to show around my Luna. I am very happy to do it," he said to them. He seemed to be getting a little snarky. He was now glaring at Ruby. She shifted from one foot to the other and then straightened and got herself together. That was odd.

"You really are such a wonderful male!" the other wolf said flirtatiously. Ruby cut the female a look. Was that jealousy? Liam smiled at the other she-wolf and winked at her, causing her to blush and Ruby to roll her eyes.

"So, who do we have here?" another she-wolf asked, looking from Kevin to Zander. A little too long for my liking.

"Oh, how rude of me. Here I am, supposed to be showing you guys around, and I forgot you don't know anyone. Aylin, this is Ruby, Heather, Josephine, and Stella," he said, pointing to each girl in turn. "Girls, this is your Luna, Aylin, her brother Kevin, and this is Zander." I noticed he left out what Zander was to me, and it seemed Zander noticed as he purposely took a step closer to me.

"It is very nice to meet you all," said Josephine. "Everyone here calls me Jo, just so you know," she said. She kept looking at Kevin and was starting to blush. However, out of the four she-wolves, she seemed to be the least snobby and most genuine.

"Yes, aren't you yummy?" Stella said, batting her lashes at Zander. I growled at her and closed the remaining distance between us. They all stared at me curiously.

"Oh, honey, I am sure you are fine with me flirting with him a little. I won't hurt him," she said coyly and winked at him. I could feel my eyes flash red, and all I could think about was ripping her and Ruby into pieces. Zander grabbed my hand, and Kevin put his hand on my shoulder to try to calm me.

"I am not interested. I have a mate, and she is all I want," Zander told her. She pouted and then smiled at him again. My stupid heart skipped a beat at his words, and I squeezed his hand.

"Well, your mate isn't here, is she? So what she doesn't know won't hurt."

I almost lost it right then. I was growling low, and the warning was clear—I was done. Not to mention, it would hurt quite a bit! The pain that betrayal creates is beyond intense, and I would wish it on nobody.

"This is my mate, and I would never hurt her by messing around with someone like you," Zander said, getting just as angry as me at this point.

All four of the girls looked between me and Zander.

"Wait, I thought you were supposed to be our future Luna," said Heather with a sneer. Ruby looked like she was just handed a gift. I wanted to wipe that look off her face so badly.

"I am," I said coldly. "I have two mates."

They gawked at me. Zander squeezed my hand. He looked at me and smiled, hope filling his eyes. I knew I shouldn't have given him any hope, but I couldn't help getting territorial with these damn she-wolves around.

"I think it is time for us to get going," Liam said. It seemed like he wanted to get us out of there. He could sense the way this was going and wanted to avoid conflict. After all, he was asked to give us a tour and keep me safe. How would it look if I got into a fight with one of the she-wolves right after saying my goodbyes to Trevor? He would have failed at the job he was entrusted with and took pride in.

"Yes, I think I would like to have that tour now, and some fresh air will do some good. It's stuffy in here," I said.

I walked past the girls while they shot daggers at me with their eyes. I didn't care. I wanted away from them and wanted them away from Zander and Kevin.

Liam led us outside and into the woods. I spent the walk breathing deeply and calming myself. I shouldn't have let them get to me so easily, and now they know they can. I had hoped things would be different here, especially with the fact that I would be their Luna, but I guess entitled she-wolves are everywhere, and nothing will stop them from wanting what they can't have.

"Okay, let's get changed, and then we will run the length of the border," Liam said, looking between us.

"Changed?" I asked.

He looked at me for a second.

"Into your wolf form," he said.

I felt stupid and blushed. I couldn't believe I didn't think of that. Obviously, that is what he meant.

"It will be the fastest way to cover the whole territory. Otherwise, it could take all day and then some," he explained.

I nodded.

I looked around for a place to strip and found a set of bushes and a large rock. I hid behind them and stripped my clothes off. This time, when I let Mona take over, it didn't hurt as bad and was much faster. I gathered my clothes in my mouth and headed over to meet the others.

When I came out, all of them stared at me, including the new Lycan.

'How is this possible?' he asked.

He was gawking at me even in Lycan form. He couldn't believe what he was seeing.

'It's one of the questions we have for the elders,' I responded, and he jerked.

'You can hear and understand me?' he asked in disbelief.

'Yes, and that is yet another question we have for the elders,' I replied.

'So, how about that tour?' I asked.

'Right, follow me. At least now I know why the Alpha didn't want anyone to see you after you shifted.'

I didn't know he didn't want anyone to see me, but if this is the response I would be getting, I understood why.

Liam led us around the border of the territory and, along the way, showed us some spots we might like to explore or get away to. Some of them were hardly used, while others were popular spots for wolves to converge. I made a mental note of the less used ones. I already knew I would need to be able to get away at times.

I liked the idea of exploring the caves. I liked being outdoors, as most wolves do, but I took it to extremes. I didn't just like to hike and run in the woods — I loved exploring and didn't mind getting dirty. Unlike the prissy she-wolves that were always trying to impress the highest-ranking wolves, I never cared about status. I just wanted a place to belong, and since I never did, the wilderness was my home, and I found it calming.

When we got back to the original spot where we shifted, we changed back and got dressed. Liam then took us around the pack, showing us where the houses were set up and explaining how they had to expand after taking in so many displaced wolves and their families. This amazed me. I was taken in but was never accepted by the pack. Here, hundreds were taken in, and it looked like everyone worked together and, for the most part, got along.

"We do have some problems when it comes to Lycan vs. wolf views, but as this is a Lycan pack, the wolves usually have to submit. Not everyone is happy that we have taken in so many wolves. However, when we first brought them here, we had a spike in mates for some of the Lycans that live here. It was a bit of a blessing in a way because they never would have found each other if this didn't happen."

Liam had just finished pointing out the last area they expanded to make room for more families.

"How many found their mates?" Kevin asked.

"Five of the Lycans that live here found mates when we took in the wolves," he said, and then his expression changed and was somber for a moment.

"What's wrong?" I asked, placing my hand on his arm. He looked at me and gave me a small smile.

"One of the Lycans came from a family that didn't believe in mixed breeding; they believed that Lycans should only breed with Lycans and never anyone or anything below them. She was set to mate with a Lycan and found out she had a mate. Her family told her if she chose to be with her mate, she was not welcome anymore. So she did something that most of us frowned upon and rejected her mate," he said, and my heart hurt for this she-Lycan. How could her family be so backward? A wolf will turn into a Lycan through the mate bond.

"Did she mate with the other Lycan?" Kevin asked.

"She went mad with the loss of her mate and passed away before she could mate with the Lycan. I am sure Trevor explained how a Lycan mate is rare and there is only one. You do not get a second chance, and very rarely can someone survive breaking a mate bond," he said, looking at me. I swallowed hard. If I rejected Trevor, he would not accept it because it could be his end. That is why he will never let me go.

I looked at Zander, and I could see the pain in his eyes as he looked back at me. He also knew I wouldn't be able to choose him, even if I still wanted to. I already knew I wanted to choose Trevor. Zander hurt me when he tried to reject me, but he was still my mate too. At least, that is how our bond felt to me. I really didn't think he would be a guardian. How or why, I didn't know, but he was still my mate.

"I am sorry for your loss. She must have been a good friend," Kevin said, finally breaking the silence.

"She was my sister," he said after a moment. "After that, I stopped talking to my family. I would rather her be with her mate and be alive than bow to old ways that make no sense," he said. My heart broke for him, and I couldn't help but wrap him in a hug. He didn't respond at first but then hugged me back.

"Thank you, my lady. I guess that kind of heartbreak is something my family is cursed with surviving," he said and then seemed to snap out of his own head. "Let's see — what would you like to be shown next?" he said to us, stepping back.

But I caught what he just said.

"What do you mean that it is something your family is cursed with surviving? Were there others in your family that have been rejected?" I knew I was prying and shouldn't, but I was curious. Besides, his sister didn't survive.

He sighed. "Yes, one of my mother's sisters was rejected, and it took her a long time to recover. And then there was one other." He paused like he really didn't want to say what came next. "I was also rejected some years ago."

That shocked me and Zander. We both stared at him in disbelief. How could someone reject him? He was handsome and funny, and he had a title. What was wrong with these Lycans?

"Who would be so crazy to do that to you?" I asked without thinking. He looked at me and gave a small smile.

"It doesn't matter. It's all in the past, and I have had time to accept it and move on," he said. "Really, no one knows about this, and I am not sure why I told you, but I have to admit it is good to finally share it."

He smiled at me again, and I couldn't help but wonder who had hurt him. He said he had had time to move on, but I could still see the hurt it had caused him. I saw it in his eyes and on his face. My heart ached for him.

"Liam, I am sorry for what happened to you, and I hope the Moon Goddess makes an exception for you and grants you a second chance," I told him.

He gave me a polite, small smile and nodded. Then he shook his head and clapped his hands together. We both knew there was no second chance for a Lycan. I will never understand why the Moon Goddess would do that. Lycans have a much longer lifespan, and you would think they would be the ones to have a second-chance mate. Yet only werewolves do.

"So, let's get to it. Where do you want to go?"

"How about the training yard?" Zander said, eyeing him.

Zander was obviously conflicted because he didn't like that I hugged Liam but knew there was nothing to the hug, as it was just meant to comfort. His wolf was warring with him about it, and I could see it. I was proud of him for not letting his wolf get the better of him. I know that right now, we are all on edge because none of us are marked and claimed, and having wolves and Lycans of the opposite sex around our mates is setting us off.

"Is that something you want to see as well, Luna?" he asked, and I couldn't help the grin that spread across my face.

"Definitely," I said, and both Kevin and Zander looked at me curiously, which caused Liam to look between us in confusion.

Not even Kevin knew about my training. I didn't like keeping it from him. We told each other everything, but I didn't want him to have the knowledge in case it was found out. I didn't want him to take any blame or get in trouble for keeping it from the Alpha or our parents.

"Okay, I will show you our training rings, courses, and yard. I think you will like it," he said, and we followed him back through to another part of the pack, ways away from the homes and on the other side of the pack house.

# Chapter Seventeen
## *Aylin*

When we got to the training area he told us about, the first thing we saw was a large open field that had an area separated into rings, another area with an obstacle course, and a track with bleachers set on both sides. They even had a large pool. This place was amazing. I could definitely see myself coming out here and trying that obstacle course. I was getting more and more excited as I looked around.

"Those are the practice rings over there. Since I have you here, why don't I see what you two got?" he said to Zander and Kevin. They both had huge grins plastered on their faces. My brother and Zander had trained with the best. My best friends back home, Lance and Layla, were omegas, and their father was one of the best warriors around. He had worked his way up to head warrior and was brutal. He was often called to help with training, even in Lycan territories. He was respected, and surprisingly, even a few Lycans feared him from what I heard. This was going to be interesting.

They went to the weapon house and grabbed a few swords, daggers, and other weapons, then headed out to the training circle. I was not very good with swords yet—I was still learning that one. However, I could hold my own against someone who knew the basics, but not against Lance. My brother and Zander, even as Alpha and Beta, barely kept up with him and could never beat his father no matter how hard they tried. Lance had been training me in secret because I was not allowed to train with the warriors. There was an irrational fear that I could be the child of a rogue and would turn on the pack one day, which is why it was kept secret, even from Kevin.

Zander went first against Liam, and they sparred. It was impressive. He really held his own against Liam, and goddess, he looked good doing it. I had always loved watching him train. Next, my brother went against him. He also held his own. My brother trained hard and loved sparring with Lance back home. He wanted to be as good as Lance's father and really looked up to him. I couldn't help but feel proud when he knocked the sword from Liam's hold. Liam looked impressed, too.

"That was really impressive. Anything else you guys want to try?" he asked.

"Hold on," I said, and they all turned their eyes on me. "I think I would like to try," I told him.

"Ay, what are you doing? You have never stepped foot on a training field. He is a Lycan," Kevin said, his face bunched up in concern.

"Don't worry. I help train some of the pups here when they are old enough to start, and here, everyone has to do self-defense and learn basic combat skills in case of an attack. Our Alpha wants everyone to be able to defend themselves,"

Liam said. I was a little shocked but really happy that it meant I would be allowed to train here.

"That is amazing," I said to him. I loved that everyone could train, and I liked that, if need be, people could defend themselves. You cannot always just count on being a wolf, and most of them did. Your wolf had instincts and could do damage, but if you went up against someone who trained, your chances of survival dropped.

"Thanks. Everyone that is of age has to take a class once a week. Every Tuesday and Thursday, we hold classes that go by age so we can break the pack into groups. The only way someone gets out of training is with a medical issue — if they are sick, injured, pregnant, or one of the wolves that work off the pack territory in a town. But they have to make it up if they cannot be there," he explained.

I nodded. "Can they take extra classes?" I asked.

"The classes are really full, so we cannot let them join other classes. However, everyone is allowed to use the training field in the evenings, and it is also open to all on Sundays. In the mornings and early afternoons, our warriors train," he replied.

"That is good to know. Now, how about we get started?" I said, grabbing the sword from my brother's hand and walking up to Liam in the circle.

"As you wish," Liam said, getting into his stance. I did the same.

I let him move first and blocked his first thrust. He nodded in approval and then did it again. When I easily deflected, he eyed me. The next move was quick, but I blocked in time and then countered, swiping up at him. He dodged, and I spun and swung out—he blocked. He lunged, and I danced out of the way. We went back and forth until he knocked the sword from my hand. I knew he was better than me, but I couldn't help the euphoric feeling I had—I had just engaged in hand-to-hand combat in a training ring with a Lycan Gamma. I was on cloud nine.

"What was that?" Kevin asked me. When I looked over at him and Zander, they were looking at me as if I had grown an extra head, gaping at me. It wasn't even a really good job. Wait till they saw what I was actually good at.

"I may have been training in secret with Lance and Layla," I told them, smiling.

Kevin started laughing, and Zander looked like he was about to pounce on me. He seemed to have liked watching me. Really liked it.

"What else did he teach you?" Liam cut in.

"Well, sword fighting was the newest thing we were learning, which is why I am not all that good at it. I had already learned hand-to-hand combat, archery, and the use of daggers. I am really good at archery and throwing knives. I am good at hand-to-hand, but Lance trains hard, and I haven't beaten him yet. I put down Layla a couple of times, though."

Kevin and Zander had seen Layla train. She was one of the best among the females, but she only did it because her father made her. She had no intention of being a warrior. She did believe that self-defense was important, though. Even so, knowing I had dropped Layla impressed them.

"Show me," Liam stated.

Kevin and Zander nodded.

"Show you what?" I asked.

"Let's start with archery, then we can do knife throwing, and then hand-to-hand," he said.

"Lead the way."

I knew I had to look crazy. I was smiling ear to ear. I was going to get to use a real archery court! Looking around, though, I didn't see it. I looked at him, confused.

"Grab a bow and quiver and follow me," was all Liam said to my confusion. I did as he said. Liam walked us to the far side of the field and into the tree line. Just past the tree line, I started to see targets. They were up in trees, hanging from them at all different heights—some were blowing in the wind.

"So you don't have a set area with targets?" I asked.

"When you are in a fight, are the other warriors going to stand still? Are they all going to be the same size? This is to get used to shooting at things that can move—targets of all shapes and sizes. That being said, we do have stationary targets for those first learning. However, you said you are good at it, so I want to see how good. As you go through the path, we have targets that are spring-loaded that will pop up, and others that are on zip lines that fly by. Like I said, I just want to see how good you are with a bow, so take a few practice shots to get used to the bow and then show us what you have." He waved his hand to the surrounding forest.

I took aim and practiced with three arrows. I missed the target twice, and then the third time, I hit wide.

"Ok, I'm ready," I told him.

He looked at me for a moment and then at the arrow that was wide of the mark.

"Are you sure you wouldn't rather take a few more practice shots?" he asked. He looked at the arrow again, debating. Maybe I should. It was wide, but at the same time, I wanted to surprise them.

"No, I'm good," I told him.

He held his hand out to the trail again and stepped back. I watched as all three of them crossed their arms over their chests and watched me.

Ok, guys, then watch this.

I knew they were doubting me with those shots, but I needed to get a feel for the bow. Now that I had, I was going to have fun.

I made my way through the path. I hit every moving target and small target I could find. I had made contact with every one of the targets. All of the stationary ones were in the bullseye; however, the moving ones were not all dead on, and I needed to work on that! I know I am getting better and will always work to improve. I want every one to hit the mark when I shoot.

When I finished, we walked the path so they could see all my hits. Liam whistled low and nodded.

"Ok, Luna, you definitely have some skills. Let's see how you do with knives."

He produced a pouch with ten throwing knives. I took them from him and held them in my hands, feeling them and judging them and their weight. Lance would bring different sets to try to throw me off, but eventually, I learned how to throw just about every throwing knife you could find. These ones were familiar to me, and I knew I could use them no problem.

I took my stance, looked around the forest, and, without saying a word, went to work throwing them at targets. Each one landed in its mark with a satisfying thud. Once again, I felt like I would have to pick Kevin and Zander's mouths up off the ground. Liam was clapping, obviously ecstatic with what I just showed him.

"You are absolutely incredible, Luna!" he praised me, and I could feel myself blushing at his words. I was not used to flattery except from my family. That was usually for my photos—never for something like this, and honestly, it felt good.

"Seriously, you didn't know she could do this?" Zander asked Kevin.

Kevin shook his head, and for a moment, he looked hurt. I knew why. Kevin and I told each other everything, and this was something big he didn't know. I felt so guilty looking at him.

"Kevin, I am sorry I didn't tell you. I promised Lance I wouldn't. You knew the rules—he would have been severely punished for training me. I swore to him I wouldn't say anything. I wanted to tell you so many times. I wanted to show you and practice with you. I felt bad for keeping it from you, but I couldn't betray Lance and Layla and risk any of you getting in trouble. You know you would have gotten in trouble or tried to stop me, and I couldn't live with either. I wanted to train. I wanted to be a warrior. I hoped I could try and show everyone that I was a part of the pack," I said apologetically. It was all true. If Kevin found out as future Beta and let me keep doing it, if anyone found out, he would be in just as much trouble, so he would have had to try to stop me from learning. However, I know my brother, and he would have tried to keep my secret and gotten in trouble if anyone found out. By not telling him, he wouldn't know and wouldn't get in trouble.

Kevin looked at me, and then before I knew it, he had me in a bear hug. "I know you wanted to keep me safe, and I love you for that, but never keep anything from me again. Even if it could get me in trouble, I am your person and will always have your back!" he declared. Goddess, thank you for blessing me with such an amazing brother.

"And I have yours," I told him. He let go and stepped back. He still looked a bit hurt, but he was also radiating pride. I could feel how proud he was of me. My heart swelled at that. At least he's not mad.

"Well, that leaves hand-to-hand. Are you ready to show us what you can do?" Liam said, getting us back on track.

"I'm ready," I told him, and we all followed him back to the training circle. I was feeling proud of myself and was happy I was finally able to show someone that I could do this. It was also a relief not having to hide it from my brother anymore, and honestly, the way Zander was looking at me with so much desire in his eyes had me preening. I liked it, and I couldn't help but wonder what else would make him look at me like that.

*Stop it, Aylin!* I chided myself. *You are choosing Trevor. You need to stop looking and thinking of Zander. Goddess, help me — this is so hard. I want him. I have wanted him for a long time. I know he hurt me, and I know I shouldn't want him, but I can't help it. Goddess, please help me be strong here.*

# Chapter Eighteen
## *Aylin*

Liam and I got into the circle and got into a stance. We were about to start when a low growl erupted from the side of the circle. It looked like Zander was starting to lose control of his wolf. He didn't want Liam touching me. Liam understood as well and backed away from me.

"Why don't you spar with her?" Liam suggested.

And I gaped at him. I don't want to spar with Zander. I mean, I do, but I don't think it's a good idea. Zander seemed to have the opposite opinion. He started toward me, and then the ass had to go and take off his shirt and throw it aside. So here he was, this hot-as-hell alpha, shirtless and mouth-watering, squaring off across from me.

This is not what I had in mind, Moon Goddess! How is this going to help me be strong?

I could hear Kevin laugh and shot him an annoyed look. He laughed harder.

Asshole, I will get you later for that, just you wait.

"Come on, my queen, show me what you got," he taunted, and I did just that.

We squared off, and I grappled with him. He tried to knock out my legs, and I spun away and then danced further out of his reach. Then I batted my eyes at him and smiled coyly. The distraction worked. He smiled at me, and I was able to spin low, kick out my leg, and knock him on his ass.

Kevin whooped from the sideline and cheered me on. Zander gave him a hard look and then looked at me with an evil smile.

"You want to play dirty?" he asked.

"You already are, so I thought I would even the score," I told him, squaring off and circling each other again.

"And how am I playing dirty?" he asked.

"You just had to take your shirt off and display all those sexy-as-hell muscles, trying to distract me," I replied.

"So you think I'm sexy?" he said.

Wait, what? Damn, I did just say that.

"Well, females don't watch you train for their health," I replied.

He moved. He was quick, but I was quicker. I jumped over him when he tried to tackle me, placing my hands on his shoulders to propel my flip over him. When I was mid-flip, I kicked out and landed a blow to his ass with my foot, sending him sailing forward and landing in the dirt.

This time, my brother and Liam were both laughing, and I noticed a crowd was starting to form.

"That's it, I'm not taking it easy on you anymore. I was trying to be a gentleman, but I think I need to teach you a real lesson in hand-to-hand combat," Zander said, swiping some of the dirt away.

"Oh really?" I said playfully. "Well then, big bad alpha, come get me."

I was taunting him, and it was working. His eyes were fixed on me, and the predator was coming out. His wolf wanted to take over and get me, and that meant he was going to try to dominate me.

We will see.

I was enjoying this, and I was going to do everything I could to show him who he was dealing with.

The more we grappled and fought, the more I realized I was stronger than the last time I did this with Lance. I was moving faster, and I had more force behind my kicks and punches. It must be the bond with Trevor. The Lycan strength was coming in.

After the twelfth time knocking Zander on his ass, he stayed down. I walked up to him and reached my hand down to help him up. This was where I made a fatal mistake. He grabbed my hand and then yanked me down, catching me off guard. Then he rolled us so he was on top and pinned me. I looked at him, stunned, and then I felt him. All of him pressed against me. His chest, his stomach, those hips and thighs against mine, and damn, I could feel HIM. Heat pooled in my core as I looked up into his face. The urge to kiss him and claim him was almost too strong. He started to lower his head to mine. I didn't want to stop him, but what about Trevor?

"That was absolutely amazing," Liam said, jolting us out of our trance. Zander looked at me for another moment, longing and desire in his beautiful golden eyes. He climbed off me and then helped me up. Liam walked over and patted me on the shoulder.

"I can't believe how badass our new Luna is," he said. He stopped between me and Zander, and I couldn't help but notice the distance he created between us. He knew what almost happened, and he was trying to keep us from doing anything in front of the crowd that had gathered. I hadn't noticed how large it had gotten, and when I looked at Zander, it seemed he didn't realize it either.

Kevin came over and hugged me. "Sis, that was awesome. I have never seen Zander get his ass handed to him this much—ever," he said.

"I was taking it easy on her," Zander said nonchalantly. Yeah, right.

"Whatever you say, Z," Kevin said to him.

"I don't know about you guys, but I am starving," I cut in, and on cue, my stomach agreed with me rather loudly.

"Alright, we can do more after lunch. Let's go eat before there's nothing left."

We made our way back to the pack house. When we got there, I looked at the others and let them know I was going to Trevor's office to see if he would join us. I missed him, and after what just happened with Zander, I thought maybe I should have him with us for a while.

I had just made my way up the stairs when I heard shouting coming from Trevor's office. It sounded like he was arguing with a female. My hackles rose. I didn't know what was going on, and part of me wanted to give them privacy in case it was pack business and I was overstepping. He could be in there with anyone discussing anything. Then I heard the female voice. Nope, that was Ruby, and my curiosity got the better of me. Walking up to the door, I opened it.

When I looked inside, everything stopped. My breathing. My heart. Maybe time itself. She had her arms around him and was kissing MY MATE! When things started moving again, all I could see was red. It completely took over everything else, and my wolf pushed me to the back. She let out a noise that I couldn't ever imagine us making. The haunted scream-like roar was eerie and scary. At some point, Ruby had tried to hide behind Trevor, and all I wanted was her blood. I wanted to rip her apart for touching what belonged to me. I also wanted to rip him apart for letting her touch him — and for protecting her.

Fuck this and fuck him! I ran. I ran from the scene, I ran from the door, down the stairs. Zander and Kevin must have known something was up because they were already at the bottom. They both froze when they took in my appearance.

I kept moving, my wolf wanting out. I couldn't hold her or contain her. She was too strong, and she was fucking pissed.

I just made it out the door when she jumped off the side of the porch, shifting mid-jump and landing on all fours. It seemed as though the ground around me shook with that landing. I could hear the tables and the contents on them rattle. I bolted into the woods and ran, letting Mona take over. We ran the perimeter and back in half the time we did this morning and then paced at the edge.

"Let's go back. I want to rip her to pieces! How dare she touch what belongs to us!" Mona complained.

The run didn't help. We were angrier than ever. Mona and I both wanted to rip apart that whore. I couldn't get the image of her all over Trevor out of my head. The more I thought of it, the more I wanted them both to suffer. Maybe I should reject him since he can't let go of his mistress. They can have each other.

That thought caused pain to rip through me, and Mona howled in agony.

"Maybe we should just go, Mona. I can't do this. It hurts too much," I told her.

"No! He chose us, and if he dares to touch another, he will fear us," Mona responded. "I am gaining my powers, and we will be feared if he thinks to betray us," she added.

"What do you mean, Mona? I don't want to be feared. I want him to love me and choose me! I don't want him to fear me. I don't want anyone to fear me. Except maybe that bitch," I told her.

"He will pay for hurting us. You will see—he will regret his actions," Mona was fuming. "You are worthy of more than you could possibly know," she added.

"Aylin? What the hell? What is going on?" Kevin called when they finally caught up. He was gawking at me again. It was a minute before I realized I was looking down at him and him up at me. Pretty far up. He took a step back, and I wasn't sure, but he looked almost afraid of me.

"He was with Ruby in his office. I can't stay here! I want to go!" I was wailing in my head, the pain and betrayal too much.

"Aylin, baby, think about this. If we leave, we are willingly walking away from a pack and will become rogues. Is that really what you want? I will follow you no matter what, and I think we can even go back to our old pack. I will talk to my dad, but whatever you want to do, I just don't want you to regret it because the choice was made out of anger."

Zander was also looking up at me, and he was beyond worried. He had to be if he was trying to get me to stay. I knew going back to our old pack would make him happy—he would be Alpha—but me? I would still be an outcast.

"Aylin, I am sure there is also an explanation. Trevor seems to really care about you! Why would he betray you so quickly, or at all?"

In my rage, I didn't want to think about the possibilities of what could have happened. All I knew was that if he didn't want her to touch him, he could have prevented it. That thought settled in my mind — he could have prevented it or stopped it, and he didn't.

When a noise came from the edge of the forest line we were standing by, all three of us turned our heads to the four Lycans emerging. They all stopped upon seeing us. Upon seeing me. I recognized two of the four and realized the other two must be Nick and Nikki. I hadn't seen them in Lycan form yet. Nick was almost as black as the other two males, and Nikki was dark brown with a small tip of white on her left ear. Definitely answered my "are all Lycans black" question.

I growled a low warning toward Trevor, who stopped and raised his front paws to show no harm. He looked sad even in this form. He took a step closer, and Zander and Kevin moved in front of me, growling. They were no match for a Lycan, but I knew they would try for me, and that brought me forward. They were reacting to how I was feeling. I didn't want them to be hurt over my anger. Mona was ready to attack and growled low and threateningly.

"What you saw was not what you think, Aylin! I would never hurt you!" I heard Trevor say in my mind.

I growled again. Some of the red haze had started to subside after the run, but with what he just said, seeing it so fresh in my head, it ramped right back up.

"Aylin, please. I had just told her she would never have what she wanted and that I chose you, and she threw herself at me. I was pushing her off when you opened the door. I swear I didn't kiss her back, and I didn't want her touch! I only want you. I only want to be with you!" he said.

He tried to take another step closer to me.

Mona took an attack stance and bared her teeth, and I knew I needed to step in before things got out of hand. It took every ounce of willpower, but I was able to push Mona back in and down. But she was right there. She was pacing in my mind, ready to go if the moment called for it. She was still sending through enough power that she had the Lycans on edge. I could feel it from her, so I knew they could as well.

I half whimpered and half growled. I wanted to believe him, but I didn't know if I could. I felt wronged, and I didn't trust him. This was the second time she did this, and I would not be some kept mate while he was with another. I knew that sounded bad coming from me, who had another mate and wanted him as well as Trevor. Maybe I am fucked up and greedy, but I was not willing to share with a female like Ruby. I didn't think I could share at all, which meant it was wrong for me to expect them to be okay with sharing me. I had tried hard not to really entertain the idea, but it was there. It just felt right. But sharing with a female like her didn't! It felt wrong and tainted.

"I don't believe you. This is the second time in just as many days I have seen her all over you. I will not compete for a place here when I can have a place at the old pack with Zander," I growled.

He growled at that last statement.

"Do you prefer the wolf to me?" he asked, hurt.

"Does it matter? I thought we were going to get answers, and you and I would figure this out and move on. It seems you had other ideas, so maybe it's time I entertain my options," I replied.

My words were meant to hurt, and they hit their mark. He looked lost, and now he was getting angry.

"You are mine! My mate, and I will not give you up to anyone!" he snarled at me.

"If you thought I was your mate, you shouldn't have let anyone touch what is mine." I snarled back.

This time, I snapped my jaws at him, causing him and the others to take a step back. It was then I realized they were also looking up at me, and I looked down at them. He huffed. He knew I was angry, and he was trying to calm me, but I couldn't clear the red. Him getting angry and shouting back wasn't helping calm me either.

"Aylin, please! I would never try to hurt you, and Ruby is going to be punished for this. I swear it to you! She was warned yesterday, and today she crossed a line that she will not be able to come back from!" he swore.

Again, I wanted to believe him, but actions speak louder than words. If I give him the benefit of the doubt and he hurts me again, I may not be able to stop Mona. Goddess help me, what do I do?

I looked to Zander and Kevin, who were both still in front of me protectively. The red cleared more from me while I focused on them. However, the power coursing through me from my wolf did not abate. She was ready to pounce if given the opportunity.

Once the red was clear, I looked back up at Trevor, who seemed to relax but only a little. I looked at the others, and they were all still a bit scared. I didn't want any of them to fear me, and I didn't know how they could, with them being such powerful Lycans.

"I am going to shift back into my human form so I can communicate with you and the others together," Trevor said. He did just that and then ran over to one of the areas Liam had shown us where we could store clothes. He came back quickly, pulling up a pair of basketball shorts. He walked a bit closer to us with his hands up, non-threateningly.

"The elders have arrived, and we should go back. Let's calm down, get some answers, and after it is all said and done, we will talk more about what happened. But, Aylin, please believe me when I say that I will never do anything to hurt you! I will always choose you!" he declared.

We had been waiting for the elders, and now that they were here and we were close to getting answers, I didn't want to go anymore, but I needed to know what was going on with me. Even if I decided to forgive Trevor or not believe him, I needed these answers. So I nodded.

"There are clothes in that area if you would like to change, and we can head back."

I shook my head. I was not ready to shift back into human form. My wolf wouldn't allow it. I may have taken the front seat back, but she would not let me change. He just nodded, then turned and led the way back through the forest, his Lycans following, with us in the rear.

The others kept looking over their shoulders like they were waiting for us to attack them. I didn't like how uneasy they seemed. Mona warned me they would fear me, but I was not sure why they did so much. I didn't even try to attack—I just growled, bit, and snapped my teeth like a rabid dog.

"Aylin, there is something you should know," Kevin said to me. "I am not sure if you are aware of this, but you are quite huge," he said, looking up at me again.

I looked down at my paws and then over at him. Mine were several times bigger than his. Why hadn't I noticed this? I mean, I noticed that they were looking up at me, even Trevor, but I hadn't put it together that I was towering over them. My wolf was at least three times bigger than Zander's, and he was a rather large Alpha wolf at that. I paused.

"Is that why everyone is so scared of me? I didn't even realize. How do I fix it?" I had stopped and was looking at Kevin. The others noticed and were looking at me, waiting.

I whimpered and raised one paw, then another, shaking them like I could shake away my size.

Trevor slowly walked over to me and placed one of his hands on one of my front legs. "Little wolf, we will figure this out."

A snort came from behind him—Kevin. I guess I could see what was funny. Trevor's nickname for me had been "little wolf," but right now, I was anything but. I whimpered again and let him continue leading me to the pack house. I was still angry with him, but his touch had a calming effect that I needed. This mate bond was a real pain in the ass.

Zander and Kevin moved in closer. Zander walked right beside me, letting our sides touch, trying to calm me as well. It was working. I was starting to relax with all of them there. However, I was still angry, and Mona was also angry and hurt. She felt threatened and still would not let us shift. She wanted to rip Ruby apart, and I had a feeling that if we saw her right now, the female would die.

When we got back to the pack house, two of the elders were outside waiting for us. One of them, upon seeing me, fell to his knees in a deep bow. The other slowly followed. This made the surrounding people, who had yet to notice me, turn to see what was going on. The many audible gasps and shocked cries rang out across the courtyard. When they saw the elder bow, many of the others followed suit.

Trevor looked between me and the elders, and I whimpered again. This time, he, Zander, and Kevin all came to me and started rubbing against me. The touch calmed me and my inner wolf with the three of them there and in contact, much like it had earlier when we were with Ruby and her friends. My wolf slowly withdrew inside, and the power radiating from me began to fade. I was no longer casting a dominant, threatening aura. Soon, when I looked at Kevin and Zander, I was no longer looking down at them.

One of the elders took off his robe and walked over to me. He held it up, and I shifted into my human form, taking the robe with a thank-you and covering my body. Shorts and clothes were brought by some of the other pack members from baskets on the porch for anyone who needed them after shifting. They brought clothes for the others as well, so they could shift back. One by one, everyone changed and got dressed.

"It is a true honor to meet you, Your Grace," the elder said, bowing.

Say what now? Did he call me "Your Grace"? There had to be a mistake. I mean, I knew I was to be Luna—was that what he meant? No, he would have said Luna.

"I think you are mistaken. I am just going to be Luna. I don't think you call a Luna 'Your Grace,'" I said, confused.

"Oh, but you are so much more, Your Grace. Come, we have much to discuss, and I am sure you have many questions to ask," the elder who had given me his robe said.

I looked around at the people staring at me in shock, wonder, and awe. Some looked scared. I hoped my large size didn't scare them. I didn't want anyone to fear me.

We all followed the elder into the pack house in silence. We were going to get our answers, and then we would figure out what we were all going to do from here. I just hoped that whatever it was, we could all live with it. I glanced at Zander and saw the worried look on his face. Out of everyone, he was the most nervous. I couldn't blame him. If there was only one, there was no choice. Trevor would not let me go, and I could not blame him — not if it was a possible death sentence. But I couldn't help the pain in my chest at the thought of losing Zander.

I gave him a small smile, and he tried to return it. He looked away from me. He walked tall and proud, with his head high, as we followed the elders through the pack house. I tried to do the same, even with the inner turmoil within. I reached over to him, grabbed his hand, and squeezed. He glanced at me, and I knew he was hoping that he would be with me. After the day we had and the moment back at the training grounds, I knew it was going to hurt if I had to let him go.

# Chapter Nineteen
## *Aylin*

The elders led us up to the third floor and to a wing of the castle I hadn't been to yet. We came upon a set of large, ornate cherry wood doors. The two elders opened the doors and led us into the most beautiful library I had ever seen. I couldn't help but stare as I walked through it after them.

It had rows upon rows and multiple levels. It had ladders that took you up to the highest shelves, and for a moment, the little pup in me came out, and I wanted to ride the ladder like Belle in *Beauty and the Beast*. Maybe later—I need to focus on talking to the elders right now. I continued to look as we were guided through. There were nooks with big, comfy chairs and fireplaces. I could see myself curling up on those chairs and getting lost in story after story.

"Here we are," one of the elders said when we came to a wall. I looked around for a place to sit so we could talk. The elders looked around, and then the elder who had spoken raised his hand to the wall and placed it upon the statue he was standing in front of. The wall cracked and then opened. I jumped. I was not expecting the wall to just open like that.

A few seconds later, there was an opening that showed a set of stairs leading down. The elders passed through, and we all followed. This isn't creepy at all—hidden doors in the castle, walking down into the dark, on a creepy-as-hell staircase. Now all we need is a ghost to float through the wall or some ominous moans in the distance.

We seemed to go down forever. I know we didn't climb this many stairs to the third level. And why go upstairs just to have to go back down? This elder definitely gets their exercise in for the day. They definitely have to do lots of cardio.

When we finally made it to the bottom of the stairs, we walked through an archway into a beautiful open chamber. Around the room were artifacts under glass and shelves of books. It looked like a library and museum in one.

Waiting for us was what I could only assume was a third elder. She was a little shorter than me, with blue eyes and graying black hair. She had a very warm and kind smile that put me at ease — like a grandmother you go to visit.

"It is nice to meet you, Your Grace," she said and bowed to me. I looked at her and then at the other two elders. The one who had handed me his robe outside looked like he would be the youngest. He also had black hair and blue eyes, but he was tall, had a strong jaw, and was definitely still fit. The other elder was a gray, wrinkly old man. He made me think of the old men depicted in barbershops who would talk about sports, the weather, and how things were back in the day. It almost made me laugh.

"Let us introduce ourselves," the tall young elder said. "I am Elder Slone, this is our senior elder, Nigel, and she is Elder Renee. We have been tasked with keeping the histories of Lycans and werewolves alike," said Slone.

"You have no idea how pleased we are to meet you! We thought you were lost or dead," said Renee. This had my attention.

"Wait, do you know me?" I asked. It was so quiet you could hear a pin drop.

"You are the missing child," she stated. "Come, we have much to discuss and show you," she said as she guided us into the next room, which had several couches, tables, and a large fire on the other side of the room. I felt cozy here.

I took a seat on a couch, and Trevor sat next to me. I got up and moved to another seat. This time, before he could move, Kevin and Zander sat beside me. Trevor growled but didn't move. He knew I was still angry with him. I needed space and time. I was grateful that he stayed where he was, even though I could see he didn't want to.

"Aylin, please, I don't want you to be upset with me. I know you got hurt, but I swear to you, I only want you, and I will show it to you every day. You have to believe me." He was pleading with me. He knew that I still possibly had a choice in front of me, and if I chose not to be with him, it could severely hurt him and this pack.

"I am still upset and need some time. Just give that to me, and we can talk about this later. I don't want to discuss it in front of an audience," I said, looking around the room. We had three elders, Nick, Nikki, Liam, Kevin, and Zander here. I didn't want them all listening to us talk about what happened in his office, even if most of them already knew.

He nodded and gave his attention back to the elders. Kevin grabbed my hand and moved his thumb in little circles on my palm. Zander watched for a moment and then copied the action with my other hand. In seconds, my anger started to subside again. I didn't even realize my anger was starting to spike. My emotions were all over the place right now. I took a deep breath, then another.

"You called me the lost child. How do you know I was lost as a babe?" I asked her.

"We were not entirely sure until Slone and Nigel saw you outside. Most of what we have learned from your mate and Beta Nick fit. The timing of your arrival to your old pack, your hair color, and the color of your wolf—it all fits. You see, you are mentioned in here," she said, holding up an old leather journal. "This is the journal of Serina Moonraiser, daughter to Alpha and Luna Moonraiser of the Crescent Moon Pack," she announced.

Nick snorted. "You brought us down here to talk about a fairytale?" he asked.

I looked at the elder in confusion.

"Young man, you should not speak of what you do not know," she said, giving him a hard look.

227

Nick shrank back. Of all the people to talk to like that, you never wanted to contradict an Elder unless you had absolute proof they were wrong—or the Lycan king, whose word is law.

"We were all told the tales of the Crescent Moon Pack and the first children of the Moon Goddess. That's what they are—stories," he tried to defend himself.

I did hope he would stop talking before he upset them and made them not want to help us.

"Most of those stories are either watered down or exaggerated, but they came from something real a long time ago. The Crescent Moon Pack is very real, and a princess of the pack sits here today in this very room," she said to him sternly.

All eyes shifted to me at that moment.

"Don't look at me. I have no idea what she is talking about," I exclaimed.

"Not yet, but you will," she said, looking at me with fondness.

"I think you are mistaken. You only just met me. How could you possibly know I am this lost child and heir to a fairytale kingdom?" I asked. "And if I am this person, then why am I here? Why has no one from that pack come for me?"

I was getting even more questions than I started with.

"I will explain it all. In this journal, Serina writes about her family. Her father, the true Lycan king of the Realm, her mother, the Luna and Queen, and a future goddess of the moon — which was one of their own children."

"Hold on. How can there be a future Moon Goddess? Isn't the Moon Goddess eternal?" Nikki asked, interrupting.

"Most gods and goddesses are eternal; however, they can die or enter a slumber. Some even go into another realm to live in peace. The current Moon Goddess is not the original; however, she is the one who created us, so she is our goddess. Her daughter, Luna Sheila Moonraiser, was supposed to take her place. However, there were complications, and the title went to one of her daughters," replied Elder Renee.

"How do you know this?" asked Nick skeptically.

Renee held up the journal.

"You're telling me someone wrote this, and you just believe it?" he asked, annoyed.

"There is no reason for someone to lie if they believe no one would ever find or read their personal thoughts. This is also not the only book or journal we have to support what I just told you," she replied.

"Now, as I was saying, she went into a little detail about her family. She also had two younger sisters. She was the oldest of the three daughters. She has been around for many, many years. Her parents had betrothed her to a god who was set to take over as the future king, as he was one of Fenrir's children and a wolf shifter as well. She didn't want to marry, and weeks before the wedding, the veil between realms thinned, and she made her way on a boat across a vast lake to our shores.

Once she was here, she hid in the forest. She talks about the things she sees, and one night, while standing by the lake thinking about going home, she was surprised by a wolf that came through the woods and approached her. She had wandered into a territory, and even though she was not a rogue and had not abandoned her pack—she just wanted to experience some of the world before fulfilling her duty—the other wolves didn't know this and assumed there was a rogue wolf on their land."

She paused to catch her breath.

"I thought you said she was a Lycan?" Liam asked.

"She is so much more than a mere Lycan. She is a shifter and a granddaughter of the Moon Goddess. She had many special abilities," she explained.

"When she and the new wolf looked at each other, the mate bond formed. She found her mate right here. According to what she wrote, that was something that was not given to them where she lived. They had mates of their choosing and formed a bond with them; it wasn't a magical bond like what we have here. Something happened to her when she came here, and she was gifted this by the Moon

Goddess. The wolf took her to his pack, and they became mates."

She paused again to catch her breath.

"Okay, so this she-wolf found a mate here but was supposed to be getting married to a god, right? Didn't she have to go back to her pack?" Nikki asked.

"She had a duty to her pack, but she couldn't let go of the gift that was given to her. She chose to stay and live with her mate, even though she had a duty to the Realm. They conceived a child shortly after mating. She made a few friends while she was living in the pack, and most of the people adored her as she was of legend—the most royal wolf, with a coat of pure white and silver. She was the only wolf or Lycan to grace these lands with a coat that color since the beginning of our kind."

She mentions a friend who was a painter and writer. She told him stories of home, and he cataloged them to share with us. She also told him how the first wolves and Lycans came to be with the help of her grandmother, the Moon Goddess, and Fenrir, the Wolf God. Fenrir loved his wolves and wanted to give them more. The Moon Goddess wanted to help and gave them the power to shift. At first, it could only be done in the light of the full moon; a wolf would gain the ability to grow legs and become a man. Over many years, they stayed as men more and more, breaking away from wolves and eventually evolving into what we are today."

She walked over and sat on one of the other couches facing us. Slone and Nigel joined her.

"How do you know she told him all that?" Kevin asked. I could tell he wanted to hear more. He used to love the stories our mom told us about a magical land where there were no humans, just werewolves and Lycans. We could choose what form to be in at any time without fear of anyone finding out about us.

"We have his journals as well," Elder Slone told him, "along with some of his artwork. He painted and drew many pictures of Serina, her mate, and her daughter."

"Serina started going into details about dreams and nightmares that plagued her, and eventually, the god she was promised to found her. They found her mate brutally murdered in their home, but his mate and their baby were gone. They eventually found her miles away. It seems she had tried to run; that is the best guess anyone could come up with. She was murdered, and the baby was missing. No one knew if the babe was alive or if it had been taken by whoever murdered Serina. Her writer friend drew a picture of them — of Serina and her baby — while they were in a field of flowers."

She looked over at Slone, and he produced another book. He opened it to a marked page and handed it to me. I almost dropped it when I saw the picture.

"It's her," I said shakily. "Kevin, that's her, and that's the baby from my dream. It's them."

I was trembling now. For as long as I could remember, I had been having dreams of my mother being chased and murdered. Kevin put it together too, and just as the tears started to fall, he pulled me to him.

"What is she talking about?" Nikki asked.

"Aylin has been plagued by nightmares of a man with red eyes chasing her through the forest—only it wasn't her. In each dream, she is running with a baby. She hides the baby and keeps running, drawing the man with red eyes away. He catches her and kills her," Kevin explained.

Tears were pouring down my face now. This was too cruel. Why was I having this dream? Why was I seeing my mother be murdered over and over?

"Aylin, my dear, there is more you should know," Elder Nigel said, speaking up for the first time. "Your mother, being who she was, had many abilities. We think you may have inherited them, especially after seeing your wolf today."

That reminded me of what Mona said earlier.

"Mona told me we were getting stronger and that her powers were coming in. I didn't think anything of it then—I was too angry," I said and glanced at Trevor.

"Did Mona mention what kind of powers?" Elder Slone asked.

"No, she didn't," I told him.

He nodded. "I am sure you all have many more questions. We will do our best to answer anything we can," Elder Renee added.

"I have one," Trevor said.

I knew exactly what he was about to ask. With everything else we had just learned, I had honestly forgotten.

"When I met Aylin and found out she was my mate, she had just been rejected by Zander." He motioned toward Zander, who was still holding my hand. He narrowed his eyes but continued. "The problem is, even though she accepted his rejection, the bond didn't break, and they are still mates. How can that be? And what can we do? I will not give her up. You know what it is like for a Lycan to lose a mate."

Trevor was definitely nervous.

"It is rare, but there are those who are destined to have more than one mate. The Moon Goddess will do this if she feels they are needed. Have you mated with either of them yet?" Elder Nigel asked.

"No, we thought it best to wait to get answers before anything happened, for fear of something bad happening to one of us," I told them honestly.

"That is good. That means a bond can still be formed between the three of you. When you meet a dual mate, usually it is not at the same time, and there can be difficulty forming a bond with all three parties. It will happen; it just takes more time. With you all being able to mate at the same time, this can be avoided," he continued.

"How? What do we have to do?" Zander asked. He was full of hope at this point, and it made me smile. Trevor, however, looked like he would rather murder Zander than have a bond with him. I understood, since I was about to rip Ruby's heart out of her chest.

"You will have to mark each other together. She will have to mark you both in turn, and then you and Trevor will have to mark her at the same time. This will form a powerful mate bond between the three of you. From what we know, you two will still be protective over her and any pups you have with her, but you will be more accepting of each other and work together as a family and unit," said Elder Nigel.

"What if we do not want to share her as a mate?" Trevor asked.

"Then you risk her life and your own," Nigel said simply. "The moon goddess would not let the bond break because she is to have you both. I know this to be true since her guardian sits next to her. If you do not do this, Aylin will not survive. Her mind will forever be torn in two, and she will go mad until she can no longer take it. She will either give in to darkness and go wild rogue—being hunted, since we cannot have a wild rogue with the type of powers she possesses—or she will be in so much pain that she will end her own life."

Kevin and Zander were both growling, and I was shaking—this time with fear instead of sadness.

"So mating to both is my only option? What if it doesn't work and they still hate each other?" I asked.

"They will still need to form their own friendship and bond, which will take time. However, they will no longer see each other as a threat and will be able to be there for you together. Them liking each other is something that will still take time," said Elder Renee.

I nodded in understanding. I felt so bad that they were going to be forced to share a mate. I felt like a hypocrite since I couldn't share them and was still mad at Trevor about Ruby.

"How did you know I was her guardian?" Kevin asked, changing the subject. And, goddess, I could have hugged him for it.

"The way you seem to know how to comfort her and when she needs it. You started to comfort her even before she got upset. Also, the way you are protecting her. Since you are not a mate, you must be a guardian. This makes sense as well. Since the goddess has chosen two mates, if she also provided a guardian, she is trying to provide Aylin with protection." Elder Slone was looking at me apologetically.

"Wait, protection from what?" Liam asked.

"That we do not know. But I have a feeling it has something to do with your mother, the nightmares she had, and the ones you are now having," said Elder Nigel.

I looked at him for a moment.

"The god that killed her. In my dream, he tried to take me from her. He was furious when he realized she didn't have me, and that was when he killed her. He could have killed her and taken the blanket bundle at any time—it would have been easier than fighting with her—but he didn't. He only killed her when he realized the baby was gone and got angry. It's him, isn't it? He is looking for me."

My very blood turned to ice, and I could feel the color drain from my face.

"After what you said, and what we know of your mother, and the fact that the god felt scorned, I do believe that to be the case. However, there is no proof, and it is just a theory. What we do know is that you will be faced with great danger. Only those who are, and who will cause great change to the world, are gifted with two mates. The fact that they are both Alphas—one werewolf and one Lycan—and that you have a guardian, means we can expect a great change. For good or bad, we cannot say, but it will affect us all," Elder Slone said, giving me a small, polite smile.

This was so much to absorb.

"So let me just see if I have all this. My mother is a descendant of *the* Moon Goddess, making me her great-granddaughter. The god she was promised to was scorned and possibly wants to kill me. I have two mates that I have to accept, or I will go crazy or die. And I am going to cause the world as we know it to go through a massive change. Is that about right?" I said, looking at the three elders.

They looked between each other and nodded.

Great. Just great.

I burst out laughing. This was just perfect. I am an apocalypse baby of some kind, and I will probably die—either by my own mates or this damn god. I didn't ask for any of this. I don't want any of this. I only ever wanted to be normal and happy. Why can't I be normal and happy?

"Aylin? Are you okay?" Zander asked, squeezing my hand.

"No, I'm really not. I went from being an unwelcome outcast to having two mates, to being a damn demigod. That is basically what I am, isn't it? Some kind of demigod or deity? Isn't that what descendants of gods are called?" I asked, and again, the elders nodded at me.

"I really do believe that the god is hunting me, and I am afraid he is getting close—if my dreams are any indication. I just want a normal, simple life where I can train in combat, help the pack, and belong somewhere. Not cause great change, or fight for my life, or anything like that," I said, breaking into tears again.

It was too much, and I was losing it.

I don't know when he moved, but Trevor was kneeling in front of me, wiping the tears off my cheeks, trying to calm me. Zander and Kevin were doing the same. Just like before, with the three of them there, a sense of calm and safety came over me. Slowly, I stopped crying and sat back.

"That is absolutely incredible—the way you were able to calm her. Did you feel that?" Elder Slone asked the others.

"Feel what?" I asked.

"Your power, my dear. When you got upset, it reached out, seeking to stop what was upsetting you—or maybe searching for aid in helping you calm down. All three of them reacted almost immediately, and the others in the room looked like they wanted to help. It was strong and un-yielding, much more powerful than an alpha aura," he said. "When they all started to calm you, the power retracted within you and dissipated."

Elder Slone was looking at me with curious amusement and wonder. I almost got the feeling he would like to do experiments on me. That will be a hard pass for me.

"It will take time, my dear, but you need to learn what your powers are and how to control them," said Elder Renee.

I just nodded. I couldn't answer anymore.

"Your mother had quite a few powers of her own, including making her wolf grow to large sizes when she was threatened. She had the ability to heal, and she could communicate telepathically with anyone in any form. She was also both wolf and Lycan. We are not sure which powers you may have, but those were just some of your mom's abilities. They are stronger at night and strongest under a full moon," she finished.

Something started niggling in the back of my mind.

"You said they are stronger at night and during a full moon. What about during a new moon?" I asked.

He looked at me for a moment, perplexed.

"My dream—the one I have of my mother being chased by the man with red eyes—it's always so dark, and I never thought about it before because I was so scared, but there was no moon. Does it mention what happens to her powers during a new moon?" I asked.

"I think we will need to look through the texts again and see if anything is mentioned," Elder Renee said. "I am sorry, my dear. I cannot remember if it was."

"Would I be able to read my mother's journal?" I asked them. After all, if they are right and it was my mother's, then by rights, it should be mine, not theirs. However, I know how important it is to preserve history for our kind.

They looked at each other like they were having a silent conversation. Then they looked at me, their faces both stern and resigned.

"As it is your mother's journal, we will allow you to have it. However, we ask that you please consider letting us have it back to keep safe and preserve it for our historical records," Renee said, extending the journal to me.

"Of course, you can have it back. I don't need to or want to keep it. I just would like to read it and see what I can learn about my mother—and maybe about myself. I know this is important to you and to our kind, so I will take good care of it and return it. All I ask is, if possible, that I can read it occasionally. It is nice to have a piece of my birth mother," I told them.

They all seemed to relax a little at that, and Elder Renee even looked at me a bit more tenderly. She smiled and nodded when she handed over the book. I took it from her, holding it in both hands as I stared down at it. Hope and wonder filled me.

This was my mother's. My real mother's.

I had wondered what she was like and who she was so many times, and now I might actually have some answers.

"Aylin."

I looked up at Kevin. He was looking at me with eyes full of concern, yet they had a stubborn set to them.

"What is it, Kev?" I asked him.

"I just want you to know that no matter what happens, you know I have your back."

I looked at him for a second and then nodded my head.

"Yeah, of course, I know that," I told him, giving him a small smile.

"No, Aylin, with everything they just said, I want you to understand that I am here, and I am willing to give my life to protect you. That is my vow to you — I will protect you with my life. Something is coming. I have sensed it, and now I know why! I will never let anything happen to you."

The dedication in his voice and in his eyes floored me. Kevin and I had always been close, but this was more than I could handle right now. The last thing I wanted to think about was my brother giving his life for mine. It was my fault he would do that, with this weird attachment he had to me because of who I was. It really wasn't fair.

That thought made me wonder further. Would he feel the same way if he weren't my guardian? I wanted to believe we would be just as close, but the truth was, he had been drawn to me from a young age and had always protected me and been there for me because of this guardian bond—even before it was solidified. That thought depressed me.

"What's wrong?" he asked.

"I was just thinking—do you think we would even be this close if it weren't for the guardian bond?"

He looked at me for a moment, then frowned as well.

"The guardian bond had nothing to do with your relationship," Elder Nigel chimed in. "The bond is a need to protect and defend. Anything more than that is a bond all your own," he explained.

That made me feel a little better, but there was still a pull to be there. Just more for me to have to accept, I guess.

"Thank you, Elders, for all your help and information. I really appreciate you taking the time to talk to us. I am going to have to ask that what you have revealed here today stays here between us. That goes for everyone here. No one outside this room is to know what was discussed until Aylin decides to let it be known. Her safety is the most important thing right now," Trevor said to everyone in the room.

Looking around, everyone was nodding in agreement. I was so appreciative that they were all willing to keep my secret safe and be there for me.

For the first time, I felt like I had a real home with these Lycans.

It's time to give it a try and see what happens.

"Thank you all so much!" I said.

It was all I could say. Talking right now was a struggle as I was still trying to rein in my emotions and not burst into tears again. My emotions were in overdrive, and I was not processing any of it very well.

Who the hell could?

The emotions kept forming a tightening in my throat, and I couldn't swallow it down.

"Aylin, are you ready to go?" Trevor asked. I looked up at him and noticed everyone was standing and looking at me. I was so lost in my thoughts that I didn't see them get up or move. He reached his hand out to me, and after a short pause, I took it. Even though I had just had my world tipped upside down, I was still upset with him. I wanted to believe him and let it go, but I knew there was something between him and Ruby—I could feel it. After all, you don't throw yourself on, kiss, or call pet names to someone you're not involved with.

After letting Trevor help me up, I moved over to Kevin and Liam, who were talking about the training fields and when they could go back. I definitely could use some more time there as well. We let the elders lead us from their hidden den and made our way to the library. We all walked out together and headed in separate directions, agreeing to meet for dinner. The time had really gotten away from us down there. I put my mother's journal in my room for safekeeping and made my way to join the others in the dining hall.

# Chapter Twenty
## *Zander*

Kevin and I must have exchanged looks about a hundred times while the Elders were talking to us. I couldn't believe everything they said about Aylin and who she is. On one hand, I am overjoyed that I can possibly still have her as my mate. I just hope they are right and that sharing her will be something I can accept. Then again, to have her at all, I think I could—but could Trevor? Trevor and I don't exactly see eye to eye, and I am having a hard time fathoming us getting along, even for the sake of our mate. The whole thing seems unreasonable to ask of anyone.

I could tell she wasn't comfortable with the idea, but I see the way she looks at me still. I know there is a part of her that still wants me, and I will prove to her that she is all I want and need. If I absolutely had to share her, then I would! I will do anything for her.

"Are you okay, man?" Kevin asked as he shoveled another bite of food into his mouth.

"Yeah, it's just a lot to take in, and I just wonder if Aylin is okay," I told him honestly.

"She's not," he said simply, and I just looked at him. I know she is not okay. That was a stupid way to say I am worried about her. But my face must have looked confused because he continued. "She is freaking out, and her emotions are all over the place. She is having a hard time accepting any of what she just found out." He shrugged.

"How do you know that?" I asked.

"She reached out to me in our mind link and told me. She is on her way down now. She just needed some time to calm down and find a safe place for her mother's journal." Kevin went back to eating his food. Then he paused. "I can also feel it if I focus on her. It's weird. I used to only feel her fear and pain, but only when they were extreme—it calls to me because she needs me. But now it is different. I still feel when she needs me, but now, when I focus on her, I can feel her," he said.

"That could be a bad thing, you know," I told him, and he stopped eating and cocked an eyebrow.

"How so? How else am I supposed to know if she is okay with something like this? Well, aside from what she tells me—because she could be telling me lies to make me believe she is okay," Kev replied.

"Yes, but say she and I are together and having some fun. Do you really want to know what she is feeling then?" I asked, and he choked on the food he had shoveled in.

"No, I do not want to know what she is feeling in that instant. I would very much rather never know that one," he said. "I will only check on her feelings if needed; otherwise, I am definitely waiting for when I sense she needs me," he said more to himself than to me.

"Yeah, that may be smart." I laughed at the expression still plastered on his face. He looked like he had seen a ghost while sucking on a lemon. The thought of feeling his sister in the throes of passion must have really messed with him. I couldn't help laughing harder.

A few moments later, her scent enveloped me, and I turned to the door where she was walking through. I could never get enough of that sweet dessert smell she carries with her. I could devour her. I plan on doing just that over and over as she cries out my name. At that thought, I gave my head a shake. I really don't know how much longer I can hold back my wolf. We want her more than we want the air in our lungs to survive. I wonder if she will allow us to mark her soon. I know we three still need to talk about this. I just hope she is receptive to us both being her mates.

I watched and tracked every move she made as she made her way to the table where we were sitting. I watched her look around at everyone, noting where Trevor was and meeting my eyes next as she located me. She made her way over to us and sat on the opposite side of Kevin, between him and Liam. I was hoping she would sit next to me, but I know that she is still upset. I was an idiot to try to give her up, and Trevor is an idiot for not putting Ruby in her place the day we got here. Both our actions were one hundred percent preventable. I just hope she can forgive me. I guess forgive us.

"Hey, how are you holding up?" I asked as she started to pile meat, potatoes, and sweets onto her plate.

"As well as I can for someone who has just found out that they are a demigod—or deity, whatever we are called—that is being hunted and can possibly change the world as we know it for the better or for worse." She shrugged and piled another piece of cake on her plate. I noticed she didn't mention the fact that she had two mates and needed to mate with both of us.

"Aylin, you know we are all going to be here for you no matter what, right? I will stay by your side and fight with you till the end," I told her, and Kevin nodded in agreement. His mouth was so full of food he couldn't form words. He just nodded and gave a grunt. Aylin looked at him, and the laugh she broke into was music to my ears.

"Kevin, you are going to choke one of these days just trying to make me laugh, you know that?" She was still laughing and shaking her head when he was finally able to swallow and respond.

"Yeah, but it will be worth it if I do."

The smile and look they shared would have had my wolf in an uproar and made me jealous if it weren't for the fact that he is her brother. I can't tell you how many times I have seen them together, laughing and goofing off, wishing it was me with her. Why didn't I just go for it? I am a future Alpha. No one should have had sway over me or my choices—let alone my sister and those below me in the pack. It was my say, and I should have had stronger willpower. I will never doubt myself or my wants again.

"He is right, though. You know we are all here for you," chimed in Liam. She looked at him and paused; she seemed to be contemplating his words.

"I know. You have all been so kind and accepting of me. It really makes me happy that you will all be there for me. I know the road ahead is going to be hard, maybe impossibly so, but knowing I have you all there helps," she replied.

"Girl, where else would we be if not by your side?" Nikki added. "You are one of us now and our Luna. We have your back!" she said.

"Not just our Luna but our friend too," Nick agreed with Nikki.

Nikki nodded emphatically. I looked around the table, and everyone was nodding, not just Nikki. They gave her something our old pack never did—acceptance. Yeah, she had a family and a few close friends, but she was never accepted by our pack, always an outsider. We have only been here for a few short days, and she has already been accepted as one of them. It made my stomach hurt that my pack was so close-minded that she was never accepted and felt like she didn't belong.

"Thank you all so much. This means the world to me."

I could tell she was trying hard not to cry. She smiled and then looked down at her plate.

"I don't know about you guys, but I am starving."

With that, she took a bite of the cake she had just put on her plate and started eating. Everyone else went back to eating and talking. That was when Thomas and Jullian arrived and sat down.

"Is everything handled?" Trevor asked them.

"The prisoner is in one of the cells and is waiting for your punishment, Alpha," said Jullian.

"Thank you. I will deal with it later, as I will need to talk with my mate about what punishment will fit best," Trevor said.

He was trying not to bring up names, but I was sure we all knew who he was talking about. Ruby crossed a line and placed hands on an Alpha without permission. That alone is cause for punishment. I didn't know what all happened in his office, but for Aylin to still be putting distance between herself and Trevor — it wasn't good.

Aylin just kept eating, almost like she was purposely trying to ignore the conversation; however, her posture was giving her away. She was tense. God, would I like to relax her. Maybe she would let me rub her shoulders. I could only hope. Gods, I want to touch and hold her.

'I can't wait to claim her,' Fin piped up.

'I know. I can't either!' I told him, watching her as she finished the cake and started on her chicken.

'You need to do it soon, or I will need to mark her. I don't like that she is unmarked with other males around,' Fin said.

I got angry at him for wanting to rush and force it.

'All you will accomplish is pissing her off. We will mark her when she is ready to accept us,' I told him.

"Another matter we need to discuss is dinner with the former Luna—my mother," Trevor said, and Aylin seemed to choke on her food.

Kevin patted her back until she was done coughing.

"Your mother?" she asked.

It was like she completely forgot that he would have had parents.

"Yes, my mother, Luna Carrie Gideon. She has asked for us to have dinner with her tomorrow in our suite. Of course, you are all welcome to attend, especially as she will be meeting you three for the first time. She was really upset with me for not allowing that to happen tonight. However, with the day we all had, I didn't want to add to it, and she can be a bit much at times," he said apologetically.

Aylin nodded and smiled at him appreciatively. After the day she had, she didn't need anything else. The fact she can wait at least a day will benefit her—and us, for that matter.

"She will probably want to talk to you about the Luna ceremony and get some of your opinions on what you want, and get to know you since you are soon to be her daughter-in-law."

She shied away a little at that. Big, brave Aylin is scared of a future mother-in-law and planning a Luna ceremony. I chuckled, and she glared at me.

"What is so funny?" she asked me indignantly.

"You beat my ass today, and now you are scared of planning a Luna ceremony. It's just a little funny," I said, shrugging my shoulders.

She went from looking like she was going to murder me to laughing.

"Yeah, I guess it is a little silly for me to get worked up over it. I just have no experience with things like that. I have been training for years, so combat and getting dirty never bothered me. Planning a party, though? Yeah, I am a little out of my element," she said, her cheeks brightening to a pretty shade of pink.

"Well, you won't be doing it alone. You will have help, and I am sure you will learn over time. Luna has many responsibilities to the pack, and I am sure you will be amazing," Trevor told her.

She just smiled and nodded. I wanted to comfort her. Seeming to read my thoughts, Kevin turned to me and shook his head. She was not okay.

Throughout the rest of the meal, we discussed plans to see more of the pack the following day and hit up the training yard again. Talking about the training yard seemed to get Aylin out of her funk, and she was smiling and talking excitedly.

After dinner, we all started to head up to our rooms. When we got to the floor for Kevin and myself, Aylin stopped as we turned to walk off.

"No," she said, and we all stopped and looked at her. "You two will not stay here," she said.

Trevor was looking at her in confusion, and my heart plummeted. Is she sending us away?

"I was told that our apartment was for us and our immediate family, is it not?" she asked Trevor.

"It is. My mother does live on the top floor along with us," Trevor answered, trepidation on his face.

"Then my family shall have rooms as well," she said matter-of-factly. "Come, let's see where you can stay. I am sure there are plenty of rooms with space and furniture that you can move into." She looked at both me and Kevin when she said this, and my heart started to race. She wants me closer?

"Are you sure about this, Aylin?" Trevor asked, glancing at me.

"It is a fact that I have two mates, so I shall do my best to work with you both. I cannot do that if one of you is always pushed aside. I think we all need to sit down and have a discussion to figure out how to work together," she added.

Trevor nodded and motioned for me and Kevin to follow. Aylin walked beside Trevor on the way up but kept looking back, almost as if to make sure we were still following. Several times, our eyes met, and I could feel the electric current between us pulling us closer. Goddess, I wanted her.

When we reached the apartment, Trevor showed us two rooms that were rather close to his and Aylin's. This surprised me, but Aylin nodded in agreement, and my heart leapt into my chest. She wanted me closer. This was good.

"I will have the staff bring up your belongings from your other rooms tomorrow so you can get properly settled," Trevor said. He was stiff and seemed annoyed. I understood why. With me here, it really seemed like we would never get along. I didn't know how we would do this, other than that we both wanted to make her happy. I just nodded.

"I am going to get ready for bed. I am rather exhausted after today and would like to put an end to it. We can all talk tomorrow. I'll see you in the morning." Aylin smiled at all three of us and walked to her room, leaving us alone in the hall.

"Thank you," I said to Trevor. He looked at me for a moment and nodded, then went into his own room. Kevin and I looked at each other for a moment, and he started laughing.

"Do you think this is funny?" I was a little annoyed.

"Yeah, I do! You really met your match this time," Kevin chuckled.

"I think you're right. I don't know what to do," I admitted.

"In this situation, I don't think anyone would. It is not something people will just understand, let alone the parties involved. Aylin is torn all the time. She is hurting and scared of everything. I know you both care very much for her, and she needs you." Kevin looked at me for a moment, seeming to assess me. "I know you will find a way to make it work," he added, then turned and walked into his room.

With my friend gone, I turned to have a look at where I was now staying.

The bedroom was large. It had a king four-poster bed with a black cover and two bedside tables made of dark cherry wood, just like the bed frame. At the base of the bed was a chest with a cushion for sitting, and a couch was against the wall to the right. To the left were two doors. When I checked, one led to a closet, the other to a bathroom.

After a quick look around, I decided to take a hot shower. The water felt good over my sore muscles, and I took my time washing the sweat and dirt from my body. As I did so, Aylin popped into my head again, and I couldn't help but imagine her on her knees before me, looking up at me with my cock fisted in her hand, pumping it and making it hard for her. Goddess, I am so hard for her.

I stroked myself firmly as I continued to fantasize about my girl—thinking of her eyes looking up at me, her tongue sliding across her bottom lip, wetting it, then darting out to catch the drop of precum off the tip of my cock, which throbbed with the need to fill her.

She opened her mouth and guided my cock between her lips, and I hissed as the sensation of her tongue and lips surrounding me made me buck further down her throat. She greedily sucked me in, and with her hand around the base, worked me until I was calling her name in a desperate plea. She worked me faster, sucked harder, and I just couldn't stand it. I exploded in her mouth while she looked up at me, her mascara running and a smile on her lips around my dick. It was the sexiest thing I had ever seen.

After a minute, I opened my eyes and relished the hot water hitting me. Maybe I should have taken a cold shower.

Looking down, I groaned, my cock already hardening again at the images I had just played in my head. I needed to calm down. I finished my shower and headed back to the bedroom. On my bed was a clean pair of basketball shorts and a T-shirt. Someone must have brought them in for me. I wondered if they had heard me getting off to my girl.

As soon as I picked them up, I could smell her on them. Aylin had brought them in while I was in the shower. Fuck. Did she hear me? What if she did and I scared her?

I got dressed and made my way out of my room, heading to hers. I needed to explain something — what, I didn't know. I just needed to make sure she wasn't put off by me if she had heard me in the shower calling her name.

I was about to knock on her door when I froze. What was I going to say? I had no clue. Maybe I could just grab a snack and think about it. I would just have to come back in a minute after clearing my head. The last thing I wanted was to stumble over what I was trying to say to her.

I made my way to the kitchen and looked for something to eat. I opened the refrigerator and saw a bowl of fruit salad. Not something I would usually go for, but it didn't sound all that bad. I grabbed it and placed it on the counter behind me, knocking over a metal mixing bowl in the process.

The loud clang made me freeze. I hoped I hadn't woken anyone. After a minute, I picked up the bowl and went to put it in the sink—but tripped over a spoon that must have fallen, causing me to drop the bowl again, making another loud clanging sound.

Well, if I got away with it before, I wouldn't now. I had definitely woken someone up.

I stood upright, picked up the bowl and the spoon, frustrated with myself, and put them in the sink. Then I searched until I found a fork, went back to the bowl of fruit salad, and hopped up on the counter. I had just taken my first bite of a strawberry when I noticed Aylin standing in the doorway.

She was in the shortest pair of sleep shorts I had ever seen and a tank top that left little to the imagination. Her silver hair cascaded down her shoulders and looked almost like it was glowing in the pale moonlight that filtered through the kitchen window. I had frozen mid-bite into the strawberry and watched her slowly come to stand before me, between my legs. She looked into the bowl of fruit and, using her fingers, picked up a piece of pineapple and took a bite, causing the juices to run down her chin.

She tried to wipe it, but I grabbed her hand and stopped her. Her eyes shot to mine, and I lowered the bowl that I had already set the fork in. Then I lowered my head to hers and licked the juice that had already started running down her neck. I traced the line the pineapple juice left from her neck to her lips. Then I couldn't stop myself. Before I knew what I was doing, my lips crashed against hers in an all-consuming, hungry kiss. It took a minute for her to respond, and I almost pulled away until she kissed me back. Her lips seared mine, and I could not get enough. The pineapple still on them only enhanced her delicious and sweet taste.

When we pulled away, there was a fire in her eyes. She smiled at me, and all reason and thought vanished. At this moment, all I saw was her fire, and all I wanted was to be consumed by it—let it burn me alive and take my very soul, for it was hers and only hers to possess. I hoped she saw what she had done to me, for there was no undoing it. I wanted her, no matter the cost, and I would have her.

Spurred on by my wolf, I could no longer hold back. I wanted her—I needed to feel her. I slid off the counter, turned us, and lifted her onto it. Her legs automatically wrapped around my body, and I groaned. Goddess, she was going to kill me before I even got to have her. I fisted my hand in her hair, pulled back for better access, and kissed her with everything I had.

I could feel her hands slide up my sides, over my chest, and around my neck, leaving a trail of electricity tingling my skin in their wake. She locked her hands behind my neck and pulled me closer to her, deepening the kiss. I was so hungry for her. My other hand explored her body, feeling the weight of her breast, then slid to her waist, where I grabbed hold and pulled her body flush against mine so she could feel the length of me between her legs. I ground against her, feeling the heat pouring from her center.

"Hope I'm not interrupting."

A low timbre exclaimed, causing us both to jump like kids caught stealing cookies out of the cookie jar. Trevor stood in the doorway now, staring at us with his arms crossed over his chest. Aylin's face turned bright red, and then a look of guilt filled it. I would not have her feel guilty for being with me. I was her mate, and this was normal for mates to be together. It was time we figured out how to work together.

"Not at all. In fact, I think maybe it's time we work together to give our girl what she needs. I think she could benefit from knowing her mates," I told him, standing tall and not backing down. He knew I was clearly challenging him. Aylin was looking at me like I had lost my mind, but my need and love for her outweighed the desire to keep her to myself. If I had to share her, then so be it—let her know I was at least willing to try for her sake.

He seemed to take only a moment to think about it, then nodded. "Very well. Why don't you bring her to my room, and we'll show her what two Alphas can do for her?"

The grin spreading across his face was filled with wicked intent, and Aylin knew it. Her body shivered under me, and I picked her up. She squealed and locked her arms and legs around me as I made my way to the door to follow Trevor.

He disappeared inside and, after a moment, came out with the bowl of fruit that had been sitting next to us. He led the way, and I followed with Aylin holding tightly to me. I followed him to his room, where he held the door open for me to enter. I made my way to the bed and dropped Aylin onto it. Trevor walked up beside me, and I could smell the fear and excitement coming from my little mate.

Goddess, this was going to be fun. I would make sure of it.

# Chapter Twenty-One
## *Aylin*

I had just gotten ready for bed when I heard a loud metallic banging sound. I opened my door to see if I could hear anything, and I couldn't. I walked out to the living room to see if anything was amiss. I couldn't see anything. Then I heard the noise again, if not a little louder, and it made me jump. I turned and headed in the direction of the noise.

Way to go, Aylin. This is how the character usually dies in a horror movie — by investigating what's going on. I gave my head a shake to dispel the thought, and I opened the door to the kitchen and watched Zander move to a bowl and hop up on the counter.

I couldn't help but admire my first crush getting ready to eat a fresh strawberry. Goddess, he looked sexy as hell. I could barely breathe. What am I doing? I should leave before he sees me.

As if hearing my thoughts, he turns to me mid-bite of his strawberry and stops. I can't help how attracted I am and start toward him without thinking. His eyes track my movements, growing hooded as he watches me walk toward him. I don't know what possessed me to do it, but I picked up a pineapple and brought it to my lips. I watch him lower his fork and watch me as I take a bite of the fruit, only to have the juices run down my chin. That wasn't sexy at all. I go to wipe it away, and he catches my hand to stop me.

I watch him as he lowers the bowl and sets it on the counter, and then he leans his head down. I can feel him start at the base of my neck, where the juices have reached, licking them off me. His tongue moves up my neck, cleaning it. My core tightens. Goddess, he is driving me crazy. When he reaches my lips, he seems to lose whatever restraint he was holding on to and kisses me.

This is no soft kiss — it is hard, hungry, and demanding. He isn't seeking permission; he is claiming me. I can feel it, and I want it. I hesitate, debating whether I should do this, but my need wins out, so I kiss him back just as hard. I reach up and wrap my hands around his neck, letting him explore my body with his hand. When he pulls me closer so our bodies are flush against each other, I can feel his hard length rub against my core. I want more.

He pulls away and looks into my eyes, assessing me. He must like what he sees because he goes back to kissing me just as hungrily. I cling to him and rub against him. I want him to take me right here and now.

"Hope I'm not interrupting."

Trevor's voice makes me jump. I look at him, and guilt fills me. How could I do this? I feel like I have just betrayed Trevor in the worst possible way. I am so caught up in Zander that I don't even think about how it will affect Trevor, and I am a horrible person for that. I can feel the shame burning on my face.

"Not at all. In fact, I think maybe it's time we work together to give our girl what she needs. I think she could benefit from knowing her mates," Zander says.

I look at him. Was he serious? Did he just suggest they both have me together? I have never been with anyone before, and he wants them both to take me? My core tightens at the thought, and I can feel myself growing wetter. It scares and entices me.

"Very well. Why don't you bring her to my room, and we will show her what two Alphas can do for her?" said Trevor.

I look at him next. What? He just agreed with Zander. Is this actually happening? Trevor's face breaks into a wicked grin that seems to promise wicked intent, and I am beyond intrigued.

I don't have time to dwell on it because Zander hoists me up into his arms, and I let out a small shriek at being jerked into the air. I instantly wrap my arms and legs around his muscular body. I don't think he will drop me, but I'm not taking any chances. Besides, now that I am wrapped around him and can still feel his hard length between my legs, I really don't mind.

Zander moves through the door, and then Trevor disappears into the kitchen. A moment later, he is back with the bowl of fruit that Zander had. Zander then follows Trevor away from the kitchen and to his room. Along the way, I can't help but rub against Zander, and I know it affects him when his grip tightens on my ass and he groans in response.

When we get to Trevor's room, the first thing Zander does is walk me over to the enormous bed and throw me down onto it. When I look up into his eyes, I can see the desire and longing in them—he is almost feral. Then I watch Trevor walk up next to him and set the bowl of fruit on the nightstand. The look in his eyes is predatory and lustful. They are both barely holding on by a thread, and so am I. It is time to let that thread snap. I grin at them both, taunting them, and they move into action.

I track them both as they climb on the bed and slowly crawl toward me. My heart is beating so loud I swear they can hear it outside. Zander goes to one side and Trevor the other. Zander puts his hand on my cheek, turns my face toward his, and kisses me. My body responds instantly, and I crave more. Then Trevor's mouth is at my neck, licking, kissing, and nipping up and down from my chin to my collarbone.

I can feel their hands exploring my body, holding and massaging my breasts, and then rubbing my pussy through my shorts. I groan, and they lay me down. Trevor turns my face toward his and starts kissing me. Then I feel hands lifting my shirt. I have no idea who is doing what to my body and clothes, and I don't care.

My skin tingles like electricity is dancing on it, and butterflies swarm in my stomach. My shirt is brought over my head, and I see it is Zander removing it. Trevor wastes no time bringing his lips back to mine. I can feel Zander's lips kissing my shoulder as he unclasps my bra and then removes it. My breasts are free, and Zander trails kisses from my shoulder to my left breast while Trevor does the same to the right. I feel their hands exploring my chest and sides, and then one of them stops.

Trevor straightens and looks down at me, tension bracketing his eyes as he looks me over. His eyes flash with anger, and I realize what he is looking at — my scars. I tense. Zander stops then and sits up. He looks at Trevor and then at where Trevor is looking. His eyes grow large, and then he, too, is angry.

"What happened?" Zander asks.

I reach for my shirt to cover myself, and Trevor stops me.

"No, little wolf, please talk to us. What are these scars from? Was it training? I don't understand why you have them. Even when you didn't have your wolf, you shouldn't scar like this," Trevor says.

"It wasn't from training," I tell them and then look away, ashamed. I don't want to talk about this. I know I won't be able to hide my scars forever, but I don't want them to see them like this.

Trevor turns my face back to them. His eyes are full of concern.

"Then how did you get them?" Zander asks again.

"I don't want to talk about it," I tell them. "Can we please just go to bed?" I ask, wanting to get away.

"Oh no, we started something, and we are going to finish it. My beast wants you, and so do I," Trevor says. "But I also need to know why my mate has scars like this on her stomach. Do you have others?"

I flame red. He notices instantly.

"Where?" he asks.

Well, I guess I better get this over with.

I sit up and turn around. I hear them both take a deep breath, and I feel like crying. I am so ashamed. I feel one of them touch my back, tracing each one in turn. There are five on my back and two on my front. They still haven't noticed the one on my upper thigh.

"Is that all?" Trevor growled, and I shook my head. I turned back around, grabbed the bottom of the shorts on the right side, and lifted them, showing the scar on my outer thigh. Trevor growled again.

"Aylin, tell me where they are from. Did someone do this to you?" he demanded.

I wanted to run. I wanted to hide. I didn't want them seeing this. I turned around again, unable to look at them. I couldn't say anything. Zander would feel like it was his fault, and I knew they would want to take it out on those who did this to me — one of whom was Zander's own sister. I couldn't get the words out.

There was a knock on the door.

"It's Kevin," I told them, and Trevor got off the bed to get the door.

"Aylin, please." Zander begged. "How did you get these?" he asked, touching my back.

I pulled my shirt over my chest as Kevin came into the room.

"What's going on?" Kevin said, rushing to me.

He stilled when he got to the bed, and I heard a growl that was more ominous than the one Trevor let out. My skin prickled with goosebumps. Only one person knew about these, and that was Layla. She helped clean and care for them, sneaking medicine from her dad's supplies in case of training or attack.

"I take it you didn't know about these?" Trevor said, crossing his arms over his broad chest.

I looked away again, unable to talk.

"No, I have never seen them before. Aylin never wears anything less than a tank top and shorts. I had no clue, but I would love to know where they came from, sis," Kevin said.

I knew he was angry. We told each other everything, and this was the second really big secret I had kept from him. I knew he was hurt that I hadn't confided in him.

"It's nothing. I am fine," I told them all.

I couldn't take any more. I didn't like them all staring at me like this.

"Aylin, please tell us how you got them," Zander pleaded again.

I looked at him and saw the pain and sorrow in his eyes. I could see the guilt there as well. He knew this had happened in his old pack.

"If I tell you what caused them, can we drop it?" I asked.

"Will you tell us who did it?" Trevor asked, and I instantly shook my head no.

"I guess, for now, I will settle for how, but I want names eventually, little wolf," Trevor said, knowing he wouldn't get them from me tonight.

I sighed. "I didn't get them all together. They are from different instances. Others healed fine, but the scars you see are from either silver blades or blades with silver dust on them."

The collective growl made me shudder, and the goosebumps returned.

"Aylin, why did you never say anything?" Kevin sounded choked up when he spoke.

I looked over my shoulder at him and saw the tears starting in his eyes.

"Because I didn't want you to know. I didn't want anyone to know. I didn't want to be weak, and who would believe me over them anyway?" I said, trying to hold onto my
own emotions.

"I would have," he said. "You know I would have."

The hurt in Kevin's voice was too much for me.

"If you knew, then so would Mom and Dad. I would
have been trapped in our house or always had to have someone with me. I didn't want any of that. I just wanted to be
left alone. I tried to fight back at first—I really couldn't. Then
Layla helped me convince Lance to train me. At first, it was
to defend myself, but then I really wanted to join the guard.
I wanted to defend those who couldn't defend themselves,"
I said.

"Kevin, I think we need to be alone with our mate. Can
you please go? I am sure you and Aylin will have time to
talk about this later, but right now, with her topless, Bane
wants to come forward with you in here," Trevor said.

Kevin looked at me one last time, nodded to Trevor,
then left the room without another word to me. My shame
only grew.

"This was going on for a while then?" Zander asked, and
I nodded.

"Is that why there were periods where you would miss
school for a few days at a time? I remember Kevin telling us
you were sick and had a high fever. Was it because of this?"

I nodded again. Wolves didn't get sick easily, but my body had to fight off the silver infection.

"Aylin, you are no longer alone — you know that. We are here for you, and you can trust us. I do hope you will tell us more, but for now, thank you for at least telling us how you got them," Trevor said.

I looked up at him, shock radiating through me. He really wasn't going to push the subject? I looked from him to Zander. They both looked like they wanted to push me for more but didn't.

"I know, and I appreciate that, but I just can't right now."

I felt the bed dip as Trevor climbed back on it. I felt his hand touch the small of my back and then move up it and around to my front. He took the tank top from my hands.

Then I felt lips gently touch my shoulder, giving me a wholly different type of goosebump. His lips trailed up to my neck, and I felt the desire I had only moments ago return in a flood. My core clenched, and a ball of need formed low in my belly. I felt hands exploring once more, and then I was turned and laid before them. They both went back to what they were doing only moments ago — exploring and touching. Zander moved to my belly, and I felt him kiss both scars. Then he moved up to my breast.

Feeling both of them suck, bite, and tease my breasts was heady. I moaned and arched my back, pushing my chest into their faces. Trevor chuckled and bit my nipple, causing me to cry out. He then let my breast go with a wet pop and proceeded to kiss his way down to my shorts, where he hooked his fingers inside the waistband and pulled them down my legs.

A moment later, he spread my legs and feasted his eyes on me. I felt Zander rise away from my other breast, and he gazed at my bare body lying before him.

"What utter perfection, little wolf," Trevor cooed.

"Yes, my queen, you truly are the most beautiful creature I have ever laid eyes on," Zander added.

"What are we to do with such a rare beauty?" Trevor asked, chuckling as his hands slowly moved from my ankles to my knees and then to my center, where he slid his fingers through my folds, rubbing against the bundle of nerves, making my hips jerk and my back arch.

"I am thinking a beauty this rare needs to be worshiped, maybe devoured. And she definitely needs to be given pleasure until she cannot even form the word to beg us to stop," Zander answered.

"That sounds like a good start," Trevor replied to him, lowering his head between my legs and replacing his fingers with his tongue, slipping it between my folds. I cried out, unable to help it. The feeling was so intense. I didn't know it could feel like this. I mean, I had played with myself before, but this was so much more. Wait—did he say that was just the start?

Then I felt Zander next to me, his hand moving in circles up my stomach to my breast, where he took the nipple between his fingers and pulled ever so slightly while pinching. A small bit of pain and a lot of pleasure came from that action, and my thoughts fell away. Then his mouth was on mine, and he was kissing me as though I would disappear. Goddess, they were not lying about devouring me. With Zander's kiss consuming me and Trevor's mouth working my bundle and folds, their hands exploring, grabbing, and more, my senses were overloaded—and we had barely just begun.

Trevor added a finger inside me, and I bucked. He groaned in response, and my hips rolled at his touch. In and out, in and out, his tongue lashed against my clit and slid down to clean the juices coming from his finger being buried inside me. He added another, and I gasped, only for it to be swallowed by Zander's mouth as he delved his tongue in and completely dominated mine. Trevor added another finger, stretching me, making me squirm.

"So tight, little wolf. We need to fix that so you can fit us inside you. How would you like us to fill you? To claim you?" Trevor asked.

My mind was so foggy from the multitude of sensations that I wasn't sure how to answer. They both stopped and looked at me expectantly. It dawned on me then, they were asking who would take me first, who I would gift with my virginity, and who I would choose first and accept my mark.

There would be no way to answer this and make everyone happy.

I looked down to where both males were fisting their cocks. They were enormous, both of them, and I wondered how they would ever fit. Zander was a little longer than Trevor but not by much, and Trevor was a bit thicker than Zander. Which would hurt more? Length or girth? I looked up at their patient, waiting gazes, both burning with lust and desire.

"I want Trevor to mark me first."

Trevor's eyes lit up. We knew that the first mark was the stronger of the bonds. In the end, we would all be bonded and connected, but I was declaring him my mate first, and it had a strong meaning in this relationship.

"And I want Zander to take me first."

Zander went from deflated to excited in a nanosecond. They looked at me and then at each other and nodded. They knew I was trying to be as fair as possible, even if they didn't like it. They were trying to work together.

Now came the tricky part. Zander and Trevor traded places. At that point, Trevor started to kiss me, and Zander pushed his fingers inside to continue stretching me to accommodate him. I was soaked and only getting wetter. I could feel myself building, inching closer and closer to that cliff's edge. Then Zander's mouth was there, licking and sucking my little bundle of nerves. I was bucking and writhing beneath his skilled fingers and tongue. Trevor was groping and kneading my breasts, squeezing them to elicit a bit of pain along with the pleasure, and then I was there — toppling over the edge of that cliff with a cry. I could feel the juices coming from me, and then he was there.

Zander thrust forward and ripped through my barrier, and I screamed. He stilled and tried to wait for me to adjust to him, but it was almost impossible. I was squirming to get away from the intrusion and needed him to get out. He started to move, and Trevor went back to touching my body and kissing me to distract me from the pain. I reached over and started to stroke him. My hand could not fit all the way around his girth, but I still stroked and pumped his cock as he kissed me like I was his air to breathe. After a moment, that pain transformed, and I was starting my climb up the mountain and toward that cliff.

I was getting close, my hips rolling to meet Zander's, and I loved the noises he was making as he took me. The moans and growls coming from him, knowing it was because he was enjoying my body, were heady. Trevor slowly moved from kissing me to kissing and licking my neck. I was a writhing mess between the two of them, and then I felt the most intense burning pain in my neck — but before I could scream, the pain turned to sheer bliss, and I exploded into a kaleidoscope of pleasure. My instincts took over, and I found Trevor's neck. I licked the area for the mate's mark and felt my canines extend before I bit into his neck. He growled in response, and then I felt his cock throb and twitch in my hand as he found his release with me.

A moment later, Zander leaned over to the other side of my neck and claimed me. I didn't have time to come down from the last orgasm when another rocked my body. I repeated the action and marked Zander next. He growled, then slammed deep into me and filled me with his release. Zander pulled away from my neck and then slowly pulled out of me. I winced a little. I felt my eyes droop. I was beyond happy. I felt whole now.

"Don't tell me you are done, little wolf," Trevor taunted. He grabbed my thigh and pulled me around so I faced him. He placed himself between my legs and, gripping his cock, rubbed it from my clit to my entrance several times, then just rubbed it against my clit for a moment, teasing me. I started to move and grind against him. It felt so good. Then he moved back to my entrance and thrust in. If I thought Zander was painful, it was nothing compared to Trevor. Girth was definitely more painful than length. I cried out, and just as before, when he started to move into me, the pain eased and the pleasure took over.

"Goddess, little wolf, you are so damn tight," he growled. Zander laughed, nodding in agreement, and then he was beside my head. He held his cock in front of my face and was slowly stroking it. I replaced his hand with my own and took over the motion. His head dropped back as he lightly rocked his hips in time with my hand. I don't know what bravery came over me, but using my other arm, I propped myself up on my elbow and then put my lips around the head of his cock and sucked. He whipped his head down and looked at me as I started to move my head, taking him deeper into my mouth. I used my tongue, rubbing it against the underside of his cock as I moved my head, and he groaned.

Trevor started moving faster inside me, and I could barely concentrate on what I was trying to do to Zander. Eventually, Zander grabbed my hair in his fist and started to move his hips, effectively fucking my mouth. I hollowed it out the best I could to accommodate him, but he was too long. He was hitting the back of my throat, and it caused me to gag. Every time I did, he would pull out a little and let me catch my breath — but only for a moment. All the while, Trevor was pounding into me relentlessly. I was a screaming, gagging mess.

"Come on, little wolf, come for me, baby," Trevor pleaded. His words mixed with Zander's growl had me on the precipice of the cliff I had come to love falling over, and I was almost there. Trevor seemed to realize this, and the next moment, I felt his thumb brush my little bundle and circle it.

"Fuck!" Zander yelled as I moaned around his cock. I knew he could feel me humming. He jerked and found his release, and I gagged again, which caused my pussy to clench tighter around Trevor's thick cock. He growled in response and worked my bundle more. I was rolling my hips, meeting his thrusts, and then Zander twisted my nipple, and

I was done. I fell off that cliff into oblivion, and everything went dark for the briefest of moments. I felt Trevor slam into me and find his own release, filling me in the process.

We lay there, the three of us, in a pile of limp limbs and bodies. I never knew this was what it could be like, and now that I know, how will I ever stop? That was the most intense feeling I had ever had, and I already craved their touch. They seemed to think the same way. They rolled over and started touching me again. Damn, did my body respond.

For the next two hours, they continued to devour and play with me. At one time, I was on all fours, taking Trevor in my mouth while Zander had me from behind. Another time, I was riding Trevor, and I had Zander behind me, kissing, sucking, and biting on my neck and shoulders. His hands reached around—one played with my breasts while the other rubbed circles on my clit. We could not get enough of each other.

Finally, after getting Trevor to fill me again, I slumped down onto his chest. I couldn't even gather the strength to climb off him and get him out of me. I was exhausted and beyond satisfied. Everything was so intense between us. I hoped it would always be like this.

"Come, little wolf, let's get you cleaned up, and then we can go to bed. We have a big day tomorrow," Trevor said, turning so I fell onto the bed. Then, removing himself from the bed, he walked to the bathroom. I couldn't help watching him as he walked away—the rippling muscles in his back and his firm, sexy ass. I just wanted to bite it. I shook my head at the thought and smiled.

Zander removed himself and then lifted me into his arms. I wrapped my arms around his neck and let him carry me into the bathroom. Trevor was already running a hot shower, the steam billowing out from the shower stall. It was definitely big enough for the three of us—maybe a few more. The water cascaded down from the ceiling instead of a single faucet. Zander walked right in, and I cried out when the hot water hit my still-sensitive body.

Zander and Trevor both chuckled at my reaction. "What's wrong, little wolf?" Trevor asked with a devilish grin on his face. "Is the water too hot for you?"

"No," I quipped back, blushing.

They both chuckled again. Zander put me down, and then Trevor stepped in, joining us. He grabbed the shampoo off the wall rack and squeezed it generously into his hand.

"Turn around, little wolf."

I did as I was told, and he started to massage the shampoo into my hair. It felt amazing. I groaned at the contact and the feeling of his fingers against my scalp. Then he lathered it into the rest of my hair and rinsed it out, then did the same with the conditioner.

Zander picked up a sponge, applied body wash to it, and started working on my front, while Trevor did the same with my back. Having them both wash me from my neck to my feet was a whole different type of erotic, and I was burning—not from the hot water, but from the need to feel them inside me again.

"What's wrong, my queen? You smell like you need some assistance," Zander said low in my ear.

I really did. I needed them to fill this need building inside of me.

"Yes, please," I almost begged.

Then they were on me. Zander's mouth crashed against mine, and I could feel Trevor kissing my neck and lingering over his mark. Every time his lips brushed it, I shivered, electricity tingling all over my skin. I could feel the wetness between my legs that had nothing to do with the water we were still under.

Trevor growled and then dropped to his knees behind me. He turned my hips until my glistening pussy was facing him, Zander's lips never leaving mine in the process.

"Hold her," Trevor growled.

Zander wrapped his arms around my upper half while Trevor placed my legs over each one of his shoulders, granting him access to my center. Then he feasted on me. I rolled my hips against his mouth, trying to get more friction. He grabbed hold of my hips and held me still. I growled in frustration, and his answering chuckle against my pussy only made me want to ride his face more.

Breaking the kiss with Zander, I cried out when his teeth nipped at my bundle. Zander had my back resting against his chest, and he started kissing my neck and sucking on his mark. This heightened everything, and I could not get enough. The noises coming from me now sounded more animalistic, and I was in a frenzy, trying to rub against him and get some friction, only to be thwarted as he kept my hips firmly locked in place.

Zander's hand moved to my breast and started to knead and play with it. Then he moved to the nipple, where he squeezed and twisted it. My back bowed, and then Zander bit over his mark again, and I detonated. My thighs squeezed Trevor's head as I rode out my orgasm on his face.

Slowly, Trevor lowered my legs to the floor of the shower, and both my mates performed the task of washing my body all over again.

After the shower, they dried me off with two very soft, fluffy towels, making sure to steal kisses around my body as they went. I was beyond exhausted, but they were driving me crazy. How could I already want more?

After they finished drying me, Trevor picked me up and carried me to the bed, where he laid me down in the center. He and Zander both climbed in and lay on opposite sides of me, each wrapping an arm around my stomach and cuddling up to me.

For the first time in my life, I didn't feel like an outsider—like I didn't belong. I didn't have a void or a hole in me. I felt whole and happy. This was everything I could have hoped for, and now that we had mated, I prayed that this was what I had to look forward to for the rest of my life.

I knew without a shadow of a doubt that I loved both of these men, and I could never give them up.

So please, Moon Goddess, hear my prayer and let them accept this. Please, let them find a way to get along so we all can make this work. Because I cannot lose either of them. Not ever!

# Chapter Twenty-Two
## *Aylin*

The next morning, I wake to find Zander cuddled up with me, still asleep and beyond dreamy. I couldn't help but stare at my mate as he slept, committing every detail to my memory. Yes, **MY** mate. I smiled at that thought. He is mine! Mated now and forever mine, and I reveled in it. No turning back now. Not that I believe I ever could have. I may have been hurt when he tried to reject me, but I never truly stopped wanting him.

I reached over and stroked his cheek. I loved the feeling of his morning stubble against my fingers. I explored further just to see what I could do before he woke up. I moved my hand down to his chest and felt his heartbeat under my palm—so strong and steady. I closed my eyes and just let the rhythm of his heart sync with mine.

I felt a hand over the back of mine, and my eyes fluttered open to meet Zander's golden ones. His eyes always fascinated me, and today they were a brilliant golden color. You could barely see the hazel in them. For a moment, I was breathless as he smiled one of his dazzling, all-teeth smiles, and I melted for him like I had so many times growing up.

"Are you enjoying yourself, my queen?" he asked, his voice raspy and deep, and I couldn't fight the shudder that ran through my body.

"Actually, I was," I smiled coyly at him. I trailed my hand down his chest toward his waist. Using the tip of my fingers, I slowly traced a line from one hip to the other. He sucked in a sharp breath.

"Aylin." My name on his lips encouraged me to keep going, and I moved on to his already hard cock. Damn, how did that fit inside me? I wrapped my hand around him and pumped it. He jerked under my touch and groaned. He rolled onto his back and put his arm over his face. I kept going, enjoying the noises he was making for me. The problem was, the more I stroked him, the more I wanted him inside me.

I adjusted myself, sitting up, and then got up on my knees. I swung one of my legs over his hips, and without waiting for him to realize what I was doing, I lowered myself onto his length, slowly taking the first couple of inches inside me. He hissed out a breath through his teeth again, and I let myself drop, sitting all the way to his base. I let out a scream as his cock impaled me deeper than it did last night.

"Fuck, Aylin!" he growled my name and grabbed my hips. "For goddess' sake, baby, you feel so fucking good around me." He groaned again as I lifted myself up and dropped back down. I did this a few more times and then started to get a rhythm of bouncing and rolling my hips. It felt amazing having him so deep within me. I enjoyed working his cock and taking what I needed, getting so close to that cliff I came to love last night.

I especially loved the feeling I got when I rolled my hips and ground against him, hitting my clit as well when I moved. It didn't take long for him to grab my hips and roll me over, thrusting into me hard and fast.

"Aylin, my queen, come for me, please." He fucked me hard, and his words were my undoing. I toppled over that cliff and let the darkness take me into a state of pleasure. When I opened my eyes again, Zander was still on top of me. He was breathing heavily and watching me with such intensity burning in those beautiful golden eyes. He lowered his lips to mine and kissed me. Unlike the kisses last night, this one was softer. I could feel his need for me, and I kissed him back, putting my heart and soul into it.

He pulled away a few moments later, leaving me more breathless than I already was, and pulled out of me. I winced at the twinge of pain. I was still sore from last night, and this didn't help. I didn't regret it at all, though. I reveled in the feeling.

We took a quick shower and got ready for the day, both sporting workout gear, knowing we planned on hitting up the practice fields for a little bit this morning with Kevin and Liam. First, however, I wanted to track down Trevor since he wasn't here when I woke up. I hoped he wasn't upset with how things worked out last night. I know he wanted me for himself, and I can't blame him because I could never share him with another.

We headed out of the apartment and made our way down the stairs. When we got to the floor with Trevor's office, I turned away and headed to check if he was there. If not, he may still be at breakfast, but I wanted to check since it was on the way.

"Where are you going? Breakfast is this way," Zander said.

"I am just going to see if Trevor is in his office. I want to make sure he is okay since he was already gone when I got up," I told him.

"Okay, I will come with you," he said, and we headed to Trevor's office together. Part of me wanted to tell him to go ahead and that I would meet him at breakfast, but having him with me gave me a sense of strength. If Trevor said he didn't want this, I would need Zander more than ever.

We reached his office, and I knocked on the door.

"Come in," Trevor called out.

I opened the door and walked inside with Zander. Trevor and Nick looked up at us. Trevor's face broke into a wide grin when he saw me, and he came around his desk and scooped me up into his arms.

"Good morning, little wolf. How did you sleep? How do you feel?"

I blushed, my eyes darting to Nick, who was doing his best to look like he was not listening. We both knew he was.

"I'm great. I slept really well," I told him.

He kissed me, and Nick cleared his throat to remind the Alpha that there were others present. Trevor broke the kiss and looked from me to Zander.

"I would like to speak with you today. How about after breakfast, you come up and we talk about your future here as a member of Blood Moon?"

Zander and I were both shocked at this.

"Yes, of course, I would like that. Thank you, Alpha Gideon," Zander said.

"It's Trevor. We are a unit now, a team. When we are in public, we can use our titles, but here we are a family, and we should act like one," he said, patting Zander on the shoulder.

Zander smiled and placed his hand on Trevor's shoulder as well. I couldn't help the tears that welled up in my eyes, seeing them get along.

Trevor looked down at me. "What's wrong?" he asked.

Everyone in the room instantly looked at me, and worry shone in their expressions.

"Nothing is wrong. I am just so happy."

I hugged him to me, and he held me tightly, breathing me in deeply. He pulled away and kissed me softly.

"You two go get some breakfast. I will see you in a little bit. And Aylin, I was wondering if you and I could go for a run later? I have border patrol since we are still down some warriors, and I thought maybe you could go with me," he asked. He almost looked worried about my answer.

"Of course, I would like that. When are we going?" I asked, excited to be included in something to help with the pack.

"After lunch. We will make passes around the south and east borders, furthest from the pack house. That is the most dangerous area if someone wants to sneak through. It is the most open and least populated area, so we try to make sure there are multiple warriors down there at all times."

I felt Zander stiffen next to me, and it didn't go unnoticed by Trevor either.

"Don't worry, Zander. I will protect her with my life. You know I will."

Zander nodded, but he didn't relax. He was clearly uncomfortable with the idea of me being near any kind of danger. I loved him for that, but I needed this. I wanted to contribute to the pack I was meant to help run as Luna.

"I will be careful and do as I am told," I said to Zander, winking at him. This made him smile at least.

"Okay, you two go to breakfast. We have a big day—lots of planning and then dinner with my mother, remember? After dinner, we are presenting our three newest members to the pack. Speaking of which, can you bring Kevin with you after breakfast? We need to discuss his role here as well," he added, looking toward Zander, who just nodded again.

With that, Trevor stole one more kiss, and I made my way out of his office with Zander.

Breakfast passed with more conversation with Kevin, Liam, and Nikki. Liam, Nikki, and I would head to the practice fields, while Kevin and Zander would meet up with us there after the meeting with Trevor. Then, after lunch, I would go on patrol with Trevor and meet up with them for dinner.

I was really nervous about meeting Trevor's mom. I really hoped she liked me.

"Okay, let's get a move on," Liam said, getting up from the table.

We all stood and followed him out of the hall. When we got to the main area, there were tons of pack members milling around, starting their day.

I said my goodbye to Kevin, and Zander wrapped me in his arms, kissing me deeply. I swooned in his arms until I heard gasps and whispers.

"How dare you!" said a shrill female voice.

Zander and I broke apart, our heads snapping in the same direction to look at the female.

"Poor Ruby is locked up like an animal for caring about our Alpha, and you show him disrespect by kissing another? Maybe you should be locked up instead!" she cried out.

It was Stella, Ruby's best friend and second in their little group. I saw Heather and Jo standing behind her. Jo looked uncomfortable and kept glancing around. I noticed that one of the places she kept glancing was at Kevin.

"You do not know what you are talking about and should probably hold your tongue, Stella," Nikki cut in. "Disrespecting our Luna is a punishable offense. Or did you not learn from Ruby's actions?"

This seemed to enrage Stella further.

"She has no right to kiss another when Alpha Gideon punished Ruby for kissing him. Why shouldn't she be punished—or him, for that matter?" she seethed.

The other pack members had now stopped and started to pay attention to the ruckus.

"First of all, he is my mate!" I seethed back at her.

I was done letting others defend or speak for me. She would learn her place. If I were to be Luna, I needed to handle situations like this myself.

She looked at me like I had two heads.

"You are Alpha Gideon's mate. You can't have two mates," she said, crossing her arms.

I smiled at her, and it was most definitely not a pleasant one.

She shifted on her feet as I let my Alpha aura out with help from Mona, who was starting to pace in my head. She hated when other females got close to our mates, and Stella had eyes for Zander—just like Ruby had eyes for Trevor.

Nope. I was so done. And I was taking care of it.

"That is where you are wrong. I have two fated mates!" The whispers started instantly. "Not only do I have two fated mates, but I have a guardian! My brother Kevin here is my protector. Do you know what that means?" I asked her as I gestured to my brother, who had his arms crossed over his chest and a look of agitation on his face. She shifted again.

"That's not possible. Only royals have guardians!" She was starting to falter, and Mona was baring her teeth, pacing, wanting to go for the kill. I laughed at her, and right there in front of the other pack members, I shifted. This time, I didn't shift into my wolf form. For the first time, I shifted into my Lycan form. Mona wanted to present the highest form of power over these she-wolves—she was as done as I was. The growl that left me would have terrified me. The power that radiated from me dropped everyone around me to their knees.

Mona reveled in the fear coming from Stella as her eyes grew as big as saucers. She, too, was forced to bow as my aura washed over her in waves. I kept it going. I wanted her to know that there would be no messing with me—that I was stronger and more powerful than her and her little group of friends here, and I would not allow her to bully me or think it was okay to continue to disrespect me. I am not the girl who hides anymore, and I need to remember that myself.

"Aylin! Would you mind letting us up?" I looked around, and by the stairs, both Nick and Trevor were on their knees as well. All of the pack members looked from him to me in complete shock. Trevor was their Alpha — he was the most dominant — but not anymore. I was. I pulled the aura back and reined it in. So many stayed kneeling out of respect, showing me their submission, while others got up and stared at me like I was a unicorn.

"Little wolf, you are the most beautiful creature I have ever seen!" Trevor exclaimed. He snapped his fingers. "Someone bring your Luna some clothes!" he demanded. Several people jumped and ran off. A moment later, I had several options to choose from.

"Thank you," I said to them, and once again, everyone froze and gawked at me. That's right — that isn't an ability they have. I can communicate out loud and through pack bonds. I shifted back and threw on a pair of shorts one she-wolf provided and a black t-shirt a male provided.

Trevor turned to the crowd of pack members waiting. "Does someone want to explain what is going on here?" he boomed.

"Oh, no need for them to be brought into this. You see, Stella here saw Zander kiss me and decided to confront me for kissing another when Ruby sits in a cell for touching you. So I explained to her that he is my mate, and when questioned, Mona asserted her dominance." Trevor looked from me to Stella.

"Stella, I would think twice before you ever question your Luna again. Ruby was given a chance, and she didn't listen. She put hands on her Alpha without consent and disrespected her Luna. She is awaiting her punishment, which has only been delayed as there are more pressing matters than dealing with a she-wolf who needs to learn respect. Her sitting in her cell should help teach her that," he growled. Stella bowed her head and looked at the floor.

"I apologize, Alpha Gideon, and I apologize to you, Luna. Please forgive my outburst. I didn't know. I was just upset for my friend," Stella said. I couldn't tell if she meant it or was putting on a show. If she was putting on a show, it was a good one. I could taste her fear, and for all I knew, she was just trying to save her own skin. She definitely assumed I was weak.

"This is your only warning. If you have any concerns, you will address them with respect formally. You disrespect us publicly again, and you will share a punishment similar to Ruby," Trevor threatened. Stella bowed her head again to both of us. Mona was satisfied, but I was leery. Just because her wolf submitted now does not mean it will stay that way. The wolf in her had no choice when I forced my aura over them.

After her show of submission, she turned and walked away with the other two in tow. As soon as they were gone, everyone started to move around like they were on fire, rushing back to what they were doing. Of course, watching what should have been a private conversation was rude, and they didn't want to offend their new Luna or their Alpha.

"I am sorry that you have had such a rough start here, Aylin. I would have thought my pack would rejoice and be happy I have found my Luna." Trevor shook his head. The pack reflected the Alpha in this situation and everything that had happened. To most, this made him look like a bad Alpha. But not to me. I grew up with women like that, and I won't let the few tell me what the pack is like as a whole. I will still give them a chance.

"Trevor, I do not blame your entire pack, and I am not going to let a few bad apples who only care about themselves get in the way of me becoming a fair Luna. Your pack as a whole did not offend me. I already love so many of you. Nickki, Nick, and Liam—you guys have already been there for me and shown support. If the rest of the pack is anything like you guys, I think we will be okay," I tell them. I turn from one to the next, and they are all smiling at me.

"Spoken like a true Luna of the people," Trevor said. The others nodded in agreement. I couldn't help the smile on my face as I looked at my new friends. I knew at that moment I could be happy here.

"All right, Kevin and Zander, we need to have a meeting about your futures here and the roles you will play," Trevor said. In turn, he and Zander kissed me goodbye and walked toward the stairs. Then the four of them walked away. I heard a few whispers and hushed voices. Really? They know Lycans and wolves have amazing hearing. Deciding to ignore them, I turned to Nikki and Liam.

"Ready to go to the practice fields?" I asked them. "I really need to let off some steam, and a good run through that obstacle course and a fight or two should do the trick." Well now, if my kissing two males didn't make them whisper, that sure did.

"Of course, girl, let's go see whose ass you can kick now. Your powers are getting stronger, and I, for one, want to see what you can do as they grow," Nikki said, full of enthusiasm. It was nice seeing her when she was more relaxed and not on duty. It could be hard to remember she was a girl like me and that we could actually become good friends. When she was on duty, though, she was just like any soldier.

"Come on, ladies, let a real gentleman escort you both to kick some warriors' backsides," Liam said, bowing at us. Yeah, there was no way I could keep my laugh in at that, and before we knew it, Nikki and I were both in fits of giggles, and Liam looked very confused.

"What? Why are you laughing? I may be a ladies' man, but I can still be a gentleman!" he said with an exaggerated huff.

"You know, only you believe you are a ladies' man. The rest of us just play along!" Nikki told him. His mouth dropped open in a big "O," and then he placed his hand over his heart, acting like he had been wounded. We laughed some more but both took one of his arms as he led us out of the pack house and toward the training fields.

# Chapter Twenty-Three
## *Trevor*

I could hear the whispers coming from the members of my pack, and it was making my blood boil. How can they disrespect me so boldly and disrespect their Luna? This is a matter that will also have to be addressed tonight. I will have to go over my speech again and make a few changes. I know the Elders think we should keep certain things quiet, but I am not sure that is wise. On the other hand, she would be hurt if the people only showed her respect because of her lineage. I know it's important for her to prove herself to the people. I need to have faith in my little wolf.

We reach my office, and the four of us enter. My trusted guards, Julian and Thomas, are already doing their rounds on this floor and the floor above, which leads to our apartment. I close my office door and invite them to sit.

"I cannot pretend to imagine what you two must be going through—giving up your home, title, and life to come here. I don't know about you, Zander, but after last night, my wolf does not want to destroy you. I don't feel any resentment. It's more like acceptance. I don't feel like killing you, but I am still jealous as a man that you touch her. Not everything can be fixed in a day, but I am sure we will grow to get along. It is, after all, the only way to truly make our mate happy. So if you are okay trying, so am I," I said to Kevin and Zander.

"I agree. I don't feel like I did yesterday toward you, and to be honest, I am also still jealous when it comes to the idea of being with you. Like later, when you go for a run and it is just the two of you. I know that this is going to take a while for us, but I am willing to try as well. I love her and want her, so I will do what it takes to keep her and make her happy. I would give it all up all over again for her. She is my world now, and I want to be there for her. Of course, I would like to contribute to your pack in the process," Zander said.

"Look, I love my pack, my family, and my friends. My best friend happens to be here along with one of my sisters. I am sure we can visit our families once in a while. So I am happy to do my part to protect someone as important as my sister is," Kevin added. He definitely was proud to call Aylin his sister. The way he puffed his chest when talking about her—he was almost boastful of her.

"Zander, I would like to make you a co-Alpha of the pack," I said bluntly, and he froze.

"What? I don't think we can do that. Especially since I am a werewolf, and this is a Lycan pack," Zander said.

"You don't realize what is happening to you, do you?" Nick chimed in.

"What do you mean?" Zander asked.

"What about you? Do you feel any different?" Nick asked Kevin.

"I have been having headaches and some pain in my muscles. That's about it," Kevin replied.

"Zander, you are now mated to Aylin. Aylin is part Lycan. When you mate a Lycan, your life ties to them, and you change with the mark she gives you," I explained.

After a minute, it's like a light bulb clicks, and his eyes grow.

"I am becoming a Lycan?" he asked, and Nick and I nodded.

"Wait. I am not mated to her, and I definitely didn't get marked by her," Kevin said to them. "So why ask if I feel different?"

"You would have been marked already. I think whatever activates in her awakens something in you. When she turned into a Lycan today, I noticed you stiffen and shake your head. For a second, it looked like your eyes glowed. Did she ever leave a mark of any kind on you?" Nick asked.

He started to shake his head and then paused.

"My shoulder." He raised his hand and laid it on his left shoulder.

"Show me," Nick said.

Kevin looked at him for a second, and then he took off his shirt and turned his back toward us. I looked at the spot on his shoulder blade. Just there, on one side of his shoulder, he had a crescent moon bite mark — a perfect indent of teeth, only smaller.

"When did she bite you there?" I asked curiously.

"We were really little; she was only a toddler. We were playing, and I was pretending to be helpless, and she was the big bad wolf."

We all chuckled at imagining little Aylin trying to be a big bad wolf. Guess nowadays, that wouldn't be hard for her to do.

"We were playing, and she jumped on my back and bit me. I remember it didn't hurt all that much, but our mom freaked out and pulled her off me. Aylin's mouth was covered in blood. My mom cleaned my back and took me to see the doctor. They thought it would heal fine and go away, but it scarred over. They figured it was because I didn't have my wolf yet, so I didn't have enough healing capabilities, even though it should have healed with what I did have." Kevin shrugged and then put his shirt back on.

"Well, now we know when she marked you. And that was probably why it didn't hurt, because let me tell you — aside from a mark, most bites suck!" Nick said, and we all laughed a bit at him.

"You are both going through the change, and it's only just starting. It will get more intense before it gets better," I told them.

"Now, about your position here. As I was saying, the events of this morning only confirmed my fears. I think it would be best to be a united front. You are a co-Alpha of Blood Moon and carry authority over all the pack. Only I can overrule you. However, in most things, we will need to be a united team—you, me, and Aylin."

"Are you sure about this?" Zander asked me skeptically. I would be too if I were him. Only yesterday, I was thinking about ripping out his spine when I saw him in the kitchen kissing my girl. Now, looking back, I just wished I would have joined right then.

"Yes, I am sure about this. I think it's the only way to keep her from getting on the wrong side of the pack. If they see we are a unit, working together, then they will be more accepting of the situation. I don't want anything that could hurt her," I said finally. That was the truth. If my pack didn't want her as a Luna because she had another Alpha mate, then she would be hurt. "I think she would like this as well," I added.

He and Kevin both nodded.

"So what would I do?" Zander asked.

"Well, for starters, we would both be involved in all pack business. Your ideas could bring an outside opinion, and we could divide responsibilities so we are not both—or only one of us—away from the pack for long amounts of time. That way, one or both of us are always here with Aylin," I told him.

He seemed to like this idea quite a bit. I knew he would, because as much as I didn't want to ever be away from her, thinking of times I get to have her all to myself had a nice ring to it.

"Sure you're not just trying to get rid of me?" Zander asked, cocking an eyebrow.

"Look, I handle multiple packs under my territory. I am in and out of here a lot anytime there is a dispute. It would be nice to have help in settling some of these matters. And with technology, we are able to call and video chat with our girl and have conference calls for work. If it's just me, I will be gone all the time. I would also like to be a part of her life, and this way, we are a team and show the pack that we truly trust each other," I explained. Everything I said was true, and honestly, I didn't like the idea of them being together all the time without me. I was accepting and didn't want to kill him anymore, but I still wanted time alone with my girl, and this could give us that time. If I had to share most of the time, fine, but now and then, I wanted her all to myself. I mean, I really just wanted her to myself constantly, but at least there was more of an acceptance now.

"Sounds good to me. When do I get started?" he asked.

"Well, this Saturday, when we have Aylin's Luna Ceremony, it is now also going to be your Alpha ceremony as well. We will say vows to the pack and to each other, much like a human wedding ceremony. Then, in the eyes of our laws, we will be one unit," I explained.

He smiled and nodded in agreement. I sighed, knowing that my responsibilities would be shared and I would get to actually spend more time with my mate. It made me beyond happy.

"Next week, we are handling a dispute between two packs. You will come with us, see how we do things, and start presenting yourself as the co-Alpha of Blood Moon. That way, they will know to respect you moving forward. However, Aylin will be traveling with us since the mating is new. I do not want to be far from her, as I am sure you do not either." I wasn't ready to be without her.

"No, I agree. So who is going on this trip?" he asked.

"You, me, Aylin, Kevin, since he is Aylin's guardian and protector — we will get to that in a moment — and then my protection, Thomas and Julian. Nick is going to stay here and see that the pack runs smoothly with Liam. It's always tricky when I have to leave right after getting back, and there is still a lot that needs to be done here. Sometimes, my pack feels neglected when my attention is so divided. I would give them all my attention like a pack Alpha should, but I have many packs to focus on, not just this one, and keeping the peace alone is a full-time job. So believe me when I say you are helping me."

He nodded, and I moved on to Kevin.

"Now, there is no higher honor I can give you than being a guardian. Here, we have protection details when we are out in public, as Lycans — especially those of power — tend to have targets on their backs. I have two. Some have more. I can't stand having protection as it is, so I took the minimum that I could. I do, however, trust Julian and Thomas with my life, as I should. Aylin trusts you, and it only makes sense that you, as her Guardian, be her protector and head of her guard."

Kevin thought about what I said and smiled.

"So my job is to babysit my sister? Is that what you just said to me?"

I frowned, and for once, I was stumped. Yeah, I didn't think of it that way, but yeah. I looked at him and grinned.

"I guess I am," I replied, and he laughed.

"Don't get me wrong, it was probably going to be like that no matter what with this need I have to protect her anyways and make sure she is safe. But to have someone else say so just makes it feel like I am babysitting. She is going to love it!"

He laughed harder, and I couldn't help but chuckle at what her reaction was going to be when we told her. I had a feeling that he was going to wish he was still just a Beta when it came to his sister.

"Now, I think we should keep all this a secret from her until tonight when we announce it. I want to see what she thinks about our plans for our pack."

"Our pack" was not something I ever thought I would say, and here I was, saying it to someone that was in love with the love of my life.

"I think we can manage that," said Zander, and Kevin snorted.

"Yeah, until she starts to think we are hiding something and uses her Alpha power to force us to tell her," Kevin said with a smirk at Zander.

That would be a misuse of her Alpha power, but I can't say I have never done something like that myself.

"I got this. She never even knew how I felt about her growing up, so we both know I can be good at hiding stuff from her," Zander quipped back.

However, his face fell just after realizing what he had said.

"I should have told her. I have so much to make up for."

"You have all the time in the world to make it up to her, and we all know you will," Kevin said, patting his shoulder.

"He is right! Stop worrying about what you did or didn't do in the past. We are here now, and the future is what matters for us all," I told him.

He smiled back at me and nodded, then did the same to Kevin.

"So tell me more about this trip we are taking and the dispute we are handling," Zander said, back to being the professional Alpha he was trained to be.

Nick stood and walked over to both Zander and Kevin, handing them folders.

"Here are the pack's details, the information about the dispute they are having, and the options we are going to be presenting to them. If you have any notes or any other ideas, we would be happy to hear them," Nick told them.

Zander and Kevin took time looking through the folders. They asked questions occasionally, and after a few minutes, they put the folders down, and we started planning how we would deal with the packs as a unit. This was, after all, the first time that Zander would be getting involved as a co-Alpha of the Blood Moon Pack.

"In the event that the packs do not agree, are you ready to destroy the orchard and have both packs help build the wall?" Zander asked.

"Yes. We do not have the resources to aid in such a build, as we have our members already spread pretty thin and have some projects of our own here that we need to finish with the pack we have taken in," Nick replied.

"What kind of things have you spread so thin?" Kevin asked.

"We have warriors that are training with the Lycan kings and serving there, and that is a regular rotation. Then, we have several that are helping other packs that have had crop damages, damages from storms, and rogue attacks. It has been pretty busy this year," Nick added.

Zander and Kevin seemed to mull this over for a moment.

"What if only one pack does not agree? Say that one is okay with what you have to offer, and the other does not—what happens then?" Zander asked.

"It would depend on what they have to say and how they respond. If they retaliate, then we will have to take more drastic measures with them. If they have ideas of their own that are not unreasonable, we may be willing to hear them out. It all depends on what they have to say and how they respond. Hopefully, this all can be dealt with amicably, but we are the law as Lycans, and if they cannot be dealt with, they can be removed," I reminded them.

Zander definitely got that reminder. He was present when I threatened his sister, reminding her who she was speaking to and that her family could be removed and replaced as the Alphas of their pack.

"Okay, I think you have a great plan in place, and I can't wait to get started as your Co-Alpha," Zander said, standing and shaking my hand.

I nodded at him. I had a good feeling about all of this.

"Is there anything else you wish to discuss?" Kevin asked.

"At this time, no. However, Zander, we usually have morning meetings to go over our daily itinerary and discuss any issues that have come to light, and you will be expected to be part of them moving forward. These meetings usually start at seven a.m. every morning."

Zander nodded in understanding.

"Kevin, as head of the Luna's guard, you will also be required to join some of these meetings if any of it includes the Luna."

Kevin nodded as well.

"Well, if that is all, then we will go and meet Aylin at the training fields. I am eager to see what she does with the sparring partners today. Liam said something about starting with others new to training and seeing what she can do," Kevin said, pride shining from him as he talked about his sister.

"Is that so?" I was intrigued. I would like to see what my little wolf can do. I did have a few things to do this morning, but some of them could wait.

"If you would like, Alpha, I can deal with some of the smaller issues this morning while you go and assess the warriors and your mate's ability," Nick said. He had a knack for knowing my intentions. He even provided me with the right words in case someone tried to question my motives for not taking care of my responsibilities. Like anyone would question me as Alpha.

"Thank you, Beta. Keep me updated on your progress." I nodded at him and turned to follow Zander and Kevin out of the office.

"Would you like me to still leave Ruby to you, Alpha?" Nick questioned. I had almost forgotten about her. I still needed to handle her punishment. I did feel that Aylin should be present for that as well.

"Yes, I do wish for her to be left alone. Aylin and I will discuss her punishment, and I want Aylin present for the sentencing," I added. Aylin may very well be the one issuing it.

"Yes, Alpha." Nick nodded in a slight bow and started going through the folders on my desk of the morning duties we had already discussed. I was looking forward to seeing my mate kick some Lycan ass. I was also looking forward to running the perimeter after lunch with her. I would have her shift into her Lycan form, which I was very eager to see again, and Bane was very eager to meet her Lycan wolf, Mona.

'You bet I am,' Bane quipped, running in the back of my mind. He was acting like a lovesick puppy. I smiled at it.

'Such a fierce Lycan you are being,' I taunted him. He stopped and glowered in my thoughts. He knew I was teasing him, but he had helped me build a reputation as a fierce, badass Lycan ruler, so questioning him when he was acting like that made him a little annoyed.

'She is my mate, and I have not yet gotten to meet her. You have kept her from me,' he retorted.

'She was not ready for you. However, she is now that we are mated, and I am sure Mona is going to be just as excited as you are to meet,' I added to placate him. It worked. He instantly went back to yipping in excitement at the thought of Mona. He had barely shut up about her since we saw her in her Lycan form this morning.

We arrived at the training fields in time to walk up and see my little wolf get tackled from behind right after she knocked one of the pack's warriors to the ground. She was facing two opponents. My hackles went up, and I growled. Kevin placed his hand on my shoulder and held on. I looked over and saw he also had a hand on Zander's shoulder.

"If you two go barreling in there to rescue her, she will be pissed, and your asses will end up on the ground. If I were you, I would wait and see what she does to the poor sap that just tackled her."

I was surprised for a second that he stopped me. The kid had some balls, that's for sure, stopping two Alphas, but he was her guardian and knew her better than anyone. Of course, I knew he was right. It just didn't sit well with me or my Lycan that someone had put their hands on my mate, even in a sparring fight.

"All my instincts say to go and protect her. This is so hard," Zander complained.

"Then be my guest. I was just giving you a warning and reminding you that she is not a prim and proper wolf that needs coddling. She will be angry with you. Not to mention, if you do go in there to try to protect her, you will damage the work she is doing to prove herself to the pack. If you want her wrath, then go ahead." Kevin let us both go and shrugged his shoulders. He crossed his arms over his chest and looked from us to Aylin like he was waiting for us to decide whether we would interfere or let her handle things herself. The struggle to stay when my Lycan wanted me to protect her was extremely hard.

"No matter how hard this is, I am not going up there. Let's see what my little wolf can do." I smiled a cocky smile at Kevin, matching his stance, folding my arms over my chest, and moving my attention back to my mate.

Aylin wasn't down long. She rolled out from under the attacker and got back to her feet in a flash, and the growl that came from her made the hair on my neck stand up. The warrior she was fighting took a few steps back and then regained his composure. He attacked, and she dodged repeatedly. It took a moment to realize that she was toying with him. She went low, swung her leg out, and knocked him on his ass. Now, the other one she had knocked down and this one were both on their feet and advancing. The urge to go to her was growing.

They advanced on her and attacked in unison. She fought them both off with ease and a grace I had never seen before. She was more coordinated in her strikes and fighting than most women are on the dance floor. It was simply amazing to watch. They landed a few hits, but she kept up with them, not letting the blows slow her down. At first, I thought they were taking it easy on her. That was until they looked at each other with shocked expressions on their faces.

Then she let them have it. No longer playing around, she attacked. She punched and kicked with precision, and in a matter of seconds, both Lycans were on the ground—knocked out. Damn, that's my girl. The pride I felt now was much more powerful than the drive to go protect her, and I was glad I stayed away. However, I wanted to see what she could really do.

I walked up to the training ring she was in as they were asking who wanted to volunteer next out of the elite warriors. Damn, already up to the elite. Let's see what my little wolf can do against me. Just as someone went to step up, they saw me enter the ring behind her, and they stopped and bowed their heads. The others quickly followed suit. She looked at them and turned around. When her eyes landed on me, I could see the lust and fire burn in them, then turn to determination. She understood I was stepping up to take her on, and I had a feeling she was going to give me her all. No games here.

Everyone got quiet. The warrior that stepped up quickly stepped back, and the anticipation around us grew.

"Are you ready for a real match, little wolf?" I asked cockily.

"Are you sure you want to do this in front of so many of your warriors? I mean, it would look bad to be taken out by your little wolf, wouldn't it?" she asked, taunting me. Oh, little wolf, someone was becoming a little too confident.

"Oh, I think I can handle you, little wolf." I smiled predatorily at her. She smiled back sweetly, and for a second, I thought she wanted to attack me in a very different way. Then she struck.

# Chapter Twenty-Four
## *Aylin*

I was both delighted and surprised when Trevor stepped into the ring. The fear that he would kick my ass and the excitement that I might be able to kick his ass were heady. He smiled at me, all cocky and sure of himself, and then I got a wicked thought. I smiled sweetly and let him see my want and need for him. Then it happened—he dropped his guard ever so slightly, and I took complete advantage.

I struck hard and fast. I tackled him to the ground. I could hear the people around us cheering and yelling.

"Get him, Luna."

"Come on, Alpha, get her."

"Whooo, Luna gonna kick some ass."

One after another, people cheered, catcalled, and even snickered.

Trevor was back to being the warrior and Alpha in no time, rolling us so he pinned me. More catcalls came from the sidelines. I think I will enjoy kicking each one of their asses after this. I was able to wiggle myself under him to the point where I could move my legs better, and then I brought my foot up in a high kick and hit him from behind. He lost his grip, and I bucked him off me. He was quick to get on his feet, but so was I.

We attacked, dodged, and struck each other. I had a feeling he was holding back, and it infuriated me. So I hit him once, almost as hard as I could, and sent him flying across the ring. Damn, I knew I was strong, but that was crazy. I laughed at the look on his face when he stood again—the sheer disbelief. I held up my hands and motioned for him to bring it.

"Come on, Alpha, show me what you got."

He smiled and struck. This time, he didn't hold back. He came at me hard, like he would an elite warrior or even an enemy. The fight went on for another twenty minutes and ended with both of us out of breath and covered in scrapes and bruises.

After taking in his appearance, I threw my head back and started to laugh. Oddly enough, even through the pain, this was fun for me. I loved it, and I was so happy that he was part of it. He watched me for a moment, looked me over, and then started to laugh as well. His laugh was infectious, and at that moment, I realized I hadn't heard him really laugh before. I really liked how it sounded.

Apparently, everyone around us hadn't really heard him laugh either. They were staring at him like they were seeing him for the first time. Even Liam was shocked and yet looked like he was trying to hold back his own laughter.

We called it a draw and decided to go back for lunch. Liam left the warriors with instructions for the rest of the training, and then we all headed back to the pack house.

Along the way, several warriors walked over to me and struck up conversations about training regimens and whether I would want to try other things. One asked me if I would try the obstacle course. I had meant to today but hadn't gotten around to it.

Everyone seemed interested to see what I could do, and honestly, I was curious myself. After all, it had only been a few days, and I had just had a one-on-one with the Lycan Alpha, Trevor Gideon, and it was a draw. He hadn't lost a fight in a really long time. Rumor had it he had even beaten his own father when he was in the mid-level ranks of training. I will have to ask him if that is true or not.

The walk was pleasant, and the more I talked to the warriors, the more I felt like I belonged here. They were impressed by what I had done today, and I had earned some respect, but the fact that they were including me and asking me to train with them made me so happy. Feeling like I belonged was foreign to me, and I couldn't stop smiling or keep my eyes from watering.

"What's wrong, my queen?" Zander said, stopping in front of me and wiping away a tear.

"Nothing is wrong. I am just happy. Really happy. I have never been asked to join so many people in anything before. I feel like I belong here," I told him honestly.

I could see the shame in his eyes for what I had gone through at our old pack. I could also see the love and happiness he had for me. He smiled and hugged me.

"You do belong here! You are going to be the best Luna for these people," he exclaimed.

My eyes watered some more, and I let him hold and hug me.

"Come on, you two, we do actually have a schedule to keep today. After lunch, we have to relieve the warriors on the borderlines," Trevor reminded us.

"You know the south and east is a large area, and if it is as you say, maybe more of us should help," Kevin said. I just think he didn't like the idea of me being somewhere that could be dangerous. I loved him, but I was sure I could take care of myself. Besides, it's not like I would be there alone.

"You are right. Why don't you and Zander take the south end of the territory, and Aylin and I will take the east? We will call on you since you will be closer if anything happens, and you do the same."

Kevin nodded, and he seemed a little more content knowing he would be closer to me if anything happened, but I could sense he was still not entirely thrilled.

"It will be okay, Kevin. I have Trevor with me, and you and Zander will not be far. I will be okay!"

He looked at me for a moment and nodded. My three overprotective men—it's surprising they even let me in the training fields. Although, I also wonder if they did because they knew it was a safe place with help if anything happened and that I would kick their ass if they denied me.

We made our way to the dining room and helped ourselves to some of the spread that the omega had laid out for the pack for lunch. I will have to be sure to do something for them. They work so hard and deserve to be appreciated. I will talk to Trevor about it later.

Goddess, the food was good. They served barbecue chicken, some sautéed Brussels sprouts with bacon, baked beans, and cornbread. It was so good that I had a second helping of it all. With my second helping, I took a bit longer than the guys to eat as I was trying to get past that proverbial wall you hit when you're full. So I was the last one done, and they were all waiting on me.

"Okay, okay, I see you all staring. I am ready, let's go," I told them, shaking my head.

Liam left, going back to the practice field to work with the warriors—they had extra training today. Nikki left to go to the library. She said something about wanting to research gods and their weaknesses. I loved that she was looking out for me. But she had a point—we would need to know if gods had weaknesses if we were going to try to deal with the one coming for me. Then Trevor, Zander, Kevin, and I made our way to the far side of the pack.

When we got to the southeast, where the borders met, I gave Kevin a quick hug and Zander a long kiss. I asked them to be careful, and they said the same in turn, and then we shifted—Zander and Kevin into wolves and Trevor and me into Lycans.

For a brief moment, they all stared at me. I know no one has seen a white Lycan in centuries, but this was a little weird for me. I huffed, and they all seemed to come to their senses. Kevin and Zander took off to cover their territory, and I turned to follow Trevor.

We had only been patrolling the border for about thirty minutes when Trevor nipped at my side.

"I think it is time for our Lycans to meet. Bane is dying to meet Mona," he said.

Mona had also just been asking when she would get to meet Trevor's Lycan and Zander's wolf. They were, after all, mates as well.

"Mona agrees she wants to meet her mates as well." So I let Mona take control, and I was pushed to the back of my mind while she took the driver's seat. It was a weird feeling watching everything through my eyes but not controlling my actions.

The moment Bane was in control, things changed. He growled at us, and I felt a little uneasy, but Mona seemed prepared. Then they started to fight — claws and biting.

'What the hell is going on, Mona? Why is he attacking us? I thought you two wanted to see each other! Stop this now!' I was shouting at her.

'We are fine, Aylin. We are fighting for dominance, and once he claims dominance over me, he will mate me,' she replied.

'Woah, wait—you didn't say anything about fights or sexy Lycan fun time,' I replied. Nope, I sure as hell didn't want this. They went back and forth, throwing each other to the ground and trying to get behind and on top. Several times, he bit us around the hind legs. Damn, that hurt. The ass just grabbed us by the back of my neck. Then I felt our body go limp.

'What are you doing? Bitch, fight back! Don't let him bite us like that!' I yelled at her.

'I cannot. Once he has us in his grip like this, it makes us compliant and calms us. He is going to mount us now,' she said in an almost wistful, longing way. She really wanted him to do this. I, however, was trying to figure out how to get control back and get the hell out of here.

Then she looked down, and I saw what she did. That fucking thing is not going to fit in us, and I lost it.

'Bitch, move! We need to run—that will tear us in half! It's as thick as a leg! Where the fuck does he think it is going to go?' I was trying to take the driver's seat back at this point. I was not going to be ripped in half by a one-eyed anaconda. Fuck this.

The problem was, I couldn't take control. His bite had us both subdued, and she wasn't willing to relinquish to me anytime soon.

I felt him grab our hind end and maneuver behind us. Then he was there. The head of the monstrous cock attached to Bane was at our entrance. He started to rub it against us, wetting it and preparing to take us.

'No, no, no, no, no!' I screamed at her in my head.

'It will feel good. You will see—he will claim us, and it will feel as good as it does when Trevor is inside us.'

Yeah, somehow, I was doubting that very much. They will have to sew me back together after this! Besides, the first time with Trevor hurt too.

'Only in the beginning, remember?'

Yeah, I remembered. After the initial pain, there was a lot of pleasure from him and from Zander.

He thrust forward, and the roar that came from Mona and the scream from me were deafening. I was right—I am going to die on his dick. He just impaled me, and now I am going to die. He stayed still inside to try to let us get accommodated, but I just wanted him out. We needed to get away and off this damn thing. I whimpered.

'Tell him to move or something because he is too big— it hurts! Bitch, do something or let me back in control so I can!' I screamed at her.

She whimpered, and he started to move. After a moment of him driving into us, he released our neck. Mona braced us on her paws and angled our ass up more. This made him go deeper, and at first, it was more painful. We were stretched further because of it, but then the pleasure she promised started, and even though it was watered down for me, I couldn't help but enjoy the sensation.

I could only imagine the pain and pleasure she was getting from this. It had to be more intense than what I was feeling, and what I felt was a lot. The sounds they were making—the growls and whimpers—were, in a weird way, erotic. Maybe I was just messed up. To someone walking through the woods, it must have sounded more like fighting.

Then I felt a searing pain in my shoulder—the same one Trevor had marked. And just as fast as the pain was there, an explosion of ecstasy followed. We went hurling over the cliff, over and over. The orgasm was ripping through me. The sensation was amazing. He was driving his huge cock into us faster than I thought possible. I couldn't stop spiraling, and then I felt him release inside of us. His hot cum sprayed and filled me, then spilled from us.

Mona was right—it felt amazing. Now I think I could die another way. Death by good dick was definitely a good way to go, 'cause I didn't know if I could stand right now, let alone patrol.

Bane seemed to have other ideas, however, as he thrust into us again. This time, the pain subsided faster, and the pleasure started to build much sooner. Mona was whimpering, which seemed to spur him on, and he was pounding harder than before.

Yep—death by good dick and orgasms, here we come.

This time, when he chased us over the cliff, the last thing I was aware of was Bane howling and spilling inside us—and then nothingness. Quiet, calm, blissful nothingness.

When I opened my eyes and started to move around, the first thing I noticed was that I was no longer in the back seat of my mind. Mona was lying there, happy and content. The next thing I noticed was the throbbing between my legs. Damn, he destroyed my pussy. That is so fucking sore. I have never been more happy to be a werewolf in my life! Thank you for rapid healing.

I may not have died, but I am positive I came close. Anacondas are deadly creatures.

Then I noticed I was no longer in Lycan form. At some point, when I was out cold, I must have transformed back. I was wrapped in a blanket, which I was grateful for since I had no clothes on my body. And that's when I noticed I was alone.

I looked around and noticed my clothes on a nearby rock. I stood on shaky legs and made my way toward them. Not only were my clothes there, but a bottle of shampoo as well.

That's when I saw a spring running just a little ways down. He must have planned for it to happen here so I could take a dip in the spring after and clean myself up a little. I just don't think he was anticipating me passing out.

I gathered my things and made my way down to the spring. I set my stuff on a flat rock to the side and tested the water with my foot. It was warm, and I couldn't stop the smile on my face — a natural hot spring, hell yeah.

I wasted no time and got right in. The water felt amazing, and instantly, my muscles started to ease up. I started to feel better everywhere — including the soreness between my thighs. I sighed as it eased.

I let myself enjoy the water for another couple of moments and then got to work washing myself. I cleaned my hair and body and swam around in the spring to rinse off. When I was done and felt better, I made my way back to where I left my clothes and blanket.

Sitting there was a very smug Trevor, just watching me in the water.

"Look here — I seem to have come across my very own water nymph," he taunted me.

"Sorry, no nymph here. My vagina was recently broken and will need some time to heal," I told him, smiling. He laughed at that, and I loved the sound. It made me laugh, but I was serious as well. I may need a day to heal after what Bane did to my lady bits.

Trevor stood and held up a towel for me. I walked out of the water into a chilly breeze and quickly dried off with the towel. After getting dressed, Trevor and I walked along the border.

"So why aren't we back in Lycan form for the patrol?" I asked as he took my hand in his and intertwined our fingers.

"It's been mostly quiet, and our time is almost up. I figured we could just walk for a bit. Besides, if anything happens, we can shift in seconds and deal with it," he said, shrugging his left shoulder.

It was getting late now, the shadows were long, and I had to wonder how long I had slept. It had to be hours, which meant he had to patrol on his own, and I knew that meant he kept checking on me to make sure I was safe. His attention was divided, which was not a good thing at all.

"I am sorry you had to take the shift alone," I told him, genuinely sorry for not being able to assist in defending our pack.

"It was fine. I usually do it alone, and I do not fault you for being tired," he said, winking at me. I really liked his fun banter. I was smiling like an idiot, even though I was red from what he implied.

We walked, content in silence, after that for a while. I watched as the colors in the sky started to change from blue to pinks and oranges. It was about seven-thirty, and our replacements showed up. I bid them a good, safe night and headed back to the pack house with Trevor.

"We have a pack meeting tonight that you will need to be present for. When we get back, you should change and meet me in my office. We will have to get a late dinner after—I apologize. But since dinner is with my mom in our suite tonight, I am okay with it being delayed," he said, and I laughed.

I was worried about meeting his mom, but she was a good and fair Luna, so I could learn a lot from her. I just hoped she liked me.

"I think it will be okay. Are Zander and Kevin joining us for that dinner?" I asked.

"Yes, they will be there, and so will Nick and Nikki. Liam is otherwise engaged tonight on rounds, taking over for the warriors on the north border."

That made me a little sad that Liam wouldn't be there, but I got it. The main leaders of the pack shared responsibilities, so we couldn't all be together all the time. I was glad that I would have some support there when it came to his mom.

# Chapter Twenty-Five
## *Aylin*

In our apartment, we all went to our separate rooms. Now that we are mated, I need to talk to Trevor about the room situation. I won't be sharing a room with one and not the other. Maybe it would be best to keep our own rooms and then just sleep together. I don't know. We will figure it out.

I took a quick shower and put on a nice dark blue evening dress. This would be appropriate for the pack meeting and to meet his mother in. Granted, you don't usually have to dress up for either, but I would like to look nice at the first one I will be attending for both.

As I finish putting on the little bit of makeup I allow myself — mostly because I do not know how to apply it — someone knocked on my door. A moment later, Trevor enters and walks over to me.

"Well, well, well, look at this! You are absolutely beautiful, little wolf," he said. He looked at me as if he would devour me. My body grew flush, and I could feel my own desire grow. Oh, my moon goddess, do I want this man! He looked amazing in his black, expensive Italian suit. I just want to rip it off and take him now. I give myself a mental shake and take a deep breath to calm myself down.

"I think you will have to come up with a new nickname for me. I am not such a little wolf now." I tried to change the subject. The last thing I needed to do was meet the pack members and his mom with wet panties.

"Oh no, to me, you will always be my little wolf. However, if you would like, I will think of something new to call you!" he said, smiling a wicked smile at me. This man had a line straight to my core with just a look. Why can't I control myself with him and Zander? He knew it too; I could see it in his expression that he had smelled my arousal.

"Do we have to do this? Can we just stay here and enjoy each other's company for a while?" I asked coyly. I wanted him, and right now I was losing the will to hold out. He groaned and closed his eyes. He looked like he was in pain, and I started to get worried.

"Ok, pet," he said with a smirk. I think I like little wolf better. "You are going to be the death of me. We have to go to the pack meeting and then meet with my mother, but after all that is done, I am all yours—I promise you that!" he said, his eyes skimming down my body, which only made me flush and want him more. "I have something for you," he said after a moment, and the distraction pulled me out of my dirty thoughts.

"You don't have to do anything for me," I told him. I was feeling a little shy all of a sudden. I never had a guy do things for me and get me gifts for no reason before.

"It goes with your dress. Here." He handed me a blue felt gift box. I opened it hesitantly, and inside were a set of beautiful blue sapphire earrings and a platinum chain necklace with a sapphire teardrop pendant. It was breathtaking.

"You really didn't have to do this," I told him. I could feel the tears starting in my eyes. Damn, I just finished my makeup.

"I already had them—for my future mate. I am so happy that I get to give them to you finally after all these years of searching for you." His words were my undoing, and I couldn't hold back my tears.

"What's wrong, pet?" he said, brushing them away.

"Nothing, I am just so happy, Trevor. I love you." The words that left my mouth shocked me. I couldn't believe in such a short time that I was actually saying them to him, but it was the truth, and I knew it with every fiber of my being. I loved this man.

His eyes were so large, with a smile that was nothing but sheer joy. He wrapped his arms around me and spun me in a circle. When he stopped, his mouth dipped to mine and kissed me as if I was the air he needed to breathe. By the time we were done, I was greedily sucking in air to replace what he had stolen from me. The look in his eyes was enough to take what little breath I still had away completely.

"I love you, Aylin. You are my life and my whole world. I have searched for you for decades, and now I never want to live a moment without you here with me." His words meant more to me than he could possibly know, and more tears fell. He gently wiped them away and kissed me on both cheeks, then the tip of my nose.

"Come, pet, let's go. We need to meet up with Zander and your brother, and then go address our pack together. We have quite a lot of news for the pack tonight," he said with a knowing smirk that had me wondering what he was planning. I let him lead me out of my room and into the living room, where Kevin and Zander were already waiting for us.

Both looked very good in the suits they had on. Zander had a black suit with a white button-up that just looked good and classy, and my brother had a gray suit and a blue shirt that I swear only he could pull off. It really complimented his boyish charm.

"You look amazing, both of you!" I said to them. They were both staring at me. Zander's mouth had dropped open, and he seemed to be lost for words.

"You are stunning, sis," Kevin said, and Zander seemed to give himself a mental shake and then gave me a smile that was so carnal that I felt myself redden under his stare. His sinful gaze promised that he would devour me, and I wanted him to.

"Yes, you are absolutely breathtaking, my queen," he added. I really didn't think I could become redder than I was at that moment, and I couldn't help the smile plastered on my face. I have never felt more beautiful in all my life. These men, in such a short time, have made me happier than I have ever been. Thank you, moon goddess, for this blessing! I have been thanking her a lot lately. My heart was so full, looking at the three most important people in my world and seeing them all smile back at me.

"Alright everyone, it's time to go," Trevor said, getting us all out of our trance. We left the apartment, and when we started down the hall, Trevor took my left arm and Zander took my right. As we walked down the hall, Liam and Nick took up spots on either side of Kevin, who was directly behind me. When we got to the main level, Thomas and Julian stepped in front of us and led the way. I was surrounded by the best of the pack, and I felt both safe and yet caged. What a weird feeling. I knew I wasn't, but for some reason, that feeling came all the same.

I was led to the back of the pack house. I looked around since this is one area I really haven't gone to yet. We stepped onto a lit patio. There were lights streaming back and forth all along the patio, and shepherd hooks with hanging lanterns throughout the lawn to cast light for you to be able to move around and see where you are going, but not too much to not enjoy the night.

We walked down one of three paths. The one to the left seemed to go into the village, the one to the right toward a massive garden, and the one straight ahead took us to a raised platform and dais where they had more fairy lights hanging overhead.

We went straight for the dais. When we got up there, Trevor had three large throne-like chairs and four others to the sides of them. Trevor had me sit dead center. As soon as I sat, there were whispers. I knew in my old pack that the Alpha was usually the center, so I started to worry. Trevor then had Zander sit to my right, and next to him sat Liam, then my brother Kevin. Nick took the chair next to Trevor's. That left one open, and I wondered who it was for. Once we were all seated and Thomas and Julian took their positions on either side of the dais to keep pack members back, Trevor looked at me and smiled.

"We are going to wait just a few more moments to make sure everyone has arrived," he told me.

"Who is missing? Should Nikki be sitting here?" I asked, looking at the empty chair.

"No, that chair is for the former Luna," he said, giving me another reassuring smile. I have not yet met his mother, as she has been out of town since I got here. I was hoping to meet her at dinner, and I don't know why it escaped my mind that she would be at a mandatory pack meeting. Way to go, Aylin. I mentally chastised myself.

After just a few minutes, the crowd parted, and a beautiful, lithe, tall blonde Lycan made her way to the dais. She was elegant and graceful and had a presence to her that screamed sophisticated. Everything that I could never possibly be. I knew at that moment I was looking at Trevor's mother. I also knew that most of his features must have come from his father. But he did get her eyes and tan skin. She was one of the most beautiful Lycans I have ever seen.

She stopped before us, and Trevor rose from his chair. I followed suit, and so did the others sitting around us. She bowed her head to Trevor and then to me. I bowed my head back in a show of respect to the Luna of the pack. When I looked up again, she was standing in front of me. Luckily, I didn't jump out of my skin. How can a woman in such heels make no noise when she moves? Seriously, those things had to be at least five inches tall.

"I am so happy to finally meet you, my dear," she said, and then hugged me. I heard the people in the crowd murmuring and couldn't bring myself to care. I hugged her back. When she pulled away, she was smiling at me, and I swear I could see unshed tears swimming in her eyes. She nodded at me and walked to her chair and sat down. The rest of us followed behind her. Trevor gave the crowd another couple of minutes to finish filling in and then stood to address the pack as a whole. I knew from pack meetings at home that he would call on those he needed to address, and only then did they rise and walk forward, so I stayed seated. I was not sure how things were done here, but I would do what I know till I am told otherwise.

"Good evening, Bloodmoon Pack. I have quite a few announcements to make tonight, as much has come to pass in a very short amount of time." Trevor's voice was loud and clear. He went on to talk about the project of the greenhouse and the playground and the ideas they had for both. He told the pack that there would be a list to sign up to volunteer for both. If there were no volunteers, then they would choose only one project, and they would be willing to pay for the labor, but at that point, only one project could be done due to the labor costs. The pack didn't seem to like the idea of only one being chosen, and there were some debates going around as to which one would be chosen.

"Please calm down, everyone. We will wait and see how many volunteers we get, and if there are not enough, we will decide at that time. The list will be in the pack house lobby if you do wish to sign up, and the list will be out till the end of next weekend. That will give us about a week and a half to see if we will have enough volunteers, and if we do, we can get started on the projects right away. If we don't, you will hear which project will be chosen by the following Wednesday so we can get started on the build before it gets too cold," he let them know.

I already knew he wanted to proceed with the playground, but the greenhouses are necessary to provide food throughout the year. I would have chosen the greenhouse because by the time the playground is done, most kids will not really be playing on it. Then again, with us being werewolves and our body temps running higher, they might. I guess he would know better than I, since I never really played on the playground back home as a kid. That is why my parents bought a small swing set for the backyard.

"Now, for the next order of business. We have two packs fighting over land, and I will be leaving next week to address this issue. I will be using it as a training tool to teach my new Co-Alpha about handling disputes with the packs I manage."

The crowd was deafening as they all started asking what he meant. Trevor raised his hand to silence them.

"As you know, I have found my true mate." He looked back at me and held out his hand for me to join him. I stood and walked over. "This is Aylin, your future Luna. We will be having her Luna ceremony this Friday, and along with her Luna ceremony, we will celebrate two others: Zander of the North Woodland Pack."

Zander stood and walked up next to me. "He was to be their future Alpha; however, as Aylin's other fated mate, he will be a Co-Alpha to me and share in the responsibilities of our growing pack."

This had the entire pack talking—some were curious, some confused, and others angry.

Trevor raised his hand again. Slowly, the crowd's chatter died down.

"This decision did not come lightly. As many of you know, this is new territory. However, after talking with the Elders and my Beta and Gamma, I do feel this is the best choice for our pack. He will be sharing in the responsibilities of helping this pack and monitoring the neighboring packs for minor disputes, freeing me to be here more often for you."

The last statement seemed to get their attention. They seemed to like the idea of their Alpha being around more.

I watched him as he continued talking about the responsibilities we three would share, and the more he spoke, the more the pack seemed to come around and even grow to appreciate that there would be more help here.

They have had the Beta and Gamma here to help when the Alpha is away — and sometimes just the Delta. But from what I gathered, the Delta goes to the Lycan King's court a lot and is there on and off for more than half the year in total with time there and travel. So, to say that there would be more help and shared responsibility seemed to put them at ease for something that is such uncharted territory.

I also could not help but feel the love I have for him grow as he paints a picture of us all working together as a family and unit.

How could I have gotten so lucky with my partners? I was so worried about them killing each other or having to choose one that I didn't want to think about what it would mean to have them both and what that family would be like. I can't wait to see how this goes now.

"I would also like to take this time to introduce someone that is extremely important to your Luna. This is another unconventional add to our pack, as usually family does not come with you when you find your mate. However, Kevin is not only Aylin's brother, but he is her guardian."

This had the pack talking and questions flying all over again. It is rare for a guardian to exist and usually only happens to royal bloodlines. Trevor raised his hand, and the chatter slowly quieted down.

Trevor told me what he wanted me to do on the way down here, and I know the pack will know soon enough — at least for those that didn't already.

I stepped forward, and Trevor unzipped the back of my dress, and I slid it down. Standing there in a tank top and hot pants, I shifted to my werewolf form.

The gasps were audible even from the back of the pack. Then, while they were all talking, before their eyes, I doubled my size.

The crowd, as one, seemed to step back. I went back to my normal size and then transformed into my Lycan form.

My white and silver fur sparkled in the moonlight. Slowly, the entirety of the pack got on their knees and bowed to me.

I shifted back to my human form, and Trevor quickly covered me with my dress again while all eyes were cast down. Zander and Kevin both stood in front of me, just in case anyone didn't have their eyes cast down.

Trevor was convinced no one would dare look up until told because that would be considered disrespect to a royal. For all anyone knew, I was the most royal being for both werewolves and Lycans, as I am the only one alive today that is pure white. The silver strands are what tie me to the goddess.

Just as he said, everyone was still down on their knees, and their heads were bowed in submission.

"You may rise and greet your new Luna, our Co-Alpha Alpha Zander, and our Luna's guardian, Kevin."

No one moved. We all looked out at the pack as they stayed where they were. Understanding dawned on me. I stepped forward.

"You may rise," I said kindly to my new pack and family.

At once, they all stood, looking at the four of us, and then the crowd erupted in applause.

My heart constricted, and I had to wipe away the tears.

They were accepting us! All of us.

I looked behind me to where the former Luna was sitting, and she, as well, was no longer sitting but clapping with the rest of the pack, with a smile across her face.

I looked around at everyone, and then to Trevor, Zander, and Kevin.

This was real.

This was happening.

We are accepted and whole, and I am happier than I have ever been in my life.

Trevor put his hand up again, and the pack silenced down once more.

"I am beyond pleased that you have accepted your new Luna and our newest pack members. Please help me in making them feel at home and part of our pack. I trust you all to work with us just as much as we will be there for you!" he said to the crowd.

"I want to thank you all for coming and showing your respect for this pack in taking time out of your busy schedules. We will see all of you Friday for the Luna ceremony, and again, anyone willing to volunteer for the projects ahead of us, there will be a sign-up sheet in the lobby. I hope there will be lots of volunteers so we can get both projects done."

He finished, and the crowd started clapping again.

We stood there for a minute, and then once the crowd stopped clapping, they did a slight bow and started to break up. Some hung around talking to friends, and others grabbed their kids and started their way home. I had asked Trevor if I should address the pack tonight, but he insisted on waiting till my Luna ceremony to address the pack. I will need to come up with a speech. That made me feel queasy. I am no good with crowds.

Several pack members walked up to the dais and bowed to us. Well, to me. Then they addressed Trevor. Trevor stood there and talked to them each in turn with so much patience and answered questions about the projects and what we realistically would be looking at when it came to the work and materials. He even listened to some of their suggestions, and I couldn't help the admiration and respect I felt for him as an Alpha. Theirs and mine.

Once they were done and the crowd dispersed a bit more, Trevor looked at the rest of us and motioned toward the house. The time had come for dinner with his mother and the former Luna. *Well, here I go. Please, Moon Goddess, let her like me.* We all made our way into the house and up the stairs to our apartment. The entire way, I couldn't help the feeling of panic I was having. *What if*'s just kept running through my head. I couldn't stop them.

*What if she hates me? Would Trevor decide not to keep me? What if she does like me but is not ok with Zander? Would she push for me to reject him?*

I felt my brother grab my hand, and I let the contact calm me. I am not sure if it was the guardian thing or the fact that he has been dealing with my emotions longer than Trevor or Zander, but he was able to pick up on my anxiety before the others. Whatever the reason, I am happy he is here with me. He ran his thumb in little circles on the top of my hand as we made our way to our apartment.

"Aylin, you have nothing to worry about, you know. I am sure the former Luna is going to love you," Kevin said, and I gave him a small smile. He knew exactly why my anxiety kicked up.

"I guess I am just worried, you know. I have a lot of *what if*'s going on in my head, and I am scared that she will either not like me or not like the two of you," I told him honestly, and he smiled down at me.

"You know even if she doesn't like you or, Goddess forbid, doesn't like Zander or myself, that it is not going to matter? She cannot do anything about it if she doesn't," he said. I knew he was trying to be reassuring, but it didn't really help. She could probably influence Trevor, and he could decide he doesn't want us or just them here. Then again, he really wants me to be happy here, so I doubt he will really be willing to get rid of anyone that could have a major effect on me.

The rest of the walk to the apartment was in silence. I didn't want to talk about all the *what if*'s—really, it was like breathing life into them. I tried to distract myself by thinking of the workout and fighting earlier. I definitely still wanted to try that obstacle course. It seemed like it was working until we got to the door of the apartment, and I had to take a couple deep breaths to remain calm.

# Chapter Twenty-Six
## *Aylin*

When we got to the dining room, the table was already set, and the former Luna was already seated to the left of the Alpha's chair. She had left the right for me; it seems as if it is the Luna's chair. As we entered the room, she rose from her chair, walked over to Trevor, and pulled him into a big hug.

"I missed you so much, my dear," she said to Trevor. Her eyes sparkled as she looked him over. "You look good, son. You look happy." She was smiling, and it lit up her entire face.

"I missed you too, Mom. I am happy now. Please allow me to introduce you properly. This is my mate and our new Luna, Aylin; her brother and guardian, Kevin; and her other mate, Zander," Trevor told her. "Guys, this is my mother, Luna Carrie Gideon." He looked at his mother fondly as he introduced her to us and then looked back at me. I smiled at her and walked forward and reached out my hand to shake hers.

She looked at my hand for just a second and then wrapped me in a hug so tight and so fast my breath was knocked out of me. It took me a moment to respond between the shock and loss of breath, but after a moment, I hugged her back. She pulled away and looked at me with a fond smile and warmth in her beautiful eyes. I instantly started to relax.

She then walked up to Zander and Kevin. I held my breath for a moment and watched. Worry flowed through me when she approached Zander. To my surprise, she smiled at him and wrapped her arms around him in a hug as well. I was relieved that she accepted him, but Mona didn't like another female touching her mate. I had to hold back the growl building in my chest and reminded Mona that we wanted her to like us and accept us all, and that is what she is doing—showing us that she accepts us. Mona relaxed, but only slightly. She was still pacing and agitated.

Next, Carrie walked over to Kevin and wrapped him in a hug as well. Kevin hugged her back tightly. When she stepped back, she looked between us and then motioned toward the table. "Let's sit. I am beyond famished. It has been a long trip and a long day," she said, taking her seat.

We all walked around the table, taking our seats. Zander, who could have had the other head of the table, chose to sit next to me instead, and I was happy for it. I liked having my guys by me. Kevin took the seat next to Zander.

"How was your trip? You said it was long. Do you mind me asking where you went?" I was curious if it was Luna-related or personal to see what I might have to do as Luna here.

"It was, my dear. I went to Ireland to visit my sister. She was traveling and found her mate over there. We talk all the time, but she finally convinced me to come. Of course, the one time I leave is when my son finds his mate, and I am not here to be one of the first to meet my new daughter." She smiled at me, and the warmth beaming from her was absolutely infectious. I couldn't help the smile that formed on my face.

"It is wonderful that you got to see her, and I wouldn't have wanted you to miss that to meet me. We have all the time in the world to get to know each other, and with such a distance between you and your sister, it is good that you took some time to visit. I know I already miss my family very much and hope to see them again soon," I told her.

There was a commotion from the living room. We all turned our heads to see what it was. Nick and Nikki came through the door. They looked a little out of breath.

"Sorry we're late," said Nikki. She was laughing and a little flushed as she walked over to Luna Carrie and gave her a hug. She took the seat next to her and gave me a big smile. Nick took the seat next to her and placed his hand on hers. What has made them so worked up and out of breath? I could only imagine, and then I stopped myself. Nope, I do not need or want to imagine anything.

We all fell into a comfortable conversation about what we did today and catching up on everyone's day. It was like being home with my family—so easy and normal. While we were talking, the kitchen aides brought in our dinner and set it before us. I took my time eating and enjoying the dinner conversation, listening to how everyone's day went.

Nikki and Nick spent most of their time making rounds on the borders today. Nick also stopped by to help at the training fields, which really sparked my interest.

"I would really like to be more involved in the training fields. There is still so much I would like to learn," I told him. I have been trained by one of the best there is—aside from his dad—however, I still have a lot to learn.

"I am sure we can work something out. You show a lot of skill, and we can build on that," Nick replied. "Who did you say you trained with?" he asked.

"The Delta and lead warrior's son, Lance. He was one of my best friends, and he and his sister Layla trained and worked with me relentlessly," I replied proudly.

"Isn't that the male that travels to train with other packs? His dad, that is. You are from the North Woodland pack, right? Their Delta is amazing. I have seen him in action when I was visiting another pack to handle a dispute. I hear he even goes overseas to train other packs and learn new fighting styles, which he incorporates into his lessons."

Nick sounded absolutely ecstatic when talking about Lance's dad. He sounded like a super fan, almost like a human going ape shit over a movie star. He shoved food in his mouth as he waited for us to respond.

"Yeah, Lance and Lynette are his children and usually go with him. They have both been trained by him and help with his classes now. That is how they were able to start training me. They are really good teachers! They understand not everyone learns the same way and can break things down if need be," I boasted. Goddess, I really miss them. I will have to call them later and see how they are doing. I can't believe we really haven't talked since I got here. Then again, I have been a little busy. I took my phone out and sent a quick text to our group chat asking how they are doing and went back to the conversation at hand.

"Maybe we can have them come here and work with our warriors sometime. Just see if there is anything we can do better or add to their skills," Liam suggested.

"That is a really good idea! They travel around and learn so much from others and incorporate it into what they train. They will get the warriors in shape and have more reflexive responses in fighting. We were going to be working on that next after I had a really good handle on all the basics."

I couldn't believe it. I may get to see my best friends again, and so soon! I know I haven't been here that long, but I really do miss them.

"I think we can reach out and see about scheduling something. I am pretty sure that he only takes a few assignments a year because he has to spend so much time away training. So he gets booked up," Trevor adds. He looks at me and smiles warmly. "However, if you would like, we can see if your friends and family would like to come to your Luna ceremony this weekend," he suggests.

I stare at him for a moment, surprised. I honestly don't know why I am so surprised—he has been nothing but generous since we met. Of course he wants to make me comfortable and happy.

"That would be great. I know we haven't been here long, but I do miss our family," Kevin added, also seeming to get excited about the possibility of getting to see our family.

"Of course! Zander, if you would like, you can invite your family as well, as this is going to be sort of a ceremony for you as well. Minding your sister be on her best behavior," Trevor tells him with sincerity.

Zander looks at him for a moment and nods.

"I am wondering if that will be a good idea," he said after a moment's pause.

"Why?" Trevor asks.

We all look at him, waiting for a response as he looks from me to Trevor.

"I was supposed to take over as Alpha. When I came here, it was with the intention to find a way to go home and take care of my pack, and hopefully bring home my Luna."

Trevor growled at that.

"With everything that has happened between us all, I no longer have that desire. I wish to stay here with all of you, with the life we have talked about. However, everything has happened so fast that I have not had a chance to talk to my father to let him know what is going on."

He looked at me again.

"Not to mention my sister is not your biggest fan, and she is not going to be happy that at the end of this, you end up with two Alpha mates when she thought one of those was going to be hers."

That last comment made me growl, and I placed my hand on top of Trevor's without thinking about it.

"You have a point," Trevor said, and after a moment he continued. "I think it is a good idea if you invite them," he told Zander.

I looked at him in confusion and disbelief.

"Hear me out," he said, raising his hands. "If they come here and start a fight over this, they are not on their land and will be held accountable for their actions. Furthermore, they need to know sooner rather than later what is going on, since he will need to find a new Alpha to replace Zander and a new suitor for his daughter, since obviously I am not taking on that nightmare.

That could actually take care of both problems at once if he found a suitable Alpha-born for his daughter to take on as a mate. They may not be okay with what is happening; however, it is happening, and they will need to come to terms with it," he said.

"Okay, if you think that is what is best, then I will invite them. Knowing you will all be there for me will make this easier to deal with after my dad lays into me," he said, looking down at his plate.

My heart clenches at the pain I can see on his face. The entire time I have known him, he has always strived to be the perfect son and perfect Alpha-in-training. I always thought he would be a good Alpha when the time came, and now he has to let his father know that his only heir is no longer going to be able to replace him. He will, in a way, be letting his father down, and that has to be getting to him more than anything.

"Zander, you are a good son and a great man, and you will be an amazing Co-Alpha here. I know this is hard on you, and I am so sorry that you have to give up taking over from your father. I hate that it is because of me, and I wish there was something I could do for you." I really wish I could just let him go and that we could both be happy with our lives. However, in my heart, I know that we won't be. We would both have a hole in our hearts if we had to say good-bye, even if he became Alpha and picked a new Luna and I still had Trevor here. We would never truly be happy without each other.

"Aylin, I am happy here! I never for a second want you to think I'm not! I want to stay. I want to be here with you and help this pack prosper and grow. I still get to be an Alpha and help one of the greatest Alphas I have had the pleasure of meeting and looking up to, aside from my own father." Trevor looks at him and nods with a smile. "I would not trade this for all my father's approval in the world. Does it make me sad to let him down and leave our pack without an Alpha? Yes, but they will figure it out! They will have to, and if they can't, then we have the ruling Alpha Lycan of this territory to help," he says, motioning to Trevor, who again nods at him as a short response, confirming what he said while stuffing his mouth.

"I have been thinking about that and may have an idea," Trevor interjects around a mouthful of food. "You said Lance, this friend of yours, is a great warrior. He seems to be a kind soul as well and does not always think like others, since even though the rest of the pack shunned you, he and his sister were some of your best friends. Is that a correct assumption?" Trevor asked me.

"Yes, he is kind not just to me, but he is that way to everyone. He helps those in need, and when he trains you, if you are not picking something up, he thinks of other ways to get you to try something. He is very versatile in teaching and training, and he is one of the smartest in our class," I boast. "Lance also is the only one that could put my brother and Zander on their asses in training. I always loved watching them train together and watching them get kicked around," I said, making a face at my brother.

"You know I did actually put him on his ass a few times. It's not like he never lost those fights, but yeah, he knows his stuff," Kevin shoots back, and we laugh.

"His sister is pretty amazing too," I add, thinking about Lynette again and hoping that she will be able to come once I tell her about the ceremony.

"I think if the Alpha cannot find someone to take over the pack, we may want to give a candidate for thought, and maybe it should be Lance. If the both of you died in battle and there were no others in line, it would go to him anyways. So, I think we will invite them all to the ceremony. I will send messengers to deliver the invites tonight. I know it may not be enough time; however, I am sure they will all attend, since it is for their ruling Lycan Luna. I am also sure they would have expected an invite anyways, with it being a member of their pack." Trevor was smiling at me, and even though I had some worries about inviting everyone, I nodded and smiled. I could handle it! I am strong, and I know that I am loved and wanted here.

"Why not just send electronic invites, so that way there is a little bit more notice?" I asked.

"The printed invitations are traditional and expected, but you can message your family and friends to expect them so that it saves them time," he suggested.

"I am not going to lie. I am nervous about addressing this issue with my father, but it has to be done. Thank you for allowing it to happen here," Zander said to Trevor, and I reached over and placed my hand on his, offering my comfort and strength. He seemed to visibly relax a little at the contact.

"Don't forget we are all here for you. I will always be there for you," I told him. I wanted to reassure him that he is never going to be alone, and at the very least, I will always have his back.

"Now that that is settled, what are you wanting for your Luna ceremony?" Carrie was looking at me with a big smile on her face.

"Honestly, I am not sure I have ever thought about a Luna ceremony, as I never thought I would ever be a Luna. What do you recommend?" I asked, knowing she probably had many ideas about it. It is usually tradition for the former Luna to plan the Luna ceremony for the new one. Some new Lunas, however, wanted to have a say. I just didn't care. I just wanted to be with my mate and be the best addition to the pack I can be.

"I have many ideas, my dear," she said excitedly.

"That's awesome. I can't wait to see what you have in mind," I told her. I loved her excitement.

"Would you like to see?" she asked. Her eyes seemed to sparkle with the excitement she was feeling.

"Sure, I would love that," I told her. I hoped I sounded as excited as she did, but honestly, I was terrified. I loved that she was like this, though, because I was worried she would not like me or even hold some kind of resentment toward me because of Zander. It is still too early to tell for sure, and she still could hold some kind of resentment. However, I am going to do everything I can to learn to be a good Luna from her and show her how much I love her son and want to be here.

"Great! I have an album put together that I have been making for the past several years, hoping to put together this ceremony, and I finally get to! I am so excited for you to be here with us at last," she exclaims. "After dinner, we can sit in the family room and go over some of it. Nikki, would you like to join us?" she asked Nikki, the only other female in the room, and I smiled at her, pleading with her to say yes with my eyes.

"Of course, Luna Carrie, I would be happy to," she said brightly and still yet a little formal.

"Nikki, what have I told you about calling me Luna Carrie when we are here?" she chided.

"I know, Luna Carrie; however, it has been ingrained in us to always be respectful of our leaders, no matter where we are. I always forget to just relax behind closed doors with you, although I guess I should get used to it, since my new friend here is about to take the title, and I am sure she will hate me if I am always addressing her as Luna as well," Nikki joked, looking at me, and I laughed. I knew how she felt, though. From a young age, as soon as we are able to understand, you are taught to respect your elders and their stations — especially in public.

"You are so right about that. I think I would have to find a new bestie if you call me Luna all the time. I have to have someone keep me grounded here! Don't want to be getting a big head," I teased back and took another bite of the delicious food that had been brought out. The roasted potatoes were sinful. The meat melted like butter in my mouth. If they feed me like this every day, I am going to get fat. Then again, we burn calories so fast that it would take ten meals like this daily to actually get me fat. As long as I keep training, I have nothing to worry about.

For the remainder of dinner, I thought about my friends and family. I missed them all, and I was excited to see them again. It's hard to believe it has only been a few days. It feels like it has been so much longer. Then there is the issue of Zander's family. His sister hated me and would even more now, knowing not only did I get the Alpha she was after, but I also have her brother. That I don't have to choose between the two, and we will be together here—meaning she will need to take on a mate to become the next Alpha of their pack, or my best friend Lance will be taking over. At this point, she will not even get a say in her mate, which I feel a little bad for. I know I would not be okay being set up and not having my mate—or a chance at finding my mate. It would have to be a second or third son with Alpha blood. Usually, a female is the one to leave, but in this case, due to the Alpha situation, the male will have to. If he is not already in line for his own pack to take over, then he will have no problems leaving anyways. Most dream of being an Alpha when they have Alpha blood, so they will jump to lead a pack.

More than anything, though, his father will be furious. He was expecting his son to come home with his Luna, not share in Alpha duties here instead. I wonder if Zander is going to truly be happy here doing that or if he is going to regret his choice to be here with me. The last thing I wanted him to do was regret that, but the choice has already been made, and we are already mated. I feel so selfish right now.

I jumped as a hand brushed over my leg under the table. "Penny for your thoughts, my queen," Zander said, looking at me with eyes full of concern. I realized he was picking up on my feelings and probably sensed I was upset.

"I started thinking about your family and how they will react to the news that you are not coming home. Then that made me think about you having to give that up to be here. With me. I just fear you are going to regret this, Zander. Regret choosing me," I told him. I looked at him, trying to gauge his reaction. He looked at me and smiled. He reached for my hand, and taking it in his, he rubbed small circles on the back of it.

"I could never regret choosing my mate and the one that will be the love of my life and future mother of my pups," he said vehemently. "You are my world, Aylin, and not choosing you is the regret I already had to face once and will never face again. I will move heaven and earth to be with you and make you happy. That is all I want, and all I need in this life is you."

He said it with such conviction my heart clenched, and I could not stop the flow of tears. He wiped them away and continued.

"Aylin, from the moment I rejected you, I regretted my actions and wanted to take them back. The Moon Goddess blessed me with a second chance, and there is nothing in this world that is going to get me to walk away now."

He wiped the tears on my cheeks and kissed them. I felt Trevor's hand on my other leg, squeezing it in reassurance.

The emotions within me were overwhelming. Thank you, Moon Goddess! I couldn't thank her enough for these two. I know that we are going to face some hard times together, but with them both by my side, I feel like we can handle anything that comes our way. I just wish I could control these damn emotions better. I feel like I look weak with all the crying I have been doing. So much for being a badass warrior.

We finished up, and then we all moved to the sitting area. Luna Carrie grabbed a binder I didn't see on one of the end tables and sat on the large couch adjacent from the fireplace and motioned for me to join her. I took one side, and Nikki took the other so we could both comfortably look at what Luna Carrie had come up with—and by the looks of it, she had been planning it for a while.

Carrie showed us pictures of the table coverings and centerpieces and place settings. She showed us flower arrangements and other decorations. Then she went into the dresses. Some were way too showy for me, so I did give some input on the dress, but everything else I was happy to let her plan. I told her I loved her ideas and trusted her opinions for the perfect ceremony. It was as if she was planning a wedding. In some ways, I guess she was. I was joined together with her son, and this was the ceremony to initiate me as his mate and the pack's Luna.

After everything was discussed and Luna Carrie made many promises to find the perfect gown for me, she gave everyone a hug and said her good nights. When she got to me, she paused when she pulled back from the hug and gave me a watery smile.

"I am so thankful that my son has found you. Very rarely are we blessed with a true mate as Alphas and need to take a chosen mate. My son will be truly happy having you by his side," she said and hugged me again.

"Thank you, and I am truly happy as well. I look forward to spending my life with him," I told her honestly. She smiled again and left. I took a deep, shaky breath and blinked back the tears her words had caused. In this moment, I felt like she had really accepted me, and I had been afraid for nothing. She even seemed to be okay with Zander. More time will tell, but for now, I was feeling less worried about our situation and more optimistic that we would all have a chance at happiness. The more people that accepted us, the more optimistic I became.

The rest of our guests decided that it was getting late and time for them to go as well, leaving me with my two handsome mates. I turn to them after saying our goodbyes. They both walk up to me with smirks on their faces, and they take my hands in theirs. They then lead me down the hall to Trevor's room.

I could feel their lust and intent, but even if I couldn't feel it, I would know what it was they were wanting. It's not like they are being discreet, and I am more than happy to reciprocate. After all, I was craving them as well.

# Chapter Twenty-Seven
## *Aylin*

The next couple of days were spent with our time being split up between showing us around the pack, introducing us to pack members that were around when we were being shown around. Most people were friendly; some were a little wary of me, and definitely of Zander. What troubled me were the ones that almost looked afraid. Then there were a few that looked outright angry. I know that the way everything is going is a big change, so I know for some it will take time getting used to.

Nikki had told me that there were some pack members that were unhappy that Ruby was locked up for what she had done and think we took it too far. Maybe they were right, but she had been warned and continued to disrespect her Alpha and future Luna. However, I had already talked to Trevor and told him that I didn't want her locked up or banished. I think what would be best is to wait until after the Luna ceremony is over, and let her go free with a final warning of banishment if she showed either of us any disrespect again. Trevor agreed that it would be best to wait till after the ceremony just in case any animosity has her wanting to do something to ruin it, which would earn her banishment no matter what. This way, the temptation would be removed.

I didn't let the people that were angry with me bother me. I focused on the people that wanted to get to know me and welcome me to their pack. As Luna, I will need to do my best to know my people and their needs, so I want them to feel free to talk to me, and I try to make that clear to them as I meet them. I know that people talk, and if they talk to friends and family and let them all know how open I am, then it will get around that they can approach me.

I never liked that you had to keep distance and make appointments to talk to the Alpha and Luna at our old pack. Even if it was about something mundane, you had to have an appointment. You were not allowed to walk up to them and talk to them unless you were close to them. The average pack member would have to make an appointment if they wanted to talk to the Alpha and Luna. I wanted any of our pack members to feel comfortable talking to me. I didn't want them to be afraid to just come up and see how I am doing or ask if I know how the projects are coming — or anything, really. It's nice to know the people and strike up conversations with them.

Trevor's pack was big. It had a town square with lots of shops, restaurants, even a movie theater and bowling alley that had an arcade and a bar. There were clothing shops, a jewelry store, and more. There were three restaurants to choose from as well: a pizza shop, a coffee café, and the bar had a grille. I loved that they had all this on the pack grounds. The human community was an hour and a half drive away with how big the pack was, so we did not travel off the pack grounds often, according to Trevor. He would go into his office to manage things with his businesses in the human world every once in a while to make appearances; however, he tried to mostly work from his office in the pack-house. That way, he could take care of the pack as much as possible, since he did have to travel a lot to manage the other packs as well. The problem was he was always having to travel to the human world and other packs, so that made it hard.

He told us he had a full team that oversaw most of the day-to-day activity at his company, and there were even wolves that lived in the human area as a preference that were on his board at the higher positions. He did not trust the humans to run his company in his stead, as humans are known for their greed. His trusted men and women were all pack members. He assured me and Zander that we would get to meet them and be more involved with the businesses as well.

I don't know how he is able to run not only this pack but oversee the others in his Lycan territory and run the businesses he had. He was definitely a badass. No wonder why in the end he was happy to have Zander here. It would definitely help with all the work he had to do. I just hope once everything is said and done, Zander gets the same respect as Trevor does when he has to handle the other packs without Trevor there.

I was also curious about the wolves and Lycans that worked at his company. From what Trevor said, some lived here and others in town. It took no time at all if a Lycan ran to the human world — they were faster than any vehicle since they didn't have to stick to the roads. He had said that they would run to the border of the pack lands, and there they would take cars to the office. This cut the time of travel in half.

There were also some that lived in the human world in apartments close to the office. Trevor said that there were only a few of them — two Lycans. One had lost his mate and didn't want to stay in his home without her anymore, and the other one ended up loving the human world and the business world. He had worked long hours and didn't see a reason to have to come all the way to the pack every day. However, he came back for pack meetings, as all had to, and would come back now and then on weekends to visit with family and friends and aid in patrol now and then. The others that stayed in the apartments were werewolves that had come from other packs. It had taken them a while to earn Trevor's trust, and they had to earn their places in the company. Trevor has the top two floors of apartments rented for those that wish to stay.

Apparently, the apartments are luxury apartments that he owns as well. The apartment tower is called the Lunary, which I love. Two of the wolves that live there run the apartment building as well. They are mates and lost their child in an attack and feel safer in the human world, where even rogues try to avoid. I can't say I don't blame them. Accord-

ing to Trevor, there are two available apartments left for anyone that wants to move there. They stay empty, as they are
only meant for wolves and Lycans of our pack. In the rest of
the building are mostly humans; however, he did say that
there was a werewolf that is technically a rogue that lives in
one of the bottom apartments, however is harmless. After
she was rejected by her mate, she ran from her pack to live
in the human world. She works at a bar in the area. I loved
that Trevor had a big heart and looked after people in such
a way.

Lastly, when it came to the apartments, Trevor told us
that we actually have the penthouse. So if he or any of us
ended up staying in the human world, we had an apartment
in town. He didn't count that as part of the top two floors, as
it was only one apartment; there were four apartments on
each floor below the penthouse, and they were all extremely
spacious. He did like keeping one apartment empty regularly for any other wolves and Lycans that worked in the
company on the ground floor. Apparently, all the employees
that did not already live there that belonged to our pack had
access to one of four keys that were kept at the reception
desk at the office. All they had to do was check one out from
the receptionist, who was one of two werewolves, and they
could stay in town. This way, if they had to work over, they
had a place to stay. There were clothes set aside in each room
for men and women, just in case, in the four-bedroom apartment. I couldn't believe the lengths he had gone through for
his employees and pack members.

Even the human employees had some pretty amazing benefits. They were all paid well—even the maintenance and janitorial staff. His companies are all that way. He believes in investing in the people that make the company work.

"What is the point of not taking care of them? Most companies want more money in their pockets. Humans are greedy that way. We make a decent profit and it goes toward our pack, which is already sustainable. Granted, we had a few hard years and have spent most of the extra on building housing for the new arrivals. This has put a limit on other projects. Some of the funds have had to go to helping other packs rebuild after attacks as well, but that is why we have those companies. Once everything is done, we will be able to start putting more away and not have to worry so much. The companies are a newer venture and were something the Alpha King had been suggesting I do for a long time. I didn't want to stretch myself thinner, but in the end, I made the choice to so that the pack had more income. It was hard starting off, and we had to make a lot of sacrifices, but we are more and more profitable every year, and business is thriving," Trevor said.

I couldn't believe it when he told me that. I thought all Lycan leaders had their hands in business around the world. It was common knowledge. However, Trevor wanted to be devoted to his role as the Alpha of this pack and the others. He didn't like the idea of having his attention divided further. I could only imagine if he had done it sooner, how profitable this pack would be now. I found myself more than eager to help when it came to all of this. I would find where I was needed and start my duties, as there were a lot of them to be had, apparently. I will say that I am very intrigued by his business. He now owned a tech company, a communication company, and two clubs—one a high-society club, the other what you could call a sinner's den that offered risque dancers, poker tables, and an attached pool hall.

Then there were his apartments. Aside from the luxury one he owned, two others in town, each on opposite ends. Apparently, there was one apartment that always stayed open in each for those who travel through and need a place to stay for a short while. Some of these are rogues, like the one staying in the Lunary. He told us that they are always offered a place in his pack; however, some are so used to living with humans that they rarely take him up on the offer. Some stay in town and even end up renting from Trevor in those apartments, but most just pass through. I couldn't wait to get started helping, and I knew Zander and Kevin felt the same way. However, there were things that needed to happen before we could do that.

The weeks following our ceremony were already filling in and very busy. Trevor was going to take Zander and me to the company and show us around. He said he was already having some space converted into an office for Zander that would be adjacent to his, as he would now be a co-CEO, just like he was a co-Alpha. I would be able to use either office I wanted, as I would also be learning and helping with the work there. Usually, only one will go, and I can go if I so choose. In the beginning, while learning, all three of us will go until we are comfortable with it. However, they want me to mostly handle the day-to-day in the pack, and I will have more responsibilities there. They only want me to learn the business in case they both need to go somewhere, as I will be officially higher than the beta and can represent the pack name. I, however, wanted to help here and with the businesses so that they could worry more about the packs they have to oversee and take care of.

Then Trevor, Zander, and I were going to visit a pack that was having a dispute over an orchard. I found this to be a trivial matter, but since it is turning into a land dispute and wolves are very territorial as it is, the matter needs to be addressed soon, or there may end up being a fight. Most pack territories are miles and miles away from each other; however, these two pretty much butt up against each other.

My nerves were really starting to get the better of me, though. Tomorrow is our ceremony, and today our families are arriving. I was feeling knots in my stomach and didn't get much sleep the night before. The sun had only just risen, and I decided I may as well get out of bed and get moving. I was not a morning person, but I threw on my workout gear and headed out the door.

I waved at a few pack members who were getting breakfast as I made my way to the front door and then suddenly found my way blocked. Standing in front of me was Stella, one of Ruby's fellow cronies. Right off the bat, the way she stood in front of me with her hands on her hips, one hip stuck out, and the look of superiority as she looked down on me, I knew it was not going to be a pleasant talk. And I was having such a good morning.

"You know you don't have to be this petty over such a small infraction," she stated, like I was the problem here.

"First of all, I am not being petty. Ruby was warned and still trespassed against her Alpha and future Luna. That is on her," I stated matter-of-factly.

"She has already been in the cells for a week. Don't you think you are being a little harsh in her punishment? She was his girlfriend and loved him, and you expect her to just drop her feelings for him just because he found you? She was to be Luna and his chosen mate. You should not be here," she spat, glaring at me.

"Look, not that it is any of your business, but she is not going to just stay down there. She is just staying there until after the Luna ceremony tomorrow," I told her. It wasn't anything she even deserved to know, since she was giving me attitude, but maybe telling her this would calm her down and get her to leave.

"So you are going to make her miss such an important event all because she can't just drop her feelings for someone? You are going to be a rather heartless Luna," she said, shaking her head like I was a disappointment to her. My temper was starting to rise. We are werewolves and Lycans.

Fated mates always take precedence, and even though I know it will hurt if you lose someone to a fated mate, a breakup is still a breakup. Everyone knows better than to come between true mates, and that you will always run the risk of losing them to a fated mate. You went in knowing that. Besides, not for a moment do I believe Ruby was actually capable of love for Trevor. She is the type that wanted power and a title.

"I would watch what you say to your future Luna, unless you are missing Ruby so much that you care to join her. There is plenty of room, after all, in the cells." Stella stiffened, and her eyes went wide. I was so focused on Stella that I hadn't heard Liam walk up behind me.

"Sorry, Gamma, I am just concerned for my friend and her unfair punishment just for loving someone," she said to him, trying to act innocent and demure.

"Ruby knew that she was his mate and that he had been looking for his mate. She was just another she-wolf to warm his bed when he needed it, and he was very honest with her about that. She was never his girlfriend, and she would have never been his Luna. Even if he did not find his fated mate, he would not have chosen her. Her actions, no matter what, are a slight against our Alpha and Luna, and that makes it a slight against our pack. In my opinion, her punishment is not harsh enough since she was already given warnings," he said, crossing his arms over his well-defined chest, making the muscles in his arm and chest pop a bit. Stella's eyes fell on that movement, and then she put her head down.

"I apologize again. I will be more careful with my words in the future, Gamma," she said. She smiled at him, then sent me a glare before walking away. Yeah, like I believe for a second she will watch what she says. The only thing she is going to be more careful about is making sure Liam, Nick, or any of the others she knows who have my back are not around.

Which, in a way, is fine with me because as Luna, I can dish out punishment as well. And if they really want to mess with me after it is official, then they will be in for a rude awakening. I am no pushover, and I will not allow them to walk on me. Not anymore. I am not the girl I was in my old pack, and Trevor wants me to show who I am here. I can be myself, and I know I am a warrior at heart. I may have been submissive in my last pack, but it took every ounce of strength and willpower to do so since it was the Alpha's daughter and her friends who were my tormentors, and I never wanted my family to pay for my actions.

"You know, somehow I just can't believe the words coming out of her mouth," Liam said, shaking his head.

"I was just thinking the same thing. You know, for a split second, I thought about talking to Trevor about letting Ruby out of the cells because I was starting to feel like it was a harsh punishment. However, now I don't think I will. We think she may try something at the Luna ceremony, and now I kind of worry that her friends will instead, since she can't be there." Maybe I shouldn't worry, but I just had this growing bad feeling the closer it gets to the Luna ceremony. I haven't been able to figure out where it is coming from.

"Well, if they do, then they will face even harsher consequences, so I hope they are ready for that," Liam said, shrugging his shoulders. "So where are you off to?" he asked, checking out my workout gear.

"I was going to head to the training yards and do some sparring to get some of my nerves out. After breakfast, that is, because I am starving," I said, and he laughed.

"Mind if I join you? Maybe I can even get some of the warriors that came back to spar with you. I know they are all out there training this morning, and most haven't seen you put the other guys on their asses." He was now filling a plate with meat and pancakes.

"I think that will be fun," I smiled at him mischievously. I liked the idea of knocking some of these elite warriors on their butts. I grabbed some bacon, eggs, and a blueberry muffin, then made my way to get my morning cup of coffee. If there was a nectar of the gods, it would be this deliciousness.

"Is that all you are going to eat?" Liam asked, looking at my plate. I looked down at the eggs, bacon, and toast for a moment, then looked up at him and nodded while digging in. I don't like over-eating before a workout, but it is still important to have protein and carbs, so I have to get something in my system. He just went back to eating his mountain of meat, and I just set to eating my food.

While we were eating, Kevin came down and joined us. He looked exhausted, like he hadn't slept last night. He also had a plate full of various meats and a large coffee. He sat there and put his head in his hands.

"You look like shit," Liam noted, looking over Kevin's face.

"I feel like it too," he said, taking a large bite of sausage.

"Did you get any sleep?" I asked him.

"Not really. I am not looking forward to tonight, let alone tomorrow," he said. I knew what he was talking about. He and Zander would both be telling their families that they would not be taking over their positions as Alpha and Beta. Which means the pack will either have to marry off their Alpha's daughter to an Alpha born without a pack to take over, like a second or third son, or find a pack member to take over. We had already discussed this with Trevor and agreed that Lance would be a good fit.

"I feel for you. It's bad enough to lose the Beta, but the Alpha too! I know the Alpha is going to be pissed his son will not be taking over," Liam looked at Kevin with pity.

"We will get through it together," I told Kevin and gave him a reassuring smile. "Want to come with us to the training fields? I am going to do some sparring with some of the elite warriors that just got back. It may be a good way to take the edge off," I told him, and that seemed to perk him up. He nodded and then started eating.

Since he found out that I had been training in secret, he has enjoyed watching me kick some serious butt with the warriors here. Every time one of them thinks they can take me, I surprise them with my strength and speed, and that is out of wolf form. I have only sparred a handful of times in wolf form, and not with the elite. I have not tried in Lycan form, and I know I need to start. Trevor said he will have Nikki and Liam start training there as soon as possible, since this is an all-new side for me. Technically, both forms were new to me, but I noticed I did prefer my wolf form, and so did Mona when we shifted.

"Sounds good to me, as long as it's not my ass you are kicking today. I am still sore from yesterday. I swear you are coming into some serious strength lately," Kevin said teasingly.

"You are all changing, but for her, she already had a Lycan part she just wasn't aware of, so her strength is going to come in faster. Your change will take longer, usually a few weeks," Liam said, smiling at me. Trevor had already explained to us that mates of Lycans become Lycans, and the elders did confirm that the same happens with Guardians. This means that Zander and Kevin will both be changing into Lycans as well. The process takes a few weeks to a month, depending on your wolf. Unlike me, however, their wolf is changing into a Lycan and will no longer be a wolf. I, however, can change into a wolf or a Lycan.

I have been trying to figure out what abilities I could have. It seems I am just going to end up stumbling across any new ones because I cannot seem to make anything happen. However, I did find that it's my wolf form that can grow rather large; my Lycan form stays as an average Lycan size.

"Yeah, well, for now, she is stronger than me and kicks my ass, so I would rather sit out today and watch her kick someone else's for a change," Kevin said, shoving food in his mouth. I laughed at his comment and manners.

"Well, hurry up and eat so we can get out there. I need to work off this anxiety," I told them. I only had my eggs left, and they still had a decent amount of meat on each of their plates. I'm surprised there are animals left around the pack with how much meat we go through here. They finished their food as I messaged Layla.

Aylin: *I am so excited you guys are coming. When do you think you will be here?*

Layla: *We are getting ready to leave now. The princess was having a meltdown.* Layla sent a follow-up annoyed face emoji.

Aylin: *So, you guys will be here by this afternoon. That should be plenty of time for us to catch up. I really can't wait to see them.*

Layla: *I am looking forward to it, girl. I have missed you so much.*

Aylin: *I have missed you too. I'll see you when you get here. I am off for training.*

Layla: *How cool is it that they allow you to train?*

Aylin: *I know, it's amazing, and I am really good at sparring.*

Layla: *Yeah, well, wait till we get there. Lance will love to put you on your ass to keep you from getting a big head. Laughing emoji*

Aylin: *We'll have to see about that. I'm getting pretty good now that I can train daily and work with real equipment. I can't wait to show them my progress. It's actually a lot in such a short amount of time, and I know it has to do with my Lycan strength and reflexes coming in.*

I put my phone away and look up at the guys who are ready to go. We all head out to the fields for training. I let Kevin know there was a delay due to the princess, and he laughed.

"Figures she would cause a problem. The attention is not going to be centered around her, so she doesn't want any part of it." I nod in agreement. Lizzie has to always be the center of attention. She even goes out of her way at celebrations and other people's ceremonies to make sure that, at some point, she is the main focus.

Just then, my phone chimes, and I pull it out of my pocket. It's another text from Layla.

Layla: *Bad news, looks like Lizzie is bringing her besties with her.*

Aylin: *They were not invited.*

Layla: *It was the only way her dad could get her to calm down since she had to leave her home and her friends. Apparently, she felt like she was going to be treated poorly since you don't like her.*

Aylin: *Just what I need — two different bands of girls who can't stand me in the same place.*

Layla: *I am so sorry, girl, but hey, we got your back. If they mess with you, just kick their ass. What are they going to do if you out-rule them now?* That thought actually did make me feel better. Aylin: *Ok, and yeah, you're right. If they want to keep up the disrespectful act, they will end up on their asses. I hear the new Lycan Luna is a force to be reckoned with and does not tolerate entitlement well.*

Layla sent several laughing emojis, and I put my phone away, annoyed. I wonder if we have enough room in the cells for all these girls. Ruby's friends are obviously not going to leave me alone, and now I have Lizzie and her cronies coming. I would say, "Can it get any worse?" but from experience, if you speak that into existence, it usually does.

"Hey, are you ok?" Kevin was looking at me and could see and feel my frustration. Sometimes, it is weird having him be able to sense when something is wrong with me. I know he is my guardian, but he seems to sense me stronger than the mate bond, yet so far, I have not really been able to sense him at all. I can only do that with my mates.

"Apparently, Lizzie is bringing her support group so she doesn't have to be all alone here without her little friends," I tell him, rolling my eyes. He understands immediately.

"Well, they were not invited, so if they cause problems, you know Trevor will deal with them." I did know this, but that could cause bigger problems than me just dealing with it for a couple of days.

"The thing is, though, if we punish them, it could cause a problem with Zander's dad, and I don't want animosity between our packs right from the start," I tell him. That's the last thing Zander needs. I know he is already stressed and not looking forward to tonight and what all we have to tell our families.

"Trevor is the acting Lycan ruler for the region, and he has a reputation for being feared. He does not tolerate much with the wolf packs, and I do not see him letting it go if his Luna is disrespected. Look what he did to Ruby. She came onto him and upset you, and she was locked in the cells for the slight, with a warning when she gets out that if she continues, she will be banished and deemed a rogue. That will weaken her Lycan, and it could end up being a death sentence since she is a female, and female rogues are brutalized when found by rogue males." I nodded. I knew he was right. I just hoped it didn't come to it, and for once, Lizzie and her friends would just shut their mouths.

Looking around at the training fields, I clear my head and move onto them with the other warriors to see who is up for sparring with their future Luna. Several of them volunteer right away, and as I look at them, my worry fades and I smile. I clap my hands together. Let the games begin.

# Chapter Twenty-Eight
## *Zander*

The past couple of days, I have been pouring myself into learning everything I can from Trevor and Nick. They are teaching me how the pack is run and handled, and how they usually go about dealing with disputes and meetings with the packs we take care of in our area. He said that, as time goes on, I will have more to learn, as we will, from time to time, have to deal with other ruling Lycans and the Lycan king himself. That, I think, is what I am most nervous about.

The Lycan king is a fierce ruler, and like Trevor, he has zero tolerance for most slights. Although I know the king has far worse punishments than Trevor seems to have, granted, I have only seen him have to punish Ruby, and she was a former lover, so maybe there was some leniency.

Today is no different. I am in the process of going over the upcoming trip to the packs that are fighting over an orchard, and we are discussing who is going to talk and when. For the most part, this is going to be a learning experience for me; however, they want me to be active and show that I am a force to be reckoned with, just like they are. This will be a way for us to show a united front and for the packs to start talking about the partnership between us.

Trevor has been adamant about one thing. Even though he tries to work with the packs as much as possible, if the disagreement cannot be resolved, there are harsh consequences for all involved. In other words, instead of everyone possibly gaining something out of an agreement, everyone will lose something instead. He does not like being away from his pack and does not like dealing with petty quarrels even more. So, if Alphas cannot come to an understanding in a timely manner, he will make the decision for them. To make sure it does not look like he is choosing a favorite, he usually makes his choice in a way that is more a consequence of actions.

Out of all the packs he oversees, only a few butt up against each other. Most of the ones that do have something in between them. One has a river, and another has a natural canyon. I have been given files on all the packs that I will be helping oversee, and to say my head is swimming would be an understatement. It is going to take me a while to learn all the pack formations and borders. I already knew the Alphas and betas and some of their children since I was supposed to take over as Alpha, and knowing the others that you have alliances or disputes with is important.

According to Trevor, I need to be firm, just, and fair with the packs, but also have a ruthless tendency. He assures me it will get easier, especially when my Lycan fully forms. I have talked to my wolf several times, or at least tried to. Mostly, he says he is resting. The transformation is taking its toll on him, and he needs rest and energy, which also explains why I have been eating so much more than usual.

I thought running a pack was going to be hard. This has my anxiety in overdrive. I don't know how I am going to help run a pack and oversee all these others. However, I guess that is the thing about it. I won't be doing it alone. Trevor is the Alpha here, and I am co-Alpha. I will have help if I need it; however, I really want them to be able to rely on me and my judgment.

However, then there are the businesses he is going to be taking me to and having me learn to help run as well. Aylin and I are both going to have our hands in them. Aylin seemed to like the idea of helping as well. She really is thriving here, and I couldn't be happier for her. She deserves this — to be seen and accepted. I will always regret not giving her that sooner. I should have stuck up for her, helped her be part of the pack, and not let others influence me so much. I will never do that again.

I need to prove to them that this is what I was born to do. I was always meant to be an Alpha to a pack. The moon goddess must have seen more in me than I did. If this is what is meant to be by her design, then I must be able to handle it. She does everything for a reason, and she would not have given me the second chance with my mate if this was not part of the plan. I will trust in her and do my best for everyone. It still does not help my nerves, however.

I knock on the door to Trevor's office and hear a sharp "enter" from the other side. Trevor is behind his desk; however, he is alone this morning. I thought Nick, at the very least, was also going to be here.

"Ah, Zander, I was just reviewing the contracts and letters that were sent to the packs over the orchard, double-checking everything. They will have time to deliberate themselves before we arrive in a few days," he said, looking over the papers. He seemed to be a little off. "I have been thinking about Aylin going with us."

"I thought that was already decided," I replied to him, thinking about her here by herself, which had me on edge, and he must feel the same way. But there is danger out there that is real, and we need to be careful.

"I know, however, there is a lot to consider," he said, steepling his fingers in front of his chin. He looked lost, and I knew this was something he was going to want to make sure is the right choice.

"If you want my opinion, I believe she should go with us." I feel better with that decision. He looks at me and doesn't speak, so I continue. "It's not just because the bond is new and I don't want to be without her. I think this is good for her to see as well, as she will be the Luna of all this territory. She will be able to meet with the Alphas, Lunas, and those that help with the pack. While there, she may be able to have input and see something that we missed. There is no telling what she is capable of, and she could be of value with us. It's also not that I don't trust the people here, but I don't feel right leaving her behind. I feel safer with her with the two of us since we will both be there. I think I would feel different if one of us stayed, but I just have a feeling this is what is right." I finish, hoping I don't sound like I just want my mate with me. Even if it is mostly for that reason, the rest of what I said is completely true.

Trevor nods and sits back in his chair, thinking about it for a moment. Then he looks up and sighs. "I think you may be right. On one hand, this will indeed be a valuable learning experience for her as well, and I have to admit, I have been feeling anxious with the looming problem and do not want her far from me." His eyebrows draw together, and then he adds, "After this issue is resolved, I think I will be sending out a mass announcement that due to finding our new Luna, we are putting disputes on hold for the short term. I want to see if we can find out more about this god that is hunting her and see if there are any ways to stop him." Trevor was right, of course. I have been thinking the same thing: if this god is coming for her and we are to have this problem, then we need to protect her at all costs. Her nightmares are more frequent, according to her brother, and even both Trevor and I holding her last night didn't calm her when she got up.

"I want to keep her safe as well. We will figure this out. She is reading through her mother's journal. There has to be some mention in there, right?" I told him. However, if there was, I think she would have found it by now. She has been pouring through that journal. She said she was only a little more than halfway through it last night, and I know it has to be hard on her, but we need answers.

"I am not sure, but I do know that gods are not to be trifled with, and this one feels slighted. I can't say I don't blame him, but he already got her mother. Why come after her?" Trevor asked.

"Maybe because she should have been his daughter. If she would have married him like it was planned, she would have borne him a child instead, and since she didn't, he feels like the child is part of the slight against him and needs to get rid of her as well," I said. It was just a theory, but it's really the only one that makes sense.

"I don't care what the reason is. I am not letting him take her from me. From us." He amended the last part, looking at me, and I nodded in agreement.

"I know she is scared. I can feel it. I just don't understand why we cannot calm her as much as Kevin can. Shouldn't we be able to do more as her mates?" I asked. Trevor has been around a lot longer than we have, and this has been bothering me. Several times, even with both me and Trevor there, Kevin has had to come in after night terrors to calm her panic attacks.

"I am waiting for another meeting with the elders. They are doing some more research with the elders in the king's library to see if there are any books about the early years and special wolves, and also about guardians and their roles with the one they are to protect. However, my theory is that he has been there since she was a baby. He has helped her through most of her nightmares throughout her life, and she has a deeper bond with him than anyone else. I am not sure that if they were not raised together, it would be him who is able to comfort her more than we could." He looked lost in thought, and I can tell he has been thinking about this as well. It is frustrating that someone who is not her mate has a stronger bond with her.

"My wolf understands but does not like it. I know he is her brother and they were raised together, but there is no real blood between them. My wolf knows this and can't stand when Kevin touches her and calms her when it should be us. I have to fight my wolf to keep from hurting him and, by extension, her." I know I shouldn't get angry, but it is a fact that even though they were raised together as brother and sister, in all reality, they are not related.

"My Lycan senses that too. Since they do not share the same blood, he gets uneasy that another male is around her and touches her. He also does not like that Kevin can calm her when we cannot." I feel better hearing Trevor say that he is going through the same thing, but only a little. Right now, I wish they really were related so my wolf would calm down, and we could try to accept the bond they share a little better. This is just going to be something we both need to do, but it is going to take a lot of patience.

"As for the trip, I am going to let her know she is coming. I will need Nick here to oversee the pack, and I am going to have Kevin, Liam, and Nikki go with us. They will be her guards and protectors, to be with her at all times, especially if we are not around." Trevor still looked uneasy at the idea of her going and not being in the safety of the pack, but with both of us gone, it will be a constant worry if she really is safe.

While we are going through the rest of the itinerary, my phone goes off. It's a message from Kevin.

Kevin - 'Aylin is really stressed and angry and is taking it out on the warriors. You are missing quite the show.' It made me smile that she was kicking some ass, but why is she angry?

Zander - 'What made her angry? I know she has been stressed with our families coming. I didn't know she was angry about it.'

Kevin - 'Nah, it's not that our families are coming, it's that your sister has her little gang of friends coming along now.' What Kevin said instantly pissed me off. I didn't want her coming, let alone her little bitch squad. I could never stand them, and the fact that they were always trying to vie for my attention with their stupid attempts to get me to notice them and want them, all while taking any other to their bed like I couldn't scent the other males on them.

Zander - 'I will not let them do anything to upset my mate!' I put my phone down and paced the office.

"What is going on?" Trevor asked, narrowing his eyes at me.

"My sister is bringing her little squad of friends for the ceremony," I told him. I was irritated.

"They were not invited. However, I suppose we can accommodate them so it is not an issue." He said. He must have thought I was worried about seating and food.

"That is not the issue. They are Aylin's biggest torturers from my pack and the main reason people stayed away from her and shunned her," I told him, my anger growing. I did not want these girls here bothering Ay. What I said got Trevor's attention as well, and I knew it pissed him off when he growled at what I said.

"If they start anything while they are here, they will be severely punished. If I were you, I would let your father know that I am not going to take any slights while he is here." Trevor's hands were balled into fists, and his knuckles were turning white. "Why didn't you stand up for her?" He was looking at me with disbelief, and even though it pissed me off, I have thought that same thing to myself over and over. The only ones that did were her family: Lance and Layla. I wouldn't let things get physical if I was there, but I didn't stop the other torment. Shame flooded me along with the anger. I looked away. I couldn't look him in the eyes because I knew I was a shitty Alpha for not stopping it. A shitty person altogether.

"I was so focused on being the Alpha the pack wanted and thinking I had to be and act a certain way, I didn't let myself be the Alpha I wanted to be. I am not making an excuse because there is no excuse for not standing up for those that are weak, and I should have." I was more ashamed of myself than angry at his words. I knew I let her down, and I started to think about the other pack members. How many more were bullied or treated unfairly?

"I have no tolerance for that here." Trevor said, and I gave him a look. He definitely needed a wake-up call as well if he thought that didn't happen here.

"Then why are Ruby's friends getting away with it?" I asked him pointedly.

"What are you talking about?" He asked, genuinely looking confused at the statement I just made.

"You really don't know? Ruby and her friends act just like my sister and her friends. They act like they are the queen bees and people should bow down to them. Not to mention, they have people in the pack already upset with Aylin over what has been done to Ruby, even though, in my opinion, her punishment was not harsh enough." I told him. I could hear the knuckles in his hand crack, and the aura he released was making me want to bow down to him. Part of me wondered, when my Lycan came in, if I would still want to bow down. He is stronger now, but we are both Alphas; would it stay that way?

I watched as his eyes glazed over, knowing he was mind-linking someone, and after a few minutes, they focused back on me. However, they only stayed on me for a moment, almost as if contemplating something, and then they glazed over again.

"Get ready to start being the Co-Alpha. It's time we show our pack that we are a united front and agree on a zero-tolerance policy for those who want to step out of line here. I will not allow anyone to show my mate or this pack disrespect of any kind. This pack thrives because we are a team and work together. I don't need or want selfish, entitled wolves here." With that, I joined him on the other side of the desk when he motioned for me and got ready for whatever was about to happen.

# Chapter Twenty-Nine
## *Trevor*

I was furious that Zander did not protect those who needed protection in his pack, letting those who thought they could get away with doing what they pleased right in front of him. Even if he was not yet Alpha, he could have stepped in or talked to his father about the issues in the pack. He could have tried to make the changes before taking over or made his stance known to the pack. But then, to find out that I had it in my pack, right under my nose, had me seeing red. I sent a mind link to Liam, who is mostly here through everything, to see what he had seen or heard.

"'Yes, Alpha.'" Liam's response to me opening the link was immediate.

"'Do you know anything about how Ruby and her friends treat the pack members here?'" I asked him. There was a pause before he answered back.

"'She was thought to be your future Luna by most, if not all, the pack, and she demanded the respect a Luna should have. If she thought anyone showed her or her friends disrespect, or didn't give them their way, she would remind them that she would be their Luna, and she would remember the slight and punish them accordingly when she finally took her place beside you.'" His words had my beast wanting to run to the cells and rip her apart. How dare she mistreat the members of this pack? I will find out just how much she has done in the name of the future Luna.

"'Why has no one told me about this?'"

"'Everyone assumed you knew since you favored her. It really seemed like you would choose her with the affection she would give you in front of other pack members.'" I thought back to all the times when I had to leave and come back and how she would hug and kiss me in the lobby like a mate or partner would.

"'I still do not understand why not one person thought to tell me how they were being treated.'" I have made it a priority to take care of my pack and show them they can come to me. Yes, at times I could be stern, but I have to be as Alpha.

"'I am not sure what she said to them to get them to stay quiet, but I do know that she only really does it when you are away.'" Unfortunately, I am away a lot with business and monitoring other packs.

"'Why have you not said anything?'" I wanted to know why those closest to me had not told me about the slight.

"'With no one coming forward to report anything, it is all hearsay and rumors, so it wasn't something that was deemed important compared to everything else you had on your plate.'" He sounded remorseful and a bit guilty that he had not brought it to my attention.

'"In the future, any disrespect to pack members needs to be followed up with. I do not want the pack members here being treated so poorly. We are a team here and thrive as such.'" There was another pause, and unease grew in my stomach.

'"Alpha, you should know that Stella approached Aylin this morning. I am not sure what all was said, however, when I arrived, it looked like she was trying to get a rise out of her.'" He said. With that, I was done. How dare the members of this pack disrespect my mate and their Luna? No matter what has happened, I know I am a fair and just Alpha, and she does not deserve to be treated poorly by anyone in this pack because a she-wolf didn't get to climb the ladder of power like she wanted.

'"Thank you for letting me know. Keep an eye on Aylin for now.'"

'"No problem. Watching her put your warriors on their asses has been the highlight of my morning.'" I could hear the pride in his voice for his Luna, and that eased some of the anger from me.

I cut the link and focused on Zander. I wasn't sure how I wanted to handle this. Should I make an announcement to the pack as a whole for a meeting? Should I handle the individual problems? I knew that Aylin has spent her days out and about the pack, talking and getting to know pack members. She is trying to make them see that they can come and talk to her and is already becoming an amazing Luna without even realizing it. I could feel the pride for my mate swelling inside me at that thought.

Mind made up, I mind-linked those in question to come to my office. It was time for me to deal with what has been going on in my pack and make an example of those who think they can abuse power. It is not for them to decide their station here and appoint themselves above others. Let's take them down a peg.

Once I was done, I turned to Zander. "Get ready to start being the Co-Alpha. It's time we show our pack that we are a united front and agree on a zero tolerance for those who want to step out of line here. I will not allow anyone to show my mate or this pack disrespect of any kind. This pack thrives because we are a team and work together. I don't need or want selfish, entitled wolves here." It's time to show our united front and start to heal the pack from the taint it has suffered due to my blindness. Zander comes around the desk, and we stand shoulder to shoulder and wait.

A few minutes later, there is a soft knock on the office door. I can feel Zander tense next to me, however, I know he is going to be fine. This is just a small problem that we are starting with. It is the first one he is actually going to deal with as an Alpha of a pack, as to my knowledge, he has not had to, as of yet, with his father. I could be wrong; it's not like we have had a lot of time to talk and know each other. I also hadn't had a lot of time to talk to his father when I was there.

"Enter." I said as formally as I could, trying to contain my anger. When it comes to my mate, I find I have a hard time doing so, with Bane wanting to lay into the people who have offended her and, by extension, him. One thing we have in common for sure is we feel disrespected every time someone disrespects our mate.

The door opens, and in walks Heather, Josephine, and Stella. My eyes hone in on Stella, knowing she is the main culprit here. I haven't heard anything about the other two, however, they are all in the close friend circle with Ruby, and at this point, I would not put it past any of them to do something.

"Do you know why you were called in here?" I asked them.

"No, Alpha." They say almost in unison. I didn't really expect Heather and Jo to know, but Stella only just harassed my mate this morning and should be very aware of what she did.

"You are here because, even after being warned, your Luna is still being harassed." I said as calmly as possible. The three girls keep their heads down, looking at their feet. "You have nothing to say about this? How about you, Stella?" Her head snaps up at that.

"I am not sure what you mean, Alpha. I have only ever tried talking to the future Luna. I have not harassed her. If she has said so, it is she who is lying. She must hate us for being friends with Ruby so much that she is trying to get the rest of us in trouble." She said, trying to put the blame on Aylin.

"Is that so? So she is, in fact, bullying you then?" I asked. Curious to see if she is going to hang herself with the amount of rope I just gave her. I can feel Zander's energy next to me and sense his anger rising. I know he can feel mine too. Since we have mated with Aylin, it is not as strong as with her, but I can get a small sense of how he feels and reacts to things. I guess the benefit of that will be we won't be able to hide things from each other.

"Yes, of course, Alpha. We have all seen what has happened to Ruby and would not want such a harsh punishment for such a minor infraction," Stella said calmly. I noticed the other two look at each other, then back at the floor.

"Jo, Heather, do you have anything to add to this statement?" I asked them. I noticed Jo jerk when I said her name. I could tell she was scared — they all were — but she was visibly trembling under the auras that Zander and I were putting out.

"No, Alpha," Heather said, but Jo stayed quiet. "We have done our best to stay away from the future Luna since your warning," she added.

"Do you agree with Stella that Ruby's punishment is too harsh?" I asked. Jo and Heather looked at each other again briefly, then looked at Stella, who was glaring at them with daggers in her eyes. It seemed that when Ruby wasn't around to boss them around, Stella took over.

"We would never pretend to know what is best, Alpha. You have never been unfair to anyone, even in punishments. You have always been just, and we do not question you," Jo said. She flinched when she looked over in Stella's direction. I could see that even the friends of the bullies were not immune to their torment.

"What about you, Heather? How do you feel about Ruby and her punishment?" I asked. Not that it would change her punishment.

"Alpha, I know you gave the punishment you think best fits the situation, but I do think it is a bit harsh. The cells are a horrible place, built for criminals and rogues. I guess we just do not understand how it is a fitting punishment for her to be kept there," Heather said. That was at least a fair analysis, and I nodded at her. Stella seemed to perk up at the way I paused, as though thinking about what Heather had said.

"Here is the thing, ladies. Whether you know the full story about what happened or not, as Alpha of this pack and the surrounding werewolf packs, I deliberate on every punishment before casting it. Ruby was to be in the cells for a month for her slight against me and my mate." That had all their heads snapping up at me. "I had warned her to stop and be respectful. You all know what happens when you find a mate and how important it is to respect the mate bonds of others. Some do step out and do not care if they hurt their goddess-given mate, and some reject them. However, when it is known that the mate bond is wanted and accepted, you are supposed to respect it no matter what. Ruby did not, and in the process, she disrespected her future Luna and severely disrespected me as Alpha. I had sentenced her to a month there." I paused, taking a deep breath. Before I could continue, Stella took a step forward.

"But Alpha, please do not keep her there that long. We thought that she was only going to be there until the ceremony," she cried. I don't know how they found out that it was only going to be until the ceremony unless that is something Aylin said during the confrontation this morning with her.

"That is true, and do you know who made it so? Do you know who defended her and had me shorten her time in the cells?" They looked at each other, then all shook their heads and shrugged their shoulders.

"Your future Luna," I said, crossing my arms over my chest. Their eyes grew wide, and Jo's mouth dropped open. Stella's lips thinned, and Heather just looked down at her feet. Their reactions were so different, and yet I was sure that, even though Aylin had a hand in coming to Ruby's aid with her punishment, Stella was still not going to let it go and would continue to act a certain way toward my mate.

"You see, most of us thought that a month was fair and that Ruby needed to be reminded of her place here in this pack. The cell she was placed in was one of the nicer ones, above the dark cells where we keep traitors and rogues," I told them. They looked at me again. "Not that I need to explain any of this to you, as I am the ruling Alpha, and my decisions should not be questioned." I looked at Stella then, making sure she understood that little vital piece of information, just in case she forgot.

"You see, ladies," Zander spoke up, "your future Luna also thought a month was too long a punishment, even though it was her that was affected the most by Ruby's antics. She still came to her defense but agreed that it would be best to wait until after the ceremony, thus shortening Ruby's sentence from a month to about a week." Zander was doing his best to stay calm.

"We did not know that Luna had been so gracious," Jo started, looking more humble than the others. Jo had always been the quieter one of the group, and I just didn't know why she hung out with them. The only thing I could think of was that she was Liam's sister, which put her as a ranked wolf. Ruby and the others were not ranked, but they were some of the most attractive in the pack, and since Ruby was with me quite a bit, that seemed to make them think they could do whatever they wanted.

"And yet you spread rumors about her and still disrespect her," Zander said flatly. Jo blanched at that and looked back at the ground. She was shaking with fear. I could tell she wasn't one to want problems and was just going along with the group. However, the group she had tied herself to was causing harm within my pack.

"This is my final warning, and it especially goes to you three since you seem to be the main cause of the things I am hearing. Whether it is all three of you or just one of you, I no longer care. If these rumors continue about our unjust Luna, or any of you continue to talk down to her, harass her, or show her anything other than the respect that girl deserves as your Luna, your punishment will be what Ruby's was supposed to be in the first place." All three sets of eyes were laser-focused on me now.

"I swear to you, my Alpha, I will show her the respect she deserves," Jo spoke up, the first fear etched on her face. The other two nodded, but I could see the disdain in Stella's eyes. She was more than likely going to have to learn the hard way. I would not allow her to get away with anything, and even when Ruby got out, she would not be able to protect her friends from me. Hell, she might even receive the punishment with them, since she was the ringleader.

"Let me find out if any of you do not, and the three of you together will share in this punishment," I said curtly.

"Wait, so if only one of us does something to disrespect our Luna or you, all three of us will be punished?" Heather asked, looking appalled.

"Unless you are willing to come forward against the guilty party, then yes. I know you three stick up for each other and for Ruby. I know that you three will say or do what you can to get out of being in trouble and try to have each other's backs. I can admire that in your friendship. However, there are lines being crossed, and if you want to be dragged down by your friends, that is up to you. So, therefore, if you come forward about their deeds and show you have loyalty to your leaders, then you will not be punished," I replied with no emotion.

"But Alpha, that is unreasonable. If we are not doing anything wrong, we should not be punished as well. Guilt by association is cruel," Heather added, looking at Stella briefly. I knew she was worried. I could sense that Jo would keep her word. I was not sure about Heather, but I also knew that through all this, Stella would only care about herself and Ruby, their ring leader.

"What part of me is supposed to care? I am cruel to the neighboring packs; however, I have rarely had to be here. You seem to forget just who I am." I stood and released a fraction more of my aura, and the little bit I did release had them all submitting and exposing their necks to me. "This isn't even a fraction of my aura, and you are already in pain kneeling before me."

"Please, Alpha, we will not disrespect our Luna again," Jo said, tears running down her face as I gave off a bit more. I pulled it back in and stayed standing. The girls rose back up on their feet. They looked from me to Zander and back again.

"You three really need to figure out if the friendships you have are really worth it and if you want to continue to be associated with those who will bring you down. I am not naïve enough to think this will be the last time one of you or Ruby does something to anger me. My mate may be forgiving, but I am not. Every time you disrespect her, you disrespect me and this pack, and I will not tolerate it," I said with finality.

"Yes, Alpha," they said together. I once again saw Jo and Heather look at each other and then at Stella.

"I will be assigning new work details for all three of you. It appears that you have all forgotten your place here in this pack and have had it far too easy because of the friendship I had held with Ruby. You will be getting your new assignments after I get back from a meeting we have with several wolf packs. If there is a real job that you would prefer, you can put in the request, and I will review it when we get back. On that note, Jo and Heather, you may leave. Stella, I would like you to stay for a minute." At these words, Jo and Heather bowed their heads and started to leave my office. Jo stopped and looked at me for a second. Whatever she was going to say, she must have decided it could wait and followed Heather out. Stella glanced up at me nervously.

"Stella, I am very aware of your run-in with the Luna this morning. I am also disappointed that you tried to make it out like she was the one trying to come after you. We both know you were lying, and I am not fond of being lied to. It is very disrespectful, don't you agree?" I said in a clipped tone.

"Alpha, I swear to you, I am not going to disrespect our Luna again, please," she almost begged. I could see the fear in her eyes now. She was fully aware that I knew the truth and that she was on her way to receiving a severe punishment.

"Oh, you are right about that. You see, I am going to let you in on a secret." She looked up at me. "Aylin did not tell me about your conversation. Liam did, and I have heard some of the rumors going around about how Aylin punished Ruby just for having feelings for her Alpha. You see, I am certain with Ruby in the cells, you are the one controlling your little group, and my promise to you is that your punishment will be worse than a month in the cells if you continue. If you or Ruby decide that you want to push this, you will be whipped, put on the posts for the pack to see, and then held in the cells for the remainder of the month." Her face paled as she looked at me, seeing my Lycan looking back at her. She looked at Zander just to find a satisfied smirk on his face.

"You have my word, Alpha!" For the first time since she entered my office, I almost felt like I believed her. Almost.

"You may go," was all I had left to say to her. She bowed her head in respect and fled the office.

"That was dramatic there at the end," Zander said, looking at me with laughter written all over his face.

"The thing is, I was being serious. I have seen in other wolf packs what can happen with jealous females that want power. I have seen smitten Alphas or betas reject their mate for these women, and I have seen fights in the packs over this. I will not allow that to happen here. I should have never taken Ruby to my bed, but I had thought I had made it clear to her that there was no chance for her to be a Luna; she was just a bed warmer." I told him, shaking my head. Greedy people, however, do not listen to reason and will continue to try to get what they want. That is something I really didn't see when it came to Ruby, and I could kick myself for that.

"I haven't seen anywhere near as much as you, but I have seen what it is to be with someone and then find their mate, and the break-up to follow is never easy. There is usually hope that they will be mates when they are young, or when they get older, they think they have time since they haven't found their mates to get to know each other and be chosen mates. No matter the age or the circumstance, it is never easy," Zander said, and I know this is true as well. Ruby had gotten attached. Whether she actually cared for me or for the opportunity to be Luna, I didn't know, but she needed to let go of her drive to be my Luna and try to find happiness elsewhere.

Speaking of Lunas, I just remembered what else Liam said to me when I mind-linked him before calling in those three. He had said that she was kicking some of our elite's asses, and after this shitshow of a start to my day, I think that watching my mate kick some ass is exactly what I needed. And like he read my mind, Zander turns to me with a smile.

"I guess our mate is relieving her anger and stress out on the elite warriors this morning. You think maybe we should go give them a hand? Or just watch her kick your best guy's asses?" He said, laughing. I was not sure how he knew that unless he had also mind-linked with Liam, or maybe he was talking to Kevin.

"You know, I think I need to see what kind of shape my guys are in," I tell him, and we head out of the office and out to the training fields with Thomas and Julian not far behind. Sometimes it is really easy to forget they are there, but I am comfortable with them. I am glad that the two I have on Aylin, she doesn't even realize, are her personal guards. Her brother Kevin is a given, and Liam is the Luna's protector as the Gamma of the pack. He is in tune with her and will do a good job keeping her safe. I know we need to get the Luna's guard going and have the ones that will be her detail for large events and for travel as well. I just don't know who to choose. All of the people I absolutely trusted are already in my circle. I will really have to vet them and see what I have to choose from for her.

Upon arriving at the fields, the first thing I notice is the large circle of warriors and pack members. What in the world is going on? As we make our way closer, the cheers and shouts get louder, and when we get up front, I can see Aylin facing off with not one but three elite warriors at the same time. My hackles rise, and I start to step forward. How can they think this is a fair fight? I stop when I feel a hand on my arm and look over at Zander, who is studying the fight.

"Wait, let's see what is happening. I don't think she will like it if we go in there, and take a look around." I did what he said and looked at the crowd and spectators, then back at the fight. They were cheering for her. And then I see Kevin and Liam on the other side of the circle also cheering her on. If they are relaxed, then I should give the benefit of the doubt. Let's see what my little wolf can do.

Standing back, I cross my arms over my chest and watch as she continues to face off against the three men. The pride I feel swells within me and Bane for that matter. Everything in us says we should be protecting her, and we also do not like other men touching her, but she wants to prove to the pack she is strong, and no matter how hard it is, I am going to let her do just that. Come on, little wolf, show them what you have.

# Chapter Thirty
## *Aylin*

I have spent the last hour going through the warriors one-on-one and beating every one of them. The best part is I don't even feel all that tired yet. The warriors started complaining about unfair advantages, so I made them a bet. Pair up your best three warriors against me, and if they can take me down, I will personally see to it that they get a week off training. However, if I beat them, they have to do an additional fifty laps around the field on top of normal training for the week.

Of course, they were willing to take that bet, and maybe I felt overly confident that I could take them on, but I also was not underestimating any of them. Going from one-on-one to three-on-one was a big jump. I could have just done two-on-one, but where's the fun in that? Besides, I want to see what I can do, and if I get put on my ass, fine, I will take it because at least I know my limits and will work to change them.

Word had spread about my deal and who was going to be taking me on. I spent about fifteen minutes getting some water and stretching out my muscles before we were ready to go. It took them that long to decide who I would be up against. During that fifteen minutes, a crowd started to form. I looked around and smiled. I hadn't even realized that in the short time I have been here, I no longer am looking to hide from people and stay out of the way. I like that people want to be around me.

"Are you sure you want to do this?" Kevin asked, looking unsure. He shifted his weight from one leg to the other. I could tell he was uncomfortable with this idea.

"Yeah, what made you decide to take on three at a time?" Liam asked. He looked just as worried as Kevin did.

"Mona wanted a challenge and said that she was bored." I shrugged my shoulders at them.

"She is bored? You just fought seven of our warriors and beat every one of them. They are out of breath, and you have barely broken a sweat. You are stronger than we realize." Liam said, shaking his head and giving a small chuckle. I grinned back at him. "I just have to be concerned because if you get seriously hurt, Trevor is going to have my head," he said.

I laughed. "So you are more worried about your head than my well-being?" I asked jokingly. However, Liam's face fell.

"No, Luna, I swear that is not what I meant! I have every faith in you to kick all three of their asses, especially with Mona's strength, speed, and agility. I only meant that on the off chance something happens, Trevor would come for me for not stopping you to begin with." He looked worried like he may have offended me, and I couldn't help the laugh that bubbled up.

"Liam, no matter what happens, I will be okay. Not only am I coming into my strength and feeling great, but I am confident that I will not lose this. And you really need to relax. I was only teasing you." I smiled at him, and he visibly relaxed. I patted his shoulder. I loved Trevor already, but if he and his pack try to hold me back, we will have issues.

"Well, let's get it over with," Kevin said with a cheesy grin on his face. "I am going to see who wants to take bets and make some money off my sister. You should help," Kevin said to Liam. Typical Kevin, although I don't think he was actually joking this time.

I headed into the circle and faced the warriors squaring off. The crowd started cheering and chanting. Some for me, and some for the warriors three. I like how that sounded in my head. Okay, warriors three, let's see what you have for me. I couldn't help the grin at the wordplay in my head, and I think the warriors thought I was laughing at them. Either way, that grin had them coming at me.

They made a formation trying to surround me instead of all attacking straight on. Smart move, guys. The warrior in front of me is tall and muscular. He is the biggest of the three and starts by rushing me. At the last second, I crouch and jump, bringing my knee up to his face, knocking him backward. The other two had taken off shortly after he did, and after my knee made the connection, I kept my momentum going into a back handspring and pushed myself out of the way of the other two, who barely stopped before colliding with each other.

The crowd is screaming, and I am walking in a circle with the guys. They both look at me with serious intent. The next moment, they rush me together. I run directly at them as well. I see when they shift—one is going to go high, the other low—so I drop and spin my right leg out in a long sweep, catching the first one. The other jumps over, but as I spin, I bring myself up and then raise my other leg in a roundhouse kick and land it across his cheek, effectively knocking him down.

The big guy had gotten back up to his feet, and so had the one I swept the leg out from under. They attack together. The big guy lands a hit to my ribs, and I can hear an audible crack. Pain radiates through my side. He must have realized how hard he hit me because, for a split second, he froze, realizing how hard he struck his Luna, and I took full advantage. I swung up and hit him under his chin and then gave a right hook to the side of his face. Then, dodging the other guy, I took a step back and hit him in the ribs a few times, which he attempts to block. Then, I swing my leg out, knocking him down for a second time.

This goes on and on; sometimes all three are coming at me, but for the most part, I am knocking them down as they get back up. I can feel the exhaustion now. Mona is excited—I can feel her inside me, and she is enjoying the fight. They have landed quite a few good hits, and I can feel the areas that are going to bruise. Thankfully, I heal quickly, and there will not be anything visible tomorrow during the ceremony. The rib may take a few extra days, though.

I have done a pretty good job of avoiding blows to the face, but some of those caused me to get a blow in another area. No matter how many times they knocked me down, I got right back up.

I have knocked two out, and they are down. Now I am facing the last one. He is the shortest out of the three but still built. He is more agile than the others, and I think this is why he is still in this fight with me. He is fast and can dodge my attacks as easily as I can dodge his.

I can tell he is also feeling exhausted. Putting on speed, I run at him. He braces for the attack. However, at the last second, I dive to the ground, somersault in front of him, and when I come around, I kick up with both feet, planting them in his torso, and he flies across the field. He rolls and comes to a stop. He rolls over onto his hands and knees, and when he looks up, he shakes his head. He concedes. The crowd erupts, and for a second, it is deafening. Then I feel familiar hands on my hips, lifting me up into the air and placing me on his shoulder.

Trevor looks up into my eyes and winks at me with a huge smile plastered across his face. Zander, on the other side, is cheering with the crowd. When did they get here? Oh well, I am happy they are here and saw me whoop those guys. Trevor brings me down and then grabs the back of my neck and steals a hard, passionate kiss that I just melt into. Goddess, the feel of him demanding and claiming was utterly breathtaking.

The moment he released me, I was pulled into Zander's arms. "My turn, my queen," he said, and then he devoured me. Any breath I may have had left after Trevor's kiss was gone, and Zander was the air I needed to breathe all over again. When he pulled away, I was briefly aware that there were still people around us cheering. I smiled at my guys and backed away to catch my breath.

I saw that the three warriors had gotten to their feet and were standing, waiting patiently for me. I walked over to them and nodded. "Thank you all for that. I appreciate that you didn't go too easy on me," I told them. They all smiled and bowed their heads to me in respect.

"Luna, it is our honor to fight with you and for you. I will gladly spar with you any day, not only to improve upon my own skill but to assist you in your growth as well. You are a fierce warrior, and I am proud to serve you. How did you know we tried to go easy on you?" The tallest of the three said with a fierceness I truly believed.

"What is your name, warrior?" I asked him.

"I am Jacob. This is Talon and Henry." He motioned toward the others.

"Well, Jacob, when you punched me in the ribs and I heard the crack, you hesitated. I knew then that you didn't mean to hit me that hard. After that, you guys all landed some good blows, but nothing so bad that it won't leave just a few bruises. So, I'll heal quickly." I gave him a knowing smirk.

"I apologize if we offended you, Luna. That was not our intent," he said apologetically. I smiled at them.

"It's quite alright. I'm grateful that you did, in a way. If I had not already fought all those others, I would have been upset that you held back, but I'm thinking for now it's a good thing since I don't want to be beat up for the ceremony tomorrow and for meeting up with my family tonight." They looked like they all breathed a sigh of relief. "Next time, however, I want you three to come at me with all you have and really make me work for it." I told them, and they nodded at me.

"It will be an honor, my Luna!" said Henry, with the others nodding in agreement.

"It's settled—next time I spar with you three first and see what happens." I nodded at them and walked off the field with Trevor and Zander. The three warriors were still bowing their heads to me and the Alphas. I don't think I'll ever get used to that, and honestly, I don't want to. I want them to be comfortable with me.

"You never cease to amaze me, little wolf," Trevor said.

"So, you're back on that nickname, huh? I thought we agreed that I wasn't a little wolf," I said, elbowing him.

"Yes, however, you will always be my little wolf. That's what you were when I met you—just this beautiful, ethereal creature that the moon goddess blessed me with as a mate. You didn't get bigger until later, so for me, you will always be MY little wolf." Trevor said, pulling me to his side and kissing the top of my head like he didn't just make my heart swell with his words and butterflies take flight in my stomach and chest.

"He has a point though, my queen. You are constantly amazing us with everything you do. I, for one, cannot wait to see what you are capable of next," Zander chimed in.

"Hey, wait for us!" I turned to see Kevin yelling for us to wait up while he and Liam made their way over to us through the crowd.

"Okay, so is anyone else starving? I'm ready for lunch. How about you guys?" I said, looking between the four of them, and they just laughed.

"We are beasts. Of course, we are hungry. We are always hungry, and watching you take down so many of our men made me work up an appetite," Liam said.

"I had you work up an appetite? How do you think I feel?" They laughed again at my expense, and we all headed toward the pack house. Along the way, several pack members stopped me and wanted to talk about the sparring, and some of the conversations led to other things. Seeing me out and about, training with the guys, seemed to make them a bit more comfortable with me. Some pack members wanted to just talk to me, others wanted to voice opinions or concerns to me and the Alphas about the upcoming projects. Some just wanted to tell me how much they enjoyed watching me spar and thought it would be fun to do it again.

I have never been so happy and felt more like I belonged than I did at this moment. I loved talking to each pack member, and even though I was starving and felt like I could eat an elephant, I didn't brush off anyone. I spent time with each and every person who wanted to talk to me.

By the time we reached the pack house, lunch was almost over. Trevor ended up going into the kitchens to see if there was anything they could whip up for the five of us. Thankfully, the kitchen staff had heard about the sparring and figured we would be famished. They put together a special lunch for me and made sure there was enough for the entire Alpha unit, even though Nick and Nikki were not here to join us.

We loaded our plates and stuffed ourselves with the delicious sandwiches and treats the cook made for us. I was beyond grateful for the turkey club, as it has always been one of my favorites, right after a good old-fashioned Reuben. The homemade chips and the rich red velvet cupcakes really hit the spot. I felt like a little girl eating lunch with the cupcakes, but I'm never going to complain about my sweet treats. I enjoy them too much.

"Damn girl, two sandwiches and three cupcakes? Are you even going to fit in your dress tomorrow?" Liam said as I finished off the third cupcake. I just shrugged my shoulders because right now, I didn't care as long as I could eat these delicious morsels!

"She will be fine; she is just replacing the calories she burned off," Zander said, bumping my shoulder with his. I grinned at him with a mouthful of food, and he chuckled and shook his head. I wondered briefly if I looked like a squirrel when they stuff their cheeks full of nuts.

"So, has anyone received an update on the arrival of your families?" Trevor asked us. Kevin, Zander, and I all pulled out our phones and checked them. I had two missed calls and four texts. Both calls were from Layla, along with three of the texts, and one text was from my mom. Layla was complaining about Lizzie and her followers, and my mom said that according to GPS, they would be arriving around two forty-five in the afternoon. Looking at the time on my phone, it was already one-thirty. I replied to both of them so they knew I got their texts.

"Mom said that they should be here just before three. So, I think I should go check on their rooms and make sure everything is in order. And do you think we should have dinner in a meeting room? I'm not sure how tonight is going to go at all. We haven't discussed when we were going to sit everyone down and talk to them or anything." I was getting nervous again, and right now, eating that third cupcake may have been a mistake. My stomach was starting to knot up.

"Their rooms should be fine. The omegas have been getting things ready all week. There's nothing for you to worry about. I have the conference room booked for tonight, and we will all be present. There's nothing to worry about. Yes, we'll talk to everyone at dinner and make all the necessary announcements. However, there is something you do need to decide, and I wanted to talk to you about it sooner, but it's been a busy week. You need to decide if you want them to know about who you are and where you come from. Our pack knows you are special, but not exactly who you are." Trevor said, and I looked down at my empty plate.

"I'm not sure what to tell them, but I know that Zander is going to have a hard time with his father. What if knowing where I come from would help with that? Would they be so willing to fight us on him staying here if they knew that staying means he is mated to the great-granddaughter of the moon goddess herself?" I asked.

"I don't know, but this is a big thing to share, and I know how worried you are with the god that is hunting you. It's something that we do not want to take lightly," he said, looking between me and Zander.

"Aylin, I don't think that they all need to know if you do decide to tell them. Maybe the announcement and all can wait until just after dinner. We can ask those on a need-to-know basis to stay, and the rest that we do not want listening to this discussion can leave." Zander was looking at me with worry in his eyes. I knew they both were. The nightmares were getting worse, and the feeling of dread was getting stronger. It's hard to breathe when I wake up, and sometimes I swear I feel like I'm still being watched, even when the nightmare is over.

"Who is it that you think needs to know? Who do you want to know?" Trevor asked me. After all, it's my secret, and I need to be careful about who knows.

"I think most of the conversation everyone can stay for. However, when it gets down to that part, I think to be safe, my sister should not be there, and I definitely do not want Lizzie or her friends there. Honestly, I don't want her friends at the dinner, but I will be nice," I said, rolling my eyes.

"So you want Lance and Layla there?" Zander said. I could hear the way he said Lance's name, and it kind of bothered me. He knows that Lance and I are close, as Lance was one of the only ones to be there for me ever, and it is his own fault that I was never that close with him. I give him a sideways glance and narrow my eyes, and he has the decency to look guilty.

"They are my closest and most trusted friends. They, above all, can keep a secret, and if they were here, I would have already told them. In fact, the only reason they don't already know is we don't know if messages and calls can be intercepted or listened in on at that moment, and I wasn't taking chances," I say with a matter-of-fact tone. "Pretty much, it's just your sister and her friends that cannot be trusted, and I am worried about what your parents will do as well when it comes to keeping this secret, since they will be pissed that you won't take over as alpha. The only reason I do not want my sister to attend is because the less she knows, the better and safer she will be." Zander looked at me with big eyes, and I realized that my words hurt him. I was so angry that he questioned Lance and Layla that I lashed out. I instantly regretted it.

"I know that it is going to be difficult to trust anyone with this, and I know it is your secret to share. I am just trying to help and look out for you," he said. I could hear the hurt in his voice as he spoke, and I knew he really was just looking out for me. Even if he was a little jealous of mine and Lance's relationship, he would never do anything to hurt me and will always look out for me. He really has been trying since we realized the moon goddess has given us a second chance to be together, denying the rejection he tried to make. I need to forgive him and let it go. I guess I didn't realize I was still holding onto the hurt he caused. In fairness, it hasn't been that long. I have already forgiven him, though, so I need to let it go.

"I know, and I am sorry I lashed out. It seemed like you just didn't want him included because of how close we are, but if there is a chance he is going to take over your pack and we are going to be allies, he should know. And if there is anyone other than the people in this room that I know for a fact will have my back, it is him and his twin," I said. I knew that for a fact, and I needed Zander to realize that he needs to let go of whatever it is he is feeling about Lance, since he will eventually be working with him.

"Okay, if you trust them, then I do too. We will have the other girls leave, and the meeting will be held after dinner. But where are they going to go while we are in a meeting?" Zander had a point. I didn't like the idea of them just roaming our pack.

"They will be escorted to their chambers, where Thomas and Julian will stand guard outside their rooms. With them having already eaten and there being a bathroom in the suites, they will not need anything during the meeting. Furthermore, they will not be allowed to freely roam my pack without a guard with them. That is how it is for most packs when visiting, and it is a sign of disrespect for one to venture off without cause. It could be looked at as they are scouting our lands to prepare for an attack. You show your allies only what is necessary," Trevor says to us.

I didn't know that when you visit a pack, you cannot just walk around. I thought back to when Trevor came to our old pack for the festival and Lizzie was supposed to be his escort, only he wanted me to show him around, and we didn't go far, only around the town square. The thought that they will not be able to just walk around makes me feel a bit better. I just feel like something bad is going to happen with them here and Ruby's friends lurking around. The last thing I need is for them all to become buddy-buddy and start messing with me as a whole. However, if they try to bully me now, they will have another thing coming.

"Where is your head?" Kevin asks, looking at me with a pinched look on his face. My emotions must be starting to get strong again.

"I just had this irrational thought that Lizzie and her friends could gang up with Ruby's friends and really have some fun at my expense." I had whispered it as low as I could, trying to make it for only him to hear, but Lycans have amazing hearing.

"You will not need to worry about that. I have taken it upon myself to talk to Jo, Stella, and Heather." I looked up at Trevor and then narrowed my eyes. I opened my mouth to tell him off for interfering, and he quickly holds up his hand to stop me and continues. "I know you wanted to deal with it on your own and that you want to show the pack that you are going to be there for them, however, I am tired of it already, and it is also a form of disrespect to me. I have a certain reputation that I need to uphold. There is a reason other packs follow me, and this pack runs the way it does. Even though my pack respects and even loves me, there is an undercurrent of fear, and I need to keep that going so they know what they will be in for if they continue to cross me," he said, and I had to think about that for a minute. Yes, you want the people to respect you, but do you want them to fear you? A little fear could be good enough that they know that if they do wrong, there are consequences, but I do believe it is better for them to respect and love you. I can see where he is coming from with the balance.

Trevor really did have a reputation about him. I had heard rumors of things he had done to other packs and their leaders, including not only stripping one Alpha of his title but also having him tied to a post and whipped, then left out there for three days before he was cut down and put in his own cells. I shivered at that and wondered if I should ask if he actually did that, or maybe I really don't want to know.

"Okay, so we are in agreement on who will attend the meeting from the other pack, but do you want us there or want us doing something else?" Liam asked, as Nick and Nikki joined us. Trevor seemed to be filling them in on what he had just missed in the discussions, then answered Liam's question.

"Since Thomas and Julian are going to be guarding the others and being escorts, we need you all with us. Liam and Kevin are Aylin's personal guards, so I don't want them far. As for you two, you will both stay with me as well. Unless something in the pack needs attention from us, in which case, as Beta, you will handle it, and Nikki will stay by my side while you do so," Trevor told them.

"You know, there are too many visitors coming for just Thomas and Julian to cover. I think we may need a few more, especially if they want to walk around but not stay together," I said, thinking out loud.

"What do you mean, not stay together?" Trevor asked.

"You know, teenagers rarely want to walk around with their parents; it isn't 'cool,'" I told him. "So, Lizzie, her friends, and my sister may end up wanting to walk around separately," I added.

"Okay, judging by the look on your face, I think you may have someone in mind," Trevor replied, and to that, I do. My mind instantly goes to the warriors I faced off with today.

"I was just thinking about the guys from earlier today, the ones I sparred with at the end. They work well together;

they are part of the elite, and I don't get any bad feelings from them. I feel a sense of duty and comfort from them. It's hard to explain, but I trust them." I'm lost in thought about the way they moved earlier as one unit. They must have been friends and trained well together.

"Then I will call them in, and we will explain the task they will have," Trevor said, and then his eyes glazed over, and I knew he was mind-linking them. Part of me did feel bad for asking Jacob, Talon, and Henry to basically babysit these girls.

A few moments later, as we were starting to talk about the plans for tomorrow, Nikki started going into details about her dress and wanting to know more about mine, and if I look as stunning as she thinks I will in it, the three that Trevor sent for walked through the door.

"Alpha, you requested to see us," Jacob said, and then his eyes landed on me. A look of unease washed over him. As soon as the others saw me, their body language changed as well. They were worried. Possibly even a little scared. Maybe they thought they were in trouble for trying to kick my ass earlier. I smiled at that.

"Yes, you are the three that sparred with Aylin this morning, right?" Trevor said, already knowing the answer.

"Yes, Alpha," they said in unison.

"Good, the Luna here said she has a good feeling about you three and chose you for an assignment," he said. You could see all three of them relax a little and then puff up at the mention that they were picked by the new Luna. Again, I smiled at the way they looked.

"We have multiple visitors that will be staying with us for a few days, and some of them were not invited. The two guards I have chosen to watch over and restrict our guests will not be enough for this task. You three will be handling the additional guests and making sure they stay out of trouble and do not wander where they should not be," Trevor said to them. All three nodded, and then Trevor looked at me.

"Basically, you three will be in charge of the visiting Alpha's daughter and her friends, and then my little sister, who is the Beta's daughter from the North Woodland pack, where Zander, Kevin, and I are all originally from. This may sound like an easy babysitting task, but these girls will try to be sneaky and conniving to get their way. I am trusting you to think with your heads and not let them sweet-talk any of you into doing anything that may get themselves and you in trouble," I said firmly. All three nodded.

"It is unlikely that these girls will want to be together, as my sister is not exactly friends with Lizzie and her friends. So, you three will be divided up. I think Jacob and Henry should watch over Lizzie and her friends, and Talon, I would like you to escort my sister. Of the three of you, you are the least intimidating, and my sister will be much easier to deal with." They looked at each other and nodded again. "Do you have any questions?" I asked them.

They all seemed to hesitate at first. "What areas are permitted or off-limits?" Jacob asked, getting right into warrior mode.

"When it comes to these girls, I do not see any reason for them to go further than the town square. They are obviously not allowed in the upper levels of the pack house either. If they want to go anywhere else, you are to verify with myself or your Luna if it will be permitted, and it will be on a case-by-case basis. The only exception to the upper levels will be for Aylin and Kevin's little sister, and only when she is up there with them," Trevor told them. They nodded in understanding. I looked at them, and I could feel the pride they felt at being picked for this, even if it is a babysitting detail.

"You three are going to be my trusted warriors now and in the future. If for any reason my personal guards are unable to assist me, one of you three will be called upon. If I need extra detail for any reason, it will be one of you three. Is this agreeable to you?" I asked them, shocking them and the people around me.

'Aylin, are you sure about this? You only just met them today,' Zander asked me through the mind link. I know he is worried, but I have to have a trusted personal guard, and again I have to trust my own instincts. I have a feeling these three will be very important to me.

'I am very sure. They are pure-hearted and have no ill will for me or this pack. Look at how proud they are to be picked for something like babysitting duty just because it was I who hand-picked them. I want them to be an extension of the Luna's guard. Kevin and Liam will not always be here, and in the case of Liam, he has other responsibilities with the pack. Which he often does. I cannot always have him with me, so this is a necessary choice,' I linked back.

'Already such a wise Luna,' Zander says, smiling at me.

"Your Luna has asked a question, warriors. This is an honor and one that is usually considered after warriors apply for the position and are gone over in great detail and interviews. I may not agree with how she is doing this; however, I trust her judgment. Do you accept this position in our pack?" Trevor asked them, snapping them out of their shock.

"Yes, Alpha! Thank you, Luna!" they said together and bowed to us. I could feel their shock, wonder, and their sense of duty. They will definitely be a good fit with our little group.

"It is settled. You three will be moving out of the Elite warriors' barracks and into the pack house. You may do this after our guests have left, so there is no distraction. Now, let me be absolutely clear on one thing. There is a reason the process for this detail is so strenuous and takes time. We want the best and most trusted for protection on the Luna. Without her, we are all vulnerable and weakened, so if anything happens to her under your care, you will be punished to the full extent of my power. If you betray us in any way, the sentence is death," Trevor looked at them, and they did not flinch. They were already aware of the consequences of this job and title. Most warriors dream of this opportunity, and all will lay down their lives to protect their Luna and pack.

"Understood, Alpha. We will serve and protect our Luna from this day forward, however she needs us," Jacob said. The other two nodded in agreement, and they bowed again.

"Your charges will be arriving tonight. However, you should not be needed until tomorrow. If that changes, I will call for you," I let them know, and they nodded again before walking out.

Now that everything settled down, we all finished lunch and talked about the plans for the rest of today and tomorrow. Where we were all going to meet up, where our places would be tomorrow, and how Zander and I would be announced. It was a good feeling to have everyone here and just be able to talk about things with people. Being included is a wonderful feeling. I look forward to doing more and being part of more with my new friends and home. I have never had this much hope for my future before.

# Chapter Thirty-One
## *Aylin*

I was so lost in thought, I didn't pay attention to who was with me when I went upstairs. I just naturally assumed that it was Kevin. So, when I felt hands touch my waist and start to travel up my sides, I tensed and then turned in the arms that held me. I was about to swing when I saw Zander looking down at me.

"Are you really going to hit me, my queen, all for wanting to touch and hold these perfect curves?" he said, amusement all over his face. I kind of did want to hit him with the smirk he had on his face. I should have realized it was him, but I was really lost in my head. That is not a good thing at all. I should not have been that caught off guard.

"I am so sorry, Zander. I don't know why I just assumed it was Kevin or Liam that followed behind me, and it bothered me when I thought one was touching me like that." I smiled at him sweetly and leaned into his embrace instead.

"Well, I am glad that you will not let anyone else touch you, but what has you so distracted that you couldn't recognize my touch or even my scent?" he asked, a little concerned. I blushed and shrugged my shoulders. Hesitating for only a moment longer, I decided that I may as well let him in; he is my mate, and we shouldn't keep things from each other. Maybe I just need to vent as well—and why not vent to him?

"It's just everything! I mean, we have been here for a week, and so much has happened, and I feel like months or even years have gone by in some ways, and not enough time in others. Look at everything we have learned and everything that is about to happen. I will be a Luna of a Lycan pack, and a week ago I was just hoping my pack would let me be a warrior and make a contribution. I never had high hopes or dared to dream other than occasionally that you could be mine, but I think all the girls fantasized about you." We both laugh at that, even though it was a pretty factual statement. "It's just—to know I have this special wolf and Lycan, and that I am actually related to the moon goddess—and then there is the fact that I am being hunted on top of learning how to control new abilities, and learn everything I can about this pack and the packs I will be aiding in leading—there is just so much!" I take a deep breath and count as I blow it out. I open my eyes and look up into Zander's.

"I know." It's all he said, and it's still enough. He is going through most of this with me. The only difference is he doesn't have to learn how to control new abilities, but he is changing into a Lycan slowly. I can even see certain features changing in him and my brother—more like they are getting sharper lines in their features. His face softens as he looks at me, and his hands run up and down my sides.

"I just wanted to make sure you are okay, and maybe even distract you a little from all those pesky thoughts that are invading the pretty head of yours." His voice is husky, and I get his meaning right away. My thighs clench, and my heart picks up pace. I can feel the heat rush between my legs, and I need him. His nostrils flare, and I can see the lust in his eyes as he leans down and starts kissing me.

The sparks from the touch of our lips shoot through me, and in the next second, a ravenous hunger and need consume me. I fist my hands into his shirt and pull him closer. I deepen the kiss. I need him—all of him—and I want it now. I moan into his lips, and something in him snaps. Whatever restraint he was holding on to vanishes.

Zander reaches down, grabbing me right under my ass, and lifts me up off the ground. My legs instinctively wrap around him, and he strides over to the couch, never breaking the kiss. He sits with a plop on the couch, with me straddling him. I move my legs from behind him to the side of his legs on the couch, and right there, already against my core, is his thick, hard cock. I can feel it pressing against his pants, and I can't help the response I have as I start rocking against it. I need the friction right there. Goddess, it feels so good.

He groans, and his fingers dig deeper into my hips. My lungs are burning from the lack of air, and my swollen nub throbs as I rub myself against him, chasing the orgasm that is starting to build inside of me.

"Take it out and stroke it, baby. I need to feel you." Zander's voice is so deep and husky it makes my pussy clench as it gets wetter just from his words. I reach down and undo his pants, reach inside, and pull his large, throbbing cock out, and it juts straight toward me. Wrapping my hands around it, I can almost touch my fingertips, and I start to stroke him. His head falls back as he hisses through his teeth. This eggs me on, and I slip from his lap and get to my knees in front of him.

"Baby, what are you doing?" he asks, but I don't answer. I just lower my head and lick the bead of precum from the tip of his cock. His body shudders, and I run my tongue from the base of his cock to the tip and swirl it around his head. Then I wrap my lips around the tip and suck. He bucks under me, and I take a little more of him in, sucking and using my tongue on the underside of his shaft, applying pressure and massaging it as I suck him in deeper and deeper until he hits the back of my throat and I gag.

I don't stop, though. I bob my head up and down, occasionally taking him as far as I can go, gagging and choking until my eyes water and I feel like I am going to be sick. I try to breathe through it, but it's too much, and I have to back off. I breathe while I work the top half of his shaft with my mouth and the bottom half with my hand. I go back and forth doing this and watching him writhe and buck beneath me. I can hear him moan and grunt and tell me how much of a good girl I am and how beautiful I look taking him like this. All his praise makes me feel empowered, and I don't let up. I am addicted to the sounds I am eliciting from him. I crave more.

I jump, startled, when I hear the door open, like a kid caught with my hand in the cookie jar. My cheeks flame red as I watch Trevor walk in. It only takes him a moment to assess the situation with me on my knees in front of Zander, my hand still around his cock, and I am not sure if I should feel worried or turned on more. My mind says it's wrong to do this without both of them together, but my body floods with heat, and wetness pools between my thighs. My panties are so wet, my need growing as I look at Trevor. He closes the door and steps in.

"Don't stop on my account, little wolf"," he says with a cheeky grin. "Go ahead and go back to what you were doing. Let me see how you please him"," Trevor said, walking closer. I turn back to Zander, who grabs his cock and aims it at my mouth, tapping it on my lips to get me to let him in. I open and take him back into my mouth. It doesn't take long, and I am lost in trying to get those sweet noises and praises from him again.

"Damn, she is a good girl, isn't she, Zan?" I only barely register that Trevor has given Zander a nickname; they must be getting closer.

"Goddess, yes she is"," Zander cries as I gag myself on his cock again and again. "Aylin", fuck!" he cries, and his head lolls back against the couch again.

"Let's see if she can keep it up while I check her cunt to see how wet she is." I already knew what he was going to find. He pulls off my pants with ease and slides my underwear down with them. I raise one leg at a time for him to help slide them off. I try to focus on what I am doing, but he is there—his fingers running through my wetness, up through my slit, and circling my clit. My hips buck involuntarily as he continues to circle the throbbing nub, then run back down into the slick mess and back again. I am a mewling mess while I bob my head on Zander's cock, saliva drenching my hand as I work him up and down, trying so hard to keep the rhythm.

This is impossible. The more I try to focus on pleasing Zander, the more often Trevor is able to get my hips to jerk from sudden sensation overloads. His skilled fingers tease my clit, and then he pushes one inside me and I groan. The reverberation of the noise I made must have felt good to Zander, because he groans in response.

"Damn, little wolf, you are so soaked and ready to be taken"," he growls, and then I hear the zipper of his pants. I don't have to wait long before he is there behind me. One of his hands grabs my hip, and the other helps guide his cock through my mess. He teases me and slides it through my folds, and the head of his cock hits my clit. He does this a few more times till I am rocking back to get more friction. He pulls back and guides himself to my opening and pushes inside me slowly, all the way to the base. He stays there for entirely too long, giving me a way-too-full sensation. I start to move and wiggle on it, and he smacks my ass. The sting of it makes me jump forward, taking much more of Zander into my mouth and down my throat, choking me, making me gag and cough.

"Yes fuck!" Zander cries out he fists his hand in the back of my hair and starts to move my head and mouth how he wants and Trevor starts thrusting hard and deep into my pussy. The wet sounds coming from both ends of me are beyond erotic and all you can hear are those noises and our heaving breathing with occasional grunts and moans.

"I am getting so close, my queen! I want you to swallow me, you understand?" He is looking down at me and all I can do is moan around his cock, which he enjoys. His hips thrusting up into my mouth and then I can feel his cock harden further and his balls tighten in my hand as he releases into my mouth. I quickly swallow every drop as it comes out. When he is done he sits back and relaxes and as Trevor loses himself into my pussy and pleasure rocks though me I clean the remnants off the tip of Zanders cock with my tongue. He smiles down at me.

"You are my good girl!" He says and watches me as Trevor fucks me harder now that I am not attached to Zander. He body punishingly pumping into mine and I scream as he fucks me with wild abandon. The pressure inside me is building and taking me higher. He reaches around and starts to circle my clit with his finger again and that is my undoing. I lose it, fall off the cliff I was climbing toward, and come undone for him.

"Fuck little wolf! Your cunt is spasming and sucking my cock in; you are so damn greedy, aren't you?" He thrusts a few more times and then slams into me, holding onto my hips with an almost painful grip, and spills inside me. I am still in a haze when I feel him pull out of me, and then I feel as though I am floating as I am carried in someone's arms.

I can hear the bath water running and I just nestle into the big strong chest holding me. Breathing in Trevor's intoxicating scent I just can't get enough and I bury myself into him as much as I can. When the water stops he sets me down and finishes undressing me. He lowers me into the tub and then both of them strip and join me. Trevor sits behind me and pulls my back to his chest and Zander sits in front of me and lets my legs fall to either side of his. They wash me together taking their time massaging the soap into my skin. Their hands kneading into my shoulder and arms over my breasts and Zander's up each one of my legs in turn.

When Zander gets to my pussy he makes sure to go agonizingly slow making sure every last bit of it is washed, while Trevor continues to rub my breasts and every now and then pull on my nipples causing my back to arch off his chest and a moan to escape from my lips.

Trevor starts kissing and sucking on my neck right where his mark is and my hips start to move on their own. Zander takes that as an invitation to push two fingers into me and start pumping them. The rhythm of my hips starts to match his fingers and the water sloshes over the side of the tub but I could care less as I am chasing yet another release. I buck more when Zander uses his other thumb and rubs circles on my clit. I am so close.

As if Trevor could read that thought, he pulls my nipples and bites down on his mark. With every sensation in overload, I explode! The sheer pleasure that courses through me has my body shaking and I see stars though my heavy lashes. It takes me a few minutes to really open my eyes and become coherent.

"Well, now, how do you feel? Are you relaxed?" Trevor whispers into my ear.

*Mmmmmmm*, is all that seems to come out. I can't even form words right now. My eyes droop and I know I am relaxed and feel exhausted.

"I think that is a yes." Zander chuckles and I try to smile. I have no clue if I succeeded.

"Well, little wolf, I think you may have a little time to take a well-deserved nap," Trevor tells me as they work together to pull me from the tub and dry me off with big soft towels. Oh my, the towels are even warm. These men thought of everything to get me to relax. They must have sensed my rising anxiety with our families coming. I was trying to hide it, but I am not quite skilled enough to school my emotions yet.

They take me to our large bed, lay me down in the center of it, and pull the blankets up over me. They both lay next to me and I roll to the side facing Zander and snuggle into his side laying my head on his chest. Trevor comes in behind me and becomes the big spoon to my little spoon. We take turns doing this but I have found that Zander likes to sleep on his back and Trevor likes to sleep on his stomach or side so this position usually works the best for the three of us and is becoming our go to.

It doesn't take me long and I am drifting off into nothingness.

'There you are! Did you think you could hide from me?' I looked around, but I couldn't find the source of the voice I was becoming all too familiar with.

'Where are you? Who are you?' I called out into the darkness. I couldn't see anything, I couldn't smell anything, it was just blackness.

'Don't worry, my little prize, I am coming for you.' The dark chuckle that followed sent dread and fear through my system. My skin felt like it was covered in ice.

'Just tell me who you are!' I screamed

'You will find out soon enough, don't be too hasty my dear.' He laughs again and then there in front of me are two red glowing eyes. I look up to see them and it is all I can see. He can't be that tall can he? I hear his chuckle and then not only my skin but also it's like the very blood in my veins turns cold. I shiver.

'Please leave me alone.' I cry. I can feel the tears streaming down my face.

'Oh no my dear I can't do that. I have big plans for you, and I can't wait to hear your cries and screams as you help me get revenge. I have been looking forward to this for some time and I must say even though I was furious back when your bitch of a mother hid you from me, I am so glad she did so. It gave me time to find what I need to aid in my revenge on your family, and you my dear are the key.' I could feel him closer now but still could not see him, and I could no longer see his eyes. I panic looking everywhere.

"Please, I am begging you, I did nothing to you," I begged

"It matters little. You are the result of the betrayal done to me, and therefore, your life is forfeit to me. You will help me get my revenge! I am coming for you, my dear.'

I bolted up screaming. Panic coursing through me Zander and Trevor are already there holding me trying to calm me.

"What is it? Tell me what happened!" Zander said as soon as he said that, the door to our bedroom swung open, and Kevin ran in. He doesn't stop till he gets to me, and he places his forehead on mine as soon as he does; his contact, along with my alphas together, calmed me.

It took me a moment to realize Trevor and Zander were both growling low. Kevin backed up and then looked away quickly. I looked down and realized I was still naked, and my top half was showing. Kevin stayed turned around, and Trevor went to the closet and pulled out a red sundress for me, and threw it on the bed. He grabbed a pair of jeans and a black shirt for himself and a pair of jeans and one of Zander's white shirts for him.

We threw on the clothes, and I let Kevin know when I was dressed so he could turn around. I didn't move from where I sat. I was still shaking, and fear still coursed through me.

"Aylin, what is going on? This one was worse somehow, wasn't it?" He was looking at me questioningly. I nodded. "What happened?"

"It was dark. I couldn't see anything, and he was talking to me. It felt like he was right there all around me." I shuddered, and Zander wrapped his arm around me protectively. "He told me that he is coming for me, that I am going to help him get his revenge, and that he is glad my mother hid me because he found a way to do that, and I am the key." I looked up at the three of them, and they were all still.

"He talked to you and told you this?" Trevor asked.

"Did he say anything else?" Kevin asked.

"Just that he is coming and that he is going to make me scream"," I added, shuddering again. "It felt so real." Tears had started to fall.

"Don't worry, my little wolf, you are safe. We have you"," Trevor said, rubbing my back. I nodded and let them comfort me. We were only there for a few minutes, and then I felt Trevor stiffen beside me. He looked down at me with an apologetic look on his face.

"What is it?" I asked.

"They are here"," is all he said, and my stomach fell. Great. All the work Zander and Trevor did to ease my mind and relax me earlier is gone just from that dream, and now I have to let everyone know that they are going to be without their future Alpha and Beta, and that I am a direct descendant of the Moon Goddess. What could go wrong?

"Don't forget, we are doing this together, and we are all a little nervous, but we will have each other's backs!" Kevin said. With that, I looked at Zander. I know he is worried, and I felt a little guilty for feeling as bad as I did about myself, knowing he feels like he is letting down his father and his entire pack.

"You're right. We are together!" I said, grabbing Zander's hand and squeezing it. He smiled at me, and I could see his shoulders drop a little. He had tensed when Trevor announced that they were here.

"Let's go downstairs. It will still be a few more minutes till they arrive at the pack house—they have just crossed onto our borders"," Trevor told us. With that, I took a few deep breaths and climbed out of the bed. I was very aware that I was still not wearing underwear, and I wanted to use the bathroom.

"Ok, give me two minutes, and I will join you in the living room, and we can walk down together","" I told him.

They all left the bedroom, and I started to walk to the closet to get my undergarments when I had the feeling of being watched. I looked around the room and then out the windows, but I didn't see anything. I shook it off and went into the closet, grabbed a red lace bra and panty set, and went to the bathroom.

Two minutes later, I joined the guys in the living room and nodded at them. We walked out the door and made our way to the first floor and out the entrance of the pack house and stood together on the large porch, waiting for them to arrive. Nick, Nikki, Liam, and Luna Carrie joined us on the porch and stood there with us while we waited.

# Chapter Thirty-Two
## *Aylin*

Three large SUVs pull up in front of the pack house. The first person I see get out is my dad. All my anxiety subsides for a moment as I run up to him and throw myself into a big hug, just like when I was a little girl.

"I missed you guys so much"," I told him, and then looked over at my mom who got out after him. I wrapped my arms around her next.

"Don't forget about me." I turned and saw my sister. We squealed and hugged each other. Next, Lance and Layla got out and took turns hugging me. I could swear I heard a low growl when Lance picked me up off my feet and twirled me around. I knew it was Zander, and I will be sure to smack my mate for it later. He doesn't get to be jealous of Lance when Lance was one of the only ones there for me other than my family.

""It's only been a week and you miss us this much"?" my mom jokes.

"So much has happened, and I couldn't talk to you about it, and I really needed to"," I told her. Her brows furrowed.

"Why didn't you call?" she asked, confused. I could have, but what I need to tell them is not exactly something you say over the phone.

"Unfortunately, due to the circumstances, this is something I couldn't talk about over the phone. But we will get into that later, I promise. Right now, I just want to talk about you guys and see how you have been"," I tell her, and she and my dad share a look but then smile at me and nod.

Kevin comes over and says hi to everyone, hugging them each in turn and shaking hands with Lance. I looked over to find Zander with his family and then couldn't hide the grimace when I saw Lizzie standing there with her little pep squad. I really couldn't stand them. Every single one was fake and had a pole shoved up their ass like they were the center of the Earth and we are all here to serve them. The way they stood there looking around at everyone and everything like it was all beneath them was really pissing me off. I took a few deep breaths to calm myself.

Two of her friends kept eyeing Zander. They were playing with their hair and pushing their chests out. My mood soured more. Nope, not happening. Trevor, who had just finished saying hello to my parents, saw where my attention had gone, and Kevin had felt my anger spike. Kevin put his hand on my shoulder and I calmed a bit. Then I felt Trevor's hand on my lower back.

"Let's get him out of the way of those knock-off sirens"," he says, and I couldn't help the laugh that comes from me.

"How can you tell they are knock-offs?" I ask curiously.

"Because I have the real thing, and she doesn't have to try as hard as they are to draw attention to her"," he said, and I blushed. He effectively distracted me and put me in a better mood. Goddess, thank you for these men. They know just how to help me in my mood swings.

Trevor keeps his hand on the small of my back, and we walk over to my old Alpha and Luna. The placement of Trevor's hands is noticed by all of them. Lizzie looks pissed, and her little friends have a mixture of emotions on their faces. The two that were flirt-ing with Zander look happy—maybe they think they have a chance with him now. Oh, just wait. The Alpha looks displeased, and Luna just looks polite, schooling her features.

"Welcome, Alpha and Luna Black, to the Blood Moon pack"," Trevor says politely, extending his hand to the Alpha. Alpha Ste-phen takes it and shakes his hand firmly. "All arrangements are prepared, and I hope they are to your liking. Please come and let me introduce you all"," he said. His tone is polite but very formal.

"Hello, Alpha Gideon. I am really happy to get to see you again, and thank you for inviting us all to your pack"," Lizzie purrs. Trevor looks at her and then to her friends. He says nothing to them but looks at me and smiles sweetly.

"Are you ready, little wolf?" he asks me, and I smile up at him and nod. Lizzie's face falls.

"Are you ready, Zan?" I ask sweetly. He looks at me, and the grin on his face spreads. He knows I am claiming them both in front of these girls, and he is all for playing along.

"Of course, my queen." He bends and kisses me. Everyone is staring and in shock. He brushes my hair back over my shoulder and shows off his mark. Then Trevor does the same to the other side, and I giggle. "Let's go inside so our guests can get comforta-ble." We three turn, and both Trevor and Zander place their hands on my back as we walk. Kevin is trying so hard to stifle a laugh along with the others. Luna Carrie is just shaking her head slightly, but I can see the corner of her lips tipped up like she too is trying to fight a smile at our antics.

We walk in, followed by our guests, and the rest bring up the back. We take them to a lounge area while we wait for dinner to be served in the small banquet room. As everyone takes seats around the room, I sit on one of the couches more in the center. Trevor sits to my left, closer to my family, and Zander on my right, closer to his. Kevin sits next to Trevor, needing to be close to me in case my emotions spike. His sitting by us did not go unnoticed. Trevor and Zander both hold one of my hands. This earns dark looks from Lizzie and her friends and curious looks from the others.

After everyone sits, Trevor goes around the room introducing everyone. Once he is done, Luna Carrie stands and welcomes everyone to the pack. She lets everyone know where they will be staying—on the second floor in the guest wing—and their guard will have beds available with our warriors.

"There are going to be some of our own warriors that will be working with your guards. As you are aware, there is no free roaming, and they will let you know if you are going into an area that is not allowed"," Trevor said matter-of-factly. Alpha Black bristled a little at that, however, kept his mouth quiet. The same cannot be said for his daughter.

"I'm sorry, I thought you just said that we will be babysat while we are here." Lizzie scowled and crossed her arms over her chest. "We do not need a chaperone like we are five years old"," she remarked snidely, and Mona bristled. How dare she come to someone else's pack and show disrespect. Both Trevor and Zander tensed as well. Alpha Black looked at her with disbelief; he, above the others, knew she had just insulted everyone here.

"Lizzie, watch your tone. This is not your pack, and you will be respectful, or you will stay confined to your room the remainder of the time we are here and, furthermore, will not be permitted to go with us to other packs in the future if you do not have the ability to show manners to the host pack and their leaders. I thought I raised you better than this!" Alpha Black said this calmly and low, but you could hear the underlying threat in his tone. Luna Molly, his mate, placed a hand on his forearm, the connection calming him, which we could see when his shoulders visibly relaxed. He is still angry with his daughter, and he gives her a look that makes me shudder.

"Dad, I was just saying we are not children and shouldn't need to be followed." She tried to defend herself, and all it did was make him more angry.

"You know very well when we have visitors from other packs, they are not allowed to freely roam. Even trusted visitors have to have someone from our pack with them. This is not out of disrespect or to 'babysit'; it is a safeguard so others cannot go around staking out the pack. Why would you think that you would get treated differently than what is expected?" He was in full disbelief of his daughter, and even his mate's touch was doing little to help his anger.

"Well, isn't it obvious? Since Aylin is going to be with Zander, that means Trevor and I are going to be mates, and this is going to be my home. So why should I need someone to babysit me when this is going to be my pack?" she said, like everyone should have known this.

My anger skyrocketed, and my wolf went extremely territorial. It was taking everything in me to try to stay calm.

I knew my guys could feel the anger building within me. Trevor leaned closer to Kevin and whispered something in his ear. Kevin nodded and moved from where he was sitting to right behind me and put his hands on my shoulders.

Our parents and sister saw this and looked more confused than ever, but the Blacks, dealing with their daughter, had not realized anyone moved.

Only a small amount of my anger had dissipated from the combined touches of the guys, but it was enough to make sure I had control over Mona, who was done with people like Lizzie and Ruby. My wolf was not having it and was becoming more and more territorial when it came to her mates.

"Lizzie, you have no clue what you are talking about, and I am going to advise you not to speak nonsense"," Trevor said, clear as day.

They all looked at us then, and I was not sure what they saw, but Alpha and Luna Black's gazes grew. Lizzie, however, didn't seem to know when to stop.

"Oh Trevor, you don't have to act like that"," she said sweetly and got up from where she was sitting, walking over to him, completely ignoring me.

"I know we will be happy together. You may not be able to reject her, but it is clear she is going to be with Zander. And even though she is your goddess mate, clearly she can't have two, and you will need a real Luna here that only has eyes for you and your pack."

She was so sure about her place here, and then she reached out and tried to touch him.

My control on Mona snapped. The guys all jumped into action, grabbing me. Kevin pulled me up and behind the couch and had his arms fully around me, his aura sending calming waves through me. Then Zander and Trevor were on either side of me, trying to calm me and Mona.

This time, even Liam had to join with his Omega powers that aid in calming the mood of his Luna.

Alpha Black grabbed his daughter and pulled her beside him, and her friends ran over and joined them, making sure to be as close to Lizzie as possible. Her friends at least had enough common sense to not try to touch anyone. Lizzie does not know when to shut up or stop. The damn entitled princess needed to be taught a lesson, and Mona was ready to give it to her.

"I advise you to stay away from me and get any silly notions about us being together out of your head. I have one mate and only one! I don't care how many she has, as long as she is also mine and accepts me!" Trevor was not playing around. He was also a little on the defensive for having someone try to touch him without permission.

"Are you serious? You are both just accepting her? You are not going to reject her, Zander? How can you be with someone that has another mate?" Lizzie was incredulous. She couldn't believe that they would both want to stay with me even though they were not the only one I would be with.

"Are you questioning the Moon Goddess?" Luna Carrie spoke up. She stood and walked over in front of the four of us. She looked appalled at the display before her.

"No, Luna, it's just that it just can't be! You cannot have two mates"," Lizzie told her, trying to sound contrite and apologetic while addressing Luna—like she just realized she had overstepped when this motherly figure of grace and beauty stood before her.

Luna Carrie looked at her like she was a rodent.

"I have never felt so disrespected in such a short amount of time from visiting pack members. I thank the Goddess that my late husband, Alpha Henry Gideon, is not here to see that someone who was considered one of his closest friends and allies would allow his own flesh and blood to be so disrespectful—not just to any pack, but to one of the royal Lycan packs."

Alpha Stephen looked like he had been struck with that comment, and his anger rose. His face was red from the anger and embarrassment.

My body was vibrating, and a soft glow was starting to appear on my skin. The guys realized something was about to happen, and they were not sure what it was. I looked up at them.

"I need to get out of here now! Mona is pissed. I can't... contain her... She feels... a threat to her mate..."

I couldn't speak anymore. All my effort to try to keep from shifting was running out. Parts of me were already transforming—my claws were extending, and my ears and tail. I could feel the fangs pushing through my gums.

"Everybody out now!" Liam yelled, and Luna Carrie backed away. The others looked at what was happening to me. Nick grabbed Luna Carrie and Nikki and backed away. Seeing this, my family got up from the couch and backed up to the far wall. Alpha Black rose and motioned for his family to move as well. Mona's eyes had not left Lizzie.

"What is going on?" my mother asked, with sheer panic on her and my sister's faces now.

"Aylin is a very special wolf. However, she is so new to her powers, she cannot yet completely control them. We also do not know what all she can do. You need to leave!" Zander yelled. Trevor and Kevin looked at him, and then he realized his mistake. He said too much about Aylin in front of those that were not supposed to know.

'Mona, I'm here. It's okay. She is not worth this anger. Please focus on me.'

It was my brother's wolf, Reece. I could feel his wolf connecting with mine. A small amount of the anger she felt subsided. I just needed a little more control.

"Guys, my wolf is going frantic. He says I need to be with Luna Aylin and I need to now"," Liam said, taking a few steps closer.

Trevor looks from me to Liam, and then understanding dawns. The Gamma has the ability to feel his Luna and is her protector. Gammas also have a calming effect on them. He nodded and motioned for Liam to come back over.

"Yes, of course, get over here now!" Trevor said without hesitating any longer. Liam moves, and he is in front of me. He puts his hands on either side of my face and makes me focus on him. He starts to push out his aura on us. That, combined with the others, did the trick. Mona relaxed enough, being surrounded by her guys and her protectors, that I could take back control. I felt myself shifting back, and then, together with Liam, I took a few deep breaths. When I was ready, I looked at each of them and nodded.

Standing up and squaring my shoulders, I addressed the room. "I apologize for scaring you. I am still learning how to handle my wolf, and she gets extremely protective over her mates"," I say, looking at everyone.

"Aylin, you were glowing. Your eyes were glowing blue, and you were partially shifted. I have never seen anything so cool before. How did you do it?" Jolene said. Her eyes were big, and she had a look of awe on her face. Looking around the room, almost everyone did. I sighed. I had wanted to wait till after dinner and not have everyone here.

"I know you are all curious about what is going on, and we are planning to tell you everything that we can. We were going to discuss some of this over dinner, and then we were going to have the leaders and spouses stay, along with Lance and Layla, while the young ladies were taken to their rooms for the night"," Beta Nick spoke up, trying to help when he saw me hesitate.

"Wait, so I can't know?" My sister looked upset, and the look on Lizzie's face was defiant. Thankfully, she kept her mouth shut. Then I noticed the Alpha's hand on her shoulder and wondered if he was giving her a warning.

"I have never seen that light before. It was mesmerizing, and I couldn't look away." The voice was quiet, and it took me a minute to realize it was Kylie, one of Lizzie's friends. She was looking at me in wonder. "I felt drawn to it. Like it was home"," she said. Then she looked at Lizzie and quickly shut her mouth.

"I felt it too"," Amber Rae said.

"I did as well"," said Layla.

I am not sure how they could feel at home when my wolf wanted to commit a murder. How can what I was giving off make them feel that way? I saw others nodding, but then Lizzie shook her head.

"What are you talking about? That is not what she could have made you feel. I felt her too, and it was not in any way like home.

It was like she was going to kill me. She is a monster!" Lizzie spat, crossing her arms. I took a deep breath, and once again, I felt my guys each put a hand on me to be safe.

"If you will please sit, we will tell you all we have learned since coming here." I gestured to the couches again. "Maybe we should have dinner brought in here since we are already here, and this is going to take a while"," I told Trevor. He nodded, and then his eyes glazed over as he let the kitchen staff know what was going on.

Everyone started taking their seats again, although hesitantly for the Blacks. I did notice the Alpha made sure his daughter sat next to him, and occasionally I would see their eyes glaze over as they talked to each other. I wondered what they were talking about, but only briefly.

"Do you wish for the ladies present to be escorted to the dining area to eat with the pack while we have this conversation?" Luna Carrie asked. I thought about it for a moment and then mind-linked Trevor.

'Are you able to Alpha command everyone in this room to silence?' I asked.

'I am; however, if they are strong of will, they can break it,' he replies.

'Well then, along with the Alpha command, we will need a warning if anyone says anything outside this room for the time being.' He nods at me.

"I will give you a choice"," I say to the room. "You can stay and hear what we have to say; however, you will be commanded not to speak of it, and if you do, the consequence will be extreme. Or you can leave and eat dinner elsewhere and retire to your rooms when you are done." Lizzie's friends look at her to see what she is going to do. Just as I thought, Lizzie doesn't want to be left out.

"Oh, we will stay"," she says smugly. I turn to my sister, and she nods. She wants to know as well. I just pray that letting her stay doesn't put her in danger.

"Let me be a little more clear about the punishment"," Trevor chimes in, looking at Lizzie and her friends. "If you speak a word of what is about to be said in this room to anyone until Aylin herself gives the OK that it can be talked about, you will be brought in front of your pack as a traitor and flogged. Then you will be brought back here and put on a traitor's post for a week or more, depending on the severity of your transgression, before finally being taken to the traitor and rogue section of our cells. There you will stay until I say you can go. There will be no set time frame for the defiance of our request, but I doubt you will leave the cells." Kylie and Amber Rae looked at each other and paled. Lizzie just crossed her arms and sat still. My mother and father looked at each other, then at Jolene, but did not move or say anything.

""OK, here's what we know so far"," it was Zander speaking. We were all going to take turns so that it wasn't all on me to have to speak. "According to the elders, Aylin is a very special wolf. She does indeed have two mates, which are Trevor and myself, and as of right now she has one Guardian, which is Kevin. We have a feeling that is going to change with who and what she comes in contact with. Even the Lycan Alpha King has multiple, and she will probably have more than him." He looked at me and Trevor. I smiled at him.

"My mother was from the Crescent Moon pack"," I say clearly. Everyone stares—some in disbelief and others in shock—and I understood why. This was a pack from fairytale books. I continued before anyone could say anything. "She was the daughter of Alpha Gerald Moonraiser and Luna Sheila Moonraiser. Her name was Sarina, and she was the heir to be the next "Moon Goddess," I told them. Lizzie snorted loudly, but Alpha Black grabbed her shoulder and she quieted.

"How did you find any of this out?" my mother asked, a little shaky.

"It appears that while Sarina was alive, she and a friend of hers kept journals. It so happens that the pack we took in almost nineteen years ago that was decimated was the pack Aylin's mother found her mate in. Our elders were given the journals for safekeeping by the one that was her mother's friend"," Trevor said. This was news to me, but maybe it shouldn't have been. There were times the elders were talking and I was lost in thought, so really I probably should have known that.

"I know this is hard to believe. I myself am having difficulty with it; however, it is true. I have abilities that come with being the offspring of the Moon Goddess herself"," I tell them, and then look at my friends for comfort. I was starting to feel like a freak.

"What do you mean, abilities?" Layla asked. She and Lance had moved closer to me to show their support, and Layla's curiosity was palpable. Goddess, she and I were so much alike—we were both too curious for our own good.

"I am both wolf and Lycan. For starters, I can take either form. My wolf can also grow to the size of a Mother Wolf—maybe even larger than that, if I am being honest." I look at the others for an opinion.

"I think you would stand just a little taller than a Mother Wolf does"," Trevor nodded. Mother Wolves were another rare wolf that came out to someone destined to affect a great change in the world. For good or bad, it was all in their choices how the outcome would go. The wolf also only arrived once every third generation.

"That is incredible! I knew you were going to be special, but damn, girl!" Layla cheered, and it broke a bit of the tension in the room. I loved her so much!

"Is there anything else you can do?" Lance asked. I nodded. His question was not out of curiosity, more so his need to have details to make assessments.

"I can speak to anyone I choose in my other forms. I do not need a mindlink. There were other abilities my mother had, but we are not sure if I will get them or if I may have others she didn't. There are a lot of unknowns here, and sometimes it is hard to contain my wolf, especially when it comes to my mates"," I tell them all, and then glance at Lizzie in warning, only for her to roll her eyes at me.

"That sounds really made up! You expect us to believe you are related to the Moon Goddess and that you have powers?" she asked incredulously.

"She has a point. How can we believe any of this?" Alpha Black said, but then shot his daughter another look.

"I am going to say this only once"," Trevor said in a low growl that caused the hairs on the back of my neck to stand up. "I am not in the habit of giving false information, and neither is anyone else here! Would you see my mother, Luna Carrie, sitting here with us and allowing us to spew lies? Are you going to question me? Question her?" he asked, and I looked at Luna Carrie, hating that she was in a position like this, being questioned. She, however, looked poised and proper.

"That is not what I meant. I truly mean no disrespect! Please understand this is a lot to take in and just believe it is real, let alone truth"," Alpha Black quickly said in a placating tone. He did have a point—we didn't fully believe it was possible either.

"Trevor, can we move the couches? I think this room is big enough"," I said, looking around.

"Aylin, you do not have to prove anything to them. They can accept what we tell them as truth." Trevor didn't like that they were being questioned by anyone, no matter how outlandish what we said sounded, but I knew that even I had trouble believing what we had found out. So I just look at him till he sighs and nods.

"Nick, Liam, Kev, and Zan, help me move the couches"," Trevor said a moment later. Lance jumped up and helped Liam move the one the Blacks were sitting on, and the others all moved the couches around the edge of the room against the walls by the entrance, and one even blocking the entrance. I knew Trevor did this on purpose—to keep anyone from entering or leaving.

"I need you all to stay on the couches and do not move. There is barely enough space here when Mona grows." I started moving to the other side of the room. I allow Mona to push forward, and first she shifts into her Lycan form, ripping the dress I was wearing. Oh well—I wouldn't take it off in front of all the people here, especially since two were my parents.

Everyone stares when they see my Lycan's pure white coat with silver strands and highlights through it. Mona takes no time zeroing her gaze on Lizzie and growling. For the first time, Lizzie shrank away from me. Even she was aware Lycans were stronger than wolves, so even if I was lying about everything else, she knew I was stronger than her and she would not win if we were to fight.

'I am Mona. It is nice to meet you all at last,' Mona said, looking over toward my family and friends. My mother and father smiled, and my sister looked like a deer in the headlights. 'Please do not be afraid. When I shift again, you will not come to harm,' Mona told them. I notice she did not glance once over to the Alpha's side. Does that mean they should worry?

Mona shifted from Lycan to wolf. Again, everyone just stared in awe. Then I could hear the gasps around the room as Mona grew before them. In no time, Mona was so large she had to lay down in the room because she could not stand to her full height. Her tail had to wrap closely around her, and she looked and felt uncomfortable. So she did not stay that size for long. She shrank to her normal wolf size and then gave me control to be able to talk to everyone here.

'I do hope that you can believe us now—that we are not exaggerating who and what I am. I also hope that you will listen to the rest of what we have to say without questioning us every step of the way,' I voiced to the room. Luna Carrie had stood up and came over to me with the wrap she had on.

"Boys, can you make a makeshift wall so my daughter can shift back and be comfortable? Especially with dinner about to arrive." My guys did just that, and I shifted back and accepted the wrap from her. She rubbed my back and gave me an encouraging smile. "You are doing very well, my dear"," she told me, and I smiled at her. She was so kind to me. I felt so lucky to have her as my mother-in-law.

I turned around and let them know I was ready to sit and talk—well, as ready as I can be. Then we moved the couches back and everyone sat. Everyone except my family, Lance, and Layla, who came to stand in front of me and bow before me. I froze.

"There is no need to do that"," I tried to tell them, but they all still bowed in front of me. Luna Black started to lower as well, only for her mate to grab her arm and pull her onto the couch next to him. They always saw me as lower than them—of course he wouldn't bow or allow anyone else to.

"Aylin, you are royalty and a direct descendant of the Moon Goddess. You should have always been bowed down to!" Lance said, looking up at me. Everyone stood, and all I could do was gawk at him—at what he said. Thinking about everything I had been through at their pack and how I was treated. He had a point, and yet it was hard to imagine that kind of a life.

"He's right, my queen. You are the highest-ranking wolf alive by blood. When you are not bowed to and shown respect like we would the king or the Moon Goddess, it's a disrespect to even the king that rules now. Were he to find out about the lack of respect that has been shown to you your whole life—or even the lack of respect in this room right now"..." He paused, looking at his family. "It is a punishable offense." He stared his father and family down, and his father turned brick red with anger.

"I guess so, but this is just uncomfortable—having people bow before me"," I told them honestly. "I appreciate it, and I love you all so much, but I don't expect that! Not from my friends and family." I added the last part just because of Lizzie and her friends. Yeah, after everything they did to me—bow, bitch! I know I shouldn't think like that ever. It is not very Luna of me, but hey, just once I want to be petty too.

"Maybe we can take a short break. Food is coming, and I think maybe you would feel better if you went upstairs and changed, my dear"," Luna Carrie suggested. I nodded in appreciation.

"Layla, Jolene, would you like to come with me?" I asked, knowing they would want to see my room and I wanted to catch up with them alone. They nodded, and we left, going upstairs. I couldn't wait to catch up with them. I wanted to hear how the last week has gone for them as well.

# Chapter Thirty-Three
## *Zander*

I watched as Aylin, her sister, and Layla left so Aylin could get changed into clothes again. I was angry that my father questioned her—questioned any of us. Why would we lie about any of this? What is there to gain if we lie and then tell them not to tell anyone? That what is said here needs to stay here in this room. If it was a lie, wouldn't we want others to know? I was also upset that not one member of my family followed Aylin's family and bowed to her. The disrespect had me seeing red, and I honestly no longer cared what happened to them and their pack. If they have no respect for my mate, then they have no respect for me.

"That was not what we were expecting at all"," Kevin's mother, Corra, said. She looked like she was in shock. Kevin walked over and sat by her, taking her hand in his. She gave him a smile, but it didn't touch her eyes. She was shaken by this, and I couldn't blame her. To find out you raised the descendant of a god—and not just any god, our moon goddess—it had to be earth-shattering to discover.

"I know, but everything that was said here is true. Aylin is special, and this is why I was always drawn to her. It's why I always felt the need to be there for her, especially when she was scared"," Kevin told them. "We suspected it before we left, but it is confirmed that I am her guardian. Zander and I are both becoming Lycans since we are bonded to her"," he added, and that caused not only his parents but mine to start with surprise. My eyes locked with my mom's and then my dad's. I knew I was already getting stronger, and I was almost as strong as him before I started changing.

"So it is true that she has mated with both of you? What does that mean for our pack? Are you able to come back? Does she have to move between packs to rule as Luna to both?" my father asked, worry clearly written in his expression.

I looked at him and my mother. I waited for the guilt I had been feeling all week to flood me, but it never came. They had taken that feeling when they continuously disrespected my mate and, by extension, me and Trevor. Thankfully, at that moment, the Omegas from the kitchen came in with our dinner, putting it all on the coffee tables around the room. I am not sure if it was such a good idea for us to stay here to eat, looking around at the tables that are being covered and nowhere to really set a plate or any-thing.

Then I saw several people carrying what looked like wooden TV trays. They set them up by each of us and set down glasses for our beverages. They went around the room, moving the plates of food to the trays, and then left several trays of fruits, cheese, and meats on one of the coffee tables for us to pick at. They had set up trays for those of us that are missing right now as well. Trevor didn't miss a beat. As soon as everyone had finished setting up our dinner and left, he turned to my father to continue the conversa-tion.

"To answer your question, Alpha Black, Zander is going to stay here and be a Co-Alpha to this Lycan pack and assist in over-seeing all packs in our territory, including yours, as needed. How-ever, this means that he will not be taking over as Alpha to your pack. Unfortunately, since Kevin is a guardian, he also will not be taking over the Beta position and will be here to do his duty to protect Aylin." Trevor did not bat an eye as he told my father that his pack has no heir and, even worse, the Beta who could have taken my position would not be there either.

My father made a choking sound and looked between us with shock, disbelief, and anger all displayed on his face. My mother tried to school her features but did not succeed. She was also shocked, and I think sad.

"This is unacceptable. He is the only heir to the pack, and to take the Beta as well—who could have at least replaced him! You are basically informing us that our pack is going to fall!" My father tried to remain calm as he spoke with Trevor, but he was getting angrier and angrier.

"When have I ever just allowed any pack under my protection to fall or fail?" Trevor asked, looking unfazed, and then took a bite of his steak. His calm exterior wasn't fooling me. I knew he was already upset with them. Right now, I really didn't care if he did let them fall. Maybe that needed to happen.

"I am sure I do not know what you would or would not allow, since you are clearly not concerned with this one." My father's voice raised slightly. Trevor looked up and narrowed his eyes. My mother put her hand on my father's leg, trying to calm him. Could he have been more stupid with his choice of words? Was he trying to get on Trevor's bad side? He was quickly getting on mine. I don't know how Trevor does it.

"I have not had a lot of time to make preparations for how your pack will be handled; however, we have talked about it, and we do have a few ideas for your pack. I will not let any pack that is under my protection just outright fall or fail! That would show me as a poor or weak leader, don't you think?" Trevor asked, and I could tell that was a loaded question and wondered how my father was going to answer. To my surprise, my sister was the one to speak up, and once again, I wanted to tape her mouth shut.

"Trevor, can't you see that this is wrong? It doesn't make sense for you to both claim Aylin! It will hurt the North Woodland pack, and besides, if you just accept me, then there would be no need for any of this! I would be Luna here, and Aylin could be Luna of North Woodland. Everyone wins and no packs have to suffer"," she said, and my father looked at her and smiled.

"She is right. You should let Aylin be with Zander and accept my daughter. You can mark and claim your goddess-given mate, and I am sure, since there could be issues with her distance from you, that she could travel to you occasionally, or you could travel to her to see each other because of the bond. But this way, we all win. That was a very wise point." He smiled at my sister again, and I just stared for a moment. I was shocked that he could agree with that ludicrous idea. Anything to gain power. I could see Trevor was trying to compose himself before he blew up, so I took over.

"First, sis, you need to get it out of your head thinking you are going to be anything to Alpha Gideon ever! The last girl that tried to say anything about him keeping his mate and making her his Luna is currently in the cells here"," I told her, and she paled.

"You locked a girl up for wanting to be with you?" she squeaked at Trevor.

"She had been warned to keep her distance and be respectful to my mate and her Luna. She did not give me or my mate that respect and overstepped her bounds by touching me and asking me to throw away my goddess-given mate." My sister closed her mouth and did not continue. My father looked appalled.

"So what are these ideas you have discussed?" My father was trying to be calm, but I knew he was worried now when it came to my sister. He would not want her to be taken to the cells for what she had said, and if she didn't stop, I just might take her there myself. I am Co-Alpha here, after all, and I have the same authority as Trevor to dole out punishments.

"So there are a few options, and as acting Alpha, you will be the one deciding on how you would like to proceed"," I told him, and my father looked at me curiously, but there was still anger in his stare. I knew he was disappointed in me, but I wish he could see what an honor it is to be here and to be the first wolf ever to be a Co-Alpha of a Royal Lycan pack.

"So what are they?" he asked again.

"First, there is the obvious, and that is an arranged marriage for Lizzie with an Alpha that is not in line to take over their pack. There are a few Alpha-born that are in the packs under our protection, and we have put together some files for you to go through if you would like to entertain that option." Lizzie's face fell, and anger and fear were all over it. She had her heart set on Trevor.

"You would want to have your sister marry a stranger from another pack?" he asked, almost incredulously, and I scoffed at him.

"Is that not what you were already trying to do with Trevor?" I said, pointing in Trevor's direction.

"That is different. I know him and his father! She has been around Alpha Gideon a few times since she was a pup. He is not a stranger to us." I shook my head at him.

"You were still trying to get a marriage out of him, and they had never had time to know each other. So in a sense, he is a stranger. She has probably met any number of these other candidates at events you held or dragged us to as well, so she would know some of them about as well as she knows Trevor. If you were to move forward with this line, we could invite the Alpha-blood wolves of your choosing here for you both to meet and choose. That way, you can get a brief feel for them and see if Lizzie also ends up liking any of them so she has an actual chance to meet him before they wed and have a choice. It will be on neutral ground. Or we can have them go to your pack. It's up to you." My father nodded. He didn't seem to mind the idea of meeting them, but I knew he had his heart set on the alliance with Trevor. Then it dawned on me. My father is all about making alliances, and in a way, already had one here.

"Furthermore, this gives you an alliance not only with this pack through me but with another pack that will be married into yours." That really got his attention. I truly don't think it dawned on him that with me being Co-Alpha, there is already an alliance with our pack as long as he remains respectful. I will have to let him know that I will not tolerate further disrespect from him or my sister and will make it to where there is no favor for the pack. He was nodding, and I knew he was thinking it over. However, Lizzie was not having it.

"No! I will not just marry a stranger because Alyin is greedy and needs two mates that she does not deserve'," she spits.

"Hush, girl!" my father says to her. I could tell he liked the idea of brokering multiple alliances. He was all about the long game as well, so he was probably thinking about the packs in the area and which ones he would prefer to broker that alliance with.

"Father, you cannot be serious?" she squeaked. "Please tell me you are not considering this?" she asked.

"I do not see what it matters to you. You just want to be a Luna, and this way you will be a Luna and of your own pack. All you have ever cared about is status and making sure you were with an Alpha"," I told her. She looked at me at first with anger, but then it was like she realized that I was right. All she ever talked about was being a Luna and in her rightful place in the hierarchy. Granted, she wanted to be Trevor's Luna and have all the additional perks that came with it, but in a way, she was getting what she wanted—just not with the person she thought it would be with. Her brows pinched, and she honestly looked kind of lost for a moment.

"So say we did decide not to go that direction, what is the other option? You said you had a couple, right?" my mother chimed in, trying to defuse the tension with her mate and daughter.

"That would be that the next in line take over. If the Alpha and Beta fall, the next to take over is the Delta, then the Gamma"," Trevor said. That is when I realized that I have not met this pack's Delta, and I would need to ask Trevor why. Maybe something happened to him. Trevor continued, "So in your case, your Delta's son Lance would be next in line to become the future Alpha of your pack." Everyone glanced at Lance, and the look on his face was nothing short of hilarious.

"I... I... uh, what?" he asked.

"You are an amazing warrior and a leader through and through. We may not have always seen eye to eye, but I truly believe you would care for and lead the pack with dignity and honor. If my father were to choose you to replace him, you will have all of our support—that is to say, Alpha Gideon's, mine, and Aylin's. She also believes that you are the best choice"," I told him, and he audibly swallowed in shock that there was a possibility that he could potentially be an Alpha.

"Wait, does that mean I would have to marry Lance?" Lizzie shrieked. Her voice and outbursts were getting to be rather annoying. The door opened then, and Aylin, Layla, and Jolene walked in laughing. It made me smile to see Aylin so happy. They took their seats, and Aylin looked around the room.

"What did we miss?" she asked, looking between me and Trevor now.

"Well, we were just talking about the possible replacements for me at home since I am staying here with you"," I tell her, and she looks at Alpha Black and then at Lance, who still looked like he was in shock. She giggled.

"I have never seen Lance so speechless"," she said. Layla looked at her brother, and then her mouth dropped.

"Wait, so Lance? He would be the next Alpha?" she asked.

"It is an option for Alpha Black to consider"," Aylin told her.

"And to answer your question, Lizzie, no, you would not marry Lance. He will be free to find his goddess-given mate or choose a mate that he deems fit to be his Luna"," Trevor told her.

"So wait, then what happens to me? Do I still get to be Luna?" she asked. Seriously, is that all she can think about? A moment ago she was appalled at the thought of marrying a stranger to be Luna of our pack; now she is worried about not being a Luna.

"You would not be the Luna of your home pack, and you would be free to find your goddess-given mate or find someone to fall in love with. Or, if you can find another Alpha that is looking to choose a mate"," I told her.

"So there is no guarantee of my being a Luna, then?" she snarked.

"Not without an arrangement of some kind with an Alpha of another pack, and you would be the Luna of his pack. However, that would be something our father would have to assist you with, and I am not sure if there are any packs under our protection that will be looking for a Luna at the moment. No one has said anything to us that I am aware of"," I told her. She looked at our dad but did not speak. She has three options. If she is dead set on being a Luna and guaranteed that role, she will have to marry one of Alpha blood—or yes, she could marry Lance, but I doubt Lance would want that. The last option would be to broker an agreement with an Alpha that is unmated or lost his mate and needs a Luna. That is usually harder to find. However, she could be free to find her mate and try to be happy with him. Why that is not an option that appeals to her is beyond me.

"Those are both decent options, and I do appreciate you taking into consideration the welfare of our pack and its needs with what you have found out. I am grateful that even though you have not had much time and have had so many other things going on, you were able to assist in even putting together these "ideas," my mother's formal tone came out poised and sure. "I think at this time it would be wise for us to talk amongst ourselves and review the options you have presented—unless there was another you were going to talk to us about?" she asked, looking between us all.

"No, Luna Black, for now those are the only two options we have come up with in the short time we have had to address this problem. It is not a normal problem we have had to deal with in the past, and we are going to do all we can when the time for the transition comes"," Trevor said. He seemed to like talking with my mother more than my father. There was definitely more respect in his tone with her, but she also has never been anything other than respectful with him.

"Why don't we take the files you have put together of the suitable Alpha blood males? We will go through them and talk about the options presented. Lance is a fine young man with a good head on his shoulders, and I am sure, no matter what is to come, he will be able to handle his part in the future of the pack—whether it is to be the Alpha or Beta, or still take over his father's spot as head warrior and Delta"," she said, smiling at him.

"Yes, my mate is right. I would like to discuss this and make a choice after we have had time to do so." My father looked at his mate and smiled. She was always the one to smooth things over, and I knew he appreciated her for how she handled herself. I also knew that my mom would be all over Lizzie later. My father may scare us sometimes with his Alpha voice and command, but my mother was who we were really afraid of.

"But what about me?" Lizzie asked again, and that was my mother's breaking point.

"What about you, Lissette?" my mother said, using her full name, and my sister blanched. My mother's tone was calm and gentle, but my sister knew better. She was quiet after that. She knew she had pushed my mother, and now she was going to pay for it. My mother hated how spoiled Lizzie was and tried to teach her how to be a poised lady so she would be fit enough to be a Luna someday. However, my father has spoiled her so much that she just became the brat she is today.

My father seemed to realize as well that my mom had reached her end with Lizzie, and like she had done for him so many times during this talk in trying to comfort and calm him, he placed his hand on hers and tried to calm her as well.

"I just thought of something else"," Beta Archwood said, looking over at my parents. "Gamma Nathaniel, you have three sons, and they are all of age now, correct?" he asked our Gamma, who was standing closer to my mother than a moment ago. He must have felt her getting upset.

"Two are of age, and my youngest, Warren, is in his last year of high school. He will be 18 this summer"," he replied.

"If you are not able to find someone for your daughter, she can choose one of our pack members to be her mate and therefore our new Alpha. The boys are of a ranked bloodline and would be able to assume an Alpha position." Aylan's father had a point—that they didn't need to go outside the pack to have a new Alpha if they wanted Lizzie to be the Luna. And Daniel and Mark were good choices as well. They were Gamma blood, so any of them—or even Lance—could take over as Alpha and mate with Lizzie to get the position. Otherwise, next in line would be Lance.

"Maybe being with one born Gamma, they will be able to help control Liz and her tantrums as well—before she causes too many problems as Luna, disgraces the family, and gets overthrown and banished"," I say in a snide remark. I see Aylin trying to fight a smile.

"Ha ha, very funny, Zander"," she said, giving me a dirty look. I just smiled back at her, sat back, and put my hand on Aylin's upper thigh. My mother cut off the jabs between my sister and me before they could escalate.

"Yes, thank you, Adam. All these options are good and will be discussed. I appreciate your help"," my mother told him and smiled at him warmly. Beta Archwood nodded in reply.

I looked around the room, and it seemed everyone had, for the most part, come to a stop with the conversation. There was a lot that had been thrown around and discussed, and it seemed everyone just needed a moment to process it all. Everyone seemed to focus on their meals for a good moment, eating in silence.

"So, are you excited for the ceremony tomorrow?" Jolene asked Aylin, trying to break the silence.

"Honestly, I am nervous. This ceremony is a big deal since it is the ruling Luna ceremony for not only this pack but the packs we protect. All of the Alphas and Lunas of the packs will be there. I am just nervous. Not to mention, we are announcing Zander as Co-Alpha of the pack as well"," Aylin told her, and Jolene nodded in response.

"You know, I have never heard of there being a Co-Alpha. How does that work exactly?" Layla asked.

"Zander and I would share the responsibilities of running this pack and assisting in the monitoring and maintaining of the packs under us. We are the largest territory in the United States other than the Alpha King's territory. So this will make it so I am not stretched so thin with all my responsibilities here and elsewhere. He is also going to be handling some of our business, so this is honestly a blessing for us here"," Trevor told her.

"The last time we saw you all, I thought you were going to murder Zander, and now you guys are going to rule together? That is quite the "turnaround," Layla said, and I laughed. Aylin looked at her like she grew a head.

"Yeah, I think once we learned that we both had to mate with Aylin, we found a way to put our wants aside. Then, after we all mated, and we each marked her and she marked us, the hate and animosity we felt for each other kind of faded. Now the only thing that matters is our pack and making our mate happy"," I told her and smiled down at Aylin. She moved over and gave me a quick kiss, showing her approval. The contact came with that jolt of electricity that I have come to crave, and it was all I could do to let her pull away from me.

"That is really cool that you guys can do that! Do you think it has something to do with the marks and bond?" Layla asked, fascinated.

"I think so, but we are not a hundred percent sure"," Trevor told her. We really didn't know why we went from wanting to kill each other to just accepting each other and our new lives together. I still get jealous when she is with him and not me, but not like before. This is more just because I want her just as much and wish it was me every time pleasing her. But the feeling never lasts. I usually find that I am just happy that she is happy, and I know that she just wants us both to be happy as well.

"So do you all enjoy a fun time together?" Layla asked, wiggling her eyebrows. Aylin choked on her drink and spit some of it out, and Kevin groaned.

"We do not need to talk about that now. Wait for your girl time"," Kevin shot back at Layla, irritated.

"I agree. We do not need to hear about that at the dinner table"," Aylin's father told her, and a chorus of agreement sounded from the room. I didn't blame them, but I wouldn't have told them anything anyway. My wolf was not okay with anyone knowing anything about our mate in that kind of way and would have put an end to the conversation if no one else did. Thankfully, an overprotective brother and father made it to where I didn't need to be an overprotective and jealous mate.

For the duration of the meal, we answered the rest of the questions they asked, which were more what we were hoping for—how have you been, how is the transition going, and even if we are happy. Aylin loved talking about the training and about the work she wants to do with the pack in helping with the projects that are going to be done. It was good seeing her so animated talking to everyone, since in our old pack she was usually quiet and didn't speak much. She has changed quite a bit in the short time we have been here. She just keeps surprising me.

She apparently was surprising everyone else as well, since they were all staring at her. Her family and friends had huge smiles on their faces; my mother was smiling at her. My father seemed to be sulking, and I think it was because he realized that she is going to be an amazing Luna! I just hope he realized she is still his Luna, as she is going to rule over his pack either way. My sister is just scowling at her, but is for once wisely keeping her mouth shut. My mother must have really scared her, and I would love to be a fly on the wall and see what my mother has to say to her later. As for my sister's friends, I wasn't sure what the look on their faces was. It could be that they were seeing Aylin for the first time and were unsure about how to feel about it.

"Can I ask a question?" Everyone looked over at Amber Rae. Aylin paused for a moment and then nodded.

"I was just curious about your wolf and Lycan. Do you have two different ones? Like, is your wolf just your wolf and your Lycan another presence inside you?" I was taken aback; I didn't even think about that. I looked at Aylin and waited for her answer. I knew my wolf, Fin, was becoming a Lycan, however, he would not be able to shift into a wolf ever again—he would just be a Lycan. She had both forms, and I didn't even think about if it was just her wolf Mona and if she could be both. However, I am pretty sure it's just Mona—that is the only name I have ever heard Aylin say.

"It is just Mona. She has told me for a long time that she is a special wolf and that we are special, but I always thought that she was just trying to cheer me up. She can take both forms, but the Lycan one is a little different. You know how when your wolf takes over in wolf form, they can push you to the back and take over?" she asked, and Amber Rae nodded at her. "Well, when we are in Lycan form, the only way she can do that is when she feels extreme emotion. Otherwise, it's like we share it—one body, one mind, one soul. It is a very unique feeling"," Aylin said, and I wondered if it would be like that for me.

"So it's not just one of you in control when you are a Lycan?" Trevor asked her, looking a bit hesitant.

"No, we are both present. We have to give control to allow only one to be there—unless, like I said, she is in extreme emotion, such as if we are in danger. Then she can try to push me back, but it's a lot harder for her to do"," she replied. "Don't worry, though. When we did patrols, it was just Mona. I let her have control." She smiled at Trevor, and he smiled back. What was that about?

"That is really cool. So it is like you each have one form and share another"," Amber Rae said, looking at Aylin in awe. Aylin nodded and smiled a genuine smile at her—something I don't think she has ever done. My sister may not like or respect her, which I hope will change; however, my sister's friends seem to be coming around slowly, and that is a good thing. We need to be able to get along and be there for each other, and they need to

show their ruling Luna the respect she is already earning and
clearly deserves.

# Chapter Thirty-Four
## *Aylin*

After answering a few more questions about my abilities, which everyone seemed to be very curious about, and talking about the upcoming projects I am going to help with, and the training on the fields—which my father seemed to not be surprised about at all, which made me wonder if he knew that I was training in secret back home—we made plans for getting ready for the coronation tomorrow.

Then, because it was only about seven in the evening and not everyone was ready for bed, we called for the guards that would be assisting with everyone so they could all meet. It only took a moment for Thomas, Julian, Jacon, Talon, and Henry to come in and line up for introductions. I looked at Trevor, and he nodded at me. He is letting me assign who is going with whom.

"Mom, Dad, this is Thomas, one of Alpha Gideon's personal guards. He will be with you and your guard while you are here. Alpha and Luna Black, this is Julian, another of Alpha Gideon's personal guards."

"Jolene, this is Talon. He is one of my royal guards that is there when Kevin or the Gamma are tending to other responsibilities or for my added protection. He will be there for you if you wish to leave the pack house and travel the grounds. Lizzie, Amber Rae, and Kylie, this is Jacob and this here is Henry," I motion to each in turn. "They are going to be there for all three of you, and you three are to stay together. If for any reason you do not need or want to stay together, you will need to let them know so they can report

back to us, and we will decide how to proceed." Lizzie looked af-
fronted by this.

"We do not need babysitters, and we should not have to ask permission for things like not wanting to be around each other"," she said snarkily. I noticed Luna Black gave her daughter a sharp look—one that I pray I am never on the receiving end of.

"First off, as it has already been explained to you, you do not have the freedom to just roam a pack you are visiting. Further-more, your friends that you brought with you were not invited and therefore are your responsibility. That means that while they are here, if they do anything, you will be held accountable for their actions as much as your own. We had to pull in extra security for you bringing along those that were not invited, and the fact that you had the nerve to bring extras without prior authorization in itself is rude and disrespectful. You have no right to question or be angry about this situation. I do not even need to let them leave the pack house"," Trevor said tersely. He, like everyone else, was done with Lizzie and her attitude.

"Lizzie, that is enough. If you speak one more word, I will have Nathaniel take you home and confine you to your room until I get there to deal with you. You have spoken out of turn and embar-rassed us far too much this evening and in the presence of not only a Royal Lycan but one that is outranking anyone else alive today— including the Lycan Alpha King! Or are you unaware of how the bloodlines work and need to go back to remedial schooling?" Luna Black said to her daughter. The color left Lizzie's face, and then the embarrassment set in, and she turned bright red. Everyone from our old pack stood there in shock. Luna Black is very reserved and does not raise her voice or let temper show. For her to even speak the way she had to her daughter in front of everyone was a complete shock.

"You will do as you are told, and you will not complain. I have obviously been far too lenient and spoiled you too much! You have no respect for me as Alpha, for your mother, for our pack, or anyone, for that matter. I am beyond appalled"," Alpha Black said to her. Lizzie looked like she was going to cry. She often did to get her way, and her father usually caved to whatever she wanted when she did.

"Alpha Gideon, Alpha Black, and Luna um"..." Luna Black paused, unsure what to call me. "Luna Archwood"," she said, using my maiden name. I realized we haven't discussed what I was to be called. I smiled at her and nodded for her to continue. "I want to apologize for my daughter's behavior. I am aware that it does not make what she has said tonight right in any way. However, I can assure you she is going to be learning her place, and if she cannot learn it, then I personally will not allow her to ascend to Luna of our pack. I would rather see the honor of the next Alpha go to Lance, as he would make a fine leader in place of our son." She then looked at Lance and smiled at him fondly.

"Dear, what are you saying? We need to discuss this in private"," Alpha Black stated. He did not like the idea of writing off their bloodline as the leaders of the pack—that I already knew. He hated that Zander could not take over, but I was sure he liked the idea of new alliances with a pack they do not already have an alliance with.

"NO!" Luna Black said forcefully, looking at her mate and then her daughter". "A Luna is the mother of the pack; she is there to nurture and guide the pack, to love and defend the pack, to put the pack's needs before her own. Today my daughter has shown she only cares about titles and herself. She has no respect for others, for her pack, or even her own parents. If she doesn't care about someone other than herself, she will not take my place as Luna!

That is final! If you dare ascend her without my blessing, I will then reject you as my mate. I will not live with those that think it is okay to show such blatant disrespect!" At her words, Alpha Black paled, his disbelief and shock evident on his face. He looked between his mate and his daughter and seemed to come to a decision.

"My mate is wise and just! It should not have taken her to make such a demand of me for me to see that she is correct. We will not allow our daughter the right to ascend and take over the pack unless she has earned it. If she cannot earn it when I am ready to step down, the title of Alpha will go to Lance Lockwood. He is a fine warrior with a kind soul that can lead our pack well!" Alpha Black stood straight, and he did not bat an eye or look at his daughter again.

Lizzie, however, had tears streaming down her face. The only thing I could think is she only had herself to blame for how this had turned out. Of course, knowing her, she will not see that and more than likely will place the blame on someone else. As if she could read my mind, she shifted her gaze from her parents to me and gave me a glare that I have come to know all too well. She did in fact blame me for what has occurred here today. She not only will not be Trevor's Luna, but now the idea of being a Luna to at least her own pack is being taken away as well.

"I believe that to be very wise of you!" Trevor told them. "I will still give you the folders we have of the suitable Alpha blood candidates for you to choose from if you find your daughter worthy"," Trevor said, nodding at them.

"Thank you, Alpha Gideon. That is very much appreciated. I do hope that it all works out for everyone involved here. I would also like to apologize for my outburst as well. I would have liked to handle this matter behind closed doors. However, it appears I was not allotted that courtesy with my daughter, who does not seem to know her place"," Luna Black said to us, nodding her head in respect.

"It is alright, Luna Black. I do not hold anything against you, or your mate, or pack! You have nothing to apologize for!" I told her.

"Thank you for your kindness, Luna Archwood. I know our pack did not give you the fair chance you should have had. I hope that it will never happen in our pack again. We should have never let fear get in the way of being good to someone in need." She bowed—not just a nod of her head, but bowed to me. Her mate then followed. Then it seemed like everyone joined in. The last to bow to me was Lizzie. I could tell she didn't want to, but when her eyes glazed over, she did so in a forced manner. She must have been commanded by her father.

Tears were pricking my eyes at the sight before me. I couldn't believe what I was seeing. Then I noticed that both Zander and Trevor and the members of our pack were bowing to me as well.

"Please, you all do not need to do this"," I told them, getting myself choked up.

"Aylin, you still do not realize who you are. You are not just the Luna to my pack. You have to understand that goddess' blood runs through your veins. You are the great-granddaughter to the moon goddess herself, and that makes you the most powerful, highest-ranking wolf or Lycan alive today"," Trevor said to me, taking my face in his hand and wiping away the tears.

"That is not entirely true"," I told him, looking from him to the people around the room. "You see, my mother was from the Crescent Moon pack. That means that that pack is a real place, and those there are higher ranking than I am"," I told them.

"Aylin, from what we know of that pack, it is in another realm. It is not a part of ours, so therefore they are not a constant presence. That means, little wolf, that you are indeed the highest-ranking wolf and Lycan in our world. At least that we are aware of. Who knows if any of your relatives ever came off that island"?" Trevor added that last part and shrugged.

Holy shit, could that really be true? Do I outrank the Lycan king? Will he be pissed about that? I hope not. I don't want the Lycan king to hate me or think that I will take away his power! I don't even know how I am going to be able to handle being Luna of this pack and the ones we take care of, let alone all packs across the world. I just don't want that responsibility. I mean, I know they have said this before, but it really was just sinking in that I outrank the king.

"If everyone is okay with the arrangements, your guards will show you to your rooms, and then if you wish to head out, they will escort you through the pack"," Trevor said to everyone in the room.

"Wait, what about us?" Layla asked. "We were not given a guard"," she said, looking at me in confusion.

"Why would you guys need one? You are coming with me!" I grin at her, and both she and Lance smile back. I felt Zander stiffen beside me but again stayed quiet. He is going to have to trust me and my friends. Lance will not overstep, and I trust him with my life. "Besides, if one or both of you do not want to hang out with me, then I guess I can ask Liam here to take you around," I said, pointing over my shoulder.

"Oh hell no, girl, you're mine for tonight!" Layla said, laughing. She walked over to me, dragging her brother behind her. "So what are we doing?" she asked.

"I was going to leave that up to you. Do you want to go to the pack square and see what there is?" Then I lean closer and whisper to them, "I could take you to our training yard. It's not on the list of places the rest can go, but I am dying to show you!" I tell them. They both grin and nod. "Excellent." I jump, clapping my hands together.

"You already kicked so much butt today. Can't you just take the night off?" Zander asked, shaking his head. He knew I wasn't just going to show them the training yard, and I couldn't help the shit-eating grin I gave him because of that.

"Oh no, no, no. Zander, this is Lance we are talking about, and Lance never lets me win! I won't have another chance like this for a while!" I grin ear to ear. The look that crossed Zander's face was priceless. A huge shit-eating grin appears, like he just realized that I want to kick Lance's ass, and he is now just as excited to see it.

"This is true. You won't get a chance like this for a while. Why don't we come along?" he said, smiling at me. I shrug and nod, not caring one way or the other. Everyone files out of the lounge area, and most head upstairs. Lance, Layla, Trevor, Zander, Kevin, Liam, Nick, Nikki, and I all head to the pack training yard.

"Do you have enough bodyguards?" Layla whispered to me.

"Everyone here has heard about Lance's abilities as a warrior and knows he is highly skilled and sought after. I have come into some of my strength, and it is still growing. I have been winning matches against elite Lycan warriors, and they are all eager to see if I will win against him and kick his ass"," I whispered back conspiratorially. She laughed and then looked over at her brother, who was walking back by Nick and Liam, asking questions about their routines and such.

Along with the invite for the coronation, Lance had a further invitation to spend a few months here to help with training. So he was talking about the styles they already knew, training schedules, and just in general what they were wanting their warriors to learn and improve on. I didn't mind the distraction so I could conspire with Layla.

"So they all want to see if you can finally beat him? Okay, I have a feeling this is going to be good!" she said, laughing again.

"So what are you two up here whispering about?" Zander questioned, catching up with us.

"Just that I plan on kicking Lance's butt, not just showing them around the practice field"," I told him, shrugging like it's no big deal.

"Honestly, I can't wait to see it"," he said with a big grin on his face.

"Really? You can't wait to see Lance grapple and touch and throw her around?" Layla said, pointing out that Lance is about to have his hands on me. Even if it is in a sparring sense and there is nothing intimate about it, the comment got Zander's attention, and a low growl vibrated from his chest.

"Oh, will you stop? Lance is my friend, and you need to get over whatever it is you have against him. He will always be a part of my life since he was one of the only people that were there for me"," I said pointedly. "And that includes you. So unless you want to be in the doghouse, you better stop!" That got his attention, and he even looked a bit guilty. He knew that he only has himself to blame for my past. If he actually cared about me like he says he did, he should have been there for me as well, instead of letting others dictate his behavior.

"Here we are"," I hear Liam shout from in front of us, getting everyone's attention. He leads us all out onto the main field and points out the different areas, arenas, and obstacle courses, and explains that they also do classes for all ages starting young so that the pups can learn the basics and self-defense, so when they are of age to really get into training, they will already have good muscle memory. They play lots of games that aid in combat training as well.

"So what do you think?" Liam asked Lance after we walked around showing him most of the field. We didn't take him through the trails.

"I think this is one of the most impressive setups I have seen in a while. I also like that you have started training young. Most packs do not think it's important and wait until about fifteen for most basic training and conditioning to start. That is not bad, since they are starting before getting their wolves. However, the younger, the better"," Lance replied. He seemed rather impressed by the whole thing.

"So, since we are here, it's been a whole week since you kicked my butt. Wanna have a go?" I asked him. Lance looked at me, and a huge shit-eating grin spread across his face.

"I thought you would never ask"," he said. "How do you want to do this? Hand-to-hand? I didn't bring the wooden swords, though, so I think we will have to wait on that one unless they have them here"," he teased me.

"Ha ha ha, very funny!" I told him. "I still need training with the sword, but I am getting better. Not using the wooden ones though, they have me using the real thing here." I gloat at him, and his eyes widen.

"I am surprised you are not cut into pieces." He is full of jokes today.

"Well, they have me going to the basics with it right now. There are a series of steps and movements to build up muscle memory, but they don't want me to get used to wielding a wooden sword since there are differences in the weight and how it moves"," I tell him.

"Yes, there is, but not by much. They are still good to use when you are first starting out sparring." He shrugs, and I know he wishes he had more time with me to help train me up. We had only just started with swords, and he had even told me he would show me the basics so I could come out to the woods and train by myself, but I begged him to show me actual movements against opponents and do it with someone. I always learned better just doing and having that person against me, so Lance caved. However, here they did not. I am sure Lance is feeling like they are looking down on his abilities for not teaching me the basics, but looking at everything else I can do, I don't think they are.

"Let's do one on one with no weapons"," I told him, and he nodded. I started to lift the blue sundress I threw on over my head and heard a low growl. I looked over at my guys, shaking my head. "Will you relax?" I lifted it the rest of the way up and over my head, revealing a sports top and shorts. I was prepared for this.

Lance and I squared up, and I waited for him to make his first move. When he did, I countered, and it was like a dance with a partner that knew your body better than you did. He could see every move I was going to make and counter it with ease, and I could see all his. We were, for the most part, equally matched, except in strength. With my Lycan, I am stronger than him, but with his skill, he can take it.

Our match lasted for a good half hour. We had people cheering and booing us. Layla would go back and forth cheering and taunting. Of course, Zander and Trevor were rooting for me, while Kevin and Liam were telling Lance he needed to kick my ass and knock me off my high horse.

"Come on, Lance, we will never be able to live with her if you can't beat her!" Liam said.

"Come on, Aylin, you got this! You have beat almost every warrior you have come across here!" Zander reminded me.

"Lance, she is still just your student, don't let her surpass the teacher! We need you to keep her in her place just a little longer!" Kevin yelled to him. "You can do it! Kick her ass!" What the actual fuck? Traitor! My brother was rooting for Lance to win? The distraction his word caused was enough for Lance to get the upper hand.

He knocked me on my back by locking one of his legs behind mine, placing a hand on my shoulder, and shifting our weight. A simple but effective move that knocked me down. I tried to roll away, and halfway through the roll, Lance pinned me. Damn, he was fast! His knee was in my back between my shoulder blades, and the other leg firmly planted next to my body.

I tried to flail around in one last-ditch effort to get free, but he pushed his knee in harder. He grabbed one of my arms and twisted it behind my back. Pain shot through my arm and shoulder, and that made anger and disbelief spike through me. I couldn't believe that he had me pinned. He had me down and restrained.

"What have I told you about focus, Aylin?" he said in my ear. "You have to block out the world around you while also staying alert to the presence of danger." He got up and let me up. I brushed myself off and then shot Kevin a look of retribution. He just smiled and shrugged his shoulders at me.

"I have been doing that, and everything that everyone else said didn't penetrate. I don't know why Kevin's did"," I said in a poor defense.

"In a real fight or battle, you will hear and see things that will throw you and cause you to hesitate. There are many distractions out there. You need to put your focus where it matters—on the danger, on the fight you are in, or the dangers around you. Sometimes all at once." I nodded at his words but was still a little confused.

"How am I supposed to block out the world around me and yet focus on the dangers around me while I am fighting?" I ask.

"You will hear cries for help, and you will see people fighting and falling. You cannot do anything about that while you are also fighting off someone. So your focus needs to be primarily on the fight you are having. However, making sure to keep your senses open to someone else that is trying to harm you is important! They could be sneaking up from behind you, or multiples could be trying to come at you at once. Always assess the situation even while you are in it, but you have to let the other things go. You cannot let outside distractions get to you. You deal with what is in front of you, then try to deal with the distractions. You do one thing at a time in battle, and the primary focus is not playing hero but to deal with the current threat and danger." What he said made sense and also sounded impossible.

I took on three warriors today and beat them all, but then couldn't beat him because I let my brother's words distract me. He is right—in a fight, that would have got me injured or killed. If I can't let his words go, what would I do if he fell in a fight? It would be no good to have both of us go down. But if I saw him get hurt or he—or anyone I knew—cried out for help, would that distract me enough to cost me my life? Then what would I be able to do to help them or anyone else? Lance is right, and I need to work on my focus more than anything else right now. I have been working on my strength and fighting but not on anything else, and it was so easy for him to beat me because I could not just focus on the task at hand.

"See what I mean? He is smart and practical and sees things that others miss. He will have our warriors looking at things in different ways and yet state things that are completely obvious that you don't think of. Not everyone trains the same, and there are things that some will need to work on more than others"," I said to Trevor and the others.

"Well, what do you say? Aylin is right, and I would be honored if you would consider staying here for a period of time to help assess our warriors and work with them. You will have lodging in the pack house and will be paid for your time"," Trevor told him, looking thoroughly impressed.

"Are you sure you do not want my father? He is usually the one that is called to do these things, especially with the larger packs and royal packs"," Lance said. He looked a little overwhelmed but also proud. I knew he would be great no matter what.

"I am sure. What you did just now and the advice you gave alone is something most overlook. Distraction is a big heel when fighting, and I will admit even I have a hard time with it"," Trevor said, and I gawked at him. "You are young and yet wise. Your father did a great job in training you to take over his responsibilities. I would like to have you work with our pack. Besides what your Alpha has learned today, I am sure your father will be needed for a while back home. Also, if you do end up getting the Alpha position, this will be the only time you will be able to help us and work with us here. You will become too busy learning to take over that position to be able to help other packs train"," Trevor pointed out.

I already forgot all about that. If Lance becomes the new Alpha, then he would carry so much responsibility and duty to the pack that he wouldn't be able to travel and spend months away training and experiencing everything he has been.

"What if I don't want to become the Alpha?" Lance asked.

"That decision is going to be a hard one. I do believe they really want their daughter to marry and take over, but if she cannot get a grip on herself, then it will have to be someone else. You are next in line and would make the pack and me proud"," Trevor told him. Lance was silent but nodded. He was all about duty and doing the right thing, so even if he doesn't want to, I knew without a shadow of a doubt that if asked, he will do what is right and become the next Alpha.

We left the training area and started to make our way into town. Nick and Nikki told us they would catch up later; they wanted to go get their stuff for the big day tomorrow. Apparently, they are last-minute shoppers. But that can be expected from people that are super busy. The rest of us started to break off into conversation while we looked around town.

It wasn't until we stopped at a bakery and ordered some pastries that Lance spoke up again. "Okay, I will train your warriors"," he said. It took us all off guard. "I have some requirements and conditions, however"," he added.

""Okay, would you like to go back to my office while we hash out the details?" Trevor asked. Lance shook his head.

"No, it's fine. It's not that many, and if these are not okay, then there is nothing to hash out"," he said firmly. The Lance Layla has told me about when he is working with his father came out—beyond formal and all business. No room for bullshit, and what will help him make an amazing Alpha if given the chance.

""Okay, what is it you require?" Trevor asked, also taking a business tone.

"First, Layla is going to be my assistant. I know you have not seen her in action; however, she is my eyes. We are a team when we train with my father, and having her there will help me keep an eye on the massive amount of warriors. Second, I will not tolerate your warriors showing disrespect to my sister or to myself. I understand we are young and are wolves, not Lycans; however, for you to ask us to assist with their training tells me that you have respect for us, and we deserve that from them as well. Anyone that shows disrespect to us will be cut from my program—no exceptions and no second chances. If we let it slide once, then in my experience, there will be more to follow. I have seen my father cut half the pack warriors from another Lycan pack on the first day because they thought it a joke that a wolf could teach them. I will not hesitate to do the same"," he said calmly, looking Trevor in the eye. I knew Lycans here that had a hard time doing that.

"Is there anything else?" Trevor asked. He was also calm when talking, but I could tell he was impressed with Lance's authority.

"Yes, there is one more thing, and this is solely for my benefit. If I become the new Alpha of North Woodforest Pack and require assistance and help of any kind, I would like it to be Zander that comes to the pack to assist us"," Lance said, looking at Zander now. For a second, I thought I might have misheard him. The others looked a bit shocked as well, especially Zander.

"What? Why do you want me?" Zander asked. Lance looked at him in confusion.

"Why wouldn't I? It is your pack—the one you were supposed to take over and love. I have seen how hard you worked in training and how you care for the people. And even though I do not agree with it, you were willing to give up your goddess-given mate for your pack, however misguided it was. I know you will only have their best interests at heart and will be willing to help and work with me when and if I need it"," Lance told him. Once again, Lance is able to see the big picture and look at things in a way that others did not. Zander was speechless.

"I find these terms acceptable. Thank you for working with us." Trevor reached out his hand and shook Lance's, sealing the deal informally. They would obviously draw up the agreement later, but for now, this would do. Lance then turned to Zander and shook his hand. Zander smiled at him and nodded—a silent show of respect. I loved that my guys would be working together, and I just hoped they would get along. I guess time will tell. I loved even more that Layla would be here and we would get to spend time together!

We made our way through the pack, and I showed my friends all the shops they may want to visit while here. We stopped at the pastry shop and got some more desserts and pigged out on them.

Thank God I am a werewolf and our metabolism burns through the calories like crazy.

We eventually made our way back to the pack house and spent the rest of the night catching up. It was like old times, and I had really missed having them around. I would give anything to keep them here with me!

# Chapter Thirty-Five
## *Aylin*

I am awoken by hands slowly traveling up my thigh toward my center. Heat and wetness are already pooling there from the simple act. Another hand is at my stomach, skimming the skin under my shirt, moving up toward my breast. I moan as they torment me, exploring my body and making me needy for more. I can't help it as my body starts moving on its own accord, my hips gyrating and my back arching for more of their touch.

I hear a chuckle and then feel the hand exploring my thigh go away. I whimper at the loss, only for them to move it to my apex and rub his fingers over my panties, running them up and down my slit. Then, he moves my panties aside and coats his finger in my wetness. He circles my clit and then moves down through my slit, pushing his finger inside me. My hips move in time with his finger plunging in and out, and another breathy moan escapes my lips. The fingers now playing with my breasts focus on my nipples as he tugs and twists them.

Another chuckle, and then lips are on mine, devouring me. Another set of lips moves to my other breast, and whoever is at my core adds another finger. My hips move with his hand, and I can feel myself climbing toward the edge of that cliff I am becoming so very familiar with. I feel him pull his fingers from me, and the mouth that was teasing my nipple leaves as well. The other hand is still playing with my breast, and the kissing doesn't stop.

I open my eyes, taking a peek, and take in Zander's soft features as he continues to kiss me hungrily. Closing them again, I let myself get lost in the feelings of him kissing me, pressing against me, and playing with my breasts.

Then I feel the bed move and know Trevor is between my legs. I feel him pull my underwear down my legs, and then I can feel him between them. My hips start to move on their own accord, grinding myself against his very hard erection. Trevor groans and then says in a breathy voice.

"Someone is eager this morning." He chuckles, and then he thrusts into me. I moan into Zander's lips, and he swallows the sound. Together, they take turns pleasing and touching me. Their hands and mouths are all over me. This morning, I felt worshipped, and I loved it. I never wanted it to end.

After two hours of lovemaking, I was starting to get sore, and we knew we needed to start getting ready for the ceremony. We showered together, and they both grabbed big, fluffy white towels and worked together to dry me off. I was loving being pampered by my mates. I don't know if it will always be like this, but I could definitely get used to it if it is.

"After today, you will officially be Luna, my Luna!" Trevor exclaimed.

"I think you mean our Luna"," Zander said, shoving Trevor's shoulder. They both laughed, and Trevor shrugged.

""Okay, okay, our Luna." He corrected, and Zander puffed out his chest. We all laughed.

"I will do all I can to care for this pack and the others under our care and help you with that burden, my Alphas"," I told them, kissing each of my mates in turn. We walked out of the bathroom and went to the walk-in. It was like a well-oiled machine, handing each other what they would need or what the other pointed to. It was a little bit of a shock when I realized this since we hadn't been here all that long, and only about a week ago, these two were ready to kill each other.

Now they get along as if they had been friends all along, and Zander almost seems to look up to Trevor like a big brother or something. I find it funny. Also, now, when I think about Zander rejecting me, the pain that I usually felt is not as sharp. It's like it happened ages ago, and now I am just thankful that he is mine and that the Moon Goddess gave us a second chance to accept the bond.

After we got dressed and enjoyed a quiet but late breakfast, we made our way downstairs to see what everyone else was doing. Most everyone else was already out and about. Apparently, my sister, mom, and dad were at the local dress shop. My sister, of course, wanted to check out the outfits we have here versus what they had at home.

Lizzie and her gang of friends were out, and I am sure the guys have their hands full watching them. I'm thinking they will regret joining the Luna's personal guard by the time those girls leave. Still, I was surprised that her friends talked to me last night and were not complete bitches to me. Maybe there is some hope there. Alpha and Luna Black were talking with Luna Carrie, and Lance and Layla were sitting in the open common room waiting for me.

"Hey guys, how were your rooms? Were you comfortable?" I asked. I looked back and noticed that Zander and Trevor had walked over to their parents when I made my way over here. They must be giving me space to catch up with my friends, which I loved and appreciated.

"It was amazing! The bathroom in my room was as big as my room at home!" Layla said excitedly. Lance chuckled, shaking his head. He has been in some nice rooms, especially when he visited the Lycan King's territory with his father. Layla doesn't always get to go, but I'm sure she has gone enough to get some really nice rooms.

""It's a standard pack house guest room"," I laugh at her.

"I don't think so. I think this one was meant for an Alpha or Luna or something"," she said. I look over at Lance, and he nods. Oh, so they got the high-ranking guest rooms. This made my heart flip that Trevor did that for my friends.

"Well, you are important guests!" I say fervently. "What do you want to do first to get ready?" I ask, and right away, Layla starts jumping up and down in excitement. Lance looks over to Trevor and Zander.

"I think I'm going to see if I can hang out with Zander and your brother and get ready with them. I definitely do not want to spend the day with you two. I would have no hearing left by the end of the day!" He said, and I rolled my eyes.

"Oh yeah, you can definitely get ready with us, no worries there. I was just coming over to see if you needed saving"," Kevin said. He had walked up behind Lance. Lance looked relieved, and I smacked his arm playfully. He feigned pain and looked at me like I had accosted him.

"You are such a jerk"," I tell him, rolling my eyes.

"When did you get so mean and violent?" Lance said, pretending to have his feelings hurt.

"Around the time you decided hanging out with my brother and Zander is more fun than hanging out with me"," I shot back.

"Hey, I am all for hanging out with you, but I'm not going to sit in beauty parlors and watch you guys get hair and nails done and ohh and ahh and screech like banshees. You guys are on your own with that"," he said, throwing his hands up.

"When you put it like that, I don't even want to do it"," I reply, laughing.

"Hey! Not funny"," Layla says, pouting and crossing her arms over her chest.

"I'm sorry, Layla. You know I love doing stuff with you, but you know I am not the extremely girly type"," I tell her, shrugging. She sighed and nodded.

"Well, today you have to be. It's important for you to be perfect today and look amazing. When is your appointment at the salon?" she asks.

"Uh, I think Luna Carrie said it's at ten-thirty for me and my guests. So that would be me, you, my mom, and sister, I suppose. Maybe Luna Carrie and Nikki. I thought she gave everyone a schedule with what is available and what some have to do." Layla pulls her schedule out and looks at it.

"Yeah, ten-thirty. You're right, we should get going. It's already nine fifty-two"," she said, checking her phone.

"Alright, let's go"," I tell her. We walk away from Lance and Kevin. I wave goodbye to Trevor and Zander. Then I see Luna Carrie hold up her finger, motioning for us to wait a minute. So, I stop Layla before we get too far. Luna Carrie finishes whatever she was talking to the others about and walks over to us.

"Are you off to the salon?" She asks, and we both nod with huge smiles on our faces.

"Good. I will go with you." Her eyes glaze over for a moment, and then she adds, "Nikki is on her way, and Talon is letting your sister and mother know to head over as well if they are not already on their way."

"Thank you, Luna!" I tell her, and she smiles at me.

"Please, just call me Carrie. After tonight, you will be the new Luna of Blood Moon"," she said. I nodded and replied.

"Yes, but you will always be a Luna. Just because you pass the mantle doesn't mean that you are to be shown any less respect. However, I am happy to call you Carrie if you call me Aylin. Since we will be family, we can be the exceptions." I smile at her, and she grins at me.

We made our way through town. Layla spent most of the trip telling Luna Carrie embarrassing stories about me, most of which were related to training with her and her brother. Some, however, were from when we were kids, and then she told her about how I had the biggest crush on Zander and would drool over him when I watched him practicing.

"That is so not true. I do not drool!" I said in defense.

"Oh, you may as well have!" She exclaimed, and Carrie started laughing.

"I have always wanted a daughter! Walking around with you, just telling stories and talking about crushes and all of that. I feel like I have missed out on a wonderful experience, but now I have you, and I am so happy to have a daughter now! I can't wait for more outings and talks with you and your friends." Carrie's eyes were bright and full of happiness and love. I felt my chest swell, knowing that she meant that. I also felt a little sad that she never had a daughter of her own.

"Well, I am more than happy to have outings and talk to you about whatever your heart desires. Hmmm, well, all except current crushes since I am mated with your son and Zander. That might get a little awkward. But hey, if you start seeing anyone, I am happy to talk to you about him." I wiggled my eyebrows at her and saw her cheeks flush. Wait a minute. Was she seeing someone?

"My dear, just because you are mated with my son doesn't mean you can't talk to me about the relationship. Believe me, he is going to piss you off, and you are going to need someone to vent to. That boy has a knack for getting under someone's skin." I laughed at her statement, but I knew that was true. He had already made me mad a few times.

"Well, I will come to you when I need advice"," I told her, hoping to placate her, and it seemed to work.

"Here we are, ladies," Carrie said as we walked up to a fancy-looking salon. We walked inside, and the girls behind the desk beamed at the Luna, Carrie. "We are here for our appointment, ladies. Has anyone else arrived for the Luna's party?" she asked.

"Nikki has arrived and is already back in one of the chairs. She insisted that we go ahead and get started, but she has only been here for five minutes, so she only just got in the chair"," one of the ladies replied. She was cute and a little short for a wolf.

"Yeah, that is Nikki for you—just wants to get this kind of thing over with"," Carrie replied.

"Huh, she sounds like you"," Layla said, and they all looked at me, and I rolled my eyes.

"Not everyone wants to spend all day doing hair and makeup"," I shrugged. There are just so many other things you can do with your time. I didn't care that I felt that way. Be happy I am here doing it today.

"Well, when we are done, you are going to be drop-dead gorgeous!" one of the girls exclaimed. They started to lead us to a back room when we heard a high-pitched voice that grated on my nerves.

"We are here to get our hair, makeup, and nails done as well"," Lizzie said with an air of superiority. Looks like her mom's threat didn't go far.

"Yes ma'am, if you would take a seat, we will be right with you once we get these ladies situated"," the receptionist said politely.

"Why don't we just go with them? We are here for her Luna ceremony; shouldn't we be pampered as well?" Lizzie told her. The lady looked from Lizzie to us, trying to figure out if that was okay. Luna Carrie stepped forward.

"Unfortunately, we had to limit the size of the Luna party, so you will need to be patient and wait for the other stylist to get to you. If it would have just been you as planned, you would be able to join us. However, since you decided to bring uninvited guests, we could not accommodate, and you were removed from the list." At Carrie's words, Lizzie turned red with both rage and embarrassment. I could tell she was having a hard time holding her tongue, but she sat with a huff, and her friends joined her.

We were led back into a room with hair stations, manicure stations, and pedicure stations. Nikki was sitting at one of the hair stations and waved to us as we walked over.

""Okay, ladies, there are chairs available for everything you need done right here. Have a seat, and as you finish each area, you will trade seats with each other"," the receptionist told us. Since sitting in the chair to do my hair is probably my least favorite of the choices, I decided to go over to the pedicure station. Layla followed and sat next to me while Luna Carrie joined Nikki in the chairs to get her hair done.

A few minutes later, my mom and sister walked in, talking excitedly. They greeted us, placed their bags down, and took places at the manicure station. We all talked animatedly, telling stories, getting to know each other, and enjoying the pastries, mini sandwiches, and drinks that were provided while we were being primped, pampered, and painted. To me, it was all torture. I did enjoy the conversation and the vibe; without it, I would be spilling my soul to my torturer. I hated sitting still.

Finally, it was my turn in the chair to get my hair done. I had already had my nails, toes, and makeup finished, and now everyone was debating on what style of hairdo to have me wear.

"How about half up and half down with big curls going down the back?" the lady offered, since it seemed half thought it would look good up and the other half thought down would be better.

"I like that idea! It would keep it out of my face but still have the length down my back"," I agreed quickly so that they could get started and I could get out of this chair. My mom and Luna Carrie both smiled and nodded at my assessment, and they got to work. After another hour and a half of them ripping the hair from my scalp and using hot torture wands on it, I was finished. I really never want to do that again.

"How does it look?" I asked. Everyone looked amazing. They did a really good job on us. I started to turn to look in the mirror when my sister grabbed my shoulder.

"No, you can't look yet. You have to wait till you put your Luna ceremonial dress on and see the full thing all together!" She was really excited about this. She was smiling ear to ear, and her joy was infectious. I loved seeing her like this.

"Why?" I asked, and she rolled her eyes at me, like I should already know the answer.

"That way, when you see it all together, you will see why this was worth it, and you will also see what your mates will see when they get their first look at you"," she said triumphantly, like she had the best idea ever.

""Okay, okay, I won't look yet, but do I look okay?" I asked, looking at everyone. The last thing I needed was to have sat here all this time being tortured and not look at least decent.

"My dear, you are breathtakingly beautiful. The boys will be beside themselves when they see you tonight"," Carrie said, clasping her hands together in front of her. I looked at my mom, who had tears in her eyes and a smile on her face.

"Mom, don't cry; you will ruin your makeup, and it looks amazing. They did a great job!" I said, and my mom looked up and tried to blink away the tears while fanning her face.

"Honey, I am just so proud of you and so happy with the woman you have become! The moon goddess sure has blessed you, and I am so happy that she guided us to you and allowed us to be the ones to raise you"," she said and gave me a big hug.

""Okay, okay, enough of that, let's get back to the pack house and get changed"," Carrie said to the group. We all went to walk out and head to the door and noticed that Lizzie and her friends were at the counter arguing with the receptionist.

""What's going on?" Carrie asked the receptionist. When Lizzie saw us, she got silent. She eyed Luna Carrie but didn't say anything.

"This young lady and her friends are disputing their bill. They said that the new Alpha is her brother and that their bill should be covered by him. I tried to explain that it needs to be addressed before the services and we need one of the Alphas or Lunas to let us know ahead of time"," the receptionist looked down, like she was afraid that she would get in trouble for not giving in to Lizzie. This upset me, and I was not going to have it. Lizzie gets away with too much, and this poor girl was just doing her job and following rules.

It really bothers me when people do everything right and follow the rules set in place by the establishment, and then one bitch with a hair up her ass that feels entitled throws enough of a fit that it ends up getting someone fired. I have seen Lizzie do that before at our pack, and I refuse to let that happen in mine.

"No, the pack is not paying for her and her friends. She invited her friends without the approval of the pack, and they need to pay for what they have done"," I chimed in. Lizzie glared at me. I knew she would have loved nothing more than to lay into me the way she used to. However, we both knew that would never happen again. There's no way, even with her followers, she would ever be able to abuse me again.

"Luna Carrie said I was originally a part of the Luna's party, which means I should at least have had mine paid for"," Lizzie replied.

"You took it upon yourself to bring your friends, which showed this pack, Luna Carrie, me, and my mates disrespect. You need to learn that this world doesn't owe you anything! You do not get what you want whenever you want it, and no one is here to serve you! If you do not have the money, then get your father over here to pay for you and your friends. At the end of the day, your daddy is the only one that will bow to you. Cause no one here ever will"," I told her. For the first time in my life, I really told her off. I felt great and loved the look on her face. The shock at what I said plastered there.

"You don't have the right to talk to me like that"," she said defiantly.

"Actually, I do. In case you missed it last night, I am the new Luna of Blood Moon, and even if I wasn't, my wolf and Lycan outrank yours"," I let out my aura. I meant to only let it out toward Lizzie and her friends. However, I haven't learned how to control it that well. I had everyone in the salon submitting to me and baring their necks. Lizzie tried to fight it but didn't last more than a few seconds. I looked around at everyone else and pulled back.

"Did you really need to do that?" Jolene said, looking at me in awe and irritation.

"Sorry, I can't control it that well; it's still kind of all new"," I said, blushing, and Nikki laughed.

"I think you should try it on Alpha Trevor. I think you'll even make him submit." She really laughed then, and Carrie joined in with the laughter. Lizzie, however, was fuming. She had never, to my knowledge, had another female do that to her.

"You think you're so special, don't you"?" she seethed angrily, with a sneer on her face that made her look like she smelled dead fish.

"News flash, Lizzie: my wolf is special, and that's the difference between you and me. I won't let the fact that I have a special and unique wolf change me or make me act entitled. However, you are not special! You're spoiled by your daddy, and there's a huge difference between being special and being a brat who throws her daddy's title—and now her brother's title—around to get what she wants. I'll make sure no one ever abuses my mate's titles to get anything, including family. There's nothing special about a spoiled brat who wants the world to bow to her just because she wants them to. You need to earn it." I spat back.

"Oh, and what did you do to earn anything here? Aside from having that wolf?" she replied.

"Actually, since you asked, even though our new Luna has only been here for about a week, she's already held audiences with our people and put in plans to help with repairs to homes, new greenhouses, and parks for the kids. Alpha Trevor was worried about the funds for all of this, and she had some great ideas to help with these problems and stretch the funds to be able to do it all." Nikki said, crossing her arms over her chest. She was getting mad, and I needed to get us out of here and away from this drama queen before we had a conflict with my old pack.

Lizzie doesn't care, and if someone here retaliates against her, Alpha Black could see it as an act of war. I looked at her, and she was actually speechless for a brief moment before she rolled her eyes, looked back at the receptionist, and handed the She-wolf her card. Her friends, however, were still looking at me with awe on their faces.

"Here, just charge it so I can get out of here"," she said. The receptionist took the card, rang it up, and handed it back with the receipt. Lizzie and her friends left and didn't even tip the girls who worked hard on them. I rolled my eyes and looked at Carrie.

"I haven't received a card or anything yet from Trevor. Do you think he would be okay if I gave these hardworking girls a tip for the services they did for those girls? They didn't deserve to be treated that way by Lizzie!" Carrie looked at me and smiled.

"No, dear, he won't mind." She then handed over her card, and when they gave her the receipt, she left each girl who worked on us—and each girl who worked on Lizzie and her friends—a fifty-dollar tip. My eyes bugged out. I was thinking fifteen or twenty, but I had never had a lot of money, and that was a lot to me when I was paying tips for multiple people. When the receptionist saw this, she seemed just as shocked as I was. She and her co-workers thanked us repeatedly.

""There's fifty for you as well, my dear, for having patience and professionalism when working with someone who was beyond rude to you"," Luna Carrie added, and the girl's eyes welled up.

"Thank you so much, Luna"," she said. Carrie nodded at her, and we walked out and back to the pack house. It made me curious as to why there was a limit on funds for the pack, but we had that kind of money to spend. I'll have to ask Trevor about it later.

We made our way back to the pack house, and everyone went to their rooms to finish getting ready. The pack house was already mostly decorated, and I couldn't wait to see what it looked like where we were having the ceremony. Trevor said it would be outside so that the whole pack could attend. He didn't want to leave anyone out. We had multiple Alphas and Lunas from other packs coming as well, and some would be staying with us here for the night, while others would go home. I was honestly nervous to meet so many of the other Alphas and Lunas. I knew I was going to, but this was becoming overwhelming now that it's here.

After we got back, I went to my room and sat on the bed. I was holding my stuffed elephant, Archie, and realized I had forgotten that I put the pendant Zander had given me around his neck. I'll have to put that up. I don't want anything happening to it, but for now, I'll leave it there. I liked how it looked on Archie.

Like my thoughts had conjured him, Zander walked into the bedroom. He stopped when he saw me sitting cross-legged in the center of the bed. I saw him look around, stopping on the dress at the end of the bed and then looking back at me and seeing the stuffed elephant in my hands.

"Are you okay, my queen?" he asked, walking over to me. His brows pinched with concern.

"I guess I'm just feeling a little overwhelmed"," I told him honestly. He nodded and sat next to me. He took my hand and held it in his own. He started moving his thumb in little circles on the back of my hand. It had a calming effect on me.

"I am too"," he said finally, and I looked up at him. I could see it in his eyes and expression. I squeezed his hand.

""It's hard to believe that you are. You seem so calm all the time, and even through our bond, I don't feel any rising panic or stress that I know you have to be feeling from me." Unless, of course, it is because I am still new to the way the bond works.

"Yeah, I mean, I've always known I was going to be an Alpha one day, but there's a difference between being the Alpha of one pack and being the ruling Alpha of multiple. There's a lot of responsibility and hard choices that you have to make, and so many things you have to oversee, trying to be fair and just to all the packs in your territory and keep them from fighting." He let out a deep breath. I squeezed his hand reassuringly.

"Well, then I guess we're going to be overwhelmed together"," I told him and tried to smile. "We'll get through this; I know we will, and one day, we'll wonder what we ever worried about, but for right now, it's scary." I said, and I could see in his eyes that he felt like I did. One day we would look back, and these fears wouldn't be anything. Today, however, they are very real and very strong.

Zander's other hand went to my elephant and to the pendant around its neck. He laughed, then grabbed my chin, turned it toward him, and kissed me. I could feel his love and desire for me through our bond. I couldn't get enough of the feeling of his lips against mine. He pulled back and caressed my face.

"You brought that pendant with you, even after I let you go?" he said, tears brimming in his eyes.

"Yes. The night you gave it to me, I put it on Archie. I planned on wearing it after the moon goddess celebration. I didn't want to lose it or risk breaking it because I knew I would have my first shift that night since it was my birthday"," I told him. The truth was, I had forgotten, with everything that had happened, that I had put it on Archie. But I am beyond happy that I did. Zander smiled at me and hugged me to him. I loved the feeling of his strong, muscular arms wrapped around me. I could just stay right here.

"I love you, Aylin. I will always love you, my queen"," he said, kissing the top of my head. I squirmed away from him, and he looked at me, confused.

"I spent hours being tortured with curlers, hot wands, and other devices of torture, and I do not want to go back, so do not mess up this hair or makeup!" I warned him, and he burst out laughing.

"That is what you consider torture?" he asked, finding it hilarious.

"I was about to spill all my secrets to them!" I told him, and he laughed harder.

"I'll have to remember that"," he said teasingly, and I glared at him.

"If you try it, I will hurt you!" I told him, and he raised his hands in mock surrender. We both laughed, and then I leaned against him. His hand gently rubbed up and down my back. We sat like that for a while in complete silence, just enjoying being there with each other. But I knew I needed to get ready. I let out a sigh and looked up at him.

"I need to finish getting ready." He nodded, kissed me, and climbed off the bed. He paused on his way to the door.

"Aylin, thank you for accepting me. I know I didn't deserve it, and I know that you could have just accepted it and never accepted me, but you did. You have shown me love and forgiveness already, and I know I don't deserve it. I am in constant awe of you and your ability to see things from others' points of view. How understanding and forgiving you are is something this world needs. You are going to be an amazing Luna! You are already an amazing mate." Zander smiled again and walked out the door, leaving me speechless for the umpteenth time today.

The more I thought about Zander's words as I climbed off the bed, the more I tried not to cry. Everyone had faith in me and believed in me. I needed to find it for myself and stop being so scared. I know I am going to give my all for my mates, this pack, and all packs. If that isn't enough, then am I really a failure? If I truly do my best and give everything I can, then no, I don't think I will be.

I went into the bathroom, took care of my needs, and checked myself in the mirror. I didn't smudge my makeup, and my hair still looked good—even after the kissing and him holding me. I went back into my room, picked up the dress, and put it on. I know I already looked in the mirror against Layla's wishes, but I was still shocked at what I looked like when the dress was on. I could hardly recognize myself. The dress was a beautiful white gown with a fitted bodice and a mermaid-tail bottom. I had plenty of give, though, and I didn't feel restricted when I moved. There were silver glitter designs all over the bottom, and on the top, there were what looked like diamonds along the neckline. I felt beautiful.

A knock at my door distracted me from myself, and I opened it. Carrie was standing on the other side, holding a white box.

"May I come in for a moment?" she asked, and I stepped back, letting her enter the room. "I have something for you, my dear. It has been worn at every Luna ceremony for this pack and every important event the current Luna attends for the last two hundred and eighteen years. Now it is yours to wear." She opened the white leather box, and inside was a diamond tiara. It was breathtakingly beautiful, but it looked like there was a piece missing in the center of it. My brows furrowed, and she chuckled.

"Why does it look like there's a piece missing? Or is it supposed to look like that?" I asked, realizing I sounded rude. "I'm sorry, it's beautiful." She laughed again.

"My dear, there is a piece missing, but this one is supposed to be. Let me show you." She closed the top lid and opened two side compartments I hadn't seen before. In both compartments, there were teardrop-shaped stones: a ruby, an emerald, a sapphire, a diamond, an opal, a pink diamond, a black onyx, and an orange-colored diamond, by the look of it.

"Wow"," was all I could say. She set the box on the nightstand, picked up the diamond, closed the sides, and opened the lid for the tiara. She then slid the diamond into place, and a small arm clasped it and locked it in from behind so it didn't move.

"This is so that no matter what type or color of dress you wear, your tiara can match it. Yes, they could have stuck with just the diamond, but honestly, my girl, what fun is that?" She had a huge grin on her face, and I couldn't help but grin back. She picked up the tiara and placed it on my head. She looked at me like she was assessing me, then snapped her fingers. "Wait right there, don't move." She said in a rather excited tone and ran from the room. I stood there and waited.

A moment later, Carrie came running back in with a blue crushed velvet box in her hand. She stopped before me and opened it. Inside was a beautiful diamond necklace, the gems wrapped the entire way around, making up the necklace as a whole. It was stunning. She took it out of the box, undid the clasp, and held it up. I gathered my loose hair and turned around so she could put it on.

"There! All done. Why don't you go and have a look?" she said, motioning to the full-length mirror I had been looking at myself in before. I walked over, and my breath caught in my throat. I looked like royalty. I glittered and shone like the diamonds I was wearing, and I felt special and beautiful. I started to tear up.

"This is beautiful, all of it. I don't think I should be wearing it"," I told her.

"Why not, my dear?" Carrie asked, looking at me worriedly.

"It's just... I never in a million years thought I would be here. All I wanted was to become a warrior, be part of my pack, and show them that I would protect them and earn my place. Now I am to be a Luna, and I am wearing this beautiful dress and a real diamond tiara and necklace. It's like I am in a dream, and I don't want to wake up. For the first time ever, I feel special and beautiful"," I tell her honestly. She walked over and, without a word, embraced me.

"My dear, you have always been special and beautiful; of that, I am certain. Your other pack lived in fear of the unknown and superstition, and it hurt you. That is not okay, and you should have been accepted. For that, I am deeply sorry. You are accepted here and are already loved and wanted, and not just by your mates!" she said with such sincerity that I couldn't hold back the tears.

She walked to the bathroom and came back with a tissue for me. She dabbed the tears away and smiled at me.

"Thank you for accepting me." I wanted her to know how grateful I was for her and her kind words. She put her finger under my chin and lifted my gaze to meet hers.

"No need to thank me. Just keep doing what you are doing, and you will see in time what I can see now: A beautiful, intelligent, and strong Luna. You belong here." She embarrassed me again and then walked out of the room. I hope I can prove her to be right. I wanted to more than ever now—for her, for the pack, for my mates, and for myself.

# Chapter Thirty-Six
## *Aylin*

After Luna Carrie left, I started to pace around my room. I had hoped that the nerves would die down, but they were building. I was supposed to wait here until they let me know it was time. Then, I would meet with Zander and Luna Carrie, walk to the podium, and wait there to be called. That is when I would take my oath, and Zander would take his.

A wave of dizziness hit me, and I walked over to the settee and sat down. It got stronger, and I started to feel sick. I closed my eyes, took a few deep breaths, and when I opened them, I was no longer in my room. I was no longer sitting on the settee in the corner. Instead, I was standing in a beautiful meadow. I was surrounded by wildflowers of all types and colors. It was beyond beautiful.

To one side, a stream flowed, and looking around at the woods, I realized they were all different. Four different seasons. One area was covered in snow, and the trees were bare. Another had buds all over the trees that looked like they were about to grow their leaves. The next area had trees full of green leaves, and some even had fruit on them. The last area had leaves of all kinds of colors—reds, yellows, and browns.

I was mesmerized! So much so, it took me a minute to realize I wasn't alone. As I turned around in a circle for probably the fifth time, I realized that off in the distance by the stream was a woman walking. I hesitated at first, but then made my way toward her. The closer I got, the more beautiful she became. There was a soft glow to her pale, milky white skin. She had raven-colored hair and startling glowing blue eyes—the same eyes I had. She watched me as I walked up to her, smiling warmly. Her hands were held in front of her, and she stood there looking like the epitome of grace and beauty.

"Hello, my dear"," she said. Her voice was like honey, yet also musical. "I am so happy to finally meet you. I have been wanting to meet you for a very, very long time." Her voice made me feel at ease. I felt like I had known this woman all my life. She chuckled. "Yes, in a way, you have known me your entire life." Wait, hold up—did she just read my mind?

"I'm sorry, but who are you?" I didn't want to be rude and was trying not to be, but how do you ask someone who they are without sounding that way?

"I am Selene, my dear. You, however, may know me better as the Moon Goddess." I couldn't believe it. This beautiful, elegant woman standing in front of me was the Moon Goddess. Oh my goddess, that means I am standing here with my great-grandmother—my flesh and blood. I had never met anyone from my family before, and to meet her as the actual Moon Goddess... I was speechless.

"We have a few things to talk about and not much time to do so"," she said with calm elegance, but there was an undercurrent of urgency.

"I have so many questions"," I finally said.

"I know, my dear, and I will try to answer a few, but we will have time to talk later. We need to discuss a few more urgent matters that you will be facing very soon." I shivered at that as warning bells went off.

"What exactly am I going to be facing?" I asked, already knowing I wasn't going to like the answer and already knowing what she was going to say.

"Amarok knows where you are and is coming for you"," she said. Her face was serious and full of fear. My blood turned to ice, and I couldn't breathe. Amarok—the once-original king of wolves who ascended to become a god to watch over all wolves. He was the one my mother was betrothed to? Are you kidding me? Even in the stories we learned about in school, he was a feared and terrifying god.

"So my mother was betrothed to the original god-king of wolves?" I asked, just to confirm what was so obvious.

"She was to be my successor and was to take him as her chosen mate"," Selene said.

"I don't understand. If you had planned the arranged marriage, why did you give her a fated mate in our world?" I asked.

"Ah, you see, once a fated mate is declared, you cannot change it. You have the choice to accept or deny it. However, once it is in place and chosen for you, I cannot undo it. She had dreamed of going to the human realm, and I knew where she could do the most good that was desperately needed. I also foresaw a child of unimaginable power out of the union. This choice was made before she became betrothed to Amarok."

This knowledge broke my heart for my mother. Talk about an impossible choice. Give up your fated mate for an arranged marriage and to ascend to the next Moon Goddess, or give up being the Moon Goddess for a chance at true love with your fated one? My mother chose to give it all up for her chance at love.

"That is so heartbreaking. Couldn't anything be done about the arranged marriage? Couldn't they choose someone else to marry him?" I asked, thinking about the mention of sisters in her journal.

"None of the others in her family carried enough ether in them to ascend to be the goddess. She was the only one." For a brief second, Selene looked like she was trying to hold back tears. "I have been the Moon Goddess for a very long time and have waited for my heir to be born. However, you are also given the right to free will, so I left it open for her to decide." She smiled at me then. "When she did decide, I went to her much like I am with you now. She never wanted to be the heir and take over as Moon Goddess, but she was raised to do so. You never got the chance to know who you are and what you would become. You see, when your mother chose to be with her fated mate, I requested a favor from her. I wanted to strengthen my line so it was not so many times removed from me when my heir arose, and she would be strong and powerful."

I looked at her as she paused, and her smile grew. My stomach dropped at her smile, and I wasn't sure I was going to like what she was going to say. She, however, continued.

"The mother that carried you agreed to be my surrogate. I placed my egg inside her womb and ensured that it would be the one to be fertilized during conception. She would still get to carry you, birth you, and raise you. She only asked that I agree that if you were to receive the right to take over as heir to be the next Moon Goddess, you would also get to choose if you would take that responsibility when the time comes or be allowed to walk away until the next heir is born. I agreed, and here we are."

She was looking at me, waiting for my response, but I was frozen. What the actual fuck did she just say? I'm sure I heard wrong, because it sounded like my mother was not really my mother—she was. But wouldn't I still be related to my mother? I am so confused.

"Wait, are you saying you're my biological mother?" I was in shock now. I really knew this had to be a dream. There was no way this was real. Then again, my mother was a direct descendant, and that didn't seem real either.

"Yes, Aylin, I am. I am so very happy to meet you and so very proud of who you have become"," she said with a warm smile.

I can't believe this. So many new things to find out. I was just starting to scratch the surface or process everything else I had just learned, only to find out the woman whose diary I had been reading was my mom—but not. She did carry me, birthed me, and protected me up until the end, and beyond that, we are related as she is also a granddaughter of the Moon Goddess herself. But she carried me FOR Selene—the actual Moon Goddess, who is my actual mother? Seriously? Oh, my head hurts. I need to sit down before I black out.

"So why wait to come to me? Why didn't you let me know who you are sooner? Why let them take me to the other pack? I was miserable there. Why not just come get me when she was murdered?" I had so many questions, and I wanted answers.

She chuckled at my rapid questions and then sat on a white wrought iron bench I hadn't noticed before. She tapped the space next to her. I moved toward her and sat, never taking my eyes off her. I really looked at her, at her features, and realized she and I had a lot of similarities. The same face shape, the same blue eyes;

however, my hair was silver and hers was as black as a raven's wing in the night.

"I wanted to come and get you the moment I found out you were in danger. However, I suspected that Amarok would come looking for you, and I felt that, for the time being, you would be safer hidden away. I watched you grow, and my heart ached for you. So I made sure to intervene just a little and put the twins in your path. They had good hearts and were not raised with the bias that others were. I could see them being good for you." She was right about that. Without them and my family, I would have been completely alone.

"I guess I can understand why you did it, why you let me stay with my family and let them raise me. I would have wanted to protect my daughter if I knew she was in danger, but I am in danger now"," I told her. I watched her smile fade as she nodded.

'Ask her about me, Aylin.' Mona was stirring inside me and wanted to talk to Selene as well.

'Why should I ask her about you? She is the one who gifted you to me; of course, she knows about you.' I shook my head.

"What is it, my dear?" Selene was looking at me with a curious eye. The look she gave me was one that the mother who raised me often would give when I wanted to talk but didn't know what to say or how to say it. She was patient and allowed me to continue.

""It's Mona. She wants me to ask you about her, and I tried to explain that you already know her." Selene smiled again.

"I am very familiar with Mona, as she was your birth mother's wolf." That caught me off guard. Man, it's just one thing after another. At this point, I am tired of finding things out. Can it be done now? Can this please be it, because I don't know how I am going to deal with any of this.

"You gave me my birth mother's wolf?" I asked. "Why?"

"Her death was horrible and before her and her wolf's time. Mona was distraught at the loss of her life so young and the loss of the life of her host. I wanted to give her a second chance to have a host that would love her and take care of her. I think this way, she has a little piece of Sarina with her by being with you." I rubbed my chest where I sometimes feel Mona and her emotions, and I had a warm, loving sensation right now that made my eyes prick with tears.

"I am honored to carry her wolf as my own"," I said through the tears and smiled. "I hope we can do her justice." I could feel that Mona wanted revenge for what happened to her and to Sarina.

"I am glad to hear it." Selene looked happy too. Happy and yet very serene. Like the knowledge that I was okay with having my birth mother's wolf put her mind at ease.

"So, how does it work if I am to be your heir?" I asked because I didn't know how it worked, and I didn't think I would be allowed to stay here. That hurt my heart and soul at the thought of never being with Trevor and Zander.

"My dear, you cannot be my heir once you are mated to a mortal wolf. Today, you will pass it on to your daughter, and she will become my heir. I wanted you to know and not have to worry about choosing between this and the love of the men who are going to move mountains to be there for you and for her. Her fathers will both love her unconditionally. Same as with her siblings." Her eyes shone then in a knowing way.

"So, when we have a daughter, she will become your heir?" I asked.

"My dear, once you take your vows to be Luna, the birthright will pass to her"," she said, and the way she said it made me hesitate.

"How will it pass to her?"

"Just as it passed from your mother to you, silly. Only this time, you don't have to wait. It will be done tonight when you take your vows, which I cannot wait to see you up there, shining as bright as the stars themselves." My heart was jackhammering, and my stomach had a weight settle in it.

"You said it won't have to wait, and it will happen tonight. Why is that different than before with my mother?" I asked hesitantly.

"Well, because it didn't pass to you until she became pregnant with you. The moment you came into existence, it passed to you." She said it as if that were an obvious answer. I went cold.

"So if it didn't pass to me until my mother became pregnant, and it will pass to my daughter tonight, that means that I'm, that I'm..." My voice trailed off as I couldn't finish that sentence.

"Pregnant." Selene smiled at me, her eyes shining with joy, and nodded just once. That rock in my stomach doubled in size. I think I forgot how to breathe at this point. Yet another bomb dropped in my lap. A madman is after me, and I am pregnant? This cannot be right! I can't be pregnant! I can't, I can't, I can't!

"My dear, are you alright?" I looked up at Selene. I hadn't realized I was shaking. My whole body was trembling, and I had been shaking my head from side to side.

"No, I am not "okay," my voice was shaking as much as my body was trembling. "My entire world has been turned upside down over and over again, and all in a week! I had my transformation during an eclipse, I found out I had a mate, was rejected by him, then found I had a second-chance mate who turned out not to be a second-chance mate but a second mate. Then I find out that I am the daughter of a woman directly related to the moon goddess and I have special abilities, and I don't even know what they all are yet. Then I have to deal with jealous exes, becoming a Luna of not one pack but a region of packs. Now I also find out the woman I was just learning about as my mother is not my biological mother, just a birth mother, that I am actually the Moon goddess's daughter, and now also that I am pregnant when I only just lost my virginity a few days ago!" I took a deep breath and continued. "So no, in no way, shape, or form am I okay. I feel like I am drowning in all of this, and I just wish I could run and hide and have time to process because all of this is shadowed by the fact that I have a psycho god hunting me down because the woman that birthed me did not fulfill her end of the deal, and he thinks to take it out on me." I was breathing fast and not getting air into my lungs.

"My dear," I felt a hand on my shoulder, and with that touch came a feeling of calm and tranquility. The sensation ran through my muscles, relaxing them; through my chest, slowing my heart and breathing; and then through my head, slowing my racing thoughts. I looked up into those startling, glowing blue eyes that were filled with concern and love.

"My dear," she repeated. "I am so sorry that so much has been put on your shoulders. You have been through so much in your life, and I wish there were a way to take all your pain and fear from you, but then you wouldn't be who you are today. I can see you, I can see your heart and soul, and I can see how brave, smart, and loyal you are to those you love. You are everything I could have hoped for and more, my daughter, and I am proud of you."""

Selene's eyes shone with tears as she wiped my own away. "You have a lot to deal with, but with the strength of your heart and mind, I know you can do this. I believe in you, my darling daughter!"

"Thank you"," was all I managed to say. I didn't realize how much I needed to hear what she said to me, and to have her say that meant more to me than I even realized it would. This is the moon goddess, and she is proud of me? No, not just the moon goddess—my mother. Then the floor dropped again. My mother—I was here with my mother. I flung myself into her arms, and she wrapped them around me. She held me so tight that I couldn't hold the rest of the tears back and let them out. She held me for what seemed like hours, even though it must have only been a few minutes.

"My dear, it is time." I looked up at her, my brows knitted."

"It's time to go back. Your brother is coming to get you to take you to your ceremony. I will be watching, my dear, and I will see you again."

My eyes widened. I wasn't ready to let her go. I didn't want to. I never thought I would get to see her and know her, and I didn't want to be without her again.

"I don't want to leave. I just found out that you are here, and I have a mother. I don't want to go—not yet."

She chuckled and brushed a stray hair back away from my face.

"My dear, I am never far from you, and I will be there, watching you as you take your vow and become the most loved and respected Luna of your time." I smiled at her. I wasn't sure if that comment was something she had seen for my future or something she was saying because she was my mom, but it made my heart swell with happiness either way.

"Will you actually be there, or is this 'watching over "me' thing?" I asked.

"I would not miss this for the world, my dear." She was stroking my hair.

"When will I see you again?" I asked.

"I will be there throughout your journey and come to you as often as I can'," she said. It was a vague answer, but I would take it. I had to.

"Thank you. I never thought I would get to meet my mother, and now I can't wait to get to know you!" I smiled up at her, and she smiled back. Her smile was full of light and warmth and made me feel safe and loved. She put her hands on both sides of my head and kissed my forehead. When I opened my eyes, I was sitting on the bed in my room. I looked around, trying to see if there was anything different or any sign that lingered of her. There was none. I was alone in my room once again.

The door to my room opened, and my brother strolled in. He stopped when he saw me and smiled.

"You look absolutely beautiful, sis." I smiled back, but it was tight, and then his smile faltered as he really took me in, looking at my face and the tear streaks on my cheeks.

"What's wrong?" he asked, and I shook my head.

"Aylin, whatever it is, you can tell me. You know I have your back no matter what. Do you not want to go through with this?"

I looked up. Then I realized that he thought I was getting cold feet about my ceremony. I almost laughed. There was no way I was backing out of this. I found my place, and I'm not giving it up.

"No, that's not it. I think you might want to sit." I looked at him. I needed to get everything I just learned off my chest, and he was probably the only one I trusted right now. Kevin walked over to the bed and sat next to me. He took my hand in his, and the look he gave me showed nothing but concern. Squeezing his hand, I dove in.

"You are probably not going to believe what I'm about to tell you, but with what just happened, you are the only one I trust! Promise me you won't say anything to anyone—not even my mates."

His brow furrowed.

"Why would you hide something from them?" he asked, and I could see he was hesitant.

""It's not that I'm trying to keep it from them; I just am not ready to tell them. Not with everything going on right now. I don't want them to worry or become extra protective of me." That really got his attention.

""I'm getting the sense that this isn't going to be good"," he said, shifting next to me.

"Actually, a lot of it is good, and I'm happy and excited, but there is a dark cloud that has already formed." He looked almost comical with his confused face, and I couldn't help it. I smiled. I really needed that.

"Aylin, what's going on? And you need to be quick if you really do want to proceed with the ceremony because I came to get you for it. Everyone is waiting and ready."

I nodded and then took a deep breath. Then I told him what just happened with the moon goddess and everything she had revealed to me.

Kevin stared at me. His jaw had hit the floor at some point and hadn't closed for the remainder of what I had told him. His eyes were like saucers. It was almost comical. He was a deer in the headlights, and that was a rarity for him since he was always quick to add opinions and comments.

"Say something, please"," I begged him.

"You... you're pregnant." He looked down at my belly, and then a huge smile crossed his face. "I'm going to be an uncle"!" he exclaimed.

"Yes"," I chuckled. "Please do not say anything." I caught his eye, and he frowned.

"Why don't you want them to know?" I knew he wasn't going to like my answer.

"I just don't want them to know yet. I still have a lot I need to do and prepare for. Amarok is coming, and he is close. I know they are going to want to keep me locked up when they find out, and I need to practice and train and keep up my strength. I also need to figure out what all my abilities are and see if any of them will come in handy"," I told him. He shook his head.

"You don't know if they will do that. Maybe they will help you train or find out what those abilities are"," he tried to reason. "And what about the part about who your mother is? Don't you think they should know? You shouldn't keep anything from your mates,

Aylin. You know that. How would you feel if they did that to you?" he reasoned. He had a point. I would be furious, and I probably wouldn't forgive them easily for keeping things from me. I sighed.

"You're right"," I said finally, and his gaze snapped to mine.

"Come again? I mean, can you say that again?" he said with a cheesy smile.

"Oh, come on. You are right. I will tell them, but at least let me wait until after the ceremony and celebration. I don't want them to spend what is supposed to be a happy and joyful night worried or "overprotective," I reasoned.

"Again, how do you know that they will be that overprotective?" I gave him a "you have to be kidding me" look, and he shrugged his shoulders.

"Kevin, they are Alphas. Have you ever known an Alpha to not be protective when he finds out that his mate is pregnant? Hell, have you ever known an Alpha to not be protective of his mate in general?" He paused and then shook his head.

"Yeah, I guess you have a point there. Okay, I can understand wanting to wait until after the ceremony. It's not like you are keeping it from them then either, so I will keep quiet until then. Promise." He smiled at me, then added, "Well then, sis, are you ready to go become a Luna?" He stood, reached out his hand, and I placed mine into it. He pulled me to my feet, and I straightened my dress.

I walked over to the bathroom mirror to make sure I looked okay. I knew I had cried and wanted to check my makeup. Surprisingly, it was not ruined, but I think maybe my mother had something to do with that. I lightly dabbed at my cheeks to try to cover the tear streaks, and when I was satisfied, I walked back into the bedroom and took my brother's hand once again.

"I'm ready." I walked with him to the door. I stopped to take one last look around, as if I could still see that beautiful meadow and my mother. Then I turned back to my brother and let him lead me out of the apartment and toward my future, toward my mates, and the ceremony that I had been waiting for all week.

We walked down the stairs with my arm wrapped through his and thanked the goddess for that because I was not a heels kind of girl, and walking down carpeted stairs in heels was hard. By the time we got to the bottom, I was cursing these stupid torture devices. How do women wear these? I will have to just get a couple of flats because I am not wearing heels like this ever again! Not in a million lifetimes could I get used to wearing these awful contraptions.

# Chapter Thirty-Seven
## *Trevor*

I looked at myself in the mirror in Aylin's old room to make sure I looked okay and headed downstairs. We were letting Aylin get ready in our room, so we got ready elsewhere. I was currently in the room she had called hers when she first arrived. I couldn't wait to see her when she came downstairs. I needed to get down there since guests were already arriving from other packs.

I left the room and ran into Kevin, who looked like he had just finished getting ready as well. He nodded at me, and I waved him over. "Why don't you head down with me?"

"Sounds good. I was hoping to run into Lance and talk to him about weapons training some more to see if he would be willing to show us some skills he has with non-traditional weapons. I heard his father took him to a pack overseas in the Egyptian area, and he learned about some of their weapons, like the khopesh sword. Wouldn't it be cool to see a display like that?" Kevin looked like a kid in a candy store.

"Do you like non-traditional weapons?" I asked curiously.

"Yeah, ever since I was little, I liked the way different cultures created different types of weapons. Ancient Egypt had some really cool-looking ones. I would have loved the opportunity to go there and learn about them. I think Lance is one of the luckiest people around. He has traveled all over and learned so much." Kevin was talking about Lance with such admiration. It made me more confident in my suggestion that he should take over as Alpha, but the more I learned about him, the more I worried about taking him away from training the packs. His father did important work, and he could continue that.

"Aylin had said that Lance and Layla had both assisted in training her, so did Layla get to travel and train with Lance and her father?" I asked. If she knows quite a bit as well and could possibly take over for her father if Lance does end up becoming Alpha, then I wouldn't feel as bad taking him from a noble job that is much needed. I need to find out and talk to Lance and possibly his father. That idea does make me feel better about the possibility of taking away a badass trainer.

"A lot of the time she did. From what Aylin told me, her mother didn't want her to, but she was very stubborn and always pushed to learn whatever Lance did. She was adamant that she could do what he could. She doesn't look like it, but Layla is a fierce warrior, and she has a lot of the same skills as her brother and some he doesn't, because some of the places they trained had separate training styles for women, catering more to their strengths like size and quickness. To be honest, I would be more afraid to go up against her than Lance, and they both worked with Aylin." Kevin grinned at me then, and it was a knowing one.

"What?" I asked.

"It just dawned on me. Aylin was trained in secret by two badass warriors in multiple styles of both men and women"," he said.

""Okay?" I wasn't understanding where he was going with this.

"If you ever get into a fight, not only is she quick and agile because of her size, but she has become powerful. You don't stand a chance! My badass sister is going to kick your Alpha ass." Kevin burst out laughing, and I stopped and gaped at him. He may be right. My little wolf may just be able to kick my ass. I will have to do everything I can not to face off against her. At this point, she could kick my ass in front of my warriors, and I am not sure I am ready for that! However, humiliating as it will be, I would also be very proud of her.

"I think I will leave the practice training to our warriors for now","  I said, and Kevin laughed. I think I may need a few lessons from Lance and Layla before I take on my mate.

"Afraid she will kick your ass in front of everyone?" He taunted.

"Hell yeah, and I am not ready to get my ass kicked in front of my warriors. Do you know how bad they will ridicule me?" I shot back, laughing. It felt good to laugh. It dawned on me that even though I had my friends here for the past couple of years, I haven't laughed anywhere near as much as I had since these three came here. It felt good. I was glad that things worked out the way they had, and that surprised me, because I would have never thought that I would be glad to have to share my mate with another. Yet here we are.

We made our way down to check on the others to see if they needed to go get ready. Nick was already in his tux and was scowling as he paced. He hated dressing up, and I knew it. He did this for Aylin, and to a lesser point, for tradition. I looked around and saw Liam and Thomas.

"Where is Julian?" I asked, looking around, thinking he may be pacing the length of the floor. I tried to keep everyone in the same general area so they could take shifts when it came to watching over everyone.

"He went to get ready. We have all taken turns going to get ready for tonight. It worked out because most of who we are watching are women, and they take forever. It doesn't take us long to get dressed, and none of us need to really do anything else. Not with these natural good looks"," Liam said, acting all cocky and posing like he just walked a catwalk. He even made a face that he thinks makes the girls swoon. I just rolled my eyes. I really let this joker around my Aylin all day?

"What are you talking about? You should have looked in a mirror and maybe taken a lesson from the girls in makeup. It couldn't hurt to improve your looks"," Nick said, and Liam brought his hand to his chest and gasped, acting like he was dealt a blow.

"How dare you! You are just jealous that I am better looking and will have all the single ladies wanting a piece of this on the dance floor tonight." Liam spun around and then swayed his hips a couple of times, with his hands in front of him, holding an imaginary woman in front of himself.

"Nah, that piece of ass you're holding right now is all you're going to get! How is your imaginary girlfriend, by the way? I keep forgetting to ask"," Thomas asked, crossing his arms over his chest, trying to act serious and losing at hiding the smile.

"Oh, don't worry, she is doing great, and she won't get jealous when I am out there with the others"," Liam shot back. Everyone started laughing, and one of the doors opened. Lance walked out and looked around at everyone, stopping his gaze on Liam, who still had his hands out with his hips mid-swing.

"Do I want to know?" He asked.

"Oh, we were just trying to figure out what Liam's imaginary girlfriend is going to wear to the party and if she really will get jealous or not if he dances with any single ladies tonight"," Thomas said. Lance looked at Thomas and then at Liam.

"Well, for your sake, I do hope she is understanding. I would hate to have a fight with someone in your head in front of a group of people"," Lance sounded serious, but you could see the humor dancing in his eyes. He is good. If it wasn't for the crinkle in his eyes, I would have sworn he was being dead serious with Liam.

"Dang, man, even the newbie is worried about you!" Nick said with a chuckle.

"You are all just jealous!" Liam said, waving us off.

"Nah, some of us don't have to worry about it, and the others just don't care"," I told him. I had Aylin and was not worried at all about what she-wolves may want to dance. It will be nice having a mate at functions now. I hated having so many she-wolves throw themselves at me, hoping I would take them as a chosen mate. Some she-wolves only cared about power, like Lizzie and Ruby. They don't care about the person, only the position. That's why I wanted to wait for my mate—that way, I knew there would be a connection.

I have to admit, part of me worried that I would have a mate who craved power as well. Even with a connection, would I have been okay with that? I don't know. Luckily, I don't have to worry about it. Aylin never wanted power; she only wanted acceptance and to help her pack. That is why she is going to be a perfect Luna here, and I couldn't wait. We were so close to it becoming official.

"Okay, guys, I need to get downstairs. Guests are arriving, and I really should be there to greet them"," I told them, waving them off. Kevin and Lance followed behind me. I could hear Kevin asking Lance all about his time overseas in the different areas. It was interesting to learn that he had also been to China and some places in Europe. There are fewer packs overseas, so the fact that they reached out and invited Lance's father over is amazing. I have to give props to the man for having such a prominent reputation. I can't imagine the things they've learned. Not to mention the fact that they've created an all-new style that incorporates the different techniques they've learned. I was eager to get him started on the training.

We finished making our way down to the main entrance, and I couldn't help but admire all the hard work of my omegas. They really went above and beyond in decorating the pack house. They made sure the red carpet was laid in such a way that it led straight through the pack house to the back. The double doors in the back were wide open, leading out to the back patio and the open backyard, where they had the stage all set up as well.

I stood by the front door and started greeting the guests as they arrived. All the Alphas under my protection were expected to attend. Then I had some Lycan Alphas who had confirmed they were coming. I was looking forward to seeing a few of them, as some were family. Unfortunately, my uncle, the Alpha King, would not be able to make it. He did send his deepest regrets and a gift for my new Luna to show his support. He also mentioned in the letter that he is looking forward to meeting my mate and had some questions for both me and her. I didn't want to dwell on that, but it could have something to do with her fur. If he found out she is a white wolf and Lycan, he could be worried about his throne. We'll address that when the time comes, though.

As members from other packs arrived, I greeted and talked to each in turn. It was good seeing everyone and not having to leave my pack to do it. It's been a while since we gathered here, and I think it might be time to change that. I'll see about hosting the next Alpha's ball here. This year, it's a special one that the Lycan King is hosting, since it's the nine-hundredth annual Alpha's ball. Every hundred years, he takes a turn hosting Alphas from all over the world. Any other time, it rotates between Alphas depending on region. I had not hosted one in a while, and I am overdue. I passed it off last time since I had just been Alpha for a few years and was still young. I didn't want to host such a huge event and mess it up, even though I would have had my mother's help. I had asked the Woodforest pack to host it, and damn if it wasn't my mate who grew up in that pack. The universe really does work in mysterious ways.

The only one who seemed to have any issues was Alpha Richardson from the Winterhaven pack. He decided now would be a good time to see if he could persuade me to extend his territory and thought he could try to get a private audience with me. In the end, I had to warn him that if he didn't drop it and just enjoy the celebration, he would be asked to leave. This was not a day for business, and I also wasn't going to have a private meeting with him to expand his territory without the Alpha of the territory he was after. He had just as much a right to be there.

"I just want to have a chance to properly make my case"," he said, and I looked at the people lining up behind him.

"Alpha Richardson, you will have a chance to discuss this along with Alpha Ashwood at the meeting scheduled in a few days. Today is a joyous occasion, and I want to keep it that way, so will you please enter and move along so I can continue greeting my guests"?" It was hard not to let my imposing aura out when all I wanted to do was reprimand him. Who comes to a ceremony like this and thinks they will be granted special treatment while holding up proceedings? Did he not see that, by trying this, he could possibly even sway my judgment against him?

Partway through people arriving, one of the omegas came to me with a problem with the stage. They couldn't get the microphone and speaker system to work, so I had to follow them out to the stage to assist. I had hooked this up a bunch of times and could tell right away that something was wrong. I unhooked everything and rewired it properly. It was like someone had just shoved cords into places and, since they fit, decided it was good enough. I would have to find out who did that later. This equipment isn't cheap.

By the time I had figured it out, I received a mind link from my mother that everyone was ready and we could get started. Then I received a mind link from Aylin that confused me.

'Trevor, when you make your speech, I need you to introduce the real me, and who I am to the Moon Goddess, but say I am a descendant.' She was scared, I could tell, even through the mind link. If she was scared, why did she want me to do this?

'Are you sure, Aylin? I thought we agreed not to reveal who you are to anyone else. That's why we told everyone last night not to say anything.' I was so confused. What changed?

'I will explain later, I promise, but for now, please do it! It is really important.' She better explain; we went through a lot with Lizzie last night just to reveal it today anyway.

'Okay, I hope you understand what is at stake, little wolf.' I told her, not sure about this, but if this is what she wanted, then I would oblige her.

'I do, and I'm sure this is what is right.' She said, and it sounded like she was trying to find her courage to go through with this. I hesitated again before I responded. She didn't sound like she really wanted to do this.

'You do not sound sure; you sound scared. Why are you changing the plan?' I asked. I didn't want to do this. It felt wrong.

"Please, Trevor, just trust me," she begged. I didn't want her to beg, and I wanted her to know I did trust her and her choices. Besides, she is going to be Luna. I need to trust her judgment.

"Okay, I will do it." I just hope she realizes how dangerous this is.

Looking out over the crowd and noting that everyone was in their seats, I stood at the podium. I had an entire speech planned, but standing up here and looking at the crowd, I decided I wanted to speak on the thoughts I had earlier. Maybe it would help calm Aylin.

""I apologize for the technical difficulties, but I have it all sorted out, and we are ready to begin. First, I would like to thank everyone who came. My mate and I are happy that you were all able to make it, and for those of you who traveled, I hope you made it here safely.

It is an amazing feeling finding your fated mate. The moment your eyes lock, the instant pull you have, is otherworldly. I had started to lose hope that the moon goddess would even grant me a fated mate. As many of you know, the elders had even started to push for me to take a chosen mate. I was never comfortable with that because how do you know, as an Alpha, if they truly care for you or for your position? Some only want power, and for some Alphas, that is enough to carry on their lineage, but not for me.

I, for one, have thanked the moon goddess every day since I met Aylin that she has granted me a mate—someone I have learned is strong, kind, a warrior, and a Luna through and through. This amazing she-wolf that the moon goddess has granted me is not only my mate but also the mate to another as well. You see, this woman is so special, she was granted two fated mates and a guardian in just the first week since getting her wolf and her Lycan. Actually, it was within the first day of receiving her wolf. That is why this is not just any Luna Ceremony. We are also celebrating my new Co-Alpha, who will be assisting in overseeing all the packs in our territory"."

The crowd hummed with gasps and whispers. If they thought that was shocking, they would really be amazed at what's next. I was surprised when she decided that we should announce who she is, but she said that we needed to, and I am still curious as to why.

""Yes, yes, please calm down and allow me to introduce you to our new Co-Alpha, Zander Black, and our very special mate, whom I have thanked and will continue to thank the moon goddess for every day for the honor of granting me and Alpha Black her descendant, our mate and Luna, Aylin Archwood"."

I held my hand out, and the next second, I lost the ability to breathe. I hadn't noticed anything going on with the crowd as the most ethereal beauty walked up onto the stage. Aylin was a vision in the white and silver dress, her hair done up out of her face with curls falling down her back. My mother's tiara and one of her favorite necklaces hung from my girl's neck. She was the most beautiful thing I had ever seen. I sucked in a breath as my lungs started to burn, and that's when I noticed the entire crowd had gone silent as well.

Aylin stepped up next to me, her smile lighting up her entire face. She seemed to be glowing—she was so radiant. I hadn't even noticed she was escorted by Zander to the stage. He was also smiling, but it looked forced. He was also uncomfortable, just like I was, about the announcement of who she is. I could feel it through our shared bond. They stopped next to me, and I presented them to the crowd, still in a state of shock. My mother stepped up from behind us, and I stepped back. Carrie approached the microphone and addressed the crowd.

"Thank you again for coming to this monumental occasion. Never before have we had someone of such purity among us. To be here and mated to one of our own is a blessing. I truly believe that Aylin will help lead this pack and those under our protection with love and understanding. In the time I have gotten to know her, I have seen her strength and selflessness. She is kind and compassionate, and she embodies the true nature we have all come to expect and strive for as Lunas. Aylin, are you ready to take your place as our Luna?"

Carrie was looking at her now, and Aylin smiled brightly and nodded.

"I am"," she said without hesitation. My awe of her was growing.

"Please step forward and repeat after me." My mother, in all her elegance, stepped in front of the podium for the crowd to see. She put down the microphone and held her hands out for Aylin to accept. Aylin stepped up to Carrie and placed her hands into Carrie's waiting ones.

""Repeat after me: I, Aylin Gideon-Black, solemnly swear to uphold the values of a true Luna"."

My mother's voice carried across the courtyard clearly so everyone could hear, and Aylin repeated her words just as loud and clearly. I hadn't missed the last name that had been given to her, and I approved. I looked at Zander, and he looked happy. However, I didn't know if it had anything to do with the name.

"I will be kind and just with all I do for our pack and territory", Carrie continued. "I will be a loving mother, provide a nurturing hand, and be a loyal and fierce Luna to all." She finished, and Aylin repeated the words back to her. There was a soft glow to their hands a moment later, and we knew that the moon goddess had blessed Aylin to be our Luna. The crowd erupted in cheers and clapping. Then it turned to awe. The glow in her hands spread, starting up her arms and then covering her entire body. I had never seen or heard of anything like this happening before, and I didn't know what it meant, but in that moment, she truly was ethereal.

Then I saw Aylin's face go from a simple smile to a huge grin as she looked into the crowd, her gaze fixed. I tried to follow her gaze but could not see what she was looking at or who. I will have to ask her later.

My mother then motioned for me and Zander to step forward. She had Zander repeat a similar promise for when an Alpha is to take over the pack, the same one I had taken years ago when my father died and I had to take over. Zander repeated every word, and then my mother turned to me, held out her hand, and asked if I would be willing to share in my responsibilities and accept Zander as my Co-Alpha and Aylin as my Luna. I stepped up, took her hand, and then took Zander's now-free hand, completing the circle.

"I, Alpha Trevor Gideon, accept my Co-Alpha Zander Black and my Luna Aylin Gideon-Black to help me lead our pack and territory from this day forward."

Carrie let go of my hand and grabbed Aylin's. She placed one of Aylin's hands in mine and one in Zander's, and we each held one of her hands with both of ours. The glow that had engulfed her then spread to us, and not just our hands, but all over. All three of us were now covered in a brilliant, warm glow that had a sensation of safety and a feeling of being at home. Then something snapped into place between the three of us. It felt like the mate bond changed—it connected all three of us the way it had connected me to Aylin. I could feel Zander before, but it was fuzzy. Now it was as if he was also my mate. It was strange and remarkable. I didn't know what this meant, but I felt joy and acceptance.

Once the glow faded, we faced the crowd with our hands still joined, and my mother walked up beside us.

"I am happy to present to you, your Co-Alphas Trevor Gideon and Zander Black, and your Luna Aylin Gideon-Black." The crowd erupted again, and I felt a sense of pride from their reaction. None of us knew how they would take a Co-Alpha, and we had some worries and doubts about it. Not all were up for change, and for anything different. Wolves were superstitious and held on to tradition more than any other race. This acceptance from our people was truly amazing.

After the crowd died down, I watched as Zander and Aylin took turns addressing the crowd, giving speeches of thanks and promising that they would do everything to be fair and just leaders.

I then walked up to the podium. "I want to thank you all again for coming and sharing in this historic moment. I hope you can all stay and enjoy the rest of the festivities. The food is ready, and, of course, the chairs will be removed shortly so the dance floor will be opened up. I hope everyone has a fun night tonight as we celebrate a new chapter for us all. Never before have we had a descendant of a god or goddess among us, and to have her here is truly a blessing."

I turned to my mates and reached for Aylin, who still had a hold of Zander. She took my hand, and we all walked off the stage and back into the pack house.

I led them both straight to my office. I wanted to know why she had changed her mind and what was going on. Something caused her to want to announce that she was a descendant of the moon goddess, and I needed to know what that was. Why say descendant and not great-granddaughter? Descendant sounds like she was even further removed. We reached the office, and I shut and locked the door behind us so no one could disturb us.

"Okay, little wolf, talk to us. What is going on? Why did you change your mind about telling everyone who and what you are?" She looked at me and Zander and then said three little words and one name that I hadn't expected to hear. One name that brought the very floor out from under me, yet I desperately needed more details.

"I met Selene."

# Chapter Thirty-Eight
## *Aylin*

As we sat in Trevor's office, my nervous energy started to ramp up. I was starting to second-guess telling them, but I knew I needed to. I didn't want them to find out later and be upset with me that I kept something from them.

"Ok, little wolf, talk to us. What is going on? Why did you change your mind about telling everyone who and what you are?" Trevor asked, and I looked between him and Zander and then said the only thing that I could.

"I met Selene." It was just her name, and it got their attention really quick.

"The Moon Goddess Selene?" Zander asked, and I nodded. "What about her?"

"She came to me right before the ceremony," I told them. They both stiffened, and I could see their eyes widen, but neither said a word, so I continued.

"She told me quite a bit. I don't know if you will believe me when I am done, but I promise this is all true. I still can't believe it all myself, as it seems completely impossible, but that is all that I have been given this last week—one impossibility after another." I paused, and they stayed silent. I sighed and continued again.

"You see, the woman that we believed to be my mother isn't. I mean, she did carry me and birth me, but she is not my biological mother. She is kind of like a surrogate and yet also related to me." They looked at me like I had sprouted a second head.

"If she gave birth to you, how is she not your biological mother?" Trevor asked.

"You know she is the granddaughter of the moon goddess. Selene told me she was supposed to become the new moon goddess and chose to be with her fated mate instead. Apparently, the moon goddess had gone to her before she mated with her fated mate and gave her that option. However, in return for her choosing her fated mate, the moon goddess requested a favor: that she would carry her daughter when she got pregnant. The moon goddess replaced one of Sarina's eggs with her own, and when Sarina got pregnant with me, she got pregnant with the moon goddess's daughter. Selene said that when she agreed to carry me for her, Sarina's only condition would be that I be allowed to choose, as she did—duty to be the new moon goddess or, if I find my fated mate, to live my life with them." I stopped and allowed what I just shared to sink in. It took a few moments, but they seemed to get it about the same time.

"So Sarina carried you for Selene, and you are actually the moon goddess's daughter and heir?" Trevor asked, making sure he was understanding what he was asking.

"Yes. My mother is Selene, the moon goddess," I confirmed.

"So you are to replace her as the moon goddess?" Zander asked.

"No, I cannot." They looked at each other and then back to me. "You see, I chose to be with you two. I cannot ascend to be the new moon goddess with mortal mates. I know we are not mortal compared to humans, but we do not live forever as a god or goddess does," I told them.

"You really chose us over that?" Zander asked in disbelief.

"Why wouldn't I? I love you!" I said, a little upset that I would have to explain that. The hurt must have shown on my face, because he quickly continued.

"I didn't mean that you didn't love us, it's just that it is a big thing to give up—being a honest-to-gods goddess. I guess I have a hard time believing that someone would do that for me," he said, brows pinching, and I could see the vulnerability in his expression, and it tore at my heart. How could he not believe that someone would choose him over that? Then again, the she-wolves he was used to were power-hungry, and if they were offered to be a Luna or a Goddess, they would choose the latter. For the power and eternal life. Not many would turn that down.

"Well, I choose you. I would rather spend our rather long lives together than forever being a goddess and watching over you instead." I would make that same choice over and over again. "Besides, if I choose that and then had to watch you both find other mates, I think I would go mad and destroy the world as we know it." I giggled, and Zander gave a little laugh and relaxed.

"Something is telling me you are not done," Trevor said finally. "You said she told you quite a bit, and as big as that news is, I am thinking there is more." Goddess, he was intuitive. He raised a brow at me, and I sighed.

"Yes, there is more." I took a deep breath and went on. "The god that is hunting me—that my birth mother was killed by—his name is Amarok. He is the original God of Wolves and the son of Fenrir, the Great Wolf. She warned me that he is close. That is why my nightmares are more and more intense. He knows where I am and is coming." The snarls that ripped from both of them were terrifying, and if they would have been directed at me, I would have been cowering before them.

"Did she say how close or when we can expect him?" Trevor questioned, and I shook my head.

"Fuck! We need to prepare. I will link with everyone and call them in, and we will discuss a plan." Trevor's eyes started to glaze over.

"Wait," I called out. He stopped and looked at me questioningly.

"There is more I need to tell you before we have people come, and to be honest, I would like today to be about us and the ceremony we just left. Can't we have this meeting tomorrow? I know you want to keep me safe, but today is important, and we need to be down there for our people and guests. Just give me this normal night where I can wear this beautiful dress and laugh and be happy." He looked at me, and with a heavy sigh, nodded his agreement.

"Ok, so what else did she tell you?" Zander asked.

"Promise me, the both of you, that we are going back down to the celebration and you will not be overbearing, overprotective Alpha-assholes." I would not tell them this last thing until after the celebration if they could not make me this promise.

"Of course. Whatever it is, we will respect you," Zander said.

"I mean it. If you do the overprotective Alpha crap at the celebration, I will transform and bite your heads off," I threatened. They both chuckled like it was cute.

"Fine then, the last thing will wait till after the celebration since you cannot make this promise to me. Besides, even if you do promise, you will probably break it," I said flatly. I truly did not believe that they would allow me any freedom once they found out about the baby.

"Come on, you said you didn't want to keep anything from us," Zander said with a smile, obviously thinking my little tantrum was cute.

"And I'm not. I will tell you just after the celebration is over. Besides, that will give me time to think about a clever way to make you guess the last thing." I smiled at that, and they both frowned.

"How would we guess what the moon goddess told you?" Trevor said, confused. I smiled back mischievously.

"Because it involves one of you." They both blinked.

"Who?" they asked together.

"That I cannot tell you. But this is going to be fun. I am looking forward to tonight more than ever now." I smiled again. "OK, now that that is settled, let's go back to our party. I promise I will tell you tonight. I just want to have fun and enjoy ourselves tonight."

They both stood, and the smiles on their faces were breathtaking. These two were my whole world. I was not ready to share them. I just got them, but I know that they will be everything to me and our pup.

"Well, I for one am going to be wondering about this the entire night," Trevor said.

"Then think about it, but I am not saying anything till we retire for the night. And no, that does not mean we are retiring now. I want to go enjoy the celebration and see my family and friends."

Both Trevor and Zander walked up to me and kissed my cheeks.

"Ok, little wolf, let's go enjoy the festivities, and we will play your little guessing game later," Trevor said, taking my face in his hands and leaning down, covering my lips with his own in a searing kiss with promises of what to expect tonight. My toes curled with that kiss.

Then I felt Zander's hands move my face to his, and he kissed me deeply, delving his tongue in and tasting me. The moan that came from me was beyond indecent, and I wanted more. When he pulled away, he smirked down at me, and then I realized what they were doing. This was not a promise of what is to come tonight—they were trying to get me to want to go now. Well, tough. I am not going to cave, no matter how badly I want their delicious kisses and exquisite touches. I smiled back at him.

"Ok, let's go," I said cheerfully. His smile faltered a little, and they both laughed. I led the way out the office door and back out to the party below, with both mates in tow behind me.

As we made our way through the crowd, we stopped and talked to as many as possible. I met some of the Alphas and Lunas that we represent, all of them congratulating me, and a lot had questions about my being a descendant of the moon goddess.

Every chance I got, I looked around to see if she was still here, even though I knew she wasn't. I no longer felt her presence. When I had taken my vow and looked out into the crowd, I had seen her. She had smiled at me, and even at the distance she was at, I could see the tears shining in her eyes and the pride in her face. Not one bit of disappointment for choosing my mates. She was happy for me and proud of me. MY MOM was happy for me and proud of me, and that happiness I felt was unlike anything I have ever felt before. I soaked it up.

As we walked around and mingled with the guests, I kept having this sense of being watched. I felt absurd since most of the guests were looking at me, at us, and tried to brush it off, but it wouldn't go away, and it was starting to bother me. But I couldn't find the source of it.

"Hello, Luna, I would like to extend my congratulations and blessings for your union." I looked at the male that had stopped in front of me, extending his hand. He was an Alpha according to his aura. I placed my hand in his, and he brought it to his lips and kissed my knuckles. I smiled at him. He was pleasant and seemed sincere, unlike Alpha Richardson, who I had just walked away from a few moments ago, who insisted we deal with the issues of his orchard. He was not going to be fun to deal with.

"And who may I have the pleasure of thanking for these kind words?" I asked.

"Forgive my manners, I am Alpha Grey of the Ashwood pack." Wait, this is Grey? The one that Alpha Richardson was just complaining about? I wonder if he is going to get into the orchard ordeal tonight as well. I really don't want to deal with this tonight. I want to have one night of fun and joy with everyone.

"Are you enjoying yourself?" I asked cautiously.

"I am, actually, although I am slightly disappointed," he said, looking around.

"Why is that? Is the party not to your liking?" I asked, folding my hands in front of myself, trying to remain polite. Is he insulting my coronation?

"To be honest, I was hoping with such a big turnout that I would find my mate here. I know it seems silly to hope for that at another's coronation, but my elder is pressing me for a mate to make our pack stronger, and much like Alpha Gideon, I do not want a chosen mate." He smiled at me, and I felt his sincerity. Out of all the males, especially the Alphas I have met today, he had been the most pleasant, and I didn't get any bad vibes from him. He did not leer at me like a prize, making me feel disgusting, and he did not make me uncomfortable to be around. Not all the other Alphas did, but more than half. Yet he was definitely the most genuine.

"Well, that won't do. If you do not want a chosen mate and want to wait for your fated, then you should have that right! You seem young, why push you into a mate so fast? How long have you been Alpha?" I was curious why the Elder would push.

"I have been Alpha for three years, and I am twenty-two. My father before me was killed when he was on his way back from a meeting with the king. There was a rogue attack. He and my mother were both taken that day." My heart clenched for him. Like me, he had lost both of his parents; however, he had their responsibilities thrust upon him.

"I am so sorry for your loss," I told him, and he gave me a small smile in return.

"It has been a difficult road, but I have managed with help and guidance. I want to be a just and fair Alpha to my pack," he said, and I could see the determination of that statement in his expression.

"It seems you already are, and I look forward to working with you anytime you need additional support! Tell your elder that I said to give you time. The Moon Goddess gives us mates for a reason, and even though you may find a good chosen mate, as an Alpha, your fated is there for a reason—to strengthen your pack and balance you. Or for you to balance her." He smiled at that and nodded.

"Thank you, Luna. I appreciate that very much. I do not wish to monopolize your time, so I will take my leave so you can visit with the rest of your guests. Have a good evening, Luna, and again, congratulations on your union." He bowed to me and walked away through the crowd.

"What did Alpha Grey have to say?" I jumped at Trevor's voice being right beside my ear. I hadn't even sensed him come up on me.

"He congratulated me on my position, and then we talked a little. He was very polite and nice to talk to. I think he will be one of the better Alphas to work with," I told him. He looked at me and raised an eyebrow.

"Do I need to worry about him, little wolf?" he said, smirking down at me playfully. I turned to him and smacked his chest.

"I only have eyes for my mates, and believe me, I do not need or want any other Alpha ass holes!" He laughed then, and it was loud. I couldn't help the smile that grew and the laughter that bubbled up.

"What's so funny?" Zander said as he strolled up to us.

"Aylin was just informing me that we are just enough Alpha assholes for her to handle and that she does not wish to handle any more than that." I turned red.

"Well, that's good then. I don't have to worry about any of these pretty boys that have been eyeing her all night," Zander said, looking around.

"You know, I am surprised you guys have kept your calm with the way some of the Alphas have been looking at me while we have talked to them." They gave each other a look.

"Well, to be honest with you, we haven't really been all that nice," Zander said. "When you walk away, Trevor and I kind of told them that if they want to keep their eyes in their head, they would need to stop ogling you like they were. Or they could find themselves needing replacements for their positions." I gawked at them, and then it was my turn to throw my head back and laugh.

"You guys didn't," I said in between giggles.

"I know you said not to be overprotective, but it is in our nature to protect what is ours," Trevor said, looking almost ashamed.

"You see, I can barely handle the two of you. I definitely don't need any more than that," I exclaimed. "No matter how pretty they may be," I added on just to rile them up. Their low growls told me that they didn't like me thinking anyone other than them looked good. I laughed again at their reaction, and they both softened. They knew in their hearts that I loved them and only wanted them.

"So this orchard thing, when are we taking care of it?" I asked. "I know we discussed it, but I would like to get it taken care of sooner rather than later," I told them.

"And it has nothing to do with Alpha Grey?" Trevor said. This time I narrowed my eyes on him.

"Actually, it's because I think we have bigger problems and would like this one that I believe to be rather petty on Alpha Richardson's part to be handled swiftly so we can focus on the larger issues. Honestly, just because the apple orchard has grown over to the land of the Ashwood pack doesn't mean they should be given rights to those trees or the land, and the more I think about it, I think they planted that orchard there on purpose." Okay, so maybe it was a little about helping Alpha Grey, but the guys didn't need to know that.

"What makes you think that they planted it there on purpose?" Trevor asked. He seemed genuinely curious.

"Wolves live a long time, and any that are smart or even cunning will play a long game, and this just seems like one of those. You see, if he started the orchard that close to the border, he would know that it has the chance to eventually spread, and if it was spreading, it would still take many more years to do so. If he didn't want the Ashwood pack having trees, they could have trimmed the line and kept them on their side. They didn't do that—they let it spread, and now they want more territory and think they have a right to it because of the food they grow." He looked at me, stunned for a moment. "I think you are definitely going to be a valuable asset and a brilliant Luna. I want you in all the meetings. We need more points of view, and I think you are going to be fair-minded and just when issuing yours." I didn't know about fair-minded, but I would try to be just—I knew that because no matter what, we want to uphold peace between all.

"I would like that. To be active and to be part of all of the planning and discussions." I could feel how big my smile was, and I was so happy that my mates did not treat me like a token Luna and actually wanted my help.

"Now, enough about business. Let's enjoy the rest of the party, because honestly, I am ready to go play your game. I am curious and want to start guessing. Have you thought of how you are going to present this to us?" Trevor asked.

"Oh, I have." I am going to have them play the game Kevin and I would play when we get each other random surprises. Speaking of the devil, just beyond Trevor striding up to us was my dear old brother.

"Hey guys, how are you enjoying the party?" he asked.

"So far so good. I was just telling Aylin that I was ready to go play her game to find out what she is keeping from us," Trevor said. Kevin looked at him and then at me.

"You haven't told them yet?" Kevin asked, and both Trevor and Zander's eyes shot to him.

"They know what I am to Selene and about Amarok, but not the last thing." I had a mischievous smile.

"He just said you want to play a game. Let me guess, twenty questions?" he asked, and I nodded. "Good luck, guys," Kevin said.

"Wait, he knows?" Zander asked.

"Of course I know. I was the one that went and got her, and she had just finished meeting with Selene. Besides, I'm her brother. Why wouldn't she tell me?" Kevin said, not hiding the smugness in the fact he got to know first.

"But we are her mates!" Zander said huffy.

"Yeah, but I'm special," Kevin said and shrugged his shoulders. I laughed at their pouty faces because Kevin knows the last secret and they don't.

"Wait, so you can tell us," Zander said, thinking he found a way around it.

"And risk her wrath? Yeah, right. You are not getting a word out of me. She will tell you when and how she wants. That is her decision, not mine," Kevin said and put his hand on my shoulder in a gesture of solidarity.

"You just don't want her to kick your ass," Zander said.

"Yeah, and neither do you. Besides, anything with teeth that are as big as my forearm, I am not going to mess with. You two are on your own." Kevin kissed my temple then and walked off.

"Yeah, I guess I wouldn't want my ass kicked either. I will wait," Zander said, huffing again.

"It's not like you have to wait long. Let's say good night to our families, and we can head upstairs," I said, and they both looked like they just won the jackpot. Oh, but we have three families to say good night to and some friends. So even though they thought this would be something we would get to do rather quickly, they were in for a surprise, because my dad was the king of long good-byes.

Over an hour later—a dance with my dad and Lance. Then, because they could not be left out, a dance with each of my mates, and lots and lots of thank-you-for-comings and goodnights—we made our way up to our apartment hand in hand in hand. Today had been full of amazing memories and huge realizations, and I was mentally and physically exhausted.

One thing is for sure: I am happy that with Lizzie here and Ruby's friends still here, there was no drama or hiccups with anything. However, I am sure I saw Lizzie and Amber Rae vying for Alpha Grey's attention throughout the night. He seemed uninterested, and I debated about saving him several times, but he held his own. I was quite impressed.

By the time we made it to the apartment, my energy was about gone. All I wanted to do was get out of all of these clothes and adornments and go to bed. However, my mates were eager to know what I was still keeping from them.

"Ok, so this game," Zander said, whirling on me when I was not even halfway to the couch to take off my shoes. Trevor must have seen the exhaustion on my face because he scooped me up in his arms and carried me the rest of the way to the couch. Then he proceeded to take off the tiara and my shoes. One by one, he took them off slowly, and when he did, he would lift my leg and kiss my shin. I giggled at his actions.

"We are going to play twenty questions till you figure it out," I told him.

"Really? Twenty questions? I thought you were going to come up with something a little more clever. Why the game you play with Kevin?" Zander asked. Trevor looked between us, and something almost like longing and then maybe jealousy morphed his features, and then he straightened out. It was then I realized that even though they are both my mates, Zander and I have an entire past together. He had known me my whole life because of Kevin and growing up in the pack together. So he has knowledge and memories with me, whereas Trevor does not. I can see why he would feel left out or hurt when we talk.

"Because I am exhausted, and we play that game whenever we have a surprise for the other, and I like it," I said haughtily. Zander threw up his hands in surrender and laughed.

"Ok, ok, so let's get started." Zander paused for a moment, then asked, "Is it an object?"

"No."

"Is it a person?" Trevor asked.

"Yes." This may go faster than I thought.

"Is it me?" asked Zander.

"No."

"Is it me?" asked Trevor.

"No." Then again, maybe not.

"You said it had to deal with one of us," Zander said, looking confused.

"It does," was the only response I could give because I did not know who the father was.

"Ok. Is this person old?" Zander asked.

"No."

"Is this person young?" Trevor asked.

"Yes," I responded. "That's six so far."

"Hmmmmm. Is this person old enough to have their wolf?" Trevor asked. That wasn't a bad question since young in wolf years is objective.

"No."

"Was this person here at the coronation tonight?" Trevor asked.

"Yes, well, kind of." In a roundabout way, but I couldn't say that.

"How young is this person?" Zander asked, a little frustrated.

"You know these have to be yes or no questions. I can't tell you outright, but I am counting that as one of your questions any-ways. That makes nine," I said with a giggle.

"Hey, no fair," he said. I shrugged at him. He knows how to play the game—ask a question and get an answer. If you waste a question, that is on you.

"Is this person related to one of us?" Zander had his brows furrowed.

"Yes," I said with a big smile. They both looked at me. Zander had a little sister, but she was of age to have her wolf; they have no other younger siblings between the two of them.

"Is it a distant relative like a cousin?" Trevor asked.

"No." They looked even more confused.

"When I said, related to us, did you include yourself in that answer?" Zander asked, and I could see that he felt like he was onto something.

"Yes, and that counts as a question as well." He gave me a look, but it did put them closer to the answer.

"Is it your little sister?" he asked like he knew that was the answer.

"Nope." They looked at each other again, brows knitted in confusion.

"There is no one directly related to any of us that is young enough to not have their wolf who would have been here tonight," Zander said, looking frustrated. Trevor, on the other hand, was staring at me now. Then, watching his features change, he looked at me with big, round eyes.

"Aylin, is this person related to more than one of us?" I smiled at him.

"Yes." Zander looked extremely confused, but Trevor was almost vibrating when he asked the next question.

"Is this a person I can see right now?" Trevor asked, a smile like no other spread across his face.

"No." I smiled bigger. "That's fifteen," I said, and Zander really looked lost at this point.

"I think I only need one more. Aylin, are you," Trevor's voice became shaky, "are you pregnant?" Zander stilled as Trevor finished his question. They both looked at me, waiting for that yes or no response. I smiled.

"Yes." A heartbeat. That is all the time that had passed—one heartbeat—before they were both by my side. Trevor had tears in his eyes as he took my hand in his and, with his other hand, placed it on my belly. Zander was kissing my cheek and nuzzling the side of my head. I giggled at them.

"Wait," Zander said, pulling back. "This baby is related to one of us, right?" I nodded at him. "Did she say which one?" he asked. My smile faded, and I shook my head.

"It doesn't matter," Trevor said, looking at me and then at Zander. "She is ours," he said vehemently. "All of ours! We are a family, and no matter who sires our pups—me or you, Zander— we will love them all together!" he said, and then he wiped away the tears that were rolling down my cheeks at his words. He kissed me softly and then rested his forehead against mine. "I mean that with all my heart, Aylin. Your pup is my pup, whether it is mine or not." And I launched myself at him, kissing him hard. He chuckled.

"I didn't mean I wouldn't love our pup. I was just curious if she said anything about who sired it," Zander said, looking a little sad, like he had dug himself a hole.

"Her," I said softly, looking at him. I grabbed his cheeks in my hands. "Our daughter, and the heir to be the future moon goddess." Zander's eyes shot to mine.

"We are having a girl?" His smile was blinding. "We have a daughter!" he exclaimed excitedly.

"So our daughter will not be able to be the Alpha of our pack?" Trevor asked. Zander's smile faded.

"Not unless she finds a fated mate before ascension," I told him. And he nodded.

"Aylin, I am not so sure I want that for her," Trevor admitted.

"It's her birthright, honey. We cannot stop it. Like I said, I gave it up to be with the two of you. I can no longer ascend to be the next goddess. That has now fallen to our daughter, as only a daughter will be able to become the goddess." Trevor just nodded.

"I guess I just don't like the idea that one day she will have to leave us." Zander's eyes shot to Trevor.

"I didn't even think of that." He looked sad then.

"I know it will be hard, but we will have time with her, and we will love and cherish her, and she will always be with us. This is an honor, and I will be proud of her no matter what she chooses for herself," I told them. They both gave a small smile, but it did hurt—the idea that one day we would lose her when she ascends and becomes the moon goddess. Till then, we would all make the most of it!

"What did the moon goddess tell you about her?" Trevor asked.

"She only told me that when I chose you, my birthright would pass to her and that I shouldn't worry about you two loving her— that you both will love her unconditionally, and the same with her siblings." I smiled at them when they gaped at me.

"She said that there will be siblings?" I smiled back and nodded.

"Did she say when or how many? Like, are you carrying more than one now?" Zander asked excitedly. I hadn't even thought of that, but she did only mention my daughter, so I didn't think she meant now.

"No, she just said that you would both love her and her siblings," I said, my brows knitted as I contemplated Selene's words to me earlier.

"Well, one thing she said is true—we will love them no matter what," Trevor said, and he pulled me into his lap and wrapped his arms around me. One of his hands trailed up and down my back as I relaxed into his chest, breathing him in and listening to his heartbeat.

Zander scooted in next to him and brought my legs up over his lap and trailed one of his hands up and down the length of my thigh. At some point, thanks to the comfort of them both being there and them rubbing and massaging different parts of my body, I drifted off.

# Chapter Thirty-Nine
## *Zander*

The rest of the weekend passed by too fast. When Aylin told us everything the moon goddess had revealed, and every piece of it finally sank in, I was overjoyed and yet terrified. She had fallen asleep in our arms, and once she was out, Trevor carried her to our room and laid her down. Then we went back to the living room and talked about everything that was revealed.

Neither of us liked the idea that this Amarok was hell-bent on our girl and was closing in, but to find that she was also carrying our pup made this situation even worse. The protective nature in me was coming out, and all I wanted to do was keep her close. Even standing in the living space and her being in the bedroom was too far for me, and I knew Trevor felt the same. I could feel his apprehension through our shared connection with Aylin. We even left the bedroom door open so we could hear better if anything were to happen in the bedroom.

We had come to an agreement that even if she doesn't like it, one of us would have to be with her at all times. Preferably both of us, but that was not realistic with the duties that were coming up. I was supposed to accompany him to the dispute with both the Winterhaven and Ashwood packs; however, we agreed that it is not safe for Aylin to leave the pack right now, and I would stay behind so he could deal with the issues at hand. I knew she would be pissed, but we just couldn't risk it. I was looking forward to getting started with my new life and duties as well, so I hope missing it will allow her to feel a little better about not being able to go, but somehow I doubted it.

Today he would be leaving alone, and we still haven't told Aylin. We didn't want to ruin this perfect weekend between the three of us. We barely came out of the room. I thought of last night again when my head was between her creamy, soft thighs, lapping at her glistening folds as she arched her back off the bed and made those delicious noises that I can't get enough of.

The sounds she made and the way her body moved for me almost had me coming undone for her. I had been so hard it was painful, but I wanted her pleasure. I wanted to worship her, and goddess did I. After she came on my face, I licked and kissed my way up her body till I was seated between those thighs and slowly pushed into her soaked pussy. I could feel it hugging my cock as I slid in and out of her. Goddess, just thinking about how good it felt had me hard and ready for more. I wanted the warmth and softness of her body against mine. I wanted her slick, wet, warm cunt wrapped around my cock again.

I needed to calm down, though. By the time we were finished with her, she was wincing when she moved, and I knew she was in pain last night. She should be ok this morning thanks to wolf healing, but I would give her a break. Besides, we had a lot to do this morning, and I wanted her to sleep as long as possible before we had to break it to her that she and I would not be joining Trevor. Goddess, I didn't want to have this talk with her. I knew it was not going to go well.

I turned the temperature of the water down, trying to cool myself down. They say a cold shower helps, but I don't think whoever came up with that had a mate like Aylin. Finally, I gave up and used my hand, replaying all the ways I took her and that she took me since she woke up yesterday. Goddess, thank you for such an amazing mate. She fits me perfectly.

I came thinking about her on her knees before me, licking and sucking my cock. My hips jerked involuntarily, and even though I tried to keep quiet, I couldn't help the grunt that left me with the release. I stood there for another minute, letting the water rush over me. Goddess, give me strength for what is to come today.

"Well, that was a waste." I jumped at the sound of Aylin's voice. I hadn't heard her come into the bathroom. I was so lost in my thoughts of her.

"What?" I was looking at her now. She was completely naked as she stepped into the shower to join me.

"I said that was a waste. If you needed release, you could have asked me." She wrapped her arms around my neck and brought her lips up to meet mine. The kiss was hungry, and I wasted no time wrapping my arms around her and lifting her. She wrapped her legs around my waist, and I seated her on my still-hard cock, filling her with one thrust. The moan that came from her, that I swallowed with another kiss, almost made me explode then and there, but I kept it together.

Pushing her back against the wall of the shower, I pounded into her relentlessly. She rescinded so beautifully. Eventually, we could not keep our lips together, and I focused on holding her up and fucking her. I could feel her kissing my neck and shoulder, digging her nails into my biceps where she was holding on. Then her head fell back against the wall, and she screamed my name like a prayer to the goddess.

I felt her pussy spasm and contract on my cock. Burying my head in the crook of her neck, I slammed into her several more times and found my release. Fuck, what this girl does to me. We stayed there for several moments till my cock softened and her pussy released it.

I peppered her face with kisses, starting at her forehead, then each temple, and across one cheek, over her nose to the other, finally landing down to her lips, where I kissed her as if she were the air I needed to breathe. Hell, maybe she was.

"Thank you, my queen!" I could hear the gravelly tone in my voice. "I didn't want to wake you, my love, but goddess did I need you." I slowly lowered her to the shower floor, and she smiled up at me.

"I needed you too," she said. She gave me another small kiss and then turned, grabbing one of the soaps and squirting it into her hand. She put the bottle down and lathered it up, and then, instead of washing herself, proceeded to wash me. She ran her hands over my shoulders and down my arms, back up and then down and across my chest, making sure she didn't miss a spot. She took time washing my stomach and then each leg. She came up my legs to my hips, and just as I thought she was going to wash my cock, she turned me around and proceeded to wash my back. I chuckled.

"What?" she asked innocently.

"Nothing, my queen. It feels good having you wash me like this. I like it when you pamper and spoil me." That was the truth, and right now, that is exactly how I felt—pampered and spoiled to have the woman of my dreams washing me and taking care of me like this.

When she was done with my back, she turned me back around and looked up at me with a smile.

"I am glad you feel that way," she said, and then she turned and grabbed a different soap and started to wash herself. I reached for the soap she had put back before and finished washing myself and my hair.

As she was washing her body, I grabbed her shampoo and started on her hair. After a brief moment, she stopped washing herself and simply enjoyed me running my fingers through her scalp, massaging it as I washed her beautiful silver hair.

"I love your hair. It reminds me of the moon," I told her, and she moaned. "The first time I saw you, I thought I was looking at an angel." I continued, and she stiffened slightly. I didn't stop massaging her head.

"We were kids when we met for the first time. I was only about four or five then. You had to be about seven."

"Yes, and even then I knew you were the most beautiful thing I have ever seen." She turned to look at me. "Aylin, I have longed for you since we were kids. I tried so hard to keep distance from you because you were my best friend's little sister, and because I was trying so hard to live up to the pack's standards and what I grew up thinking and being told what was best for the pack. But I would be lying if I said I didn't want you even then." I could see the tears building in her eyes. I tilted her head back under the spray of the water and started to rinse her hair.

"I am so sorry, my queen, for never telling you how I felt, for not giving in to what I wanted, but I knew when we got older that I didn't want you to hate me if I found a mate or had to choose one that was not you in the end. I couldn't do that to you. I tried so hard to pretend like I was indifferent, but I can't tell you how many times I saw you walk by the practice fields, catching your scent on the breeze, and had to take a cold shower to clear my head. Or how many times I thought of you while I stroked myself."

Her hair rinsed, she was looking at me intensely, listening to what I was telling her. "I have a confession to make."

"More than what you just shared?" she asked, her voice full of emotion.

"Yes." I hesitated, feeling embarrassed. She must have sensed it through our bond. She raised her hand, cupping my cheek and turned my face back to hers. Goddess, she was beautiful. I looked at her and really looked at her and took in her features—from her blue eyes to her small slanted nose, those beautiful full rosy lips, and her creamy, soft skin with just a hint of pink in her cheeks. She smiled softly at me, and I took a deep breath.

"I had never been with anyone till you," I told her. It took her a long moment before she realized what I had just said.

"But I thought—there were she-wolves that said they had been with you." She looked genuinely confused.

"I mean I had done some things, but I hadn't had sex," I admitted, and she just stared at me. Then a big smile lit up her face, and she wrapped her arms around me and kissed me hard.

"You have no idea how happy that makes me," she said finally. "I am sorry for just assuming you had been with others," she said, looking a little ashamed at just assuming that of me.

"It's ok. I let the rumors spread. I wanted to wait for my mate, but I didn't want my friends thinking I was—well..." How do I tell her I didn't want them to make fun of me for that choice?

She smiled at me again and kissed me. "It's ok," she said, and that was all she said as she kissed me passionately, letting me feel all her love and happiness through our bond.

After the second round and another quick wash, we got dressed and headed toward Trevor's office. He was just packing a few last-minute things in his briefcase when we walked in. I sat in one of the chairs across from him, and when Aylin went to sit in the other, I grabbed her wrist and pulled her into my lap. I knew she was going to be mad soon, and I wanted as much contact as I could get while I could.

"Good you're both here. I was just finishing getting ready," Trevor said. Then he looked at the two of us and sighed. "Aylin, Zander and I have decided that only I am going to go and deal with the issue between these two packs," Trevor said, getting straight to the point. Aylin stiffened in my lap. Here we go.

"Excuse me?" she asked. "And why is that?"

"With everything going on—the threat against you and now against our pup—we are worried about both of your safety," he said, trying to appeal to her using our unborn pup. I felt her anger through the bond—hot and raw.

"No." That was all she said, just no.

"What do you mean, no?" Trevor asked her. She stood then, removing my hands from her waist. She moved across the room and stood by the door.

"WE are a team and a unit. WE agreed to go do this together so that these packs can see us as a united front, and WE are going to do just that. I will not hide in an ivory tower, and you will not make me." She seethed at us while enunciating the we's as she talked to us like we were children.

"Aylin, be reasonable. It will be easier to attack us when we are out of our pack, and you need to think about the baby," Trevor continued, getting angry himself, and her nostrils flared, her eyes narrowed, and she vibrated with her anger.

"You will not use this baby against me like that. I have done nothing but think of her and what could happen. I also came to the conclusion—unlike you apparently—that nowhere is safe. This is a god, and he can come anytime, anywhere, even here. But instead of sticking together, you want to divide us. So NO! I am going with you, and WE will handle this dispute together. And if you ever think to lock me away again, YOU will regret it." Her eyes shone a brilliant blue for just a second, but damn, was it beautiful. She also had a valid point, but she needed to understand that we are scared for her and for our daughter. She is, after all, our daughter as well.

"Aylin, please understand we are not locking you away. We are just trying to protect you both. We are worried and scared for your safety and for our little girls," I told her. She looked at me then, and her anger seemed to subside some, softening her expression—but only slightly. I could still feel her rage underneath her understanding.

"I understand you want to protect us, but if a god is coming for me, unless we can figure out how to stop him, then there is nothing we can do. He is coming. All we can do is try to fight when he does, and honestly, our best chances to do that is together," she said, and I could see her point. Part of me wanted to tell these packs that we had issues of our own and can't handle the dispute right now, but I knew we couldn't do that.

"Aylin, please. I would feel better if you stayed here," Trevor said. She folded her arms across her chest and stuck out her hip.

"I am going to go grab my bag and meet you downstairs. If you leave without me, there will be consequences I'm not sure you would be able to live with," she said, and he blanched. I did not dare open my mouth at her tone, especially when I saw the glow start in her eyes. She was really pissed, and she was getting to the point where her power was coming out, and with us not knowing what she is capable of, it was a little terrifying. With that, she turned and walked out the door, not waiting for us to respond.

"Aylin... Aylin, wait," Trevor called, but the door slammed behind her, and she was gone.

"Well, that went well," I said.

"About as well as I expected it to go. I knew she would be pissed, but I really thought that with the baby, she would see that we were just trying to protect them and would want to stay," Trevor said, shaking his head.

"Are you going to leave now while she is heading up to our apartment?" Zander said.

"Do you think if I do, I really will have to face these consequences she was talking about?" he asked, looking a little worried.

"Even if she does give you consequences, how long will they really last? She will need you and want you soon enough. You know she is going to miss you while you are gone," I told him. I spoke what I felt was the truth, but I think we both were worried about these consequences she spoke of.

"What do you think they will be?" he asked, looking up at the ceiling toward the direction of our apartment.

"I don't know, but she was moving fast, so you need to decide if we are all going or just you," I told him.

"Okay, honestly I do feel that it is safer for her here. I am going to go. Tell her I am sorry and that I love her, and I will make it right." I nodded, and he got up and walked to the door. "And tell everyone they need to start searching that library for any information on how to defeat a god." I nodded again, and he left. I walked out of his office and watched him descend the stairs and go out the main door.

I went back inside his office and took a seat behind his desk, waiting for Aylin, who I knew would come back once she noticed the cars were no longer out front and no one was down there.

About twenty minutes later, there was a knock on the door. I gave a gruff "Come in," and shuffled the papers into the manila folder on the desk so whoever it was did not see what I was looking through. I knew it wasn't Aylin—she will be storming in when she gets here, not knocking.

"I'm sorry. I was looking for Trev—sorry, Alpha Gideon," a soft voice came. I looked up, and to my surprise, it was Ruby. I knew it was agreed that she would be out after the ceremony, but it was still a shock to see her.

"He has left to attend with some matters in other packs. I am here to deal with our pack. You may speak with me," I told her, motioning toward the chairs in front of the desk. She hesitated.

"I really just need to speak with him. It can wait till he comes back," she said. She turned to go.

"Ruby, please take a seat," I said to her. There is no way I was going to let her have any hope that she could do or say anything to Trevor that could potentially hurt our mate. She paused. She lowered her hand, turning to me, and then looked at the chairs for a moment. I thought she would try to leave, but then she crossed to the chairs and sat down.

"What?" she said with an air of superiority. Oh, she is going to learn.

"I am not sure what it is you are wanting to talk to Alpha Gideon about, but as the Co-Alpha of this pack, I am going to let you know—if you try anything or do anything that hurts our mate, it will be the last thing you do." She narrowed her eyes to me.

"Just because you have the title does not mean you outrank Trevor, and I know he cares about me. He was just blinded by the fake feelings the mate bond gives us," she said, and I took a deep breath.

"You are definitely delusional, I will give you that." I shook my head, annoyance showing in my expression.

"You do not have the right to talk to me that way, wolf," she seethed.

"Actually, I do. You see, I am the Alpha of this pack. I have just as much authority over the people that reside here as Alpha Gideon—he made sure of that. Also, in case you are not aware of what happens when a wolf mates with a Lycan and bears their mark"—I motioned to the crook of my neck and shoulder—"they become a Lycan as well." I let my Alpha aura out then and let it smother her. She cowered and bared her neck in submission.

"This isn't what was supposed to happen. I was supposed to be his chosen one. I was supposed to be his Luna!" she cried. She had real tears running down her face.

"I am sorry it worked out this way, but he found his fated mate, and he does love her. You need to understand that all you will do if you continue to try to chase him is cause yourself immense pain. You need to move on! Take this chance to find your fated mate," I told her, and she looked at me with a mixture of hurt and anger on her face.

"I rejected my mate for Trevor!" The breath I took stilled in my lungs. She what?

"Why would you do that?" I asked, bewildered at first, but then I thought of my choice to reject Aylin. In all reality, her choice had a better reason than mine. I thought of my pack and thought they would respond negatively, and she thought she was in love with Trevor—or at least it was the power she would gain from becoming Luna.

"I told you, it was supposed to be me. He was going to choose me before she came along!" she yelled.

"Does he know you did that? Did he ask you to do that?" I asked her, and she looked down. Then she looked really ashamed at that moment.

"No, no one knows I rejected my mate or that I even had one," she said. "Trevor was told by the elders to choose a mate and to have a Luna, that too much time had passed, and he needed to make his pack strong. I was there through all of it, and it should have been me. I waited for years for him to choose me, all while I warmed his bed and listened to him ramble on about his Alpha duties," she cried harder. "It isn't fair! It has to be me!" In a way, I felt bad for her, but from what I understood, Trevor had been clear with her from the very beginning that he did not want a relation-ship with her—that she was only that body to warm his bed. I am also certain that he would never have wanted her to reject her mate, and I couldn't help but wonder who her mate had been.

"I'm sorry." Both our heads jerked up at the word spoken; nei-ther of us heard Aylin come in. Come to think of it, I haven't been able to hear her as she approached me at all for the past several days. She is extremely quiet when she wants to be. I also thought she would slam the door open when she got here. That didn't happen either.

Ruby rolled her eyes and glared at her. "I don't know what you are sorry for. I don't want your pity." She hiccuped and tried to compose herself, straightening her spine.

"Ruby, I had no idea how much you had been through. I didn't know what you gave up, and it must have hurt like hell when you did that—and all for a man that you fell in love with that did not love you in return," Aylin said, and Ruby flinched. "I know you are not aware of this, but the day I received my wolf, I found my mate in Zander, and he rejected me as well." I blanched at Aylin's words. It really hadn't been all that long ago, a little over a week come to think of it. Damn, so much has happened—it feels like it has been so much longer than that.

Ruby looked from Aylin to me and back again. "But you are mated now? How?" Aylin crossed the room and sat down opposite Ruby in the other chair.

"The moon goddess did not accept the rejection because she knew I would need him, that I would need both of them. I know what happened is not right or fair, but the moon goddess makes these choices for a reason. It's all in what she sees when she tries to balance us." I can't help but smile at Aylin as she keeps her cool with the girl that only a few days ago had her wanting to commit murder.

"Whatever, I don't understand why the moon goddess gave me the mate she did in the first place and not Trevor." Ruby still had tears rolling down her face.

"Maybe it was for you to balance him, or maybe he needed to balance you. There also could have been something important she saw or a child of the union. She is smart in her choices and does not make them lightly," Aylin told her.

"How do you even know that?" Ruby asked. Aylin smiled at her.

"You were not at the coronation, so you did not get to hear, and I guess your friends have not told you yet," I said to her. She looked at me and then to Aylin, waiting for an answer.

"Well, tell me then," she said impatiently.

"She is my mother," Aylin said. I hadn't expected her to tell her that, only the descendant part.

"Bullshit," Ruby said, laughing, but Aylin just looked at her all serious and not flinching away. Ruby slowly stopped laughing. "You, you can't, that, that's impossible." She couldn't believe it. Then Aylin did something I hadn't fully seen before. She glowed. She fucking glowed. Her skin thinned, and a light shimmered within her, causing a silvery glow over her entire body.

"I was the heir to take over as the next moon goddess; however, I chose to be here with my mates. Now our daughter will have that responsibility," she said, rubbing her stomach. Ruby looked at her hand, and it was like she was slapped in the face with how she jerked back.

"If you are the moon goddess' daughter, why were you raised in a wolf pack?" Ruby asked. No hint of anger or sadness anymore, just sheer curiosity and maybe a little bit of awe. And to be honest, I had been wondering that myself, so I hoped she answered. If not, I will have to ask later.

"Honestly, it's a long story and one I have only shared with a few people so far. I only just found out her reasons this weekend and that she is my mother. It's been a very long week for me with many realizations. I know you are hurting, and I am sorry that I have added to it. Ruby, you deserve to be loved the way you want to love, but it isn't going to be with Trevor. I also love him, and I am never going to give him up, no matter how pissed he makes me." She glared toward the door, and Ruby and I both glanced where she looked. Yeah, she was pissed at him for leaving.

"I know, I'm just—ten years! It's so hard to let go of ten years of trying to love him and get him to love me." Ruby said, her sadness ebbing back into her features.

"The mate you rejected? Would he have you?" Aylin asked.

"No. When I rejected him, I was horrible, and he has never forgiven me for it," she said. "Before we found out I was his mate, we were actually decent friends. He would talk to me and let me vent about Trevor and life. He was nice to me." She paused. "Maybe the moon goddess didn't make a mistake after all. He would even try hard to cheer me up and make me laugh." She smiled, and then the sadness returned at the realization of what she had done and lost because of her choices.

"Maybe you will get a second chance," Aylin said. She reached over and grabbed Ruby's hand.

"Why are you being so nice to me? I tried to take your mate and said such horrible things to you." Ruby stared at Aylin like she was an alien.

"Because I know what it is like to have your heart ripped out of your chest, and I know what it is like to be in love with someone for years, only to find they do not love you in return." Aylin's words tore at me. I was the one that did that to her. Did she just say she had been in love with me for years?

"How long were you in love with him?" Ruby asked.

"Since the day I met him when I was just a child. I knew then, when he picked me up when another little girl knocked me down, that I loved him, and I swore that day that I was going to find a way to choose him as my mate." Aylin smiled shyly at that. "So you see, I know what it is like to love someone and want them to choose you as well, even if you are not fated to be together."

"I'm sorry for trying to hurt you," Ruby said finally. "I wish there was a way to fix what I had done with my fated mate. That will probably be my biggest regret in life now. I was stupid to do that, knowing we do not get second chances for our mates." She sighed.

"I am sorry too, and I hope we can move forward through this together. I hope out of this we can become friends, because no one deserves to be pushed aside, and we all need a little support now and then. I would like to be that for you, if you will let me." Aylin will never cease to amaze me. Her kindness and compassion for even those that have hurt her is unmatched.

"Will you tell me your story then? The long one only a few friends know?" Ruby asked with a small smile.

"Yeah, I think one day I would be happy to tell you," Aylin replied. They smiled at each other tentatively, and Ruby stood and made her way to the door. She looked back just before she opened it.

"Congratulations on the baby," she said to the both of us. No hint of hostility—only sincerity shone on her face. Then she bowed her head to Aylin and walked out of the office.

"I wonder who her mate was," I pondered out loud. "It has to be someone in the pack if he was there for her regularly and still has not forgiven her."

"I think I might have an idea, but I'm not a hundred percent sure," Aylin said, still looking at the door. "I feel awful for her being locked in the cells now," she said after a moment. I could feel her own guilt rising through the bond.

"Aylin, don't do that to yourself. She was warned what would happen and yet did not stop her assaults or advances on Trevor." The mention of his name seemed to remind her that before she arrived to hear Ruby's sad story, she was extremely pissed at him and also at me, since I was part of the decision to keep her here.

"I have something to do and would like you to stay out of the apartment for the remainder of the afternoon," was all she said, and then she walked out the door. Goddess, what is she up to? Please let this all blow over.

# Chapter Forty
## *Aylin*

I was done! I was on a rampage as I removed my belongings that were brought into the room I was sharing with Trevor and Zander. I mind-linked Liam and Nikki, asking for help but only if they did not have important matters to take care of. They had both come to see what I needed help with and were a little wary of doing what I asked. But when I told them I was trying to be careful because I was pregnant, they both hopped to it, not wanting me to do too much and put any kind of stress on the baby. The fact that I was pissed and stressed myself was already putting the baby in stress mode, so their hesitation in helping me because of the Alphas went to the back seat.

They helped me move things from the room I was sharing with Trevor and Zander and put them all back in my old room from when I first arrived. What I really wanted to do was find an empty room away from him and Zander altogether, and I think I still will for the first week or so, but I already know I won't be able to stay too far away from them for long—not with the bond. So moving everything here would be my backup. So when I did need to be closer to them, I would still be in my own space.

That damn bond really sucks sometimes. How are you supposed to stay mad at someone and give them the silent treatment or anything else if that bond is making it to where you want nothing more than to be in their arms and know that their touch alone will make you feel better? I don't want to feel better, however. I want to be pissed! I want to be angry, and I want them to know that they were in the doghouse and would be for a long time.

I know why they decided to do what they did and keep me here, but I will not have them making these decisions for me. I am Luna now, and I have a say, and I should be helping take care of the packs and see how these things are handled. I also knew that I was right—if a god wanted to get to me, then nowhere is safe. Once he finds me, he is coming no matter what. We still don't know how to defend ourselves against or defeat a god, and I didn't even think to ask Selene about it when I was talking to her because I was so focused on the whole "she is my mother and I am pregnant with the next moon goddess" thing.

"How long are you going to punish them?" Nikki asked me. She was in the closet with me, hanging up my clothes.

"Honestly, I am not sure. I just know I am not going to be some trophy Luna to sit there and be the pretty face of the pack. I am going to help, and if they cannot respect me, then I will handle things on my own. We will either be a team or not, and it is up to them." I was not going to back down. "If they think they can just tell me what to do, when to do it, and how, then I will do my own thing to help the people of this pack." I would not allow them to treat me like I am an object to be owned and put up on a shelf till they want to use it. That is how I felt right now.

As we hung up the clothes, I set several things aside—some dresses and shorts since it is still summer. I wasn't going to take much. I grabbed some tank tops and a few other tops and put them all in a duffel to move to another room.

"What are you doing?" Nikki asked.

"I am not staying here right away. I plan on staying in a room outside this apartment, and then I will stay here when I can't stay away because of that stupid bond. I also think I will just leave most of my stuff in this room anyways since I have a feeling I will need my space occasionally. The boys can share the closet in that room so Zander can get his stuff out of that other room so I can set it up for the baby and make a nursery," I told her.

"I really can't believe you are already pregnant. You just got here." Nikki was looking at my belly.

"I know, and to be honest, I am happy, but it sucks. I thought I would have a few years to be able to do training and all that, but no, that is not in the cards for me. I will become a great warrior—I have no doubt about that—but I guess that will be postponed for a little while. I am going to take it as a chance to really get into learning my Luna duties." She nodded at that and smiled, but when the reality of what all I was going to give up in the near future sank in, I was more than a little heartbroken. I finally belonged somewhere, I was accepted, and I was training. Now I would have to be careful, and that meant I wouldn't be able to do some of the training because if I get injured, I could lose the baby.

Now I had to take another path, so I have decided to really put my all into learning the role of Luna and taking all those responsibilities seriously. I had already talked to Carrie, and she was more than thrilled to help me set up the Luna office in a way I wanted and start helping me dive into everything I would be taking care of. I didn't really mind how it was now—it just wasn't me—and I wanted a space that was mine when I was working.

"You really didn't have all that much to move," Liam said from my bedroom. I really didn't because I didn't bring much with me, and the clothes that Trevor had gotten me were not a lot just yet. I would have to go shopping now though for maternity clothing. However, my parents did bring more up when they came for my coronation, so I was thankful for that. They had brought some of Kevin's belongings as well. Now that they know we are both in fact staying here, they will be sending most of the rest. They had said they will leave some things there—some clothes and basic items that we used—so when we come to visit, we don't need to pack much of anything. That was a good thing to know—I could visit without having to pack a ton of crap.

I had been debating on calling home and letting them know about the baby, but with the threat still looming, I don't know if I should. I also need to face the fact that if anything happens to me, the baby may not survive. That thought terrifies me, and I hope it does not come to that. I already know I will defend her with my life. Unfortunately, if it comes to that and I lose my life before she is born, then she will die as well.

"I know I don't have much right now, but I still want it here, and we are going to also move Zander's things into the closet where mine were, so both his and Trevor's are in the main suite. This way, I have my space, and they can have theirs. For all I care, if they don't get along, one of them can sleep on the couch." They both chuckled at my words.

"So you want to tell me why I overheard Ruby tell her clique of banshees to leave you alone and to stop saying shit about you?" Nikki asked, raising an eyebrow at me—just like I asked her to say via mind link when Liam was around. She had questioned it, and I told her just to go with it. I will explain if I find out that I am right. Otherwise, I didn't want to say anything if it didn't turn out to be true.

"She came to the Alphas' office today looking for Trevor and Zander, and I had a talk with her instead," I said, shrugging my shoulders.

"What about?" she asked. "Cause you don't look like you want to rip her apart anymore either," making that observation herself.

"I don't. In fact, I feel bad for her. It's really not my place to say anything, so I need you to keep it between us—and no, you cannot tell Nick either," I stated, knowing Liam could hear us.

"Ok, no problem, girl. You know I have your back. You're my Luna. Besides, if you are really worried about it, you can use your Luna powers and command me not to say anything." She chuckled, but I had forgotten I could do that. I will have to remember that for future use.

"No, I trust you, Nikki. So she basically broke down over the fact that Trevor and her cannot be together. She had been basically his companion for ten years, and she thought with her devotion and love for him that he would choose her as his mate. But Trevor never wanted a chosen mate and had told her that. She just thought she could love him enough that he would change his mind for her." I took a pause, and she nodded for me to continue.

"So I guess some time ago, because of either love or infatuation or just wanting power and position, she had rejected her fated mate."

Nikki gasped.

"I know. I couldn't believe it either, especially since she is a Lycan and only gets one, and also because a rejection from a Lycan can be fatal. But she had convinced herself that Trevor would inevitably choose her, so she rejected whoever she was fated to. Apparently, they used to be close. She would tell him everything, and he was there for her."

I heard something fall in the bedroom, and I had a feeling Liam either dropped something or knocked it over. So I raised my voice, "Is everything ok in there?"

"Yeah, yes, everything is good. I just bumped into the stand," Liam said. His voice was a bit off.

"Ok." I lowered my voice again, pretending to try to keep the conversation between me and Nikki, knowing full well he could hear me.

"Anyways, she seems to have come to the conclusion finally that Trevor is off the table, and when she realized that, she also realized how badly she messed up with her fated mate. She said that it is going to be the biggest regret that she will carry with her forever." I finished, and Nikki actually looked like she felt bad.

"Wow. I never thought I would feel anything for Ruby other than indifference and disgust." Nikki shook her head, as if to dispel the unnatural feelings she was having for a woman she really could not stand.

"I know. I even apologized to her for all of this. If Trevor had not been at my pack for the festival, we would have never known we were mates, and he may have had to choose her in the end. It really is weird how things work out," I said. "Who knows, maybe the moon goddess heard what she said and will take pity on her and find her a second chance mate—or give her a second chance with her fated mate?"

There was another clashing sound from the bedroom. This time it sounded like glass. I opened the closet door the rest of the way and peeked out.

Standing by my dresser, putting the picture frames on it that my mother had brought from home, Liam had dropped one of them and was on the floor, the glass from the picture frame shattered. Liam looked pale, and there was something else in his expression I could not quite place. Maybe unease, or was it maybe jealousy? I walked over to the spot and started to bend to pick it up, but then Liam's hands were on my shoulders, stopping me.

"Don't, I will get it," he said, and he walked from the room, presumably to get a broom. I bent and grabbed the picture from the mess, shaking it to be sure no glass clung to it, and put it on the dresser. A moment later, he was back, and he was cleaning up the glass and frame. He seemed stiff and was uncharacteristically quiet.

"Are you ok?" I asked him. He looked up at me, and it was like he did a mental shake. One moment he was a thousand miles away, and then he was smiling at me, acting like the boyish imp he is most days.

"Yeah, I am all good, just had a clumsy moment," he said, and he flashed a grin, but this one didn't touch his eyes and light up his face like his usual smiles. I was right. He was the mate she rejected, and he was still bothered by it.

"Ok, do you want to take a break?" I asked, and he shook his head.

"No, maybe I will just go grab the stuff you wanted moved out of Zander's room and put it in the other suite for you." I nodded at him, and as soon as he was done cleaning up the broken glass, he left the room.

"Clumsy, my ass. What is wrong with him today?" Nikki asked, looking toward the door he just exited through. I mind-linked with her, so I knew no matter what, he could not hear me and told her my theory.

I believe he is the mate Ruby rejected. That is why I wanted to have that conversation with you—to see what his reaction would be. He had once told me he had a mate, and she rejected him, but did not go into more detail than that.

Well, that explains a lot! A few years ago, he would even defend her when we commented on her being a leech or whenever we said anything really negative. Would tell us that we shouldn't talk about what we do not understand. I would even see them walk together now and then. Then one day, he just started to join in and make fun of her as well.

I would have to assume that the day he started was right after he found out she was his mate and she rejected him.

Timeline adds up for Lycans. We don't find out our fated mate as early as wolves. We get our Lycan at twenty-one, and we can try to find our mate around the age of fifty, and that is about how old she is. She is younger than us but still much older than you.

Wow, really? I didn't know that. I thought you got your Lycan and mate the same time wolves did.

No. Mates for Lycans are rare, and because of our long lifespan, it is said the Moon Goddess needs more time to determine the type of Lycan we will become and make the best match for us. We can live for hundreds of years until our mate is even born.

I am glad I got to find mine the day I got my wolf. I feel bad you had to wait so long.

Don't be. It gives most of us time to figure out who we want to be and get through any schooling or training without distraction. Some of us want to find love sooner and will choose mates, since the idea of possibly waiting hundreds of years kind of sucks, but some will wait forever.

That is heartbreaking. What do you think Liam is going to do with what he heard?

I honestly don't know, but if she hurt him that badly, I don't see him forgiving her easily. He was rejected and then had to watch her fawn over Trevor all the time. She did that right in front of us all quite a bit. He must have been in hell. Nikki had a point there.

I hope the Moon Goddess at least gives him a second chance. He deserves it.

I have never heard of a Lycan getting a second chance mate. It is rare to even find a fated mate as it is, and we usually covet them because of it. The fact that she rejected him is beyond mind-boggling.

"Well, that aside, let's get this done so we can go find somewhere for me to stay for a few nights." She nodded, and we finished putting the box of pictures and knick-knacks away, then went back to the closet and finished with the clothes.

A little while later, we went to check on Liam, but he was nowhere to be found. All of Zander's things were put in the closet with Trevor's, and the room had been cleared out except for the furniture. He would need help taking that out, and it can be done later—after all, I am only a few days pregnant. If it wasn't for the Moon Goddess, we would not even know for another couple of weeks, and I would have been able to go on this trip with Trevor and Zander.

I almost wish we hadn't found out yet. Or that I had kept it to myself a little longer, but Kevin was right, and they deserved to know. They would have been even more upset if I hadn't told them. But did I really care if they were upset about that if they were going to treat me like this? I knew they would be Alpha assholes, but come on.

With one more look around and the door to my room locked, I put a note in Zander's room that all of his stuff had been moved into the closet in the main bedchamber, and then I left the apartment. Nikki, carrying my bag, took me to where Kevin and Zander stayed when we first arrived.

"Which room did Kevin stay in?" I didn't want to be in any room that smelled of Zander. It would only make me crave him.

"Um, I'm not sure," she replied, looking at the rooms. So I sent Kevin a mind link.

What room did you stay in when we first got here?

Why? he replied instantly.

I just need to know.

Bullshit, Ay. I can tell in your tone, even in your head, that you are upset, and not to mention I have felt your anger since this morning. If it wasn't for me filling in for training this morning, since Nick went with Trevor and asked me to fill in his rotation, I would have come to find you. I really needed to work on my tones, apparently.

Yeah, well, I am pissed, and Trevor and Zander need to be taught a lesson. So which room was yours? I asked again.

If you can wait a minute, I can show you, he said, and I looked around.

Ok, I'm waiting by the area where your room should be. I didn't want him going up to the apartment to find me.

Ok, almost there, he said and cut off the mind link.

"Kevin is actually on his way up and will be here any second," I told Nikki, and she nodded.

"Hey, so you want to tell me what's going on and why they need to be punished?" Kevin said from behind us. Nikki laughed at the way he said that.

"Because they are Alpha assholes, and if they want to treat me like I am not a part of the team, then they can be their own team. I am not having it. I will be the Luna on my own and deal with whatever is brought to my attention."

"Ok, well, good luck with that one," he said, and then he pointed to the door on the right. "That one was mine." He opened the door for us, and we all walked in. It was a simple, small room with a queen bed and a dresser. There was a small closet, which I was ok with, and a small bathroom attached.

I lifted my nose and smelled the area, and thankfully I couldn't smell anything. The omegas did a great job cleaning it. Until I got to the bed, and there was just the faintest hint of Kevin's scent still lingering there. That I was ok with as well.

"Here is your bag. I am going to go take care of a few things that need my attention. Are you ok?" Nikki asked, looking me over in an assessing way.

"Yeah, I am good, promise. Go do your job, and I will see you later for dinner," I smiled at her.

"Sounds good. Later, Luna," Nikki said, winking at me.

"I told you not to call me that," she chuckled again.

"That's why I do—'cause I know it bothers you." She stuck her tongue out at me, and I returned the gesture. "But seriously, if you need anything at all, just link me." I nodded.

"Stop being a mother hen and go take care of things. I will be OK. I'm pregnant, not crippled." She laughed again and walked out the door. When I turned, I almost ran into the brick wall that is my brother. I took a few steps back. He was looking at me with his hands on his hips and a brow raised.

"Are you going to tell me what's going on now?" he asked.

"You already know. We were all supposed to go to the packs to talk to them about this dispute with the apple orchard, and Trevor and Zander decided that it was too dangerous now that I am pregnant. To be honest, I wish I never told them." I was livid with them, and talking about it only brought back some of that anger.

"You know," Kevin crossed the little space between us and wrapped his arms around me, "it's not a bad thing that they care so much that they want to protect you and your baby," he said, and I glared up at him.

"Look, I know all you guys think the same, and if they had made this decision with me and not for me, I would have reacted differently. That is the point I am trying to make here. They decided this for me—they didn't talk about it with me, and there is a world of difference." Kevin's brows furrowed.

"Why does it matter, though, if you would have agreed to stay behind?" he asked.

"Again, it was because they did not talk to me about it. They decided, and I wanted to go. And as I told them, whether I am out on the road or here in the pack, we are talking about a god, for cripes' sake. When he finds me, if we haven't found a way to defend ourselves or hurt him, then there is no stopping him from getting what he wants." I blew out a sigh.

"You really think you are not safer here surrounded by the warriors and all these Lycans?" Kevin asked.

"No, I really don't. Not against a god—and gods know whatever or whomever he brings with him. Not for one moment do I think he will come alone," I said, and Kevin pondered that.

"You know Trevor and Zander have multiple people looking through the library for anything that could be linked to taking down a god. He even has the elders scouring their library to see if they have anything," Kevin said. He seemed to be trying to get me to see what these guys are doing for me to try to protect me, but it's not going to distract me from my anger.

"Yeah, I know. I have been reading Sarina's journal every chance I get as well. There are a few references that I am going to look into, that I think, if I can find them in the library, they may be helpful, but I am not really sure. I am still not done reading it. I will have to set aside time later to do it, and I should have more than enough since I am not going to be kept busy," I said, looking around. Kevin laughed at that.

"Yeah, I would imagine you won't be kept busy while you are hiding out here. I will take the room next door till you decide to go back to the apartment, so if you need me, I will be close by." I really couldn't ask for a better brother, friend, and guardian than I have in Kevin, and for what felt like the millionth time, I thanked the Moon Goddess for letting me keep him.

"Thanks, love you!" I said, hugging him tight to me.

"I love you, sis, and don't hold this against them too much. They love you, and this is just the nature of a male. They want to protect their family at all costs," he said, and I knew he was right. I had to remind myself just then that it was not about them wanting to protect us—I did actually love that! No, this was about them making this choice without me, and taking my choice away, and not talking to me about any of it.

"They will get the punishment they deserve, and that is it. I don't want them to make decisions about me or my child without me, and that is the point of this. They need to work with me and trust that I can work with them. Right now, I feel like they don't trust me or my judgment, and that is why I am upset. This isn't a team—we are not partners—and out of the three of us, if I want to really be a bitch about it, I outrank them all. I could have used my command and made Trevor take me today, and I didn't." Kevin looked down at me.

"I see where you are coming from, and yeah, I keep forgetting that you outrank Trevor as well. It's kind of weird, to be honest. I am proud of you for not doing that, though," he said.

"I wanted to see if he would make the right choice, and he didn't. Why use my command when I want to see someone's actual choices and actions?" I asked rhetorically.

"I can understand that too. You never know if someone is doing something that they would choose to do or if they are only following orders at that point." His response was almost like he was just trying to appease me. It kind of angered me.

"Yeah, well, what's done is done. You know, I told him I was going to go get my bags and meet him out front, but I knew he would leave without me. Instead of going up to the apartment, I went downstairs and sat at the far end of the porch and watched him come out of the pack house and get in the car. He didn't look back or hesitate once." I shook my head. "He was so sure he made the right choice, and I have this sinking feeling that he couldn't have been more wrong if he tried." Kevin's brows furrowed at my words. His concern was heavy.

"What do you mean?" he asked, scanning my face.

"It's just a feeling, and it doesn't matter. As I said, what is done is done." I walked over to my bag that Nikki left on the bed and started to unpack it. I put the photo of my and Kevin's family on the dresser and put Sarina's journal next to it. I placed my stuffed elephant on the bed and then put the little bit of clothes I brought with me in the dresser and closet. Then I placed the bag under the bed.

"You didn't bring much down here," he observed.

"Well, I am not really trying to stay here long—just long enough to punish them—and if I do need anything, my room is only one floor up, so I can go get whatever I may need." I shrugged and then looked at the time on my phone. "I'm hungry, let's go get lunch." Kevin held open the door, and we made our way to the dining hall.

# Chapter Forty-One
## *Aylin*

Over the next three days, I helped Luna Carrie with some small matters around the pack house and the pack itself. I checked on the site for the new playground and talked to the volunteers that were going to assist in getting the equipment, and then I checked on the site for the new greenhouse. Seems like everything is moving along smoothly right now, and I was happy to be of assistance with it all.

I was still salty with the guys. I was still in Kevin's old room and hadn't needed to go back to my room. Zander had tried to convince me to come to bed with him last night and even tried to appeal to the need building inside me, but I stood my ground. He and Trevor both still felt they were in the right and had no clue what I was so upset about. I will have to dumb it down and explain it to them eventually; however, that could wait for Trevor to get back and maybe join in this form of punishment as well. It is driving Zander nuts to be so close but not be allowed to touch me and even get ignored.

Trevor should be back tomorrow. According to Liam, he is about done with the packs and only really needs to finish the paperwork between the two. Honestly, I would have told Alpha Richardson that he needed to just stick to his pack lands and leave the Ashwood pack alone. Everyone wants more power, more territory, more control. It's stupid, really. Just be happy with what you have and work on making it thrive. That is how you become a good Alpha. If something happens and you get more territory, then great, but if not, just continue being the best leaders you can. Besides, if you get along with the other Alphas, then there's really not a need to get more land. There is already established trade between the packs; just work together and don't be so damn greedy.

My favorite time of each day has been my afternoon run. I didn't stray too close to any of the borders. The bad feeling I had was getting worse. I didn't know if it was a real feeling or just because with what the moon goddess said, every day seems like a countdown to something happening.

I have finished Sarana's journal, and I think I may have found the answer to what can help us with Amarok, but I need to do more research. I entrusted Jacob, Talon, and Henry with the task of doing this research with me. They are taking turns looking through the library and remaining with me for protection.

I had been getting to know each of them. Jacob and Talon were both single and trying to focus on warrior training and moving up in the ranks. Talon wanted to be a general in the king's army one day, and Henry had a mate but no children yet. He confided that they have been trying for a little while. I felt for them. It didn't seem fair that in the first week I had been here I became pregnant, and they had been trying for so long with nothing.

I hadn't shared with anyone else about the pregnancy. It was just my mates, Kevin, Nikki, and Liam. I am sure that Nick knows—there is no way that Trevor didn't say anything, or Nikki for that matter. I had only asked her not to say anything about the conversation about Ruby. I didn't say anything about keeping the baby a secret. However, no one has seemed to say anything to the other pack members, and for that, I was grateful. I didn't need to be treated like I needed to be in a bubble by everyone, and I had a feeling that is exactly what would happen. I knew we would be announcing it to the pack soon, though. I wanted to wait for Trevor to get back to tell the others in our circle and his mother. It didn't feel right doing that without him, and I was still really early along.

Tonight, with my building frustration and lack of being at the training field, I had decided to run longer. I let Mona take control and gave over to the feel of my wolf and the excitement and joy of running through the woods. Talon and Henry were flanking me, and even though we shouldn't, every now and then Mona would put on a burst of speed and start to lose them. Then she would slow and allow them to catch up.

'Mona, you are upsetting them because they cannot protect us if they cannot keep up with us.' I giggled.

'They are fine. Besides, if I can't protect us, no one can,' she huffed. We both knew that was true, but there is safety in numbers.

'Ok, well, maybe just be nice to them. They have been doing everything they can, looking up that research and trying to be our protectors, and I kind of feel bad for them,' I told her.

'Ok, fine, just one more and then I will stop, promise,' Mona said, and before I could respond, she took off again. We just ran out of sight of them and around the bend of the waterfall when we sensed the danger. It was too late. Just as Mona went to jump out of the way, we were tackled, and teeth sank into our shoulder.

Mona howled in pain as the bite sent fire burning through us. I could hear howls in the distance, and I knew that my brother and Zander had felt my pain and rising fear. I knew they were on their way, probably with others, and I also knew in my heart that they would not make it.

Talon and Henry burst through the trees, and when they saw what was taking place, they both bared teeth and started to growl. They started to advance on the beast that had me in its teeth. I couldn't see it. Whatever it did when it bit me had me go limp, and I couldn't move. Mona whimpered.

'I wouldn't come any closer if I were you,' said a deep, gruff voice that I recognized, and my blood ran cold. My fear spiked. It was him, Amarok! Son of Fenrir and the original King of Wolves. No! No... no... no... we needed more time.

'Zander, it's him. He is here,' I sent it through the mind link. I felt the shock and fear through the bond.

'I'm coming, Aylin. Where are you?' he asked.

'I'm at the waterfall. Talon and Henry are advancing, but I can't move. He has me in his teeth, and my body is limp.' We both knew how bad that was. As the strongest and most powerful wolf here, being taken out so fast was not good.

'You are not going to make it,' I told him, my fear ramping up.

'Just watch me,' he snarled, and I could hear another howl in the distance, much closer than before. Unfortunately, so could Amarok. His attention looked toward the sound of the howl, and that distraction was just enough for Talon and Henry to attack. The moment he took his eyes off them, they leaped into the air to attack.

They collided with him, and that collision was enough for him to loosen his jaw on my shoulder, and I bolted out of his reach. My shoulder was on fire, and I could see that my white-silver fur was now covered in crimson. I snarled at him, taking him in.

He was the biggest wolf I had ever seen. He had to be all of fifteen feet high. Even when Mona grew herself large, she was measured at ten and a half. He was still larger than we were at our biggest. He was as black as night with silver fur throughout, giving the illusion of stars in the night sky. He was terrifying and beautiful. His eyes were a brilliant glowing red that I remembered from my nightmares. He bared his teeth to us, his jaw massive. My blood was still coating his white fangs.

'You are not welcome here! Leave!' I said aloud so all could hear.

'You do not have that authority, even as a newly crowned Luna. I am a god and can go where I please,' he said back. 'You are coming with me. We have some... business to take care of that your mother had left behind when she left us,' he said. Was he serious? When she left us?

'You mean when you murdered her. Unfortunately, that is between you two, not me, so kindly leave!' I wasn't going to just go with him because he was crazy.

'She forced my hand with her betrayal!' he yelled, his voice booming off the trees, and even the waterfall seemed to fall silent. 'So, my dear, it is time for us to be going.' Even in wolf form, you could see his sadistic smile.

'I don't think so,' I growled back and got ready to defend myself with Henry and Talon on either side of me. The little bit of back and forward between us was enough to let Zander, Kevin, and the warriors get to us. They burst through the trees and surrounded Amarok, the snarls and growls from them all filling the air.

'You all dare stand against me?' he growled. 'I am your god!' he bellowed. Then he howled. The sound was foreboding and eerie. Then there was a sound like thunder. Not even a moment later, we were all surrounded by wolves. Not just any wolves, but rogues. The smell was putrid, like wet dogs and garbage. He must have been gathering them for a while with the sheer number of them. There was no way we could defend ourselves against all of them, let alone a god!

I looked at Zander and then to Kevin. I took in the wolves I knew now, and I knew that this was a losing battle. If we fought, we would lose countless lives, and he would get me anyways—probably weak and battered at that point—making whatever he had planned for me that much more excruciating to deal with and harder to protect my pup. I hadn't even been to the pack doctor yet to do the pregnancy test and ultrasound.

'I see you are adding it up. Come with me willingly, and I will spare your mate and friends. If you try to fight me, they will all be punished harshly.' He laughed. He fucking laughed because he knew he had the upper hand. 'What is it going to be, princess? Are you going to come with me, or are you going to let your friends and loved ones suffer and die?'

I snarled at him. I wanted to rip him apart, not only for threatening everyone here, but for my birth mother, and for calling me princess just like he called her. That grated on my nerves.

'No, Ay! I know you! Don't do it! We are all here willing to fight!' Kevin said via mind link.

'Kev, I love you, but look around. Look at everyone here; they will all be hurt or killed or captured. I need to protect them!' I linked back.

'No, Ay, you look. All of us are here to protect and save you!' he all but shouted down the link.

'Kev, he will take me either way. How he takes me could affect the outcome of what is to come. If we fight, many will be hurt or worse, and I could be hurt as well. I have the pup to think about, and who knows what he is going to do with me when he takes me. I need my strength for me and the baby.' Kevin didn't respond right away; it looked like he was talking to Zander and some of the others.

'I am not going to ask again. Are you coming with me, or are we going to destroy this pack?'

'How do I know you will keep your word? That you will leave those here alone and cause no harm and only take me?' I asked, looking around. I could see those around us stiffen or shake their heads. Every wolf and Lycan here were ready to lay down their lives for me.

'I give my word as the god of wolves. You can believe me or not, but I do not wish for mass bloodshed of those that are sup-posed to be under my protection. I only want you,' he said, and I looked around again. I looked at Zander and opened our mind link.

'I love you! I know you will come for me! Go to the room I was staying in and grab my mother's journal. In the last ten pages, she makes two references, and I believe that in those references is the key to taking down a god. Wait for Trevor and make a plan, and please hurry!'

'Aylin, please don't do this,' Zander begged.

'I need every wolf and Lycan here to be strong and healthy for the battle that will come. We are outnumbered and need help. Now, please, this is the only way for me to be as strong as possible for what is to come. You need to reach out to our allies and also talk to Jacob and see if he found anything today. See if he found anything. I need to think of our pup as well, just like you and Trevor did for me in keeping me here. I am making this choice for you.' He flinched, and in that second realized that if I would have gone with Trevor, I would be safe right now. The god would not have gotten to me yet. Yet being the operative word—however, that could have given more time to find a way to protect and defend ourselves against Amarok.

'I will go with you,' I said to Amarok, stepping forward. I could hear the whimpers and mournful howls of those in my pack around me and the snarls coming from Zander and Kevin, as Amarok took a few steps forward.

'That's a good girl, little princess,' he all but purred.

'Don't call me that which you called my mother before you slaughtered her,' I seethed before I could catch myself.

'I am only calling you by the title in which you are, just like her. She was one of the princesses of Crescent Moon, and by extension, so are you. Princess.' He drew it out this time, and I had to take a deep breath and try to remain in control of my emotions.

'Call your wolves away,' I said, looking around. Amarok tilted his head like he didn't understand what I said.

'I will tell them to go when I decide. You don't get to tell me what to do, and that will be something I will teach you really fast.'

Ah-ha, so he isn't planning on killing me straight away. He wants to keep me alive.

'Fine,' I said, and I looked at my pack members and opened a mind link to my pack only so the others could not hear. 'I want you all to go back to the pack, go back to your homes and take care of your families and be there for each other tonight. I am thankful to you all for being here right now and being willing to lay down your lives for me, but I need each of you to be strong and healthy for what is to come. I know our Alphas will do everything they can to come for me, and I will do all I can to come back to you. All your lives are not worth this fight if he will take me either way. Please go back and get ready. There will be a fight to come, but it is not today.'

Together, the wolves and Lycans all bowed their heads to me. I could tell they were all unhappy, but they understood that we would not win this today.

Amarok looked around at all of the bowed heads that were aimed at me instead of him and huffed. I could tell he was irritated that he was challenged and then shown no respect for who he was. I couldn't help but love it, and yet I did worry that he would become wrathful toward them since he is a god.

'Come, princess,' he said gruffly. I watched as my pack members turned and made their way to the tree line. Once inside it, with enough of what could be a head start if he decides to change his mind and send the rogues after them, they will have enough of a head start to get to cover or get more aid. I knew that Zander already mind-linked with the rest of the pack, and everyone was probably getting ready for an invasion with the rogues. That would have been a standard procedure for the Alpha—to mind-link the pack and give everyone the heads-up of the danger coming.

I turned back toward Amarok as my pack members watched me close the distance between me and this beast of a wolf. They watched as he circled me and came up on the side he had bit before and, to my surprise, gently bit that shoulder again, effectively making me go lax in his jaw. Every part of me wanted to thrash and move out of his teeth and get away from him. I could hear the growls from my pack members when they saw me like this. Amarok snarled around the flesh that was in his mouth—my flesh—as a warning to them to stay back.

My pack members took a few more steps back into the trees, giving him space, but they didn't leave like I had asked them to. The rogues surrounded us as Amarok turned and started to make his way the other direction.

'Aylin, we will come for you! We will find you!' Zander said down the link. I could hear the fear and sadness in his voice. I knew he wanted to fight right now and try to keep me here. He was warring with himself about what to do, but he was smart and knew that I was right. He knew that everyone there would probably die or be captured and that they would lose me anyways. He knew the pack would suffer. So he did what I asked, even though it was killing him inside to watch me be taken by the one that killed my mother, and the unknown of what he is going to do with me was terrifying for all.

'I love you, Zander. Please tell Trevor I love him too.' That was all I could really think to say. It was one of those just-in-case thoughts. You don't want to think that the worst is going to happen, but let's face it. That is always a possibility.

'I love you, Aylin! I love you so much, my queen, and I will come for you. I will find you, I promise.'

That was the last thing Zander said to me before I felt an intense pain radiate through my body like I was being torn apart cell by cell. The pain was so swift and so intense, first causing a blinding white light to explode in my sight, and then darkness consumed me.

# Chapter Forty-Two
## *Kevin*

I watched as they walked away. Amarok carried my sister in his mouth like a dog with a toy. I saw the blood that coated her beautiful white and silver fur. Every instinct in me demanded I go to her and rip him apart for hurting her, but I can't. It would endanger her and her unborn pup, not to mention all the lives here. So I watched. I could sense her fear and resignation, and part of me broke for my sister. I have to keep it together! She is going to need me, need us!

As soon as they got to the other side of the waterfall, there was a bright white light—just a flash. I felt it, then the excruciating pain that Aylin felt. I whimpered at the all-consuming pain, and then they were gone. Amarok, the rogues, my sister, and the pain.

Zander mindlinked us all and told us to get back to the pack, that we had work to do. I knew I should do what he said, but I couldn't leave. I was rooted to the spot, looking at where they were before they disappeared. Thinking about the way she looked—vulnerable, scared—and yet when she looked back at me, I could see the determination on her face even in wolf form. She was determined to survive and get back to us! We truly didn't deserve her. I didn't deserve her. Aylin had always been so pure of heart, and now she was in the clutches of a man that is hell-bent on destroying someone so innocent and amazing. This is not right! I have to get her.

I failed her. Some guardian I turned out to be. I couldn't protect my little sister. But I would. Determination also fills me. I will find her! She will be safe, and so will her pup! She is coming home! I would make sure of it. I howled out my pain, giving myself a few minutes to feel the pain of her loss to us—even though it may be temporary—because I would travel to the ends of the earth to get her back. I didn't care.

Finally turning away from the waterfall, I made my way back to the pack house. When I got there, I made my way to the tree line area that had the crates of extra clothes. I shifted, grabbed a pair of shorts, and headed inside. When I got to the apartment, I heard the crashing and breaking of things and went to find the source I knew to be doing it.

Zander was in the room that used to belong to him, and he had completely broken the bed and the dresser. The pieces were thrown everywhere, all around the room. He stopped when he saw me standing in the doorway.

"She's gone," he said brokenly. Tears streamed down his face. I had never seen him like this before. I think the last time I even saw him cry was when we were kids.

"We are going to get her back!" I was determined to do so. I would not stop until she was home and safe. I know she is okay for now, and that is enough to keep me going. I hate seeing my best friend like this, but he can't give up. She needs him to.

"Trevor is on his way; he will be here in about an hour." Had I really taken that long out there? Zander was looking around at the damage in the room now. He just slumped and then fell to his knees. I made my way over to him and dropped to mine, and we just sat there. I had no idea how long I was out in the woods till I promised myself that no matter what, I would bring my sister home, and I was feeling guilty that I was not there for my best friend after he lost his mate, but I am here now.

"Zander, can you feel her?" I asked. Ever since that flash of light and the pain she felt, I haven't felt her. I am not sure if she was knocked out or if the bond has been severed. Zander's brows furrowed, and then he shook his head side to side.

"I can't either," I told him honestly, and his face fell again.

"What if he has already killed her?" Zander asked.

"We can't think like that! I think she may just be unconscious, or wherever they went maybe it's too far, or he has some kind of a block—I don't know—but she is not dead! I know that. I feel it in my heart and soul." I would not for one moment entertain the idea that my sister will never come home.

Zander nodded and then got up. I followed suit, and we walked out of the destroyed room and into the living space. Right after Zander took a seat, there was a knock at the door. I went over and answered it. Liam, Nikki, Carrie, Jacob, Talon, Henry, and, to my shock, Ruby were all standing there. I opened the door up and gestured for them all to come in.

They all filed in and went to the couches and took seats. Carrie took a seat next to Zander, and I sat on his other side. I watched Carrie take his hand in hers and pat it. The gesture was supposed to be comforting, but I knew Zander didn't feel any comfort. I knew he was beating himself up and damning himself for her not being here. I knew this because we were too much alike, and that was exactly what I was doing.

"We will get her back," Carrie said out loud to all of us. "I may not have spent much time with her, but I do know that this girl is strong and resilient, and she will fight to survive," she added, looking around the room at everyone. Zander took a ragged breath and shook his head.

"She isn't going to fight him," Zander said, looking down at the ground.

"You don't know," Carrie said. "She is a fighter through and through. I have seen that girl in action." Zander shook his head again.

"No, she won't. She will not do anything that could endanger the pup."

Zander's words filled the space, and for those that did not know, this bomb made it all the more stressful. The anxiety and despair that filled the space was thick and choking.

"She—Luna—is pregnant?" Talon asked.

"Yes," was the only thing Zander said as he broke down again.

"I should have done more. I should have been closer. She was just so fast I couldn't keep up." Talon hung his head. His failure at protecting Luna was definitely eating at him as much as it was for me and Zander.

"What's the plan? What are we going to do to get her back?" Jacob asked. "I will do anything you need. Just please, I can't sit here and wait!" he said.

Zander looked up at him then.

"You are Jacob, right?" he asked. Jacob nodded. "One of the last things Aylin said to me was to ask you if you found anything. Do you know what she was talking about? About some kind of reference she found in her mother's journal?" Everyone's eyes went to Jacob.

"I found a reference to a book I was about to go get when I received the link that the Luna was in danger, and for people to get to safety or stations to protect the pack from rogues that had come." He was looking directly at Zander as he spoke but then looked between me and Carrie before lowering his head.

"Then that is where we need to start." Zander seemed to collect himself almost immediately. "Aylin had said that I needed to grab that journal and that in the last couple pages there were some references, and she believes that they will be what we need to kill Amarok." He looked at me then. "We need to get started on this now. There is no time to lose." I nodded back to him.

"I will also need to notify her family of what has happened." I knew he didn't want to give this kind of bad news, but they needed to know. "Once Trevor gets back in an hour, we will discuss further measures."

"I will go to her room and grab the journal," I told him, and he nodded to me. As I made my way to the door, I heard him giving orders to everyone to get to the library, that we would start the research together and hopefully be able to start formulating a plan as soon as Trevor gets back—which would be any moment.

Down in the room she was staying in, as punishment to Zander and then to Trevor when he came home, I stood there in the center of the room. I breathed deeply of her scent, my heart aching that I was not a better protector for her... for them. I will change that.

I should have been with her. I was meant to protect her. I should have never left it to the guards that were put in place for her. We knew the danger was getting closer, and she even said multiple times that he is, in fact, a god, and if he decided to come here to get her, what can we do to stop him? She was right. We all should have listened.

'We will find her. I can still feel her, and when we get her back, we will keep her safe,' Reece replied to my thoughts. My wolf was also in distress and felt like we failed our Luna. Our sister.

'I can feel her too,' I told him, and then it dawned on me. I can feel her again. It's faint, like it's very far away, but I can feel her. She is not in pain or distress, so she must still be knocked out, but I can feel her. This revelation made me ecstatic. I needed to get back to the others.

I turned my search back to the task at hand and looked for the journal. It was sitting on the dresser next to a photo of our family. She did not bring much to this room with her, but she brought a photo of some of those she cares about most in this world.

I picked up the photo and really looked at it. It was one of the silly ones that her and Dad loved to take. In it, we were covered in dirt in Mom's garden. My arm was around Aylin, and Jolene was still kneeling, looking up at us laughing. Mom was in the background with her hands on her hips, an amused but exasperated look on her face, and there was Dad laughing.

I could remember that day we were putting together a new section of the garden for Mom. She loved her garden and loved tending to it, but when she did a big project, she would have us help.

Aylin, Jolene, and I were digging up the area, removing the old plants and getting the ground ready to put in the new ones. I got hit by a dirt clod, and when I looked up, Aylin and Jolene were still working the land, but I knew that Aylin was probably the one to throw it at me, so I grabbed a dirt clod and threw it back at her. It had hit her on the shoulder. She looked up and saw me laughing.

"So you want to play, huh?" she said, and I just shrugged.

"You started it," I retorted.

"I did not, but I am going to finish it," she replied, and she picked up a dirt clod and threw it at me. With my reflexes, I dodged it easily, but she was expecting that and had thrown a second one right where I moved to, hitting me in the chest. She giggled at my expression of disbelief. Then it was on. We just started throwing dirt clods at each other, and at some point, I missed her and hit Jolene. She looked at me and huffed, and she absolutely hated getting dirty.

"If you two want to throw dirt at each other, that's fine, but leave me out of it," she had said, which only incited me and Aylin to both pick up a dirt clod and throw it at her. She looked at us incredulously, which made Aylin and myself both start laughing again. I threw my arm around Aylin, and we laughed at the whole thing, and Jolene ended up laughing once she got a good look at the two of us completely covered in dirt.

That must have been when the picture was taken. Once we had all calmed down and our mother told us to stop goofing off and get back to work, our dad came over and told me he was the one to throw the first dirt clod at me. I couldn't believe it was Dad and not Aylin that started it.

The memory faded, and I put the picture down on the dresser. I wiped the tears that had started to fall from my face; they would help no one right now. I grabbed the journal and took one last look around. I spotted Archie on the bed, and I couldn't help it. I grabbed her favorite stuffed elephant and took it along with the journal. I headed out of the room and back up to the apartment to see what all was going on.

When I got to the apartment, only Zander was there. I looked around to be sure, but I couldn't see or hear anyone else.

"I got the journal." I held it out to them, and Zander jumped up and grabbed it from me.

"She said the last ten pages held references. We will start there, but I think one of us should read the whole thing just in case she may have overlooked something," he said, and I nodded in agreement.

"I can do that if you would like," I told him, and he nodded as he started flipping through the pages, and I walked off toward my room. He had not even noticed I had her stuffed elephant, which is fine with me. I took it to my room and placed it on my bed. I really don't know why I took it, but something told me to, and I would keep it here for safekeeping for the time being.

I walked out of my room, shut the door, and proceeded to the kitchen. I really wasn't hungry, but I needed something to do. I also knew that neither Zander nor I had eaten anything since early this morning, and we would need to keep up our strength if we were going to do anything for Aylin in the days to come. I hoped it would not take long to find her and get to her. The longer it took, the more likely we are not to get to her in time.

As I pulled stuff out of the refrigerator to make us some sandwiches, I heard the door to the apartment burst open and bang off the wall behind it. I ran from the kitchen and saw that Trevor was back. He looked wild and like he was barely holding on to his Lycan side by a thread.

"What happened?" he roared. I raised my hands as I approached the living room, as if approaching a wounded animal.

"I know you are upset. Just take a deep breath, let's all just calm down and sit down, and we will fill you in with whatever you do not know already." I tried to remain calm because if he went off the rails and hurt anyone, he would regret it, and Aylin would be pissed. I quickly sent a mind link to Nick and Liam that we may need assistance with the Alpha.

"DON'T TELL ME TO CALM DOWN!" he roared, and I could swear the very walls shook. "I want to know what happened!" he demanded.

"You want to know what happened? Exactly what she predicted! You went to this meeting without the two of us, and he attacked when she was out for her afternoon run. He had us outnumbered with rogues, and even though we were all ready to attack and try to protect her, she was the only one that could think clearly enough to make sure she would be safe in the end," Zander yelled back. Trevor's face was stone, but you could see him blanch when Zander said that Aylin was right and that they had made a mistake.

"So you let him take her?" Trevor was trying to talk and not yell, but he was not succeeding. His accusatory statement, however, pissed me the fuck off.

"Aylin demanded it. We were all ready to attack and defend her, but she had told us that it would be pointless. All it would do is cost everyone that was there their lives, or worse—that she could end up injured and still taken in the end. SHE was the voice of reason and reminded us that we needed everyone that was there and then some to get to her, to rescue her, and to fight against him and the army of rogues he had accumulated. Trevor, the rogues he had with him outnumbered us about three to one, and he is a god. What would you have done? We have no clue what his numbers are—if that was all of them or a fraction—and if that is a fraction, we are fucked." Zander was angry as well, but he was talking more rationally than Trevor could.

"That is bullshit! You should have done something!" Trevor was getting loud again.

"What would you have had me do? If we attacked and were killed, they would have gone into the pack next and hurt everyone there. It could have been a massacre! Aylin protected everyone and demanded that he not harm any of us or the pack, and in doing so, she was not hurt much when he took her. She was the only one thinking of the outcomes and which would be best for everyone. In doing this, her and the baby have a fighting chance!" Zander said, but it was the wrong thing to say.

"What do you mean, not hurt much?" Trevor retorted. His eyes were pitch black, and you could see his beast trying to push through.

"When we came across her in the woods, Amarok had her in his teeth, biting her shoulder to make her submit, and he did it again when they left. Her shoulder and arm were covered in blood, staining her fur," I told him when Zander flinched. Trevor roared again. No, not Trevor—but Bane, his Lycan. He was pushing to the front, and Trevor was losing his battle to contain the beast inside.

"Trevor, we are going to get her back!" I tried to reason, but he wasn't listening; he was trying to contain his beast. "I can feel that she is not in pain, she is not scared, she is relaxed, so she must still be out." That got both his and Zander's attention.

"You, you can feel her? I thought you said you couldn't?" Zander asked.

"Yes, I can. It's extremely faint, like it is watered down and muddled. I thought since I started to feel her again that you could too. You still can't?" They both shook their heads no.

"It is why Bane is going crazy. It's like she has vanished; she just isn't there. The bond didn't break as if she died, but she just is not there. It's like a void when I look for it," Trevor said. Zander nodded in agreement.

"I feel the same. It's like a void where she is supposed to be." He was pacing now. I didn't even notice that he had got up. I was too focused on Trevor and wondering what we would do to contain his Lycan from hurting us or anyone else. Zander and I were still in the process of changing from Wolf to Lycan and were told that it would take a few weeks to fully transform. We were already showing some features but still have a little ways to go. But the fact is, we still did not have the strength to contain Bane if he came out. I linked Nick again to see where he and Liam are.

"Nick, you need to get up here now. Trevor is losing control of Bane. Where are you guys?" I didn't want to see Trevor hurt. I knew he was already hurting in the worst possible way, but we couldn't let his Lycan out in the state that he is in.

"On my way," was all Nick said. I raised my hands again as if I was dealing with a wild animal to show no intent to harm as I walked closer to Zander.

"Trevor, Bane, I swear to you we are going to get her back, and I can let you know if there is any change to what I am feeling for her." He looked at me. I could see Bane's eyes instead of Trevor's. "She is calm, and she is not in pain. She is safe for the time being. We cannot lose ourselves; she needs us! All of us! We need to come up with a plan, and she has sent us a starting point before she was taken." I tried again to reason with him.

"She should have never been taken. You should have been with her, you both should have. We knew there was danger, and you let her go off!" He was getting angry again. He was breathing hard, and his body was shaking. I wanted to calm him down, but there was no way he was putting all this blame on us. He could have postponed the meeting or taken us all with him so we were all together all the time.

"She had two of her guards with her, and it was her usual afternoon run through the pack. She stayed closer in and away from the borders. She was caught off guard by the waterfall, and honestly, I think that even if she wasn't out for the run, he was planning to come get her inside the pack. The amount of rogues could have slaughtered everyone here. It would have been a huge fight, and we could have taken a lot of them out, but it would have been a catastrophe, and she would still be gone either way. She protected us and the pack, and I am fucking proud of her, and I am going to do whatever it takes to get her back! This was happening no matter what." I was starting to get angry. He needed to calm down. We are wasting time.

The door opened, and Nick came through with Liam and Nikki in tow. He looked around and then looked at Trevor. He could see what we did, and that was Trevor losing the fight to control Bane. At least now we had three other Lycans, and one was a Beta, so with luck, between the five of us, we would be able to subdue him if he went on a rampage.

"Bane, you need to give control to Trevor so he can help us get to your girl," Nick said, directing Bane's attention to him. Bane tracked him as he entered the apartment.

"I need to find her!" Bane's voice was guttural and gravelly, almost like he was trying not to cry.

"We will, but we need a plan. We do not know where she is or what condition she is in. We do not know anything about how to take down a god or the number of his forces. Please give control back to Trevor so we can do what needs to be done to get our Luna back! We need our Alpha to guide us!" Nick was definitely better at calming him, playing to the pack's needs and not just his own. He knew what Bane would need to hear.

Bane stared at Nick for a few moments, and then we watched as Trevor slowly stopped shaking and his eyes returned to normal. Bane had stopped fighting for control and was letting Trevor come back to us.

"So, what have we done so far?" Trevor asked.

"Aylin told us to look at her mother's journal, that in the last couple pages there were some references to what she may believe would help with defeating Amarok. I am going through them now. We have the others in the library looking up anything they can about Amarok and entrusted them to talk with the elders to look through their archives as well," Zander said, and Trevor nodded.

"Ok, I will call our allies and my uncle and see what we can do with everything else. I am going to recall the rest of our guards that are at the king's palace and have them return, along with Gio. He has yet to meet his Luna, but he will fight for her nonetheless, like the others," Trevor said. He turned and started to head toward the door. He paused as he opened it. "Let me know what I can have other elders look for—the references you mention—as soon as possible, and Kevin, if you feel anything changes with her, I need to know immediately."

"No problem," I told him, and he walked out of the room. Nick and Julian followed behind. Nikki, however, stayed with us.

"I know we will find her! I will get back to the library. Can you please let us know if anything changes or if we need to start looking for other things as well?" she asked. Her eyes were red and puffy. She had obviously been crying, and I understood why. Her and Aylin have become close in the short time we have been here. I walked over to her and wrapped her in a hug. She hugged me back, and we stood there for a few minutes taking deep, calming breaths. Sometimes you just need that contact and reassurance, and right now, we both did.

"We will keep you all updated as best we can. We are going to find a way to get her back, and we will do it all together!" I told her, and she nodded. She gave a small smile and walked out the door.

"Kev, come here and look at this," Zander called.

"What's up?" I walked over and sat next to him on the couch. Zander handed me the journal and pointed to a spot toward the middle of the page he was reading.

I am more and more grateful for those that have been helping me and my little girl. She is only a few days old and is more beautiful than I could have hoped for. I keep thinking about her safety, and I know that danger is lurking. I remember stories that my mother used to tell me when I was a little girl about a rogue god that the Moon Goddess herself and some of her allies had to battle against. In those stories, they had recruited some of the werewolves and other creatures to aid in the fight and had to give them weapons that could wound a god.

According to the stories, the gods that fought had ethereal weapons that could kill another god but were impossible to wield by one that did not have the blood of the gods in their veins. So the warriors they recruited needed something that could aid them in the fight.

They fashioned arrows and spears out of the wood of ash trees. An ash tree is the symbol of strength and protection. To make them more effective to keep this god down, they added venom to weaken him. I remember my mother telling me that "that which affects those made in their image can affect them as well."

The battle was brutal, and many lives were lost. It was a vampire named Alonzo Capriletti that struck the god with an arrow of ash tree dipped in venom. The first arrow had infuriated the god. The second had started to slow him down, and when someone got him with a third, he fell. The battle stopped, and everyone looked toward the fallen god as he drew deep breaths. One of the gods that were fighting against the fallen god raised his ethereal sword and, in one fell swoop, removed the god's head.

Once the head was removed from the body, they burned both separately till there was nothing but ash. It was one of my mom's favorite stories, and she would remind us that no matter who you are and no matter what you are, you can always fall. I think she liked to remind us as well that cruelty will always have those to rise against it and to rule fairly and justly always.

I cannot wait to tell the whole story to my daughter one day. I hoped she would become the leader I know she can be and take her place up in the heavens with Selene. I know she will do great things. I can feel it. I just hope I am able to hide her and protect her long enough to do so.

I looked at Zander. "Are these the two references she was talking about?" Zander shook his head.

"No, I think it is only one, it's a reference to weapons we can use. We either need a weapon of the gods that only a god or those with the blood of a god like Aylin can use, or the wood of the ash tree coated in that which can hurt those that are made in the gods image. So he is the original king of wolves so it would be silver and wolfsbane, but as for the other reference look here." He grabbed the journal and flipped forward a few pages. He handed the book back to me.

He is coming. I spoke to Selene last night in my dreams, and she warned me that he is close, that he has found me. She wanted to take our daughter, but I swore to her that I could protect her. I found what I needed and hid it under the floor of her room. I would protect her with my last breath if that is what it takes. Amarok will never have her!

I re-read it. "What did she hide?" I asked, looking through the pages.

"It doesn't say, but it has to be some kind of a weapon, right?" Zander surmised.

"That's what I would think as well. You want to take it to Trevor?" I asked.

"Didn't Trevor say that there was a pack that was totaled a few years back, and that is where some of the current pack members came from?" Zander asked.

"Yeah, he did, and I think it was established that that could have been the pack Aylin's father was from. If their home is still there, then we could possibly find what her mother hid," I replied, with hope sparking inside me.

"We need to go to Trevor now!" Zander said. We both stood at the same time, but I didn't even move a step before I felt terror like I have never felt before in my entire life. It consumed me, and for a moment, I couldn't even breathe. It only took a heartbeat for me to realize the fear was Aylin. She must be awake. I didn't feel pain, which is a good sign, but the fear she felt drenched me in icy shivers.

"What is it?" Zander said, looking at me with worry.

"Aylin. She is awake, and she is terrified," I said, and Zander stilled.

"Can you sense anything else?" Zander asked, and I shook my head.

"No. She is not in pain, but her fear is... it's more than anything I have ever felt before. I couldn't breathe," I told him. Zander was radiating anger, and I could see Fin come to the surface for a brief second, and then Zander closed his eyes and took several deep breaths.

"Let's go talk to Trevor. We need to find that house, and we need to see if there is any truth to what her mother said in this journal. If there is, we have a start to being able to take down this god!" I nodded and followed Zander out of the apartment and to Trevor's office.

Once we got out into the hall, we could hear snarls and yelling. I don't know what is going on, but it definitely cannot be good. We ran down the stairs, and before us were Trevor and Liam attacking each other, and you could hear the people around them screaming, including Ruby, who was begging them to stop. She was bleeding, a gash down the side of her face and arm. Luna Carrie was beside her, holding a piece of cloth to her cheek that was completely covered in blood. What the hell happened? We both ran over to assist in detaining Trevor. He was so strong, I didn't know what to do. We are going to have to knock him out.

# Chapter Forty-Three
## *Trevor*

The drive to the Ashwood and Winterhaven packs was long, and the only thing I could think of was my mate. I knew she was pissed at me. What I needed to do was figure out a way to make it up to her. I kept thinking about what she said, and I knew there was a kernel of truth to it—that we should stay together—but I can't help but feel that this decision was for the best and she will be more protected at home and in the safety of the pack than on the road.

We pulled up to the Winterhaven pack entrance, and two guards walked over to my vehicle to verify who we were. They opened the gate and let my car and the two that followed behind through into the pack. This was a nice-sized pack with a good amount of territory, but this Alpha was one of the greedier ones and constantly wanted to expand. Since it was his complaint, I had to come here instead of Ashwood. That Alpha was young, but at least he was sensible.

We pulled up to the pack house, and I took in the view. It was a large three-story house, and it reminded me of the old-style colonial homes, with the large pillars in front. The porch had wooden chairs and rocking chairs painted white. There were flowers in big blue pots spaced out along the porch. It was actually a very welcoming place. If only the Alpha wasn't such an ass. I am starting to think the welcoming vibe was thanks to the Luna.

I made my way up the porch and into the pack house. I didn't wait for the greeting since they should have already been down there. They knew we were arriving today and about what time.

The sentries at the gate also would have informed Alpha Richardson that we were here. This, in my opinion, was a show of disrespect. As I made my way inside, I had the Alpha and his Luna running up to greet us.

"I apologize, Alpha Gideon, that we were not outside to greet you upon your arrival," Luna Richardson said, bowing deeply. She looked out of breath.

"I shall let the slight slide. Please, let's just get to the business at hand." They both blanched at my notation of the slight delivered to me, and Alpha Richardson nodded and motioned toward his office. This was already not going in their favor, and he knew it.

"Come, let's discuss this in my office. My Beta will be joining us shortly. He was just making rounds of the borders." I nodded to Alpha Richardson and followed behind him to his office. We entered his office, which he had decorated with a large obscene redwood desk and gaudy artwork, such as gold statues and pictures of the Lycan King. I sat in one of the chairs opposite his desk, took out the manila envelope, and slid it over to him. "Now, we have come up with several options, and we would like to discuss them with you and Alpha Grey preferably together, but I have sent my Beta ahead to the Winterhaven pack to deliver the options to Alpha Grey instead, so you both can read through them and be aware of what there is to discuss," I said, waiting for him to open the envelope and read through them.

He set the envelope down on the desk and looked at me. "I am sure these will be fine ideas, but there is only one course of action. The orchard belongs to my pack, and no matter what, we will have it all." I could not believe his audacity. He did not even look at the proposals. I smiled a very unfriendly smile, and I could see him work on a swallow—the only indication that he was at all affected.

"I suggest that you read through those carefully, for if we cannot come to an arrangement, I will have the entire orchard burned to the ground." The Luna's hand flew up to her mouth in shock, and the Alpha glared at me—the look of utter disbelief on his face.

"You can't do that. It took years and years for us to grow that orchard. It would cause untold repercussions to our pack—that's jobs and food gone." He was so angry his face was turning purple.

"Oh, I can and I will. I am in no mood to argue with you and would much prefer to be back home with my mates than here over something as petty as a few trees, so I suggest before you respond again, you open that envelope and look at the proposed ideas. Of course, if you can think of any other ideas that benefit BOTH packs, I am open to them, but you will not gain territory at the cost of nothing." I was not playing, and he knew it. Huffing in response to what I told him, he opened the envelope, pulled out the documents, and began reading.

As he read through them, his expression kept changing between disbelief, anger, and confusion. He read through each proposal and then set them down—one next to the other.

"No offense, but none of these will do. I am not going to give up my land for what is rightfully mine to begin with, and the others won't do either," he said.

"Then you have made my choice very easy. I will let my men know to grab the cans of lighter fluid and gas from the cars, and we will begin the task of clearing the orchard," I responded. His face went purple again. However, it was the Luna that spoke up next.

"What if you just burned the part that is on the Ashwood side?" she asked.

"We did think of that as an option. However, that will not prevent the orchard from growing back onto their territory, and I am not going to come back to deal with this in a few years all over again. Also, how is it right to torch the land of another pack who has done nothing wrong in this situation and not to the pack that caused the situation in the first place?" I told her, and she nodded and looked down at the ground, trying to show respect. It wasn't a bad idea—like I just said, we did think of it—but between the reason I just gave and the fact that we would have to destroy the earth and land on a pack territory that has done nothing to deserve it doesn't sit well with me when it comes to the Winterhaven pack making out without any harm.

"I will not have you burn that orchard to the ground. Why can't you just give us that little bit of territory?" Alpha Richardson all but demanded.

"First of all, I settle disputes fairly—that you already know. You will not get something for nothing! Second, if you cannot take this seriously and work with me, then I will decide the fate of that orchard and the land it sits on. You are right—burning it to the ground is harsh—but I could always just take that orchard and give it and the territory it is on to the Ashwood pack." This really had the Alpha seeing red. "I suggest you look over those options again and see what would work best. We will be meeting with Alpha Grey at the orchard in an hour." He fumed at my words. His Luna walked over and put her hand on his shoulder, and you could see him visibly relax—but only slightly. Though he was still mad, he was more in control.

"I will take another look," he said, picking up the documents.

"Very well. I would like to take a look at this orchard in question before the meeting starts. Do you have someone that can show us to it?" I asked, and the Alpha nodded. His eyes glazed over, and a moment later, a tall boy came in and stood before us with his hands behind his back.

"Yes, Father," he said tentatively. The Alpha glared at him. "Sorry—yes, Alpha," he corrected himself. The boy had to be in his late teens. I could not sense his wolf yet. He was tall and a little lanky, but he shared a lot of features with his father now that I look at him. However, he has his mother's nose and mouth.

"Take Alpha Gideon and his guests to the orchard and show them around. I will be joining you shortly," he said. His son bowed his head to his father and then turned and bowed to me.

"If you would follow me, please, Alpha Gideon." The boy straightened and walked out of the office. I followed behind. We exited the pack house, and I motioned to the men that came with me to move out. Only two would stay behind with the vehicles for now, just in case they needed to start bringing the rest of the gas and lighter fluid. All of the others went to the back of the car and grabbed some of the cans of gasoline, then followed me and the young Alpha-born to the orchard.

I could see the boy was nervous. He kept looking back at me and then at the men—more at what they were holding. He was scared and didn't really know what was going on. It took us about thirty minutes to walk to the orchard. It was a pretty good distance away, and that alone bothered me. Why would you put the orchard that provided so much food and so many jobs all the way out here?

Aylin's words came back to me about the long game, and I knew she was right. I would not have started an orchard this far from the pack and this close to the border. Whether it be a border that a rogue could go through or one that was against another pack's territory, it is just too easily raided. If a rogue went through here and someone was out here, they could easily pick them off as well. This is a very poor design and choice.

"Do you know when this orchard was planted?" I asked the young boy who led us here.

"It was before I was born. I guess my mother had a love of fruit trees, and there was a random apple tree out here, and my father asked her to be his Luna under that tree. They decided that they wanted more of them, and as long as their love grew, so too would the orchard. They started planting many apple seeds, and before you knew it, the orchard grew like their love," he said, looking around.

That did more to explain why the Luna had reacted the way she had to the orchard being burned. I had just assumed it was because of the jobs and food, but she also wanted it for the memory it held—the meaning being the start of the orchard. Alpha Richardson may not have the sentimental aspect of it, but still fair reasoning for the jobs and food. I looked around again. I could very well see lots of open areas moving closer to the pack, but the orchard spread closer to the border.

"Do you know which tree was the first?" I asked him. The boy looked at me for a moment, then nodded. He hesitated, looking at the men with the gas cans. "I am not going to destroy anything here unless your father cannot come to an agreement that is fair for all parties. If that is the case, the tree will be gone whether I see it or not. I just want to see if I can get a starting point from where the trees grew." I could see him tense as I told him what would happen if his father continued to be stubborn, and then he nodded and gestured for me to follow.

As I suspected, the tree in question was along the edge of the grove. That means when they planted, they purposely went closer to the border. They could have gone a little way closer and also moved some of it further toward the center of the pack—there is more than enough room. He saw an opportunity and took it, and his Luna believed it to be a gesture of their love.

"Will you really burn it all if he cannot agree to work with Alpha Grey?" the boy asked tentatively.

"I will. I am not going to punish the Ashwood pack because your father decided to grow the orchard toward their territory. I also do not see a reason the packs shouldn't be able to work to-gether. Greed for the sake of greed will never be tolerated under my rule. Even the King does not tolerate such behavior," I told him, and he looked around a bit, then back to me.

"My father does not like when I speak of working with others. He wants me to become a strong, independent Alpha that can take what we need, but I don't see that being the best course of action. Working with Alpha Grey has more benefits than harm, but being enemies when we are this close to each other never made sense to me." What a wise kid. I have a feeling when it is his time, he will be a great Alpha.

"Listen, you already seem to have more sense than your father. If you keep it and don't let him beat it out of you, then I believe you will become a great Alpha to your pack one day," I told him. He gave me a small smile and nodded. I went back to the task at hand and started looking around more. I walked the length and then went to walk the width of the orchard. It had indeed grown quite a bit onto the Ashwood pack territory. They have a small area that separated the packs that is neutral space—only about a hundred and fifty feet wide—and the orchard went through that space and onto the Ashwood pack. I really could not believe that the orchard had spread this far on its own. It was about another hundred feet into the Ashwood pack.

I started walking back toward the Winterhaven pack, finishing my assessment. There is no way this was just by it growing on its own, and there is definitely no way that they could have not known it was happening. I could understand a few trees possibly growing into the neutral zone, but this was not something that just happened. And I had a feeling that this Alpha was needing to retire if he thought for one moment that he could try to pull one over on me. What he was asking for was all this neutral area and the Ashwood pack. I am not having this. The more I thought about Aylin's assessment of the long game, the angrier I got.

"Trevor!" I turned to see Nick waving at me. He and Alpha Grey were on their way to the neutral area for the meeting.

"Ah, Beta, were you able to come to any agreements that Alpha Grey here would be interested in?" I asked, looking between the two. Surprisingly, Alpha Grey did not bring anyone with him. He must have trusted that we would have his back and keep him safe in the event talks went south. Or maybe I just didn't see them and they were hiding, which is a smart play.

"He actually liked parts and pieces of each deal and is willing to come to a compromise. He does like the idea of a fence along the border and has even offered to just build one along his territory. He said he was already thinking about doing that anyways around the entirety of his pack territory," Nick said, and I nodded.

"Well, if he cannot come to an agreement, you may need it, as I am going to burn the orchard on his side to the ground," I said, and Alpha Grey balked. He opened his mouth to reply when we were interrupted.

"I hope this is not the start of the negotiations without me," Alpha Richardson said. His tone indicated hostility. I am really getting to a breaking point with this Alpha. I know I shouldn't be this testy, and I know that it has more to do with not being with Aylin when danger is so close, but he is openly being disrespectful.

"No, Alpha Richardson, I had just gotten here myself and have not had the opportunity to voice any opinions or concerns, let alone talk through negotiations," Alpha Grey replied calmly. I had to give it to him—for such a new and young Alpha, he was respectful and held himself with grace and dignity. I liked him and his attitude. Time will tell if this is a facade or really him, and if it is really him, he will have my support and respect in all things to come.

"Since you are here for the meeting, let me just clarify a few things with all present so that we are aware of the situation in its entirety and can be fair with the terms that will be agreed to," I said. I looked at Luna Richardson for a brief second. I knew this would either hurt her or, if she was in on it, would irritate her.

"What do you mean?" Alpha Richardson asked.

"I came out here to do a walkthrough. Your son told me how this orchard started, and I must say it is a beautiful story." The Luna blushed, and a soft smile graced her lips.

"What does that have to do with the part of the orchard in question?" Alpha Richardson asked, growing irritated.

"You see, I had your son show me which tree was the tree that started this beautiful orchard, and to my lack of surprise, it was on the farthest edge closest to your pack. The orchard was purposely started heading toward the border of your pack. This, of course, makes no sense to me. I, for one, would maybe go a little ways over toward that direction to maximize the output, but I would have planted it more in this sprawling valley here." I motioned toward the large open area before the tree line of their pack.

"This is one of the areas where we host large get-togethers," the Luna piped up, trying to explain why they didn't plant it there.

"I see, and how many of those areas do you have?" I asked. She looked at her mate, who was glaring at her for speaking out. She bowed her head and cast her eyes down.

"It is one of two areas we have gatherings at," he answered, and she pressed her lips together. I didn't think he was being honest. I looked at the Luna.

"Is this correct, Luna Richardson?" I asked. Her eyes shot to mine and then to her mate. She was just put in a hard situation. She knew there would be consequences for lying to me if she did, but she would not want to go against her mate.

"I would like it if you kept the questions and discussions about this with me and left her out of it. In fact, my dear, why don't you go back to the pack house and I will let you know how this turns out," he said, trying to keep her from answering.

"Oh, I don't think so," I said, and then I looked at her and used my Alpha command. "Tell me how many areas you have for celebrations." I demanded, using my Alpha tone, and her body tensed. I could see she tried to fight my command and knew it was hurting her. A tear rolled down her face, and Alpha Richardson grew angry.

"There are four areas on the pack, not including the pack house and yard behind it," she answered. She looked at her mate and then lowered her eyes, knowing he was angry.

"Ahhh, I see. So you thought to lie to me to make it seem like this area would have more importance, that you actually would need it for large events, when in reality there are multiple others that you can use and therefore no reason that you could not have planted the orchard there." The Luna looked at her mate again, this time confusion in her stare as if she hadn't really thought of that.

"It is the largest of all the spaces, and I like using it for the larger celebrations," he said pointedly, not even caring he was caught in a lie. This Alpha is going to learn today.

"I see. Is that why you also planted trees into the neutral area and on the Ashwood pack?" I asked, and I watched as the Luna's brow drew together, even more confused.

"I do not know what you are saying. The orchard grew with the storms we have had in the last several years, spreading into those areas. Those trees would not exist if it were not for our orchard and rightfully belong to me," he insisted.

"You see, as someone that has studied agriculture, I will have to disagree," I replied. Alpha Richardson looked at me again, and this time I saw a flash of concern spread across his face. It was brief, but it was there, and I knew I was right.

"What are you saying, Alpha Gideon?" Alpha Grey asked.

"I could see there being some trees that went into the neutral area; however, the neutral area is a hundred and fifty feet wide, and the distance into your pack that the orchard has taken over is about an additional hundred feet. Not to mention there is a decent length to it. Even if a storm were able to blow apples off the trees and those apples roll away, growing new trees and so on, they could not go that far. And even if they spread over time, there would not be this many. It would take hundreds of years for it to do so, and then there is still no guarantee it could do this. Also, if they saw the trees growing and didn't want them to spread, they could have easily removed them as saplings." I motioned around me at the amount of trees we were standing under. "So therefore, someone had to help it along," I surmised.

"That is not possible. The orchard grew on its own; no one here would have done this without my permission," Alpha Richardson argued.

"Oh, I don't think for one second that it was done without your permission. I think you had it done. Slowly, over time, you spread it out and blamed it on the storms. It seemed believable—at least until it got to the point where you thought it could benefit you and you could lay claim to more territory. Since what you are asking for is over two hundred and fifty feet of territory to be added to yours—and that is just the width to be added, not the length," I surmised. "That is not all that much territory; however, it is still not yours, and you do not deserve it just because some trees grew over. And if what you say is true—that it was all just from storms and heavy winds over the years—it still does not make it yours by default. Only those that grow on your land are yours. Everything else is not, and you should know that as Alpha. Anything in neutral territory is neutral, and anything on another pack belongs to them. If you didn't want the Ashwood pack to have access to the trees, then you should have pulled the saplings."

"That is not all that much territory, like you said. It is not like I am asking for much. Just what is rightfully mine." Alpha Richardson was looking around the orchard. He really thought that he

was in the right, that he wasn't asking anything that was unreasonable.

"Well, if you are sticking to the story that the storms caused
all this to grow over time, it is still not rightfully yours. That falls
under nature and/or acts of gods. You cannot claim any of it as
rightfully yours since it was the wind and the rain that helped
these come into creation," I told him, and I could see the vein in
the side of his neck stand out.

"The fruit came from the trees that we planted here, and that
is enough of a reason that they should belong to me," he retorted.

"I take it, then, that even though I gave you extra time to look
at the proposals, you are still not going to agree to any of them—
even the one where you can have the land the orchard rests on if
you forfeit land that the Ashwood pack can use. I am sure there is
an area along the border they would enjoy. That would be if Alpha
Grey would be willing to accept that one as well," I said.

"No, I refuse to give up any of my territory." He was so red and
angry, I could almost see his head exploding from the pressure.

"Yet you want them to give up their land," I said, steepling a
finger against the side of my face. He huffed.

"You are twisting it—that I am just taking from them," he replied, and I laughed.

"You are just taking from them. You are trying to take the neutral area between the packs and part of their territory. Unless you
are willing to compromise, you are not getting any of it," I replied,
and I really thought he was going to give himself an aneurysm.
"Okay, since there can be no agreement—Alpha Grey, if you are
willing to put up the fence as you have stated before, which you
do not need permission to do on your territory—you have my

blessing, and I can even send you some aid. As for this area—boys," I said, twirling my finger in a circle. "Light it up. Leave the Ashwood pack alone. We will not touch anything done from acts of gods."

The faces of those that were not part of my group all dropped in shock. The warriors I brought with me grabbed the gas cans that we had walked out here—that Alpha Richardson must not have seen—and started walking toward the trees.

"No. Please. I beg you to stop!" Luna Richardson cried. I held up my hand, and the warriors halted.

"Luna, if we cannot come to an agreement that is fair to all parties—not just you and your pack—then I will make sure that this orchard cannot overgrow again," I told her. I know I seem to be cold-hearted, but I am not coming back in a few years to deal with this again.

"Alpha, please, this place means so much to me!" she begged. I crossed my arms over my chest and looked at Alpha Richardson. She turned to her mate as well, tears streaming down her face. "My love, please. This is our spot. This is where you proposed to me to be your Luna—please!" she begged. He looked at his mate, and maybe it was seeing the tears in her eyes or realizing he would lose everything and gain nothing at all if he would not settle on some kind of agreement. He sighed a deep sigh.

"Fine. What if we just added the neutral area and left their lands alone?" he asked. He still really wasn't getting it.

"I am not going to allow you to add territory. The neutral area between the packs was an agreement placed over a hundred years ago. It is so anyone not in your packs can travel safely without trespassing, and it is also so there is space between your packs so that there is no dispute over the territory lines," I told him. "What if we just burned the area between the two packs? Then you will have your orchard, and the Ashwood pack will not have to worry about your pack members trying to do anything on this side of the orchard," I offered.

"It is just such a waste," Alpha Grey spoke up. I looked at him, and he was looking around the area thoughtfully.

"Do you have an idea, then?" I asked.

"Actually, I have two ideas. One will have to have more cooperation than the other, and the other is more work," he said.

"I am all ears, since no one else has suggested anything of value." My dig at Alpha Richardson hit its mark. I wonder if he can get any darker in the face.

"Okay. The first one is we both put fences at least along our borders and keep this the neutral zone, in which we can all utilize—even those just passing through. Obviously, there would be doors on the fence that we can enter through, but this way we don't accidentally go on their territory and vice versa. The second idea is that we clear out this area by digging up all the trees and placing them on the Winterhaven territory in the field you mentioned, expanding his orchard further inland. We can still put fences up—I know I am either way. Also, there will be a very clear line, not mistaking the neutral area and the territory lines," he said. Both ideas were great, and I could go for either one.

"I like them both. I will allow you to decide which to utilize." I looked between the two alphas.

"How do you expect us to dig up all these trees and replant them?" Alpha Richardson said, crossing his arms over his chest.

"It is just an option for you. If you do not want to do it, then the other option is still very viable. It will be easier to build fences, and you can still have people access the neutral area for that fruit. You just cannot stop others from taking it, since it is a neutral territory to all," Alpha Grey said.

"I should not have to put up a fence, and I should not have to allow access to the trees that belong to me anyways," he huffed.

"I can always burn it and make you put up a fence anyways," I told him, and I could tell it was getting to him. Alphas didn't like taking commands from others, even though they were not at the top of the hierarchy. Even I had to answer to the King, and the King had to consult major decisions that affect all wolves with a council of elders. That way no one person has complete control.

"I am just trying to be as reasonable as possible. I would even send my people to help dig them up for you. I do not need or want them. We have plenty of fields with food and greenhouses with more. We have utilized the land here to be completely self-sustaining, turning half our land into viable farmland." Alpha Richardson gawked at him.

"How would you help?" he asked hesitantly.

"We had to get some rather large machinery, and I believe it could be of assistance if you do wish to replant these trees onto your territory. That way, you have most of the trees that came from your orchard, and you can look at us keeping these trees as a payment for that service," Alpha Grey said. His offer was beyond fair; in a way, he was giving up time, work, and resources for something that is technically his anyways. I admired this Alpha more and more, while I detested Richardson more and more.

"I have to say, you are in all actuality giving up quite a bit just to make your neighbor happy," I said, trying to see why he would do such a thing.

"I do not wish to be so close to a pack that looks at us like an enemy. I would like to strengthen the bond between the packs and be allies. As we all should be under your rule and under the king. I understand that there are territories out there that we have to worry about and will always be enemies, but being this close to one another, working together is better than fighting each other. And if it helps take steps toward being allies, then I am all for it," he said, shrugging his shoulders.

"Well, I for one consider you an ally, and if I ever need an outside perspective, I may just have to give you a call," I told him, clasping him on the shoulder. He gave me a nod, and then we turned to Alpha Richardson.

"Maybe I have gone about this the wrong way, and for that I apologize. I know it is the more selfish route, but I would like to replant the orchard onto our territory. Even if it isn't all of them, if we could get most of them, I would appreciate that help," Alpha Richardson said.

"It will take some time to move the trees after you have the majority replanted. I want fences lining both territories. I don't care if you do it only between your two packs or if you place it all the way around your territory. Originally, the idea of the fences was just too much in case humans stumbled upon them, but I think it's needed at this time. In fact, after this and the growing numbers of rogues, I think it's time to decree that all packs start the work of building fences around their borders." Both Alphas nodded. "Ok, if we are all in agreement, let's hash out the details and draw up the agreements for you both to sign. If there are further issues, action will be taken that I will decide, and that will be the end of it," I told them. Both Alphas nodded, and then it was the Lunas' turn to surprise me.

"Alpha Grey, would you like to come over for dinner? I am sure you are all hungry, and you can finish the discussion in one of our conference rooms while you eat." Grey smiled at her and nodded.

"I would appreciate that very much," he replied. She led the way back to the pack house. When we got there, I had my warriors go to the actual chow hall, and I joined the Alphas and Luna along with my beta. Nick would help keep me in check or point things out if I miss them, which rarely happens, but it's always good to have an extra set of eyes and ears.

The dinner passed rather quickly. Alpha Grey was going to have his machinery out there ready for use tomorrow morning so they could get it started, and Alpha Richardson was going to have his men ready with trucks and other gear to start getting holes ready for replanting more on their pack. They also agreed that, with how extensive it is, they would leave the section closer to the Ashwood pack in the neutral area that both packs will have access to, along with passerbys.

When everything is said and done, and the trees are all moved, they will both be working on the fences. Alpha Grey, to my surprise, was already putting up fencing around his territory and had been for a while but had left this area between the packs alone because of the dispute over the orchard, which had apparently been going on longer than I was aware of. Now that the dispute is over, he is going to have the fence on his side finished while they are digging up the trees and helping. He planned on having a gate put in on this side as well so the pack members can get through, even with vehicles if needed.

I was very impressed during negotiations with Alpha Grey. He always kept his cool, he never gave any indication of trying to take anything, and he was more than fair when it came to just accepting the trees on and around his territory as a type of payment so Alpha Richardson didn't feel like he was losing part of the orchard—instead, more like selling it. That was a very clever maneuver on his part. This Alpha was indeed smart. If I am wrong about him and his kind nature, and this is all a ruse, I would have to keep my eyes on him. But for now, he does seem genuine.

# Chapter Forty-Four
## *Trevor*

The following days, we stayed to supervise and help where needed with removing trees and replanting them. I got to know Alpha Grey a bit better and had a few chats with the future Alpha of Winterhaven. I had more hope for a better peace between the two packs when he takes over for his father, as long as he keeps his level head. I even saw him talking with Alpha Grey a couple of times. They seemed to get along pretty well, and that gave me more hope for a good, strong alliance one day—unlike the rocky one they had now.

On the third day, I was ready to get home. I planned on staying till the end of the week, but I wanted to see Aylin. She had not responded to any of my calls and texts, and Zander said she was avoiding him to the point she wasn't even staying in our apartment. She had also moved all her stuff out of our room, put it in her old room, and moved Zander's stuff into my closet. It didn't sit well with me that she moved her stuff out of there, but I would give her that space. Besides, she will need a closet of her own with all the clothes and other things she would be getting soon enough. But not staying in our apartment, in our bed, bothered me.

I wanted to go home and make it right. I wanted to apologize and tell her that I love her and will do better in the future to talk to her about things. According to Zander, Aylin told her brother that she was angry about us just making the decision for her and not talking it through together. Knowing that she would have agreed to stay if we sat down and talked about it—and not forced it upon her—made me feel like an ass and like I let down my mate by disrespecting her. That also did not sit well with me. I had a lot to make up for. I also was surprised when Zander told me she had also told Kevin that she knew I would make the wrong choice, that she watched me leave from the porch. That she had told Kevin she could have commanded me to let her come and didn't because she wanted to see what I would do. Knowing how badly I messed up, I would be paying for this for a long time. I just prayed she would find it in her heart to forgive me.

I was in the middle of helping replant another tree, laughing with Alpha Grey and Nick, when I felt fear and distress down the mate bond. It was strong, and it was from Aylin. Then I felt Zander's panic pick up, and I knew instantly something was wrong. I looked at Nick, and he was by my side in an instant.

"What's wrong?" he asked.

"It's Aylin. Something's not right. She is terrified, and Zander is scared and full of panic," I said, and my own panic started to rise.

"We need to go now!" Nick said. He whipped out his phone and tried to call Zander—no answer. Then he called Kevin—again, no answer. He tried Liam, and yet again, no answer. Last, he tried Nikki. She picked up almost right away.

"What's going on?" Nick asked as we started walking back toward the cars. Alpha Grey was following behind, and soon Alpha Richardson joined as well.

"He's here. He brought an army of rogues. I am helping get our pack into shelters and round them up, but most of the warriors went to the falls to try to stop him," she said. Nick froze as he looked at me. He knew with my hearing I heard what she had to say, and my entire being stopped.

"No!" was the only thing I could get out. She was right. I left her behind, and she was attacked. How could I let this happen?

"What? What is going on?" Alpha Grey asked. He was starting to get uneasy.

"Get everyone to safety, including yourself. You will need to be there in case the rogues get through the warriors," Nick said and cut the line off as we raced toward the pack house. I mind-linked with the warriors here that I wanted half to stay and the other half to get back to the pack house, that the Luna and the pack were in danger. All the warriors, of course, protested. There is not one that has not seen the Luna at practices and wanted to protect her and their pack. And even though it is hard, I needed some here in case there is an issue.

"Will someone tell us what is going on? Is there anything we can do to help?" Alpha Grey said again.

"Our Luna and our pack are under attack. Amarok has come for her, and he brought an army of rogues to aid him," I said, trying to hold onto Bane. It was getting to be tremendously hard to do so.

"Amarok? You don't mean the god?" Alpha Richardson said in disbelief.

"Yes, I very well do mean the god himself has come for my mate and Luna," I yelled as we ran as fast as we could, getting back to the pack house in minutes.

"That isn't possible," he replied, turning pale.

"It is, and I need to get to her now!" I replied.

"What can we do to help?" Grey asked.

"I will let you know as soon as I know the full extent of what is going on, but for right now, I need to get back to my pack, and I need—" My heart stopped, along with everything else. Where I should feel my mate, there was nothing. Just an empty hole. A void. It isn't like what my mother said a mate's death feels like, where you lose your bond—no, it was still there, but she wasn't.

"What is it?" Nick was panicking as he looked at me, as all the color drained from my face. "Trevor, what is it?" he demanded.

"She... she's gone." I fell to my knees. The sorrow in my heart and in Bane's was more intense than anything I have ever felt before. This can't be. She should be safe. I should have kept her safe. I failed my mate! And then I remembered—I didn't just fail my mate but my pup as well. Bane howled, the sound so mournful and painful, and the warriors from our pack joined in the sorrowful call. Then Bane started to push forward, trying to take control.

'Stop. We need to get back to the pack, and you need to stay calm,' I told him.

'I need my mate and my pup!' he howled back to me.

'So do I, but we have to make sure everyone is safe, and we have to try to stay calm,' I reasoned. 'This is killing me too!' I reminded him.

'I don't care! You took us away from her. I didn't want us to be separated, and I told you. She made sense—that we needed to stay together!' he whimpered. 'I want my mate!' He was howling again.

I felt hands on my arms as Nick and Grey helped me to my feet, and then we were walking again. Two of the three vehicles we came in were pulled up and waiting for us when we got there.

Nick helped me into the passenger seat and ran around. We waited for the warriors that were coming with us to get into the rest of the seats.

"Let us know what you need. I will see to it that all my resources are at your disposal," Grey offered, and I nodded absently. I really couldn't pay attention. All I could focus on was that void inside me.

Nick took off toward the gate that was already opened, waiting for us to leave, and sped toward the road outside the pack. In no time, we reached the highway, and as soon as we hit the highway, my phone went off, and I answered before it could ring a second time.

"Yes?" I asked.

"She's gone. He took her," Liam said on the other end.

"How many casualties?" I asked.

"None," was all he said. What? How were there no casualties?

"What do you mean?" I asked.

"She sacrificed herself and let him take her as long as he left the pack unharmed."

My rage exploded.

"YOU LET HER GIVE HERSELF OVER TO HIM!" It was more a demand for answers than a question.

"Alpha, we were all ready to fight, but she told us not to—said that if we fought, there would be too much carnage, and she too could end up hurt. That she had to think about us, the pack, and the pup. She told us to get ready for what's to come and that we needed to all be strong and healthy—and so did she if she stood a chance to survive. That she would be taken either way, and she didn't want to be injured and worried."

Aylin was smart. So damn smart. I would have attacked without a second thought to try to keep her safe and keep her with me. But she saw the outcome of what could happen and chose the safest option for all—including our baby. I sighed.

"So everyone else is safe? No one is injured?" I asked.

"There were a few minor injuries as people scrambled for the shelters, but other than that, everyone is safe, thanks to our Luna," he said, and I could hear the pain and pride in his voice.

"We should be back in a few hours. I want full reports when I get there," I told him.

"Yes, Alpha." And the line went dead.

"She sacrificed herself to keep the pack safe," I said to the car, even though I knew everyone in the car could hear what Liam had said.

"She is a Luna through and through. So brave!" Nick said, and I could hear the pain and pride in his voice as well. She has touched all of us in the short time she has been here. We will fight for her! That, I had no doubt in my heart.

The rest of the ride home was quiet. I mostly fought to control Bane, who seemed to think he could run off, find where she is, and rescue her all on his own—taking down anyone that stood in his way. I had to repeatedly tell him how much of an idiot he was being—that we needed a plan and needed help. I was getting tired of arguing with him and tried to just block him out, to no avail.

We finally made it home, and before the vehicle even stopped, I was out of the car running toward the pack house. I didn't stop for anyone. I ran straight to the apartment and burst through the door.

Only Zander and Kevin were there, and I couldn't control the rising anger at seeing them and not our mate. Why didn't they protect her? I went off. I listened to what they had to say, but I couldn't control the rage that was humming through me, and having Bane's fury added to mine was pushing me over the edge.

We talked for just a few minutes, and I agreed to handle things to aid in getting ready for what is to come. Most everyone is doing some kind of research, but I was going to make calls to my packs and to my uncle and see what kind of aid I could get. If my uncle will not help, then I will just pull my warriors, as is my right when it comes to needing them for war—and like it or not, that is exactly where we are headed.

I almost made it to my office when I heard someone calling me. I didn't stop. I kept walking. Whoever it was could fuck off— I had shit to do. I felt a hand on my arm and whirled around. Standing there looking up at me with big eyes was Ruby. Of all the fucking people to stop me right now.

"Alpha, I just wanted to see if you are okay and if there was anything I could do for you," she said timidly.

"You? The person that tried to come between me and my mate? You are asking what you can do for me? Or do you mean to ask, since my mate is not here, if I will spread your thighs again?" She blanched.

"No, Alpha, I don't want that, I just want to help my Luna!" she said, and I laughed. It was not friendly at all.

"You want me to believe that you care about her?" I said, and I wrapped my hand around her neck and squeezed. "What fucking games are you playing, Ruby?" She clawed at my hand and then wheezed out.

"I... am... not... playing... any... games... I just... want... to... help..." She could barely breathe, and I couldn't care less. Then I was hit with the force of a truck and lost my grip on her. She fell to the floor, and so did I, with someone on top of me. I looked up to see my Gamma, Liam, standing to get off of me and walk over to Ruby to help her up.

"I know you are hurting, but you didn't need to hurt her. She did nothing wrong and had actually been becoming friends with Aylin while you were away! You would know that if you didn't piss your mate off to the point where she didn't talk to you!" he yelled, and I went on the defensive.

"How dare you attack me? I am your Alpha!" I roared.

"You were hurting a pack member for no reason other than you were hurting and angry!" he yelled back. "I don't care who you are, we do not hurt the innocent, remember?"

"You want me to believe that this whore, that did nothing but hurt my mate since she arrived, is now friends with her?" I seethed. My rage was all-consuming, and I was trying to understand what he was saying, but it just did not seem possible.

"Don't you dare call her that! And yes, she has been becoming friends. You have no idea what's been going on the past couple of days, and that is on you!" Liam was breathing heavily and had put himself between me and Ruby to protect her. I saw red, and what little restraint I had left of Bane snapped. He was free, and he lunged for Liam.

Liam was quick and shifted, fighting against Bane. I tried to calm Bane, to get him to back off, but the more I tried, the more he pushed me to the back of my mind. I could vaguely hear screams and shouts. I felt multiple hands and teeth on me. I was being subdued, and Bane wasn't having it. Finally, everything went black.

My limbs and eyes were heavy as I started to come to. I could hear monitors beeping around me. I opened my eyes and saw I was in the pack hospital. I looked around and noticed the call button for the nurse and pressed it.

Within moments, a nurse came in. She looked like she would be about mid-forties, which for us could be a couple hundred years old since she was Lycan. She gave me a warm smile and bowed her head.

"Good afternoon, Alpha. Let me get the doctor for you. Would you like anything to eat or drink?" she asked.

"Some water would be good," I rasped. My throat felt like I swallowed the Sahara.

"No problem. The doctor will be with you in a moment," she said and walked out the door. She came back not even two minutes later with the cup of ice water and left it on the stand by the bed and walked out. I grabbed the cup and started to drink, letting the ice water soothe my throat. It only took a few minutes for the doctor to show up.

"Dr. Langston, what's going on? Why am I here?" I asked, since I have no memory of coming to the hospital. I remember coming home, talking to Zander and Kevin, and then on my way to my office, I ran into Ruby and lost control of Bane.

"You're here because you had to be subdued. Bane was causing harm to your friends and pack members, and one of them was able to shoot you with a tranquilizer that we usually use on rogues. It is a good thing that you implemented the use of them with some of your guards, otherwise you could have caused way more damage," he said. I gulped.

"Did I hurt anyone? Is anyone... that is, did I...?" I couldn't get it out. I was starting to panic that I had killed someone in my pack.

"Everyone is fine, thanks to the quick actions of the guards you keep with you. The Gamma had multiple injuries and is in the room next door healing still, but he will make a full recovery within another day or two and be fit for duty."

Memories started to come back of Liam defending Ruby. I can't believe I attacked him the way I did. I was so angry, and Bane was feeding into my emotions and then losing control of him like that. I am thankful that Liam was not lost to my rage. I nodded at the doctor.

"Thank you for letting me know about his well-being." Dr. Langston nodded and then looked at his charts. "How long have I been out?"

"Well, Alpha, you had to have a few doses of the tranquilizer to subdue you, and you have been out for about two days. Honestly, I was not expecting you to wake up till tomorrow at the earliest, but your Alpha blood is strong and cleaned out your system fast. In fact, if you are feeling up to it, you can get out of bed. I need you to be able to use the bathroom and walk at least two laps around the floor, and we can discharge you." I looked at the doctor and cocked my head.

"I feel fine," I told him.

"It is just standard procedure," he replied, and I nodded again. When he left, I got up and used the bathroom. I didn't feel any lingering effects from the sedative, aside from a bit of the heaviness still. I know some did feel more, but with my Alpha blood, it is pretty much out of my system. I got dressed and did the two laps and made sure the nurse saw me so it could be marked. Then it only took about twenty minutes to get the papers for discharge.

When I got them, I walked to the room next door and knocked before opening it. I walked in to see Liam laying in bed, and to my shock, Ruby was sitting beside him. They both froze when they saw me standing at the door. Seeing Ruby made my anger rise, but I kept it in check and kept Bane in the back of my head. I would not let him get the better of me again.

"Liam, I just wanted to tell you that I am sorry I couldn't control Bane or the rage that we were both feeling. And Ruby, I apologize to you as well. I should have never laid a hand on you." I was no good at apologizing. I rarely made them.

"I understand it was a hard situation losing your mate like that, but we will get her back. You need to believe that and have faith we will get our Luna!" Liam said and gave a small smile. Ruby reached over and grabbed his hand. He looked back to her and smiled.

"I also forgive you, Trevor. I am sorry for all of my behavior since Aylin arrived. I was so stuck in my head and believed that you would change your mind and look at me one day the way I had looked at you that I hadn't realized what I gave up in the process, and I guess I just couldn't give it up." She looked at Liam again. "I am so sorry to both of you." A tear slid down her face, and Liam wiped it away.

"I take it you two are a thing now?" I asked, trying to keep the sarcasm out of my voice.

"Actually, yes," Liam said. That seemed to shock Ruby. Her eyes lit up, and the smile that crossed her face was actually quite beautiful.

"Really?" she asked. Liam smiled back at her and nodded his head.

"It will take time, but I choose you, Ruby. Even if the bond we could have had is not there, we can choose each other and see if the Moon Goddess will accept that. Who knows? With Aylin being related, maybe she can see if there is any way to get it back. If not, I have always felt a connection with you," he told her, and the tears just kept coming.

"I don't deserve you, Liam. I truly don't," she cried and then flung herself into his arms.

"I feel like I am missing something," I said, and they both turned their heads almost like they forgot I was there.

"She was my fated mate," Liam said, and she looked away. She could not look at me, and I could see she was ashamed.

"When did you find out?" I asked.

"It was after I had started seeing you. I convinced myself that you and I should have been fated to be together and that you would eventually choose me. The day I got my Lycan and found out Liam was my mate, I rejected him to be with you," she said, still not looking at either of us.

I was floored by what she said. I couldn't believe she had done such a thing. Fated mates are coveted, and you almost never hear of one being rejected as a Lycan. I had told her from the beginning that I was only looking for a bedmate, and when I found my fated mate, that would be the end of everything. I could not believe she would have done that. She knew I would not take a chosen mate.

Liam turned her head to face him. "I was angry for a long time, but I forgive you and will not hold it against you ever. I promise you that." She kissed him, and I took that as my cue to leave.

"I will see you in a few days, Gamma." I turned and walked out the door and toward the pack house. Along the way, I kept reaching out to the bond to see if I could feel her at all. It was the same. I could feel a pull on the bond, like it is still there and stretched but not broken, as if she were dead, so I took a deep breath and relaxed the best I could. She's not dead. She's not dead. I repeated it over and over in my head.

I didn't even notice that I had made it to the pack house and was on my way up the stairs till I heard someone call for me. I turned to see Nick and Nikki walking toward me.

"Alpha, are you ok?" Nick was definitely concerned; you could see it all over his face. I had never lost control of Bane before, and I am sure it scared everyone. "I'm as good as I can be right now. I think it's time we have a meeting and see what all has been found out so we can start putting together a good plan for what is to come. We need to get a plan going and get them home and safe!" I said. Nick nodded, and we made our way up to the apartment.

When I went inside, it was dead silent. I couldn't sense anyone inside. I looked around to be safe and then went back to the living area. I mind-linked with Kevin and Zander to meet me here, and if they were with anyone else in our group that knows the full extent of what is going on, to bring them with.

It's time to get our girl back. The thought of her being gone now for two days already has my stomach in knots. I can't imagine how afraid she is or what she is going through. I just have to remember that I can still feel a bond, even if I can't feel her, and that is a good sign. Aylin, wherever you are, just know we are coming!

# Chapter Forty-Five
## *Aylin*

My head was pounding, and my shoulder felt like it was on fire. I didn't want to open my eyes. I was so tired and groggy. I tried to roll over and felt the edge of the bed I was resting on. It was not comfortable, and the blanket was scratchy. Why is it scratchy? Why does my arm hurt? Then it came back to me in a rush. I was taken.

I shot upright, opening my eyes and took a look around. I was in a cell. One random cell in a large room. Panic surged through me. What am I going to do? How am I going to get out of here? I couldn't breathe, my fear turning into a panic attack. No! I need to calm down, I need to focus. I took a few slow, deep breaths.

I got up and started to look around. The cell was against one wall in the center of it. On both sides of the cage were tables that I could reach through the bars and touch. The cot—not a bed— was against the bars, with the head of the bed against the wall to the left of the cage, and to the right was a small table and chair with about a foot in between it and the bars that the table on the other side sat at. That table had a chair as well.

When I tried to move the chair to see how sturdy it was or if I could potentially use it as a weapon, I found that it, along with the small table, was bolted to the floor. Looking around, I saw that everything was bolted down.

The wall the bed was against had an opening that led to a small room with a toilet and sink, nothing else. There was a roll of toilet paper and a small soap, similar to the ones you would see in

hotel rooms, and a hand towel. There was no door to the bathroom, so I made a mental note that I would have to take the blanket with me or something to cover up in case someone came in
while I was using the bathroom.

On the table next to the bed, I noticed there was a lamp. I
went over to see if I could lift it, but besides the fact I could barely
reach it, I could really only reach the switch on the bottom that
turns it on and off. It was bolted down. Next to it was a book.
Why would they leave me a book? On the other table, I noticed a
paper cup. I walked over and reached through the bars to grab it.
The cup was full of water. I smelled it, hoping if there was poison
or something in it, I would be able to sense it, but I couldn't smell
anything. I took a tentative sip to see if it made me sick at all, but
nothing happened, so I took another, and then another. When it
seemed like it was safe, I quickly drank the rest.

Now that I had explored my cage, I looked around, taking in
the room I was in. The wall across from me had several shelves
with books and a large desk in front of it, like the kind of desk you
would see in an Alpha's office. To the right, closest to the table on
that wall, were two doors. I had no idea where they went, but one
had to be the way out. Then the wall closer to my bed had a large,
ornate fireplace. The room was pretty bare. There was no art, no
pictures, nothing to indicate anything about the person that lives
here.

I looked down, seeing that I was in unfamiliar clothes. That's
right—I was in my wolf form, running when he took me, so I
would have had no clothes upon my arrival. I shivered at the
thought of him dressing me. I felt like throwing up. It was a simple, soft pink peasant dress. It had a few stains, and I couldn't help
thinking it may have belonged to another captor of his. I really

wanted to take it off, but not having anything else to wear, I would keep it on.

I jumped as I heard the sound of footsteps getting closer to one of the doors, my fear and panic rising. I couldn't remember the last time I was this afraid, aside from when he took me. I ran back over to the bed and laid down and pretended like I was still asleep. I heard the door open, and staying still when my entire being wanted to flinch was the hardest thing I have done. I focused on my breathing, keeping it even, and waited. I heard the sound of something soft being set down across from me. Something must have been placed on the table on the outside of the cage.

I heard the soft steps retreating back toward the door, and I cracked my eyes to see if I could make out the figure. It was a man, but he looked pale and lanky, like he hadn't had a full meal in months or even years. I wanted to stop him, but I didn't know if he would run and tell Amarok that I was awake, and I wasn't ready to see him.

When the man left, I got back up and walked over to the table. The paper cup was replaced with a new one, and there was a paper plate with a sandwich on it. I picked up the sandwich and peeled it apart. It was just peanut butter. That was fine with me. Just like the water earlier, I took a small bite and waited a few minutes to see if I got sick at all. I did that once more and then ate it. I did the same with the water again. I was not taking any chances. The moment I let my guard down, they could slip me something.

They would obviously know I had been awake, with the water being gone and now this food and water as well. I can't pretend to be asleep forever. Sooner or later, they would come into the cage, and I really didn't want him anywhere near me. I didn't know how long before anyone else would come back, so I quickly went to the bathroom and used it and washed my hands and face. The cold water felt good. I filled the paper cup with water and drank some more and then left that paper cup in the bathroom so I could get water whenever I needed it. I wish there was a mirror so I could see the wound on my shoulder better, but I guess they don't want someone to break it trying to make a weapon.

Looking at it the best I could, it was already healing. It was a very angry red; he had gone deep with his bite to make sure I couldn't move. That was the worst thing I have ever felt—not being in control of my body, forced to submit against my will. My anger surged forward at the thought of being forced to submit. I hate him. Before everything was said and done, I would show him exactly how it felt to be forced to submit.

I paced the width and then the length of the cage. I had no idea how long I had been out for, and I needed to find out what the endgame was. Is he going to kill me? Use me? I have no idea what I am in for, and the more I thought about the possibilities, the sicker it made me. I just continued to pace and rub my stomach. Don't worry, little one, we will get out of this.

I looked around for the hundredth time, looking for a clock or something to tell what time of day it was. I had not heard or seen anyone since the person came with the sandwich earlier, and I didn't know how much time had passed since then. It felt like hours, but with no way to tell time and my mind running wild, it could have been minutes.

I finally gave up pacing and sat on the bed. I reached for the book and started reading. Why not? If I am to be trapped here, it would be nice to get my mind off the unknown and the million different scenarios of what could happen to me—or the endless wondering about how my mates, friends, and pack are all doing.

The book was rather boring, some old romance novel about a countess whose husband died and she found comfort in the arms of her butler. These books were a dime a dozen. However, it was enough to kind of preoccupy my mind. I was about a third of the way through the book when I heard footsteps coming from outside the room.

I sat there and continued to read the book. The footsteps sounded the same as the ones from earlier, so I was not going to pretend to be asleep this time. It wouldn't help anyway if they decided to wake me up.

The same man from earlier came through the door to the right on the wall closer to the shelves of books. He looked up after the door closed, and his eyes rounded when he saw me awake. He snapped his mouth closed and walked a tray over to the table. He removed a plate that had another sandwich on it and a cup of what I assume is water.

"What time is it?" I asked timidly. I allowed myself to sound scared and vulnerable, trying to appeal to any sense of decency this guy might have. He looked at me and then looked down. He was obviously told not to talk to me. He turned to walk away.

"Please, I don't know how long I have been here or what time it is. I don't know if he kept his word about leaving my pack alone, please." I begged. He looked up at me, and I could tell he was scared. He shook his head and continued to walk to the door. I have no idea if he was shaking his head in regard to anything I said or if he was just shaking it because he can't talk to me. I sighed and went back to my bed. I looked over at the sandwich, my stomach in knots—I didn't feel like eating.

I picked up the book and started reading again. At first, I couldn't get past the paragraph I was on. I must have read it six times before actually seeing what it said. Finally, I was able to concentrate on the book and try to get lost in the pages. When I was able to calm down enough and my stomach didn't hurt as bad, I went ahead and ate the sandwich. Again, it was just a plain peanut butter sandwich and a cup of water. After eating, I went back to reading till I felt tired. I put the book face down on the table outside the bars and laid down to go to sleep.

Sleeping did not pan out very well for me. I tossed and turned; my mind would not shut off. When I finally woke, I looked to see if anyone had come, but the room was empty. No new plate of food or anything. Maybe it was still night. Maybe I only slept for an hour. I had no way of knowing.

I picked up the book and started to read to pass the time. After I finished the book, I got up and used the bathroom. I really wanted to take a shower. I felt gross. I had gone for a run before I was taken and usually would have showered after getting back from my run. Not being able to do that and not knowing how long I have been in here made me feel disgusting, and not knowing who probably wore this dress they put me in was also adding to the gross factor.

I started pacing the cage again, and when I got bored with that, I started to exercise. I know I should conserve my energy, but I didn't want my muscles to cramp up, and I needed to stay limber and loose. I hated the idea of getting even more sweaty and not being able to shower, but I would do what I needed to.

In the middle of going through practice stances and moves, I heard footsteps again. I stopped what I was doing. I didn't need them seeing me practice defense and attack moves.

The same man that has come before walked through the door. He glanced at me and then dropped his gaze to the floor. He put another paper plate with yet another sandwich on the table and a paper cup full of water next to it. He walked away, and I stopped him again.

"Wait," I said, and he stilled, his body tense. "I am getting the impression you cannot speak to me or that you can't speak, but can I ask you to get me a different book?" He looked over at me. I walked over to the bed and reached through the bars and grabbed the book that was sitting on the table. I walked it to the edge of the bars and put it through them closer to the man. He hesitated for a moment, and I bent down, putting the book on the floor and then stepped away. "There, just in case so you won't accidentally touch me, and I will stay back so you won't get close to me or I close to you." He nodded, and his shoulders relaxed a bit. I could see that he was scared to be anywhere near me.

He walked over toward my cage, picked up the book that was about a foot outside it, and walked over to the bookshelf. He looked at the book and looked at the shelf. He put the one he had in a spot I hadn't really noticed was empty, grabbed one next to it, and walked it over to the table beside the bed and set it down. He nodded to me and started to walk back to the door.

"Thank you," I called, and he stilled, looked back, and nodded once. Then he left. I sat down on the bed and grabbed the new book. It was another romance. It's not that I didn't like a good romance, but it just didn't seem like the best thing to read in the situation I was in. I would have to ask if they had any other styles. I doubted Amarok read romance novels. My mind spiraled again to the idea that I am not the only one to be held here in this cage, and I was beginning to suspect any other tenants were probably females.

Again, I don't know how much time had passed, but I started a routine. I would read for a while, and then I would get up and pace the cage. Read a little more, then get up and do some of my workouts. I made sure every time I got up, I would try to use the bathroom and grab a drink. I wanted to stay hydrated, and I didn't want to chance someone being here and then I have to use the bathroom with no privacy. I did this till I got tired and fell asleep.

The next time I woke up was when I heard the door open. The man that had been bringing my meals was back with the next one. Judging by the meals, if I am getting three a day, I have only been here a day and a half since I woke up, but there is no guarantee that I was getting three meals a day. Somehow, I doubted it with how far in between he was coming. At least, that is how it felt.

He sat down the paper plate. This time, along with the sandwich, was an apple. He pointed at it and gave me a small smile. I couldn't be sure, but I think he was being nice to me. Why, I didn't know. I smiled back and held up my finger, indicating one minute. I walked over to the book and picked it up. This one was shorter than the other, and I finished it already.

"Can I get a new one? Maybe one that is not a romance? If that is all you have, it is fine. It's just kind of weird reading them while I am locked up like a Disney princess waiting for a prince to rescue me. Not that a prince really would, but reading romance novels kind of gives that vibe in my head." I gave a small laugh at my reference, and he smiled back. I placed the book down like I had before and stepped back. I didn't want him to think I was going to get him in trouble, but I was beyond restless with needing to know what was going on. "I wish you could talk to me," I said, sitting on the chair away from the bed so he felt safe going over to the table.

He paused for a moment at the bookshelf and looked at the book he had pulled down. He looked at me and put it back, grabbing a smaller book. He walked over and sat it down, and keeping his head down, he uttered two words so soft I almost didn't hear him.

"Next time." He left the book and walked toward the door with his head down. I called another thank you and went over to the food he brought. I ate the apple first. It was delicious, and then I ate the sandwich. I was growing tired of peanut butter, but I would take what I could get. I had to keep up my strength as much as possible, so I would eat it and like it.

I sat down on the bed and opened the book. It was only about two hundred pages. I knew I would finish by the time he came back with how far in between the times he came in were. Maybe that was the idea. He said next time, after all. Maybe he would say more when he gave me another book.

I continued my routine, only focusing on what I was doing in the moment I was doing it. I only let myself contemplate escape ideas, but it would not matter if I didn't know where I was. I had no idea about the place I was being kept in and how to get out of not only this room but the building. Was it a small house or a large mansion or a castle? He was a king and a god, after all.

Then, once I made it out of this place, how would I know where I am at? Am I close to home? Across the country? Or somewhere even further? I was unsure how I would find all this out since the man that would bring my meals is too scared to talk to me. I doubt he would give me inside information to aid in my escape, since something like that could get him in trouble, and by looking at him, he definitely knows his place here, so he will not be so keen on helping me.

Maybe I could try to trick it out of him. Maybe if I could get him to talk to me, I could get him to unknowingly tell me where I am at. I would really have to think about how to do that. I knew I could. It was all a matter of having the right conversations and wording. First, of course, I had to get him to open up and talk to me.

Time passed by, and I couldn't tell, as usual, what time of day or night it was. I finished the book and had gone through my exercises multiple times. I was bored out of my mind. I tried to feel for my mates through the bond we shared, but I kept coming up empty. I was getting frustrated and started to feel more and more desperate. I had no clue what was going to happen to me here. I just wanted to go home.

I lazily rubbed my stomach and thought of my little girl. I wanted her to be happy and healthy, but more than anything, I wanted her to live. To have a chance at life. I hated the idea of her being a goddess more and more. No matter what, though, it would be her choice. I would allow her to grow up and be trained and do everything she needed to do to take on the role once it came, but in the end, if she decided she didn't want to, then that was it. I wonder how many of the lineage would decline becoming a goddess.

I heard footsteps approaching and sat at the table waiting for the man that usually visited. However, it was not the usual man that entered—it was a woman. A rather beautiful woman with midnight hair, fair skin, and big dark brown eyes with luminous streaks of gold through them and full red lips. She looked otherworldly. Was she a goddess? I then looked at her dress, or rather lack of dress. It was borderline see-through. Can you say trying too hard? Anyone that needs to dress in a way that leaves nothing to the imagination is definitely looking for attention.

"So," she drawled in a lilting voice. "You must be her. The one he's been looking for, the one that will help him bring down that bitch that betrayed him." She said. I rolled my eyes. Yippy, another bitchy female with possessive issues. I was so done with this. Everywhere I went, I had to deal with one of these types of cunts.

Ignoring her, I walked over to the bed, grabbed the book I already finished, opened it to the last couple chapters, and pretended to be reading. This seemed to aggravate her. She placed her hands on her hips and glared at me. I looked back at the book, letting her know how little I thought about her presence.

"That is no way to treat someone better than you," she scoffed. "You should be bowing to me. I, after all, am a goddess and soon to be Amarok's consort." She beamed at that last part like she was trying to brag and not realizing that I didn't give a shit about Amarok.

"Cool," I said and went back to rereading the end of the book I had already finished. My dismissive response pissed her off more.

"How dare you not show me the respect I deserve," she seethed at me. "Wait till Amarok hears about this. He will punish you greatly." She crossed her arms. As I glanced up at her with a bored look on my face, she smiled. "That is unless you cower and beg me for forgiveness." She added, her smile widening. I laughed.

"Go ahead and tell him. See if I care. He will either torture me or take my life, both of which I am already expecting. That is unless you are bluffing and you won't tell him because you are not supposed to be here and definitely not supposed to be talking to me." Her smile faltered. Yup, I guessed right. There was a reason the man that brought me food wasn't talking to me, and I bet that everyone was ordered to stay away or, if they came in, to not interact with me.

"I can do whatever I want here. He would not deny me if I wanted to see the whore he captured." She was definitely a petty one.

"Ok, well then I suggest you go tell him that I was rude and refused to apologize, because you sure as hell are not getting one from me. And by the way, I really don't care who or what you are. Respect is earned, and you have not earned mine in the brief time you have been here, coming in and posturing around here and demanding anything from me. I don't know who you are, and you can bet if you are a goddess that I have respected in the past, seeing how you are now, dressed like a whore unlike myself, and worshiping a lunatic that you can't wait to be the latter half in a relationship with, I will have lost any and all respect I could possibly have had for you." I smiled viciously at her, letting her see how little I truly cared about the situation I am in and about her.

My words did the trick: the smile was completely gone, along with any composure she could have had. She started stomping her way to the cage, and when she was up close to it, she reached through the bar and held out her hand like she was waiting for me to take it or put something in it. Her brows furrowed, and she seemed to concentrate a bit harder. She looked comical, and I started laughing.

"Are you wanting me to hold your hand now?" I laughed again. She glared at me.

"Of course not, you dumb bitch," she said, lowering her hand. She turned toward the bookshelf, held out her hand like she had just done, and a book flew off the shelf and into her waiting hand. "I was trying to bring you to me. However, I could not feel a way to do so." She chucked the book at me, but I dodged it easily.

"Thanks. I needed a new book to read. I already finished the one I was rereading to ignore you." I smirked again. I was really enjoying pissing her off.

"I can't wait to watch him play with and torture you," she said through gritted teeth.

"I am sure that is all he actually allows you to do is watch." It took her a moment to get my insult, but eventually she did, and she let out a frustrated growl.

"You will get what you deserve for this insolence. Even if I don't say anything to Amarok, he is going to have so much fun playing with you." She was once again trying to scare me, so I smiled broader.

"I can't wait," I said, and then, not taking my eyes from hers, staring her down like she is trying to do with me. "Maybe I will even let him know how much I appreciate him letting me have company." She faltered for just a minute, and I saw the fear in her eyes. Yeah, I was right. She wasn't supposed to be in here. "Who knows, maybe with all that playtime, he will prefer my company instead. After all, wasn't it my birth mother that he wanted so desperately to marry? Wasn't it her that he truly cared for? He wouldn't be wanting revenge this bad if he didn't want her! I bet he doesn't even care for you. You are just, after all, going to be a consort with no real title. He is the one that people will look to. Did you know he would have been her consort? And he was ok with that? You are just pitiful. So run along and tell him, oh great goddess." I knew my words were affecting her.

"Whatever," she said, acting as if it didn't matter one way or the other. I turned from her and walked over to where the new book lay on the ground and picked it up. At least it wasn't a romance. It was titled A History of War. Well, this should come in handy. I waved the book in the air. "Thanks again, like I said, I needed a new read." She rolled her eyes and walked from the room. I got way too much enjoyment in pissing her off.

I sat down and began reading the book she gave me. It was boring and interesting at the same time, which, in my opinion, is a weird combination. The facts were lengthy and boring, but the content was the interesting part—the types of wars between different gods, who won, and how. Ancient weapons forged in the heavens. Some of which were lost on Earth. If only we knew where any of these weapons were.

There were pictures and art renderings of some of the gods involved, and even of the weapons lost to time. Then there were references to the power or ether within gods that can be wielded like weapons. The stronger the god, the more ether they possessed. It was described as a glowing silver essence that can be used by mere thought and is essentially an extension of the gods' will. I have seen this glowing light from me a few times. Could I potentially use it like a weapon? Until I figure that out, it would be smart to keep that bit to myself. After all, I don't know what he does or does not know about my abilities. Maybe I can find a way to practice.

I heard footsteps again, and I looked around. I didn't think it would be wise to be caught with this book. Somehow, I believed that I was not supposed to see this, and it must have been an accident for that goddess to throw it at me. I hid the book inside the pillowcase and sat straight up on the bed. I would have to find a better spot for it later if I could.

The door opened, and the man that had come so many times before with food walked in. I grabbed the book he had given me and walked over to the table he set my food on, and left it there and walked away, and sat back on the bed.

He sat down a plate that had a sandwich and some slices of carrots. I had a feeling I was not supposed to be getting the sides, just the sandwich. He sat down the cup as well. I waited for him to grab the book and walk toward the bookcase.

"I wish I knew your name so I knew what to call you other than 'that man that brings food.'" I chuckled to myself, and I could have sworn I heard him laugh a little too. I watched him exchange that book for another. It was also a thinner book. I watched him open the book and close it. He walked it over to the nightstand, and as he set it down, he mumbled one word.

"Johnathan," he whispered. His name—he actually gave me his name.

"Aylin," I said. He glanced up and gave me a small smile, almost not noticeable, but with the rest of his features softening, I did. He quickly looked down and walked to the door without looking back.

I grabbed the food and sat down on the bed. I grabbed the book he had given me. It looked like a mystery, which I was cool with. I opened it and almost missed the small piece of paper that was wedged in between the cover and first page. I held it like I was reading the book. It was a note, and it gave some answers I had been wanting. It read:

Today marks four days since you arrived, and the time I wrote this before bringing this meal is six thirty p.m. I have only been ordered to bring two meals a day: breakfast and dinner, if that helps keep track. I can try to answer questions. This is the only way, but you need to destroy these letters. I am sorry you are here. Thank you for being kind to me when you didn't have to be.

I couldn't believe he risked his safety to give me this letter. I was not sure how I would destroy it. Maybe I could just flush it? No, what if it backs up the toilet? Then again, it is just a small piece of paper. I could tear it up and then flush it. No, that could leave pieces floating, and then what would I do? Maybe I could leave it in the book and let him take it back? No, 'cause what if that goddess or someone else came and found it? I didn't want him to get in trouble when he did this out of kindness. Then it came to me. Albeit a disgusting idea, but it was all I could think of. I could just swallow it. So I crumbled it up and put it in my mouth and swallowed it.

I ran over to the table and grabbed the cup and took a drink. It was not water. It was sweet and fruity. I looked at the cup—he had brought me juice. Grape juice, if I had to guess. I truly hoped he didn't get himself in any trouble. I finished off the juice and sat back down on the bed. I ate the carrots first in case someone came in and then munched on the sandwich while I read the book he gave me.

Three more days passed with this. I would talk out loud when he came in the room, just trying to sound like I wanted someone to talk to or wondering out loud about things like where I am and when I would see the god that took me, who the goddess that paid me a visit is, and more. I would reiterate that I was scared and worried about my pack and family, and beg for him to respond to me like he hadn't been for the past couple of days, just in case someone was watching somehow. And each day, when I got a new book, I would have a small note with scribbles on it.

From my understanding, he kept his word, and your pack was left alone. The goddess you saw comes here a lot to see the master. Her name is Discordia, and she is very vindictive. You should be careful with her.

You are not on Earth. You are in the realm of the gods in Amarok's castle. I wish I could give you more information, but I can't. I have been kept here against my will, so I don't know much about this realm.

The master has been hunting. When he came back with you, he was in an uproar about his people not loving him the way they should. He considers himself to be a fair god, but only to those he truly cares for, which are his wolves. He does not even really care for the Lycans. I do not know when he will return.

Each time Johnathan gave me the book with the new note in it, he would give a slight nod. I would grab the book before I even looked at my meal, and eventually that paid off. The last note he gave me scared me.

Don't drink the juice. I think Discordia put something in it. Some of the guards were talking, and he is going to be back in the next day or so, according to them.

He had no idea how appreciative I was to see that note. I walked over to the table and lifted the paper cup to my nose. Sure enough, just barely there, I could smell the wolfsbane under the smell of the grape juice. I grabbed the sandwich and opened it. There was nothing that looked discolored, and when I sniffed it, there was no smell other than the peanut butter. So I ate the sandwich and left the juice.

More tired than usual, I laid down, deciding to take a nap. I was restless. I couldn't get images of my mates out of my mind, and my heart hurt from missing them so much. I slept restlessly, tossing and turning. I didn't really dream, but at the same time, I did—it was just like being blindfolded. I kept looking around and seeing nothing, but I could feel a presence, and it had my skin pimple with goosebumps.

I slowly grew aware, as I was waking up, of a presence. Opening my eyes, it was dark. The light had been turned off. I turned over on the cot to turn it on and froze. Right next to my bed, on the other side of the bars, were the eyes that have haunted my dreams for as long as I could remember. The eyes I saw when I was running through the woods as my mother, carrying my newborn babe, tried to get to safety. The eyes I saw as he brought that dagger down that ended her life. The eyes that have become a staple in my nightmares, that I still saw when I woke. My blood turned cold, and my breathing stopped. Amarok was back.

"I told you, Princess, that I would come for you. That you would be mine. It's time to get ready and start preparations for what is to come. We are going to have so much fun together, you and I."

I sat there, frozen. I couldn't move. I couldn't respond. He was here, and I was out of time.